My Husband and I Sleep in a Coffin

1

My Husband and I Sleep in a Coffin

我和老攻睡棺材

WRITTEN BY

无水不渡
Wu Shui Bu Du

ILLUSTRATED BY

Oniku
AND
Chikage

TRANSLATED BY

Liting Xiao

Seven Seas

Seven Seas Entertainment

MY HUSBAND AND I SLEEP IN A COFFIN VOL. 1

Published originally under the title of 《我和老攻睡棺材》 (Wo He Lao Gong Shui Guan Cai)
English edition rights under license granted by Shanghai Shunduo Network
Science and Technology Co., Ltd
English Translation copyright ©2025 by Seven Seas Entertainment, Inc.
Arranged through JS Agency
All rights reserved.

Seven Seas press and purchase enquiries can be sent to
Marketing Manager Lauren Hill at press@gomanga.com.
Information regarding the distribution and purchase of
digital editions is available from Digital Operations Manager
CK Russell at digital@gomanga.com.

Seven Seas and the Seven Seas logo are trademarks of
Seven Seas Entertainment. All rights reserved.

Follow Seven Seas Entertainment online at
sevenseasentertainment.com.

TRANSLATION: Liting Xiao
ADAPTATION: Athena Michaels
LOGO DESIGN: Mariel Dágá
INTERIOR DESIGN: Clay Gardner
COVER DESIGN & INTERIOR LAYOUT: M. A. Lewife
COPY EDITOR: Nino Cipri
PROOFREADER: Cheri Ebisu
SENIOR EDITOR: Nibedita Sen
PREPRESS TECHNICIAN: Salvador Chan Jr., April Malig, Jules Valera
MANAGING EDITOR: Alyssa Scavetta
EDITOR-IN-CHIEF: Julie Davis
PUBLISHER: Lianne Sentar
VICE PRESIDENT: Adam Arnold
PRESIDENT: Jason DeAngelis

ISBN: 979-8-89373-692-2
Printed in Canada
First Printing: August 2025
10 9 8 7 6 5 4 3 2 1

TABLE OF CONTENTS

A Casket With a Sliding Lid is Totally Worth Having

*H*ELLO *EVERYONE, my name is Wang Xiaomie.*

I'm currently lying in a casket, wearing a red wedding dress, after having been reincarnated as a thousand-year-old dead zongzi[1] (jiangshi). I'm seriously panicking right now. Not only am I too scared to move, but I also need to pee.

Why, you ask? Because I've realized this isn't even the scariest part. The scariest part is that I just noticed this isn't a one-person casket... it's a mother-fluffing double bed!

Wang Xiaomie squeezed his eyes shut. The truth was he'd actually been awake for a good while now, but there was just something about opening your eyes first thing in the morning to find that you were no longer yourself, but a guy in an ancient wedding dress. (And by "guy," he meant the dead kind.)

Beside him lay a beautiful man who looked almost as lifelike as the actually living, dressed in a gorgeous red-and-black robe with tons of fancy detailing.

(This guy was also the dead kind.)

Wang Xiaomie's eyes rolled back into his head. He'd fainted from fear.

When he woke up again, it was to discover...th-th-th-the dude next to him had moved too?!

---

1 Zongzi: A glutinous rice dish, here used as slang for an undecayed living corpse.

WTF!

Wang Xiaomie squeezed his eyes shut again, too scared to look.

So what if he's hot?!! No matter how hot he is, that's still a dead guy right there! And he can fluffin' resurrect himself, too! Oh Jade Emperor, Tathagata, Sakyamuni, Mary Mother of Jesus...

Scenes of jiangshi, Daoist priests, and the like flashed wildly across Wang Xiaomie's mind. He was afraid the bigger zongzi beside him would break his neck with one bite.

But the dude next to him only grew more restless. Suddenly, something ice-cold pressed against Wang Xiaomie's neck.

AAAAH—!

He desperately restrained both his bladder and his voice, feeling goosebumps spread across his neck—

Huh? Wait, could dead people get goosebumps?

Wang Xiaomie had this bad habit where the more frightened or nervous he was on the inside, the calmer he'd look on the outside. Even better, when he was *really* frightened or nervous, it got easier to make him laugh. For example, when he was a kid getting a shot at the doctor, the other kids were tearfully wailing while he sat there laughing his little head off. The nurse had been worried the injection had somehow turned him stupid. He was a profound example of what people meant when they said "Steady as an old hound without, actually freaked out within."

Relying on his years of practiced cowardice, Wang Xiaomie managed to endure the itch on his neck. He didn't move until that cold sensation ceased. But before he could breathe a sigh of relief...the hot zongzi started trying to pull off his clothes.

That's right—he was stripping him.

Eff your granddad, you stinkin' perv—! His icy claws've gotten far enough in to start rubbing at my skin! If I don't jump up and start stompin' on your knees then I might as well write my family name backward!

...Though "Wang" written backward looks exactly the same.

Wang Xiaomie had only just gathered the courage to defend his honor and integrity when the super-sexy zongzi in the ancient outfit gently hugged him. He sighed, chilly breath whispering over Wang Xiaomie's forehead. "Mian Deng, another day has passed in the mortal world. How many more will pass before you wake?"

So the zongzi could speak! Wang Xiaomie silently thought: *Who is Mian Deng? Don't tell me that's the owner of the body I'm in now? Guess this body's only preserved against rot—it didn't actually come back to life.*

Just as he was thinking this, an icy pair of lips approached him, bringing with them the scent of aged eaglewood. Those lips came right up against his mouth, and then pressed down in a soft and affectionate kiss.

WTF—that was my first kiss!

Internally, Wang Xiaomie was crying a river. He'd never imagined his first kiss would be destined for an unfamiliar zongzi—because the guy *was* still a zongzi, no matter how sexy he might be!

Weh, I was saving my first kiss for my future boyfriend...

But as much as this pained him, nothing was more important than staying alive. Not daring to reveal himself, Wang Xiaomie kept his eyes shut and laid there in the darkness, feeling the careful intimacy of the kiss on his lips. The love and protectiveness he sensed behind the kiss made him feel somewhat bashful—he was a young man, after all, still in his adolescence, which was the one stage of life where you had the least resistance against this sort of excitement.

As Wang Xiaomie unwillingly accepted the stranger's kiss, he inwardly rejoiced at the fact that the super-sexy zongzi's chilly lips didn't smell like a rotting corpse. If his breath had been as rotten as it was in the movies, he definitely would've vomited in the guy's face.

This kiss went on for half an hour. If it weren't for the fact he was a corpse too now, he'd probably have suffocated to death. Though considering this grave's owner and the wedding garb he was dressed in, plus the intimate behavior going on right now...

These two couldn't be ancient gays, could they?!

I, an upstanding young citizen of the modern-day motherland, am suffering the single life, while even ye olde corpses over here got to have romantic partners.

Sigh...

After a while, Wang Xiaomie gradually started to enjoy the kiss. He wasn't brave enough to use his tongue, merely opening his mouth wider to accept it. The super-sexy zongzi's careful and deeply heartfelt actions made him suddenly emotional. He and this body's past owner must have been an extremely lovey-dovey couple once upon a time, or they wouldn't have gone so far as to be buried together when they died. He made sure to kiss his wife every day, even after becoming a zongzi. And kissed him so compassionately, too! What a good man! Too bad he was dead...

Wang Xiaomie, lost in thought, inadvertently swallowed once.

The soft and affectionate kiss instantly came to an abrupt halt.

As those icy lips left his mouth, the terrified Wang Xiaomie broke out in a cold sweat. *Oho, I'm done for.*

The atmosphere was deathly still.

Wang Xiaomie cracked his eyes open just a bit, using the light of a glowing night pearl inside the casket to sneak a peek. He found that the super-sexy zongzi was wearing a red-and-black ancient robe, with a red crown perched on his raven hair, and a bit of bright-red patterning between his eyebrows. He had a face that was delicately contoured but not without sharpness, blue lips, and long and narrow eyes with far more black than white, which were currently looking at him with an extremely complicated expression of mingled happiness, excitement, and a whole lot of trepidation.

Oh my god!

Wang Xiaomie hurriedly shut his eyes again in a foolishly hopeful attempt to pretend that hadn't happened. Meanwhile, the undead hottie pressed something, somewhere, causing the casket to emit the sound of a mechanism activating.

And then the casket lid unexpectedly began to slide slowly open.

Bro, who woulda thunk your casket was the sliding-cover model...

Piercing light filtered in through the opening. When Wang Xiaomie finally opened his eyes again, they gradually widened in disbelief. He sat up like he'd forgotten where he was and looked around the outside of the casket.

They were in a rounded cavern so massive it was like a mountain had been hollowed out. The space was enormous, bigger than the Bird's Nest Stadium. Cantilevers attached to the towering walls supported a thickly dotted expanse of buildings and palaces. They looked just like those temples built on cliffs in scenic areas, with the added ability to look down upon all the buildings below them.

In the middle of this massive space, surrounded by mushroom-like buildings, stood a single gigantic stone pillar wrapped in tree roots. Growing from the wide platform attached to that stone pillar was an old tree so wide you'd need seven people to circle it.

What shocked Wang Xiaomie wasn't the old tree, though, but the clouds of delicate pink peach flowers blooming from it. No leaves, only flowers! And to what degree were these flowers blooming, you might ask? Intensely enough that it looked like a blazing red fire merrily licking at the tree. The light shining down from above only served to give the tree an even more saintly aura.

Their casket was located smack-dab beneath this blazing red peach tree.

It took quite a long time for the shaken Wang Xiaomie to finally regain his senses, after which he suddenly turned his head.

A youthful zongzi gege with a gaze even hotter than those peach flowers was currently smiling at him.

The two of them stared at each other in silence for a while.

"Ji—jiangshiiiii!" A trembling Wang Xiaomie let out a loud scream, his eyes rolling backward.

And just like that, he fainted.

Please,
Let Me Go, Boss!

WHEN WANG XIAOMIE woke up, he discovered that he was lying in someone else's embrace. Though the chest pressed against his back was icy cold, it was also very sturdy, and its owner had even adjusted their position to make the hug more comfortable for him.

A few peach blossom petals landed on him, looking like little sparks of flame amidst the gorgeously detailed patterning of his ancient wedding robe. It was enchantingly beautiful.

If an outside observer saw this—a pair of men in red-and-black wedding robes in such an embrace beneath an ethereal peach tree, atop this towering terrace high above the glorious and colossal underground tomb—they would surely have the impression of soul-stirringly deep love. If a fujoshi were to see this scene, she would have instantly conjured a few thousand little ficlets in her head.

If the man embracing me with such intense possessiveness didn't happen to be dead, I'd be pretty happy myself.

And not just happy, but horny as well.

But Wang Xiaomie was quite panicked right now—so panicked that his face was completely expressionless and his body shook like someone with Parkinson's disease, or one of those old washing machines that kept vibrating loudly as they worked.

There was a sound of low, husky laughter from behind him. Wang Xiaomie felt his embracer's arms tighten a little more. Not only that, but the guy brushed something soft and chilly down along his neck in an extremely lewd fashion. He tentatively guessed that that something was the guy's lips.

Wang Xiaomie's eyes widened to the size of saucers. His shaking got so bad he was all but ready to shake his own head right off his neck.

"D-d-dage, if you have something to say, then say it nicely!" *As long as you don't bite me, I'm good with anything you do!*

"Mian Deng, how wondrous is your cuteness in this life." The husky voice, with its hint of chest-rumbling laughter, then quietly continued: "Mian Deng, that stupid old bastard wasn't lying after all—this pining tree has finally brought you back to me."

Wang Xiaomie was shaking too violently to hear a single word of that. All he could hear at this point was the sloshing of water inside his head.

The stranger waited a while. Then, apparently dissatisfied with Wang Xiaomie's lack of response, he turned him around to face him.

Now the two were really and truly making eye contact. Wang Xiaomie had been so focused on his fear of jiangshi that his teeth were chattering. But the zongzi dude facing him—with that red crown and raven hair, that bit of bright-red patterning between his eyebrows, and those long, narrow eyes that were more black than white—had an unnaturally seductive air.

He'd been laughing just a second ago, but now that face looked totally savage. "Why won't you speak, Mian Deng?"

But what scared Wang Xiaomie most of all was the emotion in those eyes, so intense it was almost distorted—like he'd just witnessed the resurrection of a dead loved one, but also like he'd transformed that love into hatred, such pure hatred that he could tear the other person to pieces with his teeth and swallow him bite by bite!

This time Wang Xiaomie was *truly* about to vibrate out of his own skin. *Allow me to take back what I said earlier about being a lovey-dovey husband and wife. This is clearly one of those shit-uations where the wife crossed a boundary, so he choked said wife to death in a moment of rage and offed himself after!*

Wang Xiaomie felt his entire body seize up under that gaze. His mind had been a total blank, but now he was yelling like he was incapable of proper speech. "Spare me, jiangshi-dage! I'm not Mian Deng my name is Wang Xiaomie I live in Nangang on Wutong Road I've never been in a relationship or acted improper or fooled around with women even once in my twenty-plus years of life, I might not have any way of explaining why I'm inside this corpse's body, but!"

After blurting out all that, he hurriedly gasped for breath before continuing, "Dage—you've got the wrong guy! Please let me go!"

Wehh, I'm kneeling at your feet here, Dage!

Don't off me, I haven't lived long enough. Plus—Wang Xiaomie tearfully added in his head—*I'm afraid of ghosts!*

After all that, the would-be tyrant across from him softened somewhat. There was a very strange expression on his face, something like doubt, but also a little bit like happiness.

He pulled Wang Xiaomie—who was currently as stiff as a wooden stake—into his loving embrace. The devil's scary aura was replaced with a soft voice and gentle demeanor as he quietly asked, "Mian Deng, do you not remember anything?"

The speed with which this guy could switch vibes was practically magical, a fact which only served to scare Wang Xiaomie worse, though he continued to explain in a panic, "My—my name is Wang Xiaomie, not Mian Deng..."

"You really did forget everything..."

If you remembered the past, would you ever have allowed me to act as intimate as I have with you? Wen Fengjin looked down at the face of his beloved, whom he held in his arms. Though his body was still that of an eternally preserved corpse, it was enough that his soul had returned. Perhaps, as far as he was concerned, being unable to remember anything was actually a blessing from above...

"Oh, Mian Deng...I've been watching over you beneath this pining tree for 1,200 years. Legend has it that, under certain conditions, this tree can summon the souls of bodies buried beneath it from their tenth lives..."

The man's face had an unhealthy pallor, but this wasn't enough to influence his overall appearance. When those unusual eyes looked at him, brimming with emotion, Wang Xiaomie actually felt his heart beat for a moment. Pressing his hands over his wildly pounding chest, he silently opened his mouth, then finally said, "You waited in this underground tomb? For over twelve hundred years..."

"That's right. And it was all worth the wait." The man closed his eyes and pressed his forehead against Wang Xiaomie's with what seemed like genuine love and affection.

Even if he didn't need to eat or drink, waiting all alone in a grave for your lover to come back to life really was an extremely touching idea. Wang Xiaomie wasn't as afraid of him anymore. After all, such a tale of unrelenting passion was moving to hear.

And also...I'm that Mian Deng guy's tenth reincarnation?

Wang Xiaomie asked, "Then what about me? You mean I'm dead?!" *No way. I remember being asleep in bed... How could I have suddenly just kicked the bucket?!*

Pitch-black eyes opened as the man before him replied, "That should be correct."

Wang Xiaomie's eyes widened too. "I was safe and sound at home. How could I have just died like that?"

The man smiled back at him. "Calamities do happen, both natural and man-made. Besides, vermin who sneak into homes to kill their occupants for money can be found in any era."

Wang Xiaomie, dumbfounded by this answer, had to lower his head in silence while he tried to accept it. In doing so, he failed to catch the deep emotions hidden in the man's eyes.

After a good long think, he let out a sigh, then timidly asked, "So what's going on...between me and you?"

"You and I?" The man half closed his eyes, concealing his emotions, and slowly began to tell him a tale of long ago.

My Husband and I Sleep in a Coffin

3

Ten Lifetimes
of Pining is a
Bone-Deep Pain

THE MAN WAS NAMED Wen Fengjin. He and Wang Xiaomie's previous incarnation, Mian Deng, were fellow disciples of a spiritual sect. They'd had earnest feelings for each other since they were young, and been in a romantic relationship even as children. In Wen Fengjin's words, they were a perfect and natural pair.

The two originally planned to travel the world together for three years before returning to the sect to have a big wedding ceremony. But their departure had proved permanent...

Of course he died, Wang Xiaomie thought. *Just look at that little "we'll get married when we return" flag you raised!*

People were very superstitious in ancient times. Some chased ambitions of immortality, creating all sorts of medicine and causing all sorts of trouble in the process, exhausting the common folk and draining the national treasury. The emperor and nobility were the biggest believers of all, and sent a great many people out in search of a drug that would confer eternal youth.

Meanwhile, the traveling couple just happened to rescue a blood-soaked stranger. According to Wen Fengjin, his past self—in other words, Mian Deng—was a cold-faced but warmhearted person. He not only treated the stranger's wounds, but even fought off many waves of incoming assassins to protect him.

But to their surprise, the assassins only continued to increase in number. Despite their efforts, the stranger still died in the end. With his dying breath, he finally explained that he was one of the people the emperor had sent out in search of an elixir of immortality, after which he gave the pill he'd found to Mian Deng.

Mian Deng and Wen Fengjin knew the item would bring them nothing but trouble. The immortality seekers would never just let them go. Even if the elixir was destroyed, they'd refuse to believe it. The pair immediately headed back to their sect to ask for help. But before they could get there, they were encircled by four separate waves of attackers. The two of them were unable to fend off an attack of such ferocity alone, and by the time they escaped into the remoteness of the mountain, Mian Deng was already heavily injured and on the brink of death. Wen Fengjin wasn't doing much better, forcing himself to keep going entirely out of sheer desire to save Mian Deng. Their pursuers, meanwhile, were clearly playing a game of cat and mouse with them, looking on as they fought to save each other's lives.

At this point of the story, Wen Fengjin's arms suddenly tightened so forcefully around Wang Xiaomie that it hurt. He seemed to be overcome by the memory. His eyes turned bloodred so abruptly that a panicked Wang Xiaomie shrank as small as he could, too terrified to speak.

Wen Fengjin continued, saying that the two had decided to eat the elixir in the name of survival. They had no idea whether the pill was real or not, but they'd already been pushed to their limit. At this point, if even one of them lived, it would still be a win.

Back then, the two of them were so close that the idea of either of them living without the other was unthinkable. After much argument, they finally made the decision to have Mian Deng live...

only for him to trick Wen Fengjin, using his own mouth to give the pill to him instead.

The elixir turned out to be real. But a magical pill that could turn you into an immortal came with downsides. One glance at all the people who'd studied the Dao and consumed immortality pills through the course of history was enough to prove as much. Although Wen Fengjin survived, Mian Deng did not. On top of that, Wen Fengjin became a corpse-like monster without a heartbeat, incapable of suffering pain or death. He killed all of the assassins, then disappeared from the world, carrying Mian Deng's body in his arms.

Many years later, a vengeful Wen Fengjin established his own organization and began wantonly plundering rare and exotic medicines and treasures. Anything rumored to have powers of resurrection was especially likely to be the target of his unscrupulous grasp. By the time he was done, he'd amassed a legendary amount of ill-gotten wealth, built an underground mausoleum, and managed to find the legendary pining tree.

No one knew whether this tree could truly bring Mian Deng back from the dead. But, having exhausted all other options, Wen Fengjin had no choice but to lay himself down beneath the earth, sleeping within a coffin and next to a corpse.

Beneath this pining tree, ten lifetimes of pining had passed in bone-deep pain. But now Wang Xiaomie, this body's tenth incarnation, had truly returned and woken from his eternal slumber...

After hearing this story, Wang Xiaomie was momentarily at a loss for what to say. He didn't have even a subconscious distrust of Wen Fengjin's words—after all, the pain and hatred he'd expressed when speaking of Mian Deng's death certainly hadn't seemed fake, and the guy having lain inside a grave waiting for him was all the more reason to dismiss any doubts he might have had.

But...

"I really don't have any memory of that period of time...and I've always been Wang Xiaomie, so even if you say that I'm Mian Deng now, I..." *I can't put on an emotional act and tearfully say "Hubby I'm back, thanks for everything," okay!*

"It's no trouble." Wen Fengjin lowered his head, revealing a shallow smile. "My heart's desire has already come to me. No matter your identity, or your form, it's still you... We can start over from the beginning."

There was profound meaning in the boss jiangshi's smile. Wang Xiaomie wanted nothing more than to cry out—*Boss, we've already become zongzi, what kinda romance can we even have? Are you planning for us to become Mr. and Mrs. Zongzi?!*

Wait, that's not the problem here!

Wang Xiaomie suddenly thought of something. "If you ate the elixir of immortality, doesn't that mean you're an immortal now? So you're not a zongzi?! Do you have any way to turn me back into a human, too?!"

When he first woke up and realized he lacked body heat and a heartbeat, he'd nearly scared himself to death. Wang Xiaomie didn't want to be a jiangshi—if he was a jiangshi, he'd never be able to go to the surface world ever again!

"Zongzi?" Wen Fengjin tilted his head as he asked, "What do you mean?"

Wang Xiaomie bashfully scratched his head. "Oh, by 'zongzi' I mean 'jiangshi,' heheh. Sorry, I've read too many novels."

"Jiangshi?" Wen Fengjin furrowed his brow, wrinkling the red pattern that adorned his forehead. "Taking that drug was the equivalent of death for me. I don't need to eat or sleep, and any injuries I sustain heal very quickly, but my heart does not beat and my body is cold, making me barely different from a corpse. You, too, have gone through the coffin pit and the divine tree's preservation to become an undecaying jiangshi. At present, I have no way of reviving your body."

D-didn't that mean he was still a zongzi then? Wang Xiaomie's head drooped with discouragement.

"Don't worry. You may be a zongzi, but you're the sweetest one of all." Wen Fengjin fully wrapped Wang Xiaomie in his embrace, sniffing at him and touching him with his nose and lips.

Wang Xiaomie was speechless. *Heh...men. Always saying they're happy just to have met you, when really they want nothing more than to strip you naked, press you into the bed, and ravish you with all the energy they can muster.*

Wang Xiaomie looked at the boss-man's handsome face, with its hotness index akin to a demon lord's...then suddenly stuffed his hands into the front of the boss's outfit.

Only an idiot would refuse to take advantage of something that's right there for the taking!

Though he still couldn't make heads or tails of all the past life stuff, Wang Xiaomie was in his twenties. If he didn't feel up the beautiful guy he'd been presented with, it'd be a total waste! So he pressed his hands against that big ol' boss's chest and felt him up real good!

Wen Fengjin was struck dumb by this development at first. But after a moment those eyes practically bloomed with a brilliant luster, and he even bent his waist to allow Wang Xiaomie better access. *Mian Deng... To think there'd come a day when you felt desire for me...*

Wang Xiaomie felt the touch on his back grow increasingly gentle. Having been queer for years but thoroughly discouraged by the gay community's focus on casual relationships, Wang Xiaomie couldn't help but feel like being dead with a zongzi husband who loved him this deeply (and most importantly, had a damn good-looking face) wasn't all that bad.

It was just... he wasn't sure if a jiangshi could do *it*...

I'll just take a look...ahem. I've got no other intentions, I'm just taking a teensy-weensy peek out of curiosity, is all...

Wang Xiaomie lowered his head to take a cautious glance at the boss's lower body. Despite the looseness of his clothes, he could still see a noticeable lump down there...

Heheh~

One Disagreement
and They Dig Up
My Grave

WEN FENGJIN HAD NO IDEA of the uncouth thoughts running through Wang Xiaomie's mind as he embraced him, nor did he know how daring people could be in modern society (boys gotta make sure to protect themselves when they go out). As always, he used that husky voice of his—so magnetic that just the sound alone was enough to knock you up—to gently coax him. "Mian Deng, call me Fengjin just once..."

What would one call a husky, sexy top's voice? What would one call being subjected to such masculine wiles? Wang Xiaomie didn't know. All he *did* know was that one of his shoulders had gone numb just from listening to this. His face exploded into a burning shade of red: "Feng, Fengjin..."

What the hell am I getting red for?! I've been a fudanshi for six years. This ain't my first rodeo. How could I go to my knees so easily? Ready to start lapping at this guy's hotness? Heh, I—this zongzi's seriously good-looking!

"N-now you can try calling me Wang Xiaomie, too." Getting called Mian Deng made him feel a little bit like he was being used as a replacement.

Wen Fengjin tilted his head, a blaze of peach blossoms at his back. With his raven hair, red crown and the bloody pattern on his forehead, his long and narrow eyes that were far more black than white...he really did look a lot like the big boss of an online game Wang Xiaomie had played back in the day.

The big boss opened his mouth and said, "Xiaomie."

Wang Xiaomie was speechless. The way that sounded, it was like he was saying it as a joke! He sighed. "...Forget it, let's just stick with Mian Deng."

The boss was about to say something when an unnaturally graceful sound suddenly rang out around them. It sounded like a woman quietly singing, which was all the more terrifying when you heard it coming faintly from the depths of an underground mausoleum.

Wang Xiaomie startled. He clung unconsciously to the big shot beside him before belatedly remembering that guy wasn't alive either—in fact, Wang Xiaomie had become a zongzi himself, so what was there to be afraid of?

And so he lowered his hands, still somewhat frightened, as he looked around and asked, "What's going on?" It couldn't be that other "people" also lived in this mausoleum, could it?

Wen Fengjin shook his head as he smoothly helped Wang Xiaomie back to his feet, one arm wrapped around his waist as he flung out his other sleeve in a dramatic gesture, expression darkening. He said, "Grave robbers have activated one of the mausoleum's mechanisms."

"Grave robbers?" Subconsciously, Wang Xiaomie's mind filled with images of a bunch of TV dramas and novels he'd seen. There was a time when he'd been a real avid fan of this genre of novels, too.

"Yes. I once traveled across the land in search of unusual treasures, all for the sake of building a mausoleum in which to revive you. This mausoleum contains countless legendary items as well as ordinary gold and silver. I originally intended them to be our grave goods, thinking they could all be my betrothal gifts to you in death, since we were never able to marry in life..."

Wen Fengjin then turned and lovingly stroked his cheek with a hand: "But now that you're awake, none of those things matter to me anymore." His expression stayed as gentle as ever, but his eyes filled with a twisted and murderous intent as he continued, "On the other hand, you just woke up. That they chose today of all days only speaks to their inability to tell good from bad... Mian Deng, don't be afraid, I'll go take care of them right now, okay?"

The boss smiled gently. His voice was soft and affectionate. Wang Xiaomie nearly couldn't stop himself from vibrating out of his skin again. *Fucking hell! Mama, there's a pervert here!*

Wen Fengjin was like some kind of horror movie monster right now. The aura he gave off was sinister enough to make your flesh crawl. The average person would get goosebumps just looking at him. It was like he'd been born a rank above them all—like he was supposed to be sitting on a throne, smiling down at his subjects as they trembled in fear.

"Could you wait here for me?" Wen Fengjin pointed at the casket. "Once I've dealt with all of them, I'll come right back to you."

"I have to sleep in the casket again?" Wang Xiaomie scrunched up his face. This thing honestly gave him the heebie-jeebies.

"Hm..." Wen Fengjin frowned. "I could have you accompany me, but as you are right now, you seem to have forgotten the martial arts you previously learned. Also, your body isn't like mine. You are in essence still a corpse, so it would be best for you to stay beneath this tree and continue absorbing its power. If you leave its presence for too long, it's possible your body may rot."

Rot? Wang Xiaomie looked at his pale-skinned palm, then felt at his face, before silently crawling into the casket and waving a hand at Wen Fengjin from inside it. *Seeya, Boss. You can see yourself out, Boss.*

"Heh."

Wen Fengjin laughed low, sparing a moment to watch his foolish behavior before stepping onto the great chain that connected the towering stone pillar's terrace to the cliffs and palaces in the distance. With a few graceful leaps, he left the area as easily as if he were taking a walk in the park.

Meanwhile, having laid back down in the casket, Wang Xiaomie looked up at the sea of peach blossoms which covered the tree. Unexpectedly, he found himself in the sort of leisurely mood where one might say things like "Ah, what nice weather we're having today." His mind was a mess: tangled in thoughts of his past life, what Wen Fengjin had said to him, and what his life would be from here. He thought and thought, until finally he closed his eyes without realizing it.

The scene: A big red coffin decorated with exquisitely carved images of ascension, placed beneath a gently swaying peach tree as thick as six or seven men, the body within it possessing a waterfall of raven hair, his scattered locks not only full and soft, but also reflecting the faint light from above onto the gold-embroidered, soft red cloth which lined the coffin. A gem-studded phoenix crown made of coiled gold was firmly attached to this delicate beauty's head, and his snow-white skin was smooth and soft. The fallen peach blossoms floating across that tranquil sleeping face made him look even more like a real living person.

The black-and-red wedding dress he wore was slightly rumpled. A peach blossom landed in the casket. Even in this hidden underground tomb, one could not possibly resist the desire to kiss this waiting bride awake...

Elsewhere, a number of grimy but heavily armed men equipped with flashlights and large packs were resting on the ground. Some of them even carried guns. Every last one was male, and each wore a malicious expression on his face. One look was enough to tell you they weren't the kind of guys you wanted to mess with.

The middle-aged leader pulled out a map and started talking with the man next to him.

"Uncle, where are we now? How come we still haven't seen the big guy?" the man next to him asked in a low voice.

The middle-aged man frowned. "We're currently at this position." He pointed at a spot on the map. "This mausoleum covers an area as large as three mountains, and its master's identity is still a mystery to this day. I can't tell you how many lives were sacrificed just to make this simple map. We've only gotten this far—there's practically a million miles to go before we get to the main tomb! Where we are right now might as well be just the little courtyard at the entrance of their house!"

"Huh?! But we've already lost seven men! You sure this is gonna be worth it?"

"Worth it?!" The middle-aged man's eyebrows shot up as he replied, "Lemme fuckin' tell you, we could do nothing but pull a rock off the front door in there an' still come out on top! This tomb's been known for ages—how many people do you think have been comin' in here? But aside from a couple guys with a real talent for running, all of them lost their lives! Those talented runners are also the ones who recorded the tablet inscription at the entrance of the main tomb, and that more than made up for what they lost!"

The middle-aged man indicated a number with his fingers, sneering. "Heheh...all we gotta do is set foot in that main entrance and we'll have struck it rich! We'll never have to do this kinda dirty work again. It'll be easy livin' for the rest of our lives!"

He hadn't bothered to lower his voice. His words caused the men around him to stare at their leader, eyes glowing with greed and excitement as they waited to hear more.

The middle-aged leader, meanwhile, knew perfectly well that they'd lost too many people on the way here, and that his gang was probably chickening out. With that in mind, he purposely played to the crowd by telling them about the inscription on the tablet.

5

It's All Thanks to Shixiong's Guidance

"**A**CCORDING TO THE INSCRIPTION on the tablet, this mausoleum—which I'll remind you is even more impressive than the imperial tomb—has two people buried in it. One dead...and one alive!"

Some of the men laughed heartily. "Huh? Haha, you're such a kidder, Uncle! If you bury a live guy in the dirt, won't he become a dead guy too?"

But the middle-aged man shook his head. "No, this said the living one really is alive... The tablet records that the tomb master and his fiancée once acquired a pill of immortality, but then found themselves the target of all kinds of forces trying to snuff them out. In the end, they were backed into a corner. The fiancée got killed, while the tomb master ate the pill and transformed into a monster that never ages or dies."

He purposefully lowered his voice at this point, building up the scary atmosphere as he continued, "But there was writing on the other side of that tablet, too. It said that that person actually wasn't the tomb master's fiancee at all, just someone he was madly in love with. In the end, they got into an argument over these unrequited feelings, and he accidentally killed his love while fighting over the immortality medicine... By the time the other person was dead, it was too late to repent.

"Many years later, that tomb master brought together a team of extraordinary fighters to help him seek justice. They traveled across the entire country in search of treasures that could bring the dead back to life, and amassed incredible riches while they were at it. In the end, after failing to find a way to revive his lover, the tomb master went berserk, leading his team in a bloody massacre that cost countless lives. Young or old, every last person related to his enemies was dragged into this mausoleum, strung up, and tortured to death!"

"You mean those dried-up corpses we saw outside the door earlier were..."

"They're probably the murdered people that tablet mentioned..."

"That, that sure is something." One of the grave robbers gulped. Remembering those dense piles of bones at the entrance made this pitch-dark mausoleum suddenly feel a lot chillier than before.

Nobody in their line of work was afraid of bones, but it was another matter entirely to have millions of dessicated corpses hung swaying above your head like wind chimes. The place was clearly cursed like nobody's business, especially considering how many of their compatriots had died here.

"On top of everything else, they say he used drugs to turn a bunch of his subordinates into monsters who could guard the mausoleum for him, then had his beloved spend his eternal slumber beneath a divine tree. The tablet says the main tomb is filled with not just mountains of riches, but legendary treasures too—if we got our hands on just one of those, we could start our own reign of terror!"

The mention of treasure brought the greed back to everyone's faces. Seeing that he'd gotten the mood he wanted, the middle-aged man continued, "Our backer this time around is looking for something called the Fish Pearl that's hidden in this tomb. If we can just get our hands on that..." His expression practically glowed as he thought of the sum their client had agreed to, his mouth cracking open in a smile.

"The lady this tomb master set his eye on sure was unlucky, though. He seems like the kinda guy you seriously wouldn't wanna mess with," the man who'd started the conversation earlier muttered. He kicked at a companion who laid on the floor, saying, "Hey! Everybody up! Shit, you think we came out here on vacation or something?!"

The middle-aged man got up as well, laughing as he said, "Who said it was a lady? According to that tablet, the person this tomb master fell in love with was a shixiong from his own sect!"

"Huh?!" Some of the men expressed revulsion at this. One made a disdainful noise as he said, "So they're a pair of dead fuckin' gays! That tomb master's a real degenerate."

"How do two guys even get it on with each other?"

"Heheh, you must still be wet behind the ears—there's all kinda ways they could mess around."

"Tch! Fuck off!"

The men teased each other as they pulled their equipment back on, quickly quieting under their leader's gaze and continuing their forward march.

Wen Fengjin stood in a corner of the mausoleum. The sound of low, constrained breathing could be heard throughout the dark and gloomy passage. The source of this sound was a man laying prostrate like a lizard on the floor by his feet—if it could even be called a man. The figure on the floor didn't have a single patch of skin or hair on him, with what looked like raw muscle and veins being all one could see. On closer inspection, however, it appeared this layer of veins was in fact his skin. The blood that covered it actually seemed to be a viscous fluid secreted from his body.

A cackling sound emitted from the lizard-like monster's throat, leading Wen Fengjin to laugh grimly, as if he'd understood what he said. "You've done well. Drive them toward the passage to the tomb, and make sure none survive but that middle-aged man..."

"Gegege..."

The red lizard monster moved extremely fast, disappearing within moments as it scurried off to do Wen Fengjin's bidding.

In about half the time it took to burn a stick of incense, the stumbling sound of frantic running came from the depths of the passage. The middle-aged man was entirely devoid of his earlier composure and complacency. Something had ripped his right arm straight from his body. His left arm staunched the terrifying injury, and spatters of blood covered his face and body.

"Shit! *Shit!*" In excruciating agony, the middle-aged man fell head-first in the passage, flung into a panic by dangerous levels of blood loss and the monster pursuing him.

The fall managed to jar his already horrific injury. *"My aaaarm aaaahhh!"* The middle-aged man covered the stump of his missing arm as he wailed and rolled on the floor.

Suddenly, a soft-soled black boot with gold lining stepped into his field of vision.

This boot was beautiful, but clearly not something a modern person would be wearing—especially considering they were in a tomb right now! The middle-aged man immediately forgot about wailing, his body breaking out in a cold sweat. His bloodless face was paler than that of a dead man.

The owner of those boots squatted down in front of him. A thin and icy hand pressed down against his head, then lifted him entirely off the floor.

What he saw next was a man dressed in an ancient-styled red-and-black outfit. This man was very handsome, holding one arm behind his back while he lifted the middle-aged man with the other. A smile lifted the corners of his lips like he was looking at an amusing toy.

But there was a tint of red in those pitch-black eyes. It was a zongzi! A real, honest-to-goodness zongzi!

The middle-aged man opened his mouth to yell, only to discover that he suddenly couldn't move at all. He couldn't even speak!

"Little creature, how did you get in here? Hm?"

The middle-aged man struggled with all he had, but it was as if something had been stripped from his body, making all his efforts pointless.

"Answer me. How did you and those rats crawl into my mausoleum?"

Wen Fengjin slightly tightened his grip, nearly making dents in the man's skull. His mouth opened wide as he let out a pained scream. He yelled with all his might: "A—A map—I have a map!"

"Oh?"

"It's in my backpack! Honest! I'm begging you, please let me go—"

There was a muffled noise. Some sort of liquid sprayed against the mausoleum wall, and the sharp smell of blood filled the passage. The headless body collapsed to the floor, twitching a few times before going motionless.

Wen Fengjin shook his hand. Viscous liquid stuck to those pale, slender fingers and dripped onto the floor. He dug a map out of the corpse's pack, giving it a cursory glance before expressionlessly using it to wipe the blood off his fingers.

Right at that moment, his entire body suddenly began to shake. "Don't be angry, Mian Deng!" The expressionless, handsome man grew flustered as he said to the empty air, "I won't kill any more people, okay, I only did it because they were bullying us..."

Whatever his imagination supplied was enough to make him calm again, for he delightedly said, "I knew you wouldn't truly be angry with me—those outsiders could never be as close as the two of us, after all."

Wen Fengjin had suddenly turned into a madman, talking to himself while gently smiling at thin air. If Wang Xiaomie were to see this, he'd probably end up running away on his hands and knees while pissing his pants in terror.

After a while, Wen Fengjin calmed down again, seeming to switch personalities like flipping a switch as he said, "A tablet inscription? It seems the artisans who built this mausoleum all those years ago weren't as well-behaved as I thought, if they actually recorded all this."

He looked down and smiled at the corpse on the floor. "I should thank you for telling me. Who knows what might happen if Mian Deng were to see that thing? Mian Deng also happens to like polite people, so I should make sure to give you a good reward."

He squatted down again to grip the corpse's hand, as polite as an elegant young noble, smiling as he said to the headless body before him, "You have my utmost gratitude."

He stood up, expression unchanging, as he issued an order to the dark tomb before him. "Mu Yi, destroy anything with inscriptions on it, and make sure to properly reward our guest here as well. He is fond of riches, so take his corpse to one of the side halls where jewels are stored, and satisfy his desires—don't be stingy, understood?"

Cackling calls echoed out from within the empty tomb.

He said aloud: "Look, Mian Deng, did I do well?" Then his face turned beet red, and he bit at his lip in embarrassment. "You don't need to commend me like that, Shixiong, this is all because you taught me well..."

His mouth lifted in a smile as he spoke to the air, apparently having gained someone's praise as he somewhat bashfully turned to leave. The spreading puddle of blood wet his boots, leaving bloody footprints in the gloomy tomb passage. In the moment he turned around, the corpse on the ground instantly disappeared from sight.

Mian Deng is still waiting for me. He's returned to my side again.

This time...

This time...

I won't let him escape again...

My Husband and I Sleep in a Coffin

Hunger

WANG XIAOMIE'S DIARY:
Today is my second day playing wife for a guy in a mausoleum. I'm hungry...

Standing beneath the great tree, Wang Xiaomie looked up at all the peach blossoms. He was so hungry his eyes practically glowed with desire. He swallowed a mouthful of saliva, saying, "Is this thing edible?"

"This peach tree is mutually linked to your body for the moment. If the tree were to suffer damage..." Wen Fengjin said uncertainly. "Why do you ask, Shixiong?"

"Because I'm hungry!" Wang Xiaomie looked around at the only edible things in the vicinity, crying tears of sorrow. This was the second day he'd been here, but why was he so hungry if he'd turned into a jiangshi? And not just that, but this hunger was worse than anything he'd ever felt when he was human. This tremendous feeling of lack nearly drove him mad from starvation!

But as far as the eye could see, the only edible thing in this mausoleum was probably tree bark. Now that he'd become "Wang Tree-man," leaving the old tree for a certain period of time would cause his skin to turn ashen gray, which was a pretty frightening sight.

The hunger filling his mind told him that he needed to find food as soon as possible, or else something bad was definitely going to happen...

Wang Xiaomie, swallowing his spit in a frenzy, squatted down on the floor and started chewing on his fingernails, oblivious to the fact that his eyes were gradually taking on a glowing shade of scarlet.

I'm so hungry... so hungry... I want to eat...

Wen Fengjin watched all this from behind him, the corners of his mouth slowly turning upward. He donned a gentle expression, embracing the person squatting on the floor as he said in a low voice, "This underground palace *is* a tomb, after all. It doesn't contain a single bite to eat, nor did the ancient texts ever record those revived from death experiencing feelings of hunger. It's all my fault, making Shixiong suffer like this..."

Even dizzy from hunger, Wang Xiaomie still retained a measure of rationality. He waved a hand, thinking to himself, *How could I blame the guy? I never thought a jiangshi could get hungry either.* "It's not your fault..." He cradled his stomach as his mouth produced an endless stream of saliva.

"Mian Deng...you're still just as considerate as you were in the past," Wen Fengjin said. "But you look unwell to me. It might be unwise to let this hunger continue... There *is* one thing in this mausoleum which can be eaten."

There's food?! Wang Xiaomie's eyes widened. "What is it?!"

Wen Fengjin's mostly black, narrow eyes curved in a smile as he pulled aside the collar of his elaborately decorated robes to reveal a deathly pale neck, raised a finger, and sliced his own flesh open with a razor-sharp nail. Rather than the expected fountain of fresh blood, what appeared to be quite a deep injury only leaked a few small drops. "If Mian Deng is amenable, feel free to partake."

Fuck! D-drinking blood?! "I won't drink it!"

How could he drink another person's blood? It wasn't like he was a man-eating monster. What little sanity remained to him loudly condemned the idea in his head, while his starving appetite burned away at his stomach.

Wang Xiaomie had no idea that the red light in his eyes was growing even stronger as he stared at that blood. His hands began to shake as the scent of it reached his nostrils. His formerly soft and delicate features turned savage, with ghastly pale skin and crimson eyes, blue veins creeping from his neck toward his eyes, and that bloodred wedding dress to top it all off.

Human? This was clearly a terrifying evil spirit!

Yet Wen Fengjin continued to treat this form of Wang Xiaomie's with the utmost gentleness, even gazing at him with a doting look in his eyes. He threaded a hand into Wang Xiaomie's long hair, then forcefully pressed him against the wound on his neck. "You and I are husband and wife. Ensuring that you eat your fill is a duty I am obligated to fulfill, as your husband." His husky voice and gentle laughter carried with it a sense of unspeakable joy.

Meanwhile, Wang Xiaomie's mind went hazy the instant his lips touched blood—all he knew was that he was hungry, so hungry, hungry enough that his stomach was killing him with pain. Wang Xiaomie—who had never so much as killed a chicken before, who trembled in fear at horror movies—opened his mouth viciously wide, firmly latched onto Wen Fengjin's neck, and began sucking in large mouthfuls of blood, even sticking his tongue into the wound and licking it like a madman!

Wen Fengjin hugged the evil spirit in his embrace who cared for nothing except eating, leaning back against the fully blooming peach tree behind him with his eyes narrowed in a smile. The occasional hoarse grunts and laughter he emitted sounded almost like noises of pleasure. When that tongue stuck into his neck, his face flushed bright red, and he gently pressed his fingers against the back of the insensate Wang Xiaomie's head to hold him still. He pressed him down with even more force than before...

"Shixiong, ah, Shixiong... Mian Deng, ah Mian Deng, look at you, you once hated me for so much as touching you, but now? Now you approach me all on your own. I'm so happy, Shixiong... Go on, drink... Does it taste good? You'll grow addicted to my blood, and never be able to leave me... I'm the one who brought you back..."

The scarlet pattern on Wen Fengjin's brow became brighter than ever before, and his already terrifying black eyes flashed with an excited red glow.

"How did I fall asleep?"

Wang Xiaomie scratched his head as he looked up at the blooming peach tree above him, then pushed himself up into a sitting position in the casket. The last thing he remembered was hungrily chewing on his fingernails beneath this tree. How was it that the next time he opened his eyes, he was sleeping in the casket?

Oh fuck, don't tell me I fainted from hunger! Wang Xiaomie knew he had some problems with low blood sugar, but how could he still have low blood sugar after turning into a zongzi? He subconsciously smacked his lips, then suddenly froze.

Hm? What's this taste in my mouth? It's bitter and kinda medicinal, but also a little bit sweet?

Rubbing his belly, Wang Xiaomie realized with astonishment that he wasn't the slightest bit hungry anymore—in fact, he actually felt quite stuffed.

"You're awake?" said a familiar masculine voice from beside him. Wang Xiaomie turned his head to discover Wen Fengjin lying flat within the casket, clothes rumpled and face somewhat pallid, but with a smile no less vibrant than usual.

From the moment Wang Xiaomie first met him, he'd barely seen any other expressions on the man's face. And looking at him now, Wang Xiaomie felt a particular closeness for some reason, like he'd gained an added beauty filter.

"What happened to you?" Wang Xiaomie asked in surprise. The guy looked like he'd been sucked dry or something.

"Call me Fengjin, Shixiong. You kept sticking your hands in my clothes while you slept just now. I couldn't pull you away, no matter what I did." There was a hint of a teasing look on Wen Fengjin's cold and handsome face, his gaze carrying profound meaning as he looked at Wang Xiaomie.

Wang Xiaomie was speechless. Thankfully it was impossible for a jiangshi to blush, or else his face would probably be as red as a baboon's butt right now!

Wang Xiaomie mentally scolded himself. *Pick up your integrity, man, it's scattered all over the floor! So what if you have a thing for good looks? So what if you've never had a boyfriend in the twenty-plus years you've been alive?! Control yourself!*

"Fengjin, well, uh, sorry about that, ahahaha. I tend to move around a lot in my sleep," Wang Xiaomie somewhat awkwardly explained.

"It's fine, you made me feel quite good."

You're trying to take liberties with me here, aren't you?

Thanks to this interruption, Wang Xiaomie completely forgot his original intention of asking Wen Fengjin why he was no longer hungry, assuming instead that his being a jiangshi now meant that he could simply take a nap to eliminate his hunger, without needing to eat anything.

It sure is strange, though—what's up with this taste in my mouth? Wang Xiaomie asked himself in confusion. *Could it be...because I didn't brush my teeth?!*

MY HUSBAND AND I SLEEP IN A COFFIN

Wen Fengjin

EVER SINCE SHIXIONG DIED—*ever since I killed all those involved, tortured my enemies to death before the entrance of this mausoleum, and used failed elixirs created by a Daoist priest to turn my most capable subordinates into exceptional tomb guardians who would watch over the four corners of this mausoleum—*

To make this mausoleum meet the requirements necessary for the divine tree to summon Shixiong, it was constructed with the circular main tomb at its center, set within a square which was then cut into countless layers. Even I have yet to walk the entirety of this labyrinthine grave. Mechanisms, underground flower gardens, towers and palaces, a subterranean river, decorative rocks with flowing water, innumerable riches... It's as if the entire imperial palace were moved underground. Only a building of this scale and grandeur would be worthy of acting as our wedded abode.

Yes, that's right. I will have Mian Deng wear a wedding dress here in this underground mausoleum. Even though death has claimed him, he will still sleep in my arms, become my bride, and lie with me in the same casket.

Black boots with gold embroidery leisurely strode through a tomb flowing with blood, under the watchful gazes of formerly human but now monstrous tomb guardians. He carried a dormant figure in his arms as he stepped across a steel chain as easily as if he trod on flat ground, until he stood beneath the red flowers of a pining tree in full bloom...

And there they were finally buried together.

In the gloom of the casket, watching Mian Deng's sleeping figure, I felt a kind of happiness. So it wasn't a lie that Mian Deng would only be with me in death: no longer swatting away my hand, speaking to me with a cold and indifferent gaze, calling me abnormal, or choosing to travel the world just to evade me...

"Shixiong, I really do have powerful feelings for you. From the first moment you began teaching me in Shifu's place... I've always been the most special person in your eyes, haven't I? So what if I killed Shifu, and killed all those so-called sectmates? They wouldn't let me be with you, Shixiong. Was I not allowed to resist? They all looked down on me, despised my background. Even though Shifu allowed me to be his disciple, he never once gave me any serious guidance! Those sectmates? Heh... They all deserved to die! They deserved it!

"Only you, Shixiong—only you ever treated me fairly, never isolating me or looking at me with any sort of disgust, selflessly teaching me all that you learned, even coaxing me to sleep when I was a child still trembling with foolish timidity.

"So why did it all change? You promised you would stay by my side for eternity, so why did that change?"

A twisted laugh accompanied this oppressive demand for an explanation.

But none of that matters anymore—I'm sure Shixiong was wrong. He misunderstood me. He definitely made a mistake. The truth is he really does love me—just look at how happy he is lying next to me.

Wen Fengjin smiled as he turned on his side, reaching out a hand to flip open the wedding dress that Mian Deng wore.

"None of that matters anymore, Shixiong. We're going to consummate our love. I've always dreamed of this day. You feel the same way, right? I'm truly so happy..."

The corpse—preserved through time by countless mystic potions and extraordinary treasures—looked like it was alive. As if any moment now, it might open its eyes. Its plaited red belt with its strings of pearls was pulled off, placed to one side by thin and pallid fingers and soon joined by a corset. A jade pendant and jadeite beads were scattered randomly around the vicinity.

The wide, red-and-black wedding dress was like the elegant wrapping around a candied treat, pulled open to reveal the soft, sweet prize within. The smooth-skinned body—slender and pale, yet also somewhat stiff and cold—was gently covered by another, slightly more lively body.

"Shixiong really is beautiful, the most beautiful person I've ever met, I'm so happy... You finally belong to me, Shixiong..."

He affectionately pressed his face against every inch of skin on that body. What kind of sensation was it—using one's own ice-cold flesh to feel another, even colder body? Wen Fengjin didn't know...

In the aftermath, the expression on that peacefully sleeping face was hard to determine. It could have been a virtuous sneer, or a smile of exasperated indulgence.

He tightened his arms around the stiff and icy corpse, their bodies intertwined with each other.

"From now on, we are husband and wife, Mian Deng. Eternally husband and wife... I'll always love you, and you'll always love me. We will never part again..."

My Husband and I Sleep in a Coffin

8

Take Some Pity On This Child

WANG XIAOMIE'S DIARY:
Today I picked up garbage underground, weh... It feels like I've forgotten a lot, but even though I'm surrounded by mystery, I feel perfectly satisfied with this inconsistency.

With his parents and past life seemingly obscured by a layer of white cloth, Wang Xiaomie looked, expressionless, at the unfamiliar reflection in the huge brass mirror before him. A handsome face with soft and gentle eyes... Even without smiling, this was someone whose appearance could make people feel at ease.

Wang Xiaomie slowly frowned. He'd died, become a jiangshi, even gained a thousand-plus-year-old lover, and was now living in an underground mausoleum. And somehow, he'd accepted all of this surprisingly quickly.

No matter how bizarre the things he saw, he found himself feeling neither fear nor suspicion, as if he'd lost the ability to feel such emotions...

This was both impossible and unscientific!

"I haven't been possessed, have I?" Wang Xiaomie stood there in the great and cavernous palace, mocking himself as he gazed into the full-length oval mirror. The stark shadows cast by rows of lit candles around him made for a creepy sort of atmosphere. In the past, he would have peed his pants by now, but he was currently as comfortable as if he'd lived here for hundreds of years.

Wang Xiaomie muttered to himself, "There's something fishy going on here..." *What the heck is wrong with me?*

"What are you doing, Shixiong?" A pair of hands landed on his shoulders, A gentle smiling face, which looked surprisingly sinister in the yellowed reflection of the brass mirror, pressed close to his ear.

Wang Xiaomie could feel the great force being exerted by the hands on his shoulders. The long and slender fingers were like iron hooks ruthlessly digging into his flesh. If he weren't a corpse right now, he'd probably have screamed in pain.

Anyone else would have been scared out of their wits to be so suddenly approached or have their shoulders grabbed so forcefully. A few might even have automatically slapped the guy's hands away, and added a "Fuck, are you crazy?!" But Wang Xiaomie looked at the face in that mirror and somehow couldn't bring himself to feel any anger—not even the barest ember of fury. Instead, he docilely allowed himself to be pulled into the man's embrace.

"You need to behave, Shixiong. When I woke up and didn't see you there I really was very worried. You shouldn't stray too far from me from now on, understood?" Wen Fengjin sighed, his tone of voice one of doting exasperation, icy hands carefully carding through Wang Xiaomie's hair. He really did look like the perfect lover.

Wang Xiaomie twitched his fingers, somewhat irritated by the way he was looking at him. *It's none of your dang business where I go! You might as well have me strapped to your belt these past few days, you've been so clingy!*

But when he opened his mouth, what came out instead was a sweet-voiced "All right, I won't do it again."

Wang Xiaomie was stunned. *Fuck, when'd I get to be this much of a hypocritel?!*

"Why did you come over here today?"

"I was bored and walking around at random."

The first time he saw the mountain of gold, jewels, and other riches in the side hall he'd been excited enough to throw himself in and yell that he'd struck it rich. But now, he was spending every day expressionlessly tossing these things around in boredom. This mausoleum, secluded as it was underground, was silent. So silent it almost seemed to swallow sound itself. It was awfully depressing.

"If only there was Internet and phones and games for me to play... I haven't watched a TV series in ages!" Wang Xiaomie let out the howl of a dying overweight otaku.

"Are those tools modern people carry with them?" Wen Fengjin replied. "If that's what you're looking for, there's a good many in one of the nearby side halls, all left behind by grave robbers. They died in the palace's various traps, and their equipment was all carried to the side hall by my little pets. Come, I'll take you there."

Wang Xiaomie followed Wen Fengjin as they repeatedly crossed more towers and stone stairs. As they went, Wen Fengjin would occasionally fiddle with a wall or a stone carving.

Perhaps because of how quiet the atmosphere was, Wang Xiaomie asked in a tiny voice, "What happened to the bodies?"

Wen Fengjin blinked as he looked back at him, then replied with a smile, "I ate them."

"...D-did they taste good?"

"Heh, I was kidding."

Wang Xiaomie had nothing to say to that. *Somehow I get the feeling that wasn't a joke.*

When they reached the side hall on the farthest outskirts of the mausoleum, Wang Xiaomie's mouth dropped open in shock, at a loss for words once he beheld all the equipment waiting to be looted. He noted that these bags of equipment varied in age from ancient to new, and some even looked like modern-day backpacks. Some were just like those green canvas packs from the nineties, and there were others so old they were falling apart, the tattered fabric turning to dust at a single touch.

He found a lot of ancient weapons like Tang swords and the like. It was hard to say whether they were used by modern grave robbers for exorcizing evil spirits and chopping up zongzi, or if they were weapons left behind by the earliest grave robbers long ago. Picking one up and wiping off the dust, Wang Xiaomie unsheathed it. His eyes glimmered at the sight of a blade still bright as snow after so many years!

After that, he hurriedly opened one of the newer-looking backpacks and, like a hamster stealing snacks, promptly let out a marmot-like screech of excitement as he spread its contents out on the ground. "Whooaaa! A light stick, a flashlight, a lighter, a diary—there's even food tins and crackers! And they haven't passed their expiration date yet! This is great!"

Wang Xiaomie also dug up some powered-off cell phones, impatiently turning them on, only to discover that the majority of them were password-locked. Only one was unlocked, and it was in such poor shape that the screen barely flashed for a few seconds after being turned on before its batteries died. Tears of sorrow ran down Wang Xiaomie's face as he looked at the sacrificed phone.

He had to admit, though, picking up trash and digging for treasure really was pretty addicting. Wang Xiaomie finally understood why so many gamers would do anything for loot. He laughed mischievously as he tugged open one bag after another, stacking the edible food tins atop each other, and treating all the hardtack and jerky as if they were the most precious things on earth. As for personal items like watches and photos and things, he neatly organized them and put them back in their respective owners' bags.

As he sifted through the things, he repeatedly said things like "Why did this bag's owner pack so much beef jerky, wasn't it heavy? I think this can's about to expire soon, so I'll have to make sure to eat it later! Ai, get me some more notebooks and pens, I'm going to write down my experiences and post them online, ehehe. I might even get to become the next Robinson Crusoe!"

In the next backpack, Wang Xiaomie's hands touched something red and soft, and when he pulled it out his face turned red as a tomato. "What'd this grave robber bring a woman's bra with him for?! To ward off evil with or some shit?"

Hurriedly stuffing the undergarments back into the bag, Wang Xiaomie next unearthed some black donkey hooves, along with an alcohol heater and fuel tablets.

"Not bad, not bad, we can stew some donkey hooves to eat! Wait, no! I'm a zongzi now! Is this stuff even edible?!" Wang Xiaomie looked up at Wen Fengjin, waving a black donkey hoof in his hand, and asked, "Fengjin, can I eat this?"

Wen Fengjin was currently squatting right in front of him, resting his chin on a hand as he cheerfully watched him rummage through things. At the question, he said, "Those grave robbers are always carrying these things, but they don't actually have any use—you can eat them."

"That's great! I'll stew it up today! Aiyo, can you believe this guy even brought a bunch of hot pot condiments? Looks like they're all special blends he made himself, too... but it doesn't seem like they brought meat or anything else, and I can't imagine them wanting to just drink hot pot soup base..."

Someone brave enough to drink hot pot soup base by itself? Wang Xiaomie felt pain in his chrysanthemum just thinking about it—*Dude, you were one amazing bastard! Your chrysanthemum must've been tough as iron!*

Despite his garbage-picking adventure getting into full swing, Wang Xiaomie was still able to find time to feign innocence in his success, tut-tutting as he wiped a fake tear from his eye out of self-pity. "To think I used to be a foodie with a full membership on Meituan...and now I've fallen to the level of picking out food from a trash heap... Sob, sob... Dude! Who brought this self-heating hot pot?! Fuck! It smells so good!"

As Wen Fengjin watched the man scurrying about on the floor like a little mouse hoarding grain, his mouth tilted upwards into a faint smile.

He's so cute. (I kind of want to f♥♥k him.)

9

Black Donkey Hoof Hot Pot

WANG XIAOMIE'S DIARY:
Today I ate hot pot inside my own grave...

A river bathed in faint mist flowed along man-made canals and rocks, its banks marked by piles of pebbles and the red-roofed wayside pavilions commonly featured in classic scenery. The stone ceiling above his head was even inlaid with glowing pearls, and the walls all around were lit with undying mermaid-oil lanterns, making the area bright as day.

Little zongzi Wang lifted up the lower hem of his ancient and overly fancy wedding dress and stuffed it into the waistband of his pants, rolled his sleeves all the way up to his shoulders, and squatted down by the river to stew black donkey hooves, looking for all the world like one of those uncles who hang out at building entrances sucking on popsicles.

The seasoning for these donkey hooves had also been dug up from some grave robber's backpack. The hot, bright-red, eye-wateringly spicy soup base bubbled merrily away, the very sight making Wang Xiaomie's chrysanthemum hurt despite him also holding back drool with hungry anticipation.

"Fengjin, stop washing, come and eat some hot pot," Wang Xiaomie shouted off to the side.

Wen Fengjin had his long hair tied up and his clothes pulled out of the way in the same manner as Wang Xiaomie's. Just one look at the messy way his sleeves had been rolled back was enough to tell you who'd done it. The man once renowned as the most terrifying demon to ever exist was now squatting by the riverside with a gloomy look on his face, wordlessly scrubbing clothes.

Years ago, he'd trusted the words of that elmwood-headed subordinate of his and picked out the best flaming-red clothes to make a good many backup wedding outfits. But when he mentioned this, Wang Xiaomie absolutely refused to keep wearing the one he'd had on, insisting that it had to be washed clean.

"How could you not wash an outfit after wearing it for a thousand years?" Wang Xiaomie's clear disdain at the concept caused Wen Fengjin to subconsciously swallow what he'd wanted to say.

The truth was, these clothes actually had a dirt-repelling effect on them. But for the sake of watching Wang Xiaomie as he changed, he still smilingly presented him with a new outfit.

And then reality proved that immoral behavior never led to good endings. After changing his clothes, Wang Xiaomie handed the old ones to him, rubbing his nose as he asked, "Boss, do you know how to do laundry?"

Wen Fengjin was struck speechless. How could you expect a man who'd historically been the most powerful person of his era to be able to do such a thing? But as it happened—he actually could. Wen Fengjin—once a miserable child himself—had washed his own clothes back when he was very young. It was a very long time ago now, but he still remembered how to do it. Faced with Wang Xiaomie's pitiful expression, Wen Fengjin could only nod stiffly. Ultimately, urged on by a cheering Wang Xiaomie, he'd fetched

a wooden tub from a side hall, squatted down by the river and started scrubbing the clothes.

The greatest devil the world had ever known did laundry while listening to Wang Xiaomie mutter, "Later, we can get those decorative clothes racks placed in the side hall and turn it into a laundry room. It'll make it easier to hang clothes out to dry."

Wen Fengjin thought: *Those aren't clothes racks, they're sword racks.*

When Wang Xiaomie called out to him, he cast a glance at the red wooden washbasin in front of him, then quickly got up, neatly arranged the laundry, and walked over.

Wang Xiaomie hurriedly stopped him. "Don't let down your sleeves! You've gotta keep washing later!"

Wen Fengjin looked at his terribly unsightly sleeves, then quietly rolled them back up again.

This completely medieval-looking pair thus squatted around the hot pot like a couple of old uncles, creating a sense of dissonance that was as laughable as it was hard to look at. Just like witnessing the monk Xuanzang in his kasaya, squatting on the curb with his three disciples and smoking cigarettes.

Wang Xiaomie sniffed the aroma from the hot pot and suddenly thought to himself: *A pair of big zongzi eating black donkey hooves and hot pot in the middle of a tomb? If a grave robber happened to come across us right now, he might just faint on the spot.*

A grave robber would be great, especially if they could bring some more donkey hooves with them!

A few days ago, he could never have imagined he'd be eating hot pot in his own grave!

Wen Fengjin watched as the steaming, pungent concoction churned bubbling red. After a moment of silence, he said, "This stuff looks rather like the cinnabar those Daoist priests use in their alchemy. Are you sure it's edible?"

Wang Xiaomie pulled out two freshly cleaned empty food tins, handing him one to use as a bowl as he replied, "Don't worry, this is real tasty stuff. People these days can't live without a little spice! Here you go, have a taste!" Wang Xiaomie obstinately pushed chopsticks and food at him, then impatiently served himself some as well, stuffing his face without even waiting for it to cool. The food's delicious flavor and the accompanying spice immediately made Wang Xiaomie's mouth go numb and his eyes redden, but the long-missed taste also gave him the sensation of being alive. "Gods, that robber must've been from Sichuan! This is seriously freakin' spicy!"

Wen Fengjin watched as Wang Xiaomie continued stuffing his face despite the fact his tears wouldn't stop flowing, then looked down at the tin in his hands. He stared at the strong-smelling meat inside, and finally picked up a piece to put in his mouth.

Wang Xiaomie watched as Wen Fengjin slowly chewed in a refined manner, his face gradually turning red, nose scrunching from the spice. Finally losing all decorum, he hurriedly swallowed the meat, a tortured expression appearing on his pretty, somewhat feminine face.

Wang Xiaomie, still holding his bowl, laughed aloud at the look on his face. "I didn't know you couldn't handle spice."

Struggling to quash the spicy feeling in his throat, Wen Fengjin replied with a frown, "I've always preferred sour foods."

"I hate sour foods myself." Wang Xiaomie could handle soy sauce and vinegar, but even a slightly sour fruit would set his teeth on edge.

The two blew on their donkey hooves to cool them as they ate the tendons. As they were eating, Wang Xiaomie spoke up. "Since

I'm now the living dead and have no plans to leave, I'll stay here and keep you company. It's not like I've got any aunts or uncles who love me up there, anyway, and when my parents found me dead they probably just handed some money to a random relative to get my body taken care of.

"I still don't fully believe what you told me before, but you're single, I'm single, and I won't lie to you, I'm gay—that's what you call a cut-sleeve—so if you treat me with honesty, then we can start off as friends, and if we feel like things are working out, then we can couple up and spend our days in the mausoleum together. So you don't need to hide things from me... I've been feeling myself getting more and more strange of late, and I was wondering if it had something to do with you."

Wang Xiaomie had laid everything out in a single breath, and hadn't stopped moving his chopsticks for even a second. Despite his nerves, he tried to question Wen Fengjin in a way that kept the mood light.

The guy's an old zongzi who's lived for over a thousand years, after all! What if he realizes he's been exposed and accidentally bites me to death? I've only got my twenty-something years of memories under my belt; all that stuff about past and present lives honestly isn't the slightest bit persuasive. Unless Wang Xiaomie one day recovered his memories and discovered that he really was Mian Deng in the past, it was going to be really difficult for him to turn himself into someone else entirely.

Wen Fengjin's chopsticks paused in the air, and he lifted his eyes to gaze at Wang Xiaomie.

Wang Xiaomie swallowed somewhat nervously.

After a moment of silence, Wen Fengjin's expression suddenly turned gloomy, the corners of his mouth twitching downward as he said, a sad look on his face, "I'm happy to hear you say you'll stay with me. I promise I won't hurt you, and have not done so prior to this."

Wang Xiaomie frowned suspiciously. "You really haven't done anything?"

Wen Fengjin clenched his fists as he lowered his head, his tied-back hair falling to cover his face.

"I didn't get the wrong person. Mian Deng, you're still you. It's very clear to me that you're the one I was waiting for." With a self-mocking smile, he continued, "Yet you doubted me even in your past life, because of my monstrous eyes and the negative comments I received from others. Why is it that even now, I still cannot obtain your full trust? I waited for you for a thousand years! How could I bear to hurt you?"

His husky voice trembled slightly, almost as if he were crying. Wang Xiaomie had nothing to say. *I'm feeling kinda like a scumbag right about now.*

MY HUSBAND AND I SLEEP IN A COFFIN

This is Just the Kind of Hooligan I Am

WANG XIAOMIE'S DIARY:
I don't want much, a serving of mala hot pot is enough~~~

Wang Xiaomie couldn't see the twisted, savage look on Wen Fengjin's lowered face, or the scarlet veins spreading across those black eyes to the point they were nearly about to cover the entire socket.

That old bastard—! How dare he deceive me! Why did Shixiong have to notice? Why, why, why?! The rites I performed should have been correct! That old bastard must have lied!

Wen Fengjin bit his lip, forcing himself to breathe calmly. If that old man weren't long dead by now, he'd definitely torture him to death!

"Uh hey, I didn't mean anything by it..." Wang Xiaomie hurriedly put down his food, rubbing his hands together like a fly as he squatted by Wen Fengjin's side: "I really didn't mean it. Wh-why is a big boss man like you acting like a shojo character?! Wait! Don't tell me you're a bottom, that's not gonna work! Two bottoms won't equal a happy ending!" Wang Xiaomie's face paled at the thought, becoming a scumbag to his own kind at the drop of a hat.

Though Wen Fengjin didn't know what he meant by "tops" or "bottoms," he still got the gist, raising his head to say, "Mian Deng, you're overthinking it..."

Oh good, that's a relief... You practically scared me into a cold sweat.
Wang Xiaomie cleared his throat, saying with some embarrassment,
"Like I said earlier, I'll probably die if I leave the divine tree, so
I won't be going anywhere."

At present, he had truly become "Wang Tree-man, good for two
hours after a minute of charging"—whenever he left the divine tree
for too long he had to come back and recharge his battery. Even his
ability to taste anything in this hot pot was thanks to him having
hugged that big tree for a good long while beforehand—otherwise,
every bite he ate out of his little tin can would've tasted no different
from dirt.

"Hey, uh, there isn't really anything I'm going to miss back on
the surface, and you're absolutely certain I'm the guy you want.
With all that in mind, we can partner up and live out our days
together without any disdain between us, and if I really do get my
memories back, then we can be together for real. Or if one day you
discover I'm not the guy you were looking for, then we'll split up,"
Wang Xiaomie said tentatively. "What do you think?"

Wen Fengjin shook his head, saying, "That day won't come. I've already said you're definitely the one I want."

"How are you so sure?" a puzzled Wang Xiaomie asked in return,

Wen Fengjin didn't reply, staring silently at the blazing red hot
pot instead. It was clear that he had no intention of explaining.

Wang Xiaomie had grown up under the care of his paternal
grandmother. As a child, his parents had paid no attention to him,
and other relatives were constantly telling his grandmother that he
was a burden. If he did the slightest thing wrong, they would simply
say, "Oh, it's *that* boy."

Perhaps it was having a family like this that led Wang Xiaomie
to be so good at looking past things. He had nothing, and therefore

had no fear of losing anything, which made him especially good at accepting unfamiliar things or situations.

Back when his grandma had asked him a few questions in hopes of having a heart-to-heart talk, he'd been just as taciturn as Wen Fengjin was being now. What was it she'd said back then?

"Let's just eat... It's enough as long as you know what's what in your heart."

Wang Xiaomie tapped his chopsticks against his tin, smiling somewhat helplessly. He then said, with a loud sigh, "Don't you worry—the two of us will be depending on each other for survival from now on, heh! I've actually never depended on anybody for survival before in my life!"

His grandma hadn't even taken care of him for two years before she was gone too. The thought that he'd be able to find a man—whoops, sorry, that he'd be able to find a zongzi—to make a living with in this lifetime, while a little melancholy, had a much greater part in making Wang Xiaomie feel strangely fortunate.

Compared to dying of old age after a lifetime of loneliness, being stuck in an underground mausoleum with someone to keep him company was a far kinder way to go. A frighteningly strange daily life involving two zongzi eating hot pot together was a happiness beyond Wang Xiaomie's wildest dreams. So even if all of this was just a fantasy he was having in the moments before death, Wang Xiaomie considered it to be a positive event borrowed from someone else's good fortune, and would shamelessly cling to this opportunity until the day he had no choice but to let go...

Fuck! What the hell am I getting all sentimental for?!

Wang Xiaomie mentally called himself out, then went back to shoveling tendons into his mouth, occasionally putting some into Wen Fengjin's bowl while he was at it. "Come on, eat, eat! It feels like the flavor in my mouth's dampened a lot—I've probably been away from the divine tree for too long, and my sense of taste is about to die."

Wen Fengjin looked at the meat in his bowl, then at this version of Mian Deng, so different from his previous life, feeling the pungently spicy steam from the pot wafting against his face in a daze as he thought. How long had it been now? How long had it been since those trying days when Mian Deng stopped treating him with warmth, or willingly approaching him? Now he was right by his side, drawing near in a manner that was as foreign as it was familiar.

Wen Fengjin picked up a piece of meat and set it in his mouth, a heat he hadn't felt in ages spreading across his tongue at the same time that a relaxed, smiling expression gradually spread itself across his face. It was different from his usual, perfectly flawless smile. It was the kind of emotion which people tended to inadvertently reveal due to feelings of warmth...

"Mian Deng, as long as we live, as long as you do not betray me, I will make sure never to betray you," Wen Fengjin suddenly said, putting down his bowl and chopsticks.

Wang Xiaomie laughed at that, replying with a wink, "You know, you've got this habit. When you're happy, you call me Mian Deng, and when you're not, you start calling me Shixiong. So I'm guessing that our past relationship wasn't as perfect as you told me it was. That's fine, though—if you were able to wait for me for this long, I think that even if I got my memories back, I'd still be willing to know you again, and accept you."

Wen Fengjin gazed at Wang Xiaomie's smiling face, the expression on his own face one of blank astonishment. After a long moment, his smile slowly widened, and he quietly said, "All right."

A big zongzi and an old-ass fake zongzi squatted close to a steaming hot little pot, desperately seeking the sensation of what it was to be loved by one another, and becoming inextricably addicted to that sensation...as well as intangibly deepening the relationship between two pitiful creatures.

Afterward, Wang Xiaomie expressed deep gratitude toward the grave robber bro who'd sent them homemade hot pot soup base and helped this to happen! Sichuan hot pot was amazing! Homemade hot pot soup base was the bomb!

He thought: *As master of this tomb, I welcome any and all grave robbers to continue bringing soup base with them when they come in to play, okay. And if you bring fresh black donkey hooves I'll even give you a free gold coin! You say something too, Fengjin!*

And Wen Fengjin would say, *Welcome, welcome, we have many gold coins, which I guarantee will be presented to you.* But as an aside: *Heh~ It's not as if any of you will be leaving again once you enter.*

He could imagine the grave robber bros going *We're not falling for your tricks! You two zongzi are rotten to the core!*

After they'd finished the hot pot and Wen Fengjin had finished doing the laundry, the two of them returned to the divine tree. Traces of blood vessels were already beginning to show themselves on Wang Xiaomie's arm as his skin turned pallid. He clucked his tongue at this. It was exactly two hours of usage for an hour's charge—he couldn't squeeze even an extra second out of it!

Wang Xiaomie rolled up his sleeves, hugged the vigorously blossoming divine tree, and began his daily activity of tree-fuc— wait, sorry, of tree nuzzling.

This thing really was miraculously effective. When Wang Xiaomie approached the great tree, he could clearly sense power entering his body from where he touched its bark, giving his quickly rotting body a new lease on life.

After nuzzling it for five minutes, a fully charged and fully sated Wang Xiaomie plopped into his casket. Speaking of which—it was weird how, every time he laid down in the casket before the heart-to-heart they'd just had, the big guy next to him would hug him with a perversely captivating smile on his face. But now that they'd had the talk, this guy actually seemed to be getting bashful. He lay there as stiffly as a piece of wood, even keeping his hands properly placed on his own lower belly.

Looks like I'm not getting any chance to take advantage of him today, huh? Wang Xiaomie tutted regretfully to himself as he lay back in the casket.

That's right! Normally, when Wen Fengjin pressed close to embrace him, Wang Xiaomie kept his face expressionless while actually secretly laughing to himself every time, even faking resistance just to steal a grope in return, using the chance to get his claws in on some action. At this point he'd even felt out exactly how many abdominal muscles Wen Fengjin had!

Wang Xiaomie thought, *That's right! This is exactly the kinda good-for-nothing I am! Ain't nothin' you can do about it!*

A shameless yet self-righteous Wang Xiaomie lay there in the casket, head against a hard jade pillow, and nodded right to sleep.

Jiangshi Poop Too?!

WANG XIAOMIE'S DIARY:

How might I describe what happened today, ai... Would you believe me if I told you that I could get diarrhea as a jiangshi, and that as I was poopin' away, a whole grown man dropped from above to watch me?

A shameless yet self-righteous Wang Xiaomie lay in the casket, head against a hard jade pillow, and snored right to sleep. Right up until the middle of the night, when his stomach was suddenly hit with a familiar pain.

Wang Xiaomie sat up, cradling his stomach, his face contorting.

"What's wrong, Mian Deng?" Wen Fengjin didn't need to sleep, and was thus always only pretending. He hurriedly got up when he heard movement beside him.

"I—I—I! I think I upset my stomach...fuck, how can a jiangshi get the urge to shit?!" As he cradled his stomach, Wang Xiaomie wanted to cry but lacked the tears to do so. "Hurry and open the lid!"

Wang Xiaomie crawled out of that casket like his life depended on it. But Wen Fengjin, having opened the casket's lid, said with a frown, "But mausoleums don't have bathrooms."

Wang Xiaomie was struck speechless. That's right—who'd ever think to build a bathroom in the family tomb? Putting aside the matter of cleaning an ancient mausoleum pit latrine in the first place, why would anyone in this mausoleum even be taking a shit?! They'd already be dead and buried! Who'd ever imagine the resident of the grave might one day suddenly wake up for a late night potty break?!

"Wh-what do I do then...?" Wang Xiaomie tearlessly cried as he covered his butt with both hands and pressed his legs tight together, his normally good-looking face twisting in an ugly manner. "You gotta think of something, Boss!" The shit-uation had already gotten critical. If he didn't deal with it soon...

This was the first time Wen Fengjin had been faced with such a situation as well. He looked at the savage expression on Wang Xiaomie's face, coughed once into his fist, and said, "This place is rife with traps. We could look around the outermost area of the mausoleum and see if the artisans who built it might have set up—pfft—ahem—set up outhouses near the halls."

Fucking hell, don't think I can't see you laughing over my misfortune just because you've got a hand over your mouth... Wang Xiaomie said through gritted teeth, "Then what are we waiting for?! Let's get going!"

"But...due to the size of this mausoleum, it would take two shichen by horse, galloping all the way. As for an average person's walking speed..." Wen Fengjin changed the topic in a way which seemed to Wang Xiaomie to be entirely survival instinct. "While the mausoleum is massive, I can take you there myself—you need only hold it in for another half shichen."

Wang Xiaomie couldn't have told you if his hands were shaking out of anger or constipation as he said, "Why'd you even make this tomb so big?! Hurry up and take me there—I'm gonna—"

At this point the look on Wang Xiaomie's face changed and he immediately clamped his legs tight. Wen Fengjin lifted him like a princess and rushed out as quickly as a soaring swallow.

The surrounding scenery was left behind them at record speeds as Wang Xiaomie lay in Wen Fengjin's arms, the resulting wind causing his hair to fly wildly.

Once Wang Xiaomie was finally put down, he woodenly leaned against the wall and patted Wen Fengjin's shoulder. "Bro, you sure are a good driver...*hurk...*" *Thanks to going two hundred miles an hour, my stomach's churning up a storm—hworf—!*

After vomiting, Wang Xiaomie waved a hand in response to Wen Fengjin's confused look, saying, "You can leave now, Boss. I'll squat here for a bit. Just in case there's nothing to wipe my butt with, go dig through those grave robber guys' backpacks and see if they have any white paper."

"All right." Wen Fengjin nodded. But as he was about to go, he suddenly stopped in his tracks, turning his head to look at Wang Xiaomie with a blossoming smile and say, "Shixiong wouldn't purposely lie to me about stomach pains in order to leave the mausoleum, would he?"

Wang Xiaomie froze in the middle of anxiously hurrying to pull up his robe and untie his pants. He then expressionlessly gave him the finger. "Get outta here, unless you wanna see how bad I can gross you out right in front of your eyes."

Wen Fengjin laughed lightly but did in fact leave, though not without a last parting word: "The mausoleum is filled with dangers, so I'll have Mu Yi come over to accompany you. Don't worry—he's a guardian of the mausoleum, and the cutest of my little pets."

Wang Xiaomie muttered to himself as he squatted over the pit. *Isn't that just another way of saying you don't trust me?! Hmph! But what did he mean by Mu Yi being a little cutie? Is he as cute as me?*

Ever-shameless Wang Xiaomie curled his lip at the thought, only for his body to stiffen just a few seconds later. Hold on, he was pretty sure Wen Fengjin had said there weren't any normal living creatures in this tomb, or something to that effect. Plus, what exactly could a big zongzi be raising as pets? Huskies?! There was no way these things were gonna be normal!

Wang Xiaomie curled up in fear, internally screaming wildly for the big boss to love him again.

But ten minutes later, Boss Wen had not returned to love him again—because he was currently lost in thought as he stared at a few rolls of toilet paper packed in waterproof bags. Please forgive the boss—he had never seen toilet paper like this before.

Meanwhile, Wang Xiaomie had a frosty look on his face, ruthlessly pinching his arms to prevent himself from yelling aloud. He had a habit of acting increasingly calm the more scared or nervous he got—a quirk commonly known as "getting scared silly." Which was exactly what he was going through right now.

Wang Xiaomie looked at the bloody, seemingly skinless lizardman "little cutie" before him, also lost in thought. Even the need to shit had been scared back into him.

After a long moment of silence, he looked up at the skinless lizardman who'd already climbed onto the ceiling above him, and quietly called out through chattering teeth. "Mu Yi?"

The lizardman above his head immediately cracked its mouth open into a smile so wide it stretched from the base of the left ear to the base of the right, and let out a laugh like a dropped barbell, its meaty tail happily starting to wag...

This is your effin' little cutie?! How the heck is this any kinda little cutie! The little pets you're keeping are seriously unique, dude!

And this wasn't even the most terrifying part—the most terrifying part was that just as he was tremblingly but assiduously struggling with this life-or-defecate situation, there was a loud noise overhead and the entire tomb passage began to shake!

Little cutie Mu Yi made a terrifying "gegege"-like call, similar to the ghost girl from Ju-On, while quickly spinning in irritable circles up on the ceiling, as if it was on alert about something while watching Wang Xiaomie with an incredibly intelligent gaze, as if saying, *Hey bro, why aren't you getting up yet? Don't you see there's danger going on here?!*

Bare-cheeked and squatting, Wang Xiaomie was speechless. *Bro, it's not like I don't want to get up, but I don't have any paper.*

He gripped the waistband of his pants, hesitating a good long while between the two options of getting crushed to death in an earthquake, or getting straight-up stunk to death after not wiping his butt.

Just as he decided to abandon his integrity, and was preparing to firmly pull up his pants and stand up—after all, if he died in the latrine, it wasn't entirely guaranteed that the big boss could dredge him back out—right at that moment, the violent noise above his head suddenly got worse!

Then a flagstone located about three feet from Wang Xiaomie's head suddenly flipped open, revealing a dark void, followed by an unfamiliar man's heartrending scream. A whole guy came rolling out of the hole like a man-sized ball and crashed against the floor with a thud not even eight inches from Wang Xiaomie.

"Aiyo...why must there be traps even at the mausoleum's *border*..." The guy must have been pretty tough, since he squinted and picked himself up without the slightest sign of dizziness from his fall...

Only to find himself face-to-face with a certain zongzi right in the middle of pulling up his pants.

The two stared at each other. And stared. And stared... Wang Xiaomie clutched his pants tight in embarrassment: "Hey, uh... mister, do you have any paper?"

The honestly rather pretty mister was absolutely speechless.

The pair went back to staring at each other for quite a long while, before the other guy suddenly let out an ear-piercing scream. "Oh my gooood it's a big red-clothed zongziiii and it fuckin' taaaaalks! *Save me, Ge!*"

Wang Xiaomie, fast approaching deafness, thought: *I'm mindin' my own business using the restroom in my own tomb, when a whole-ass man comes falling from the sky and won't stop yelling, scaring me so bad I can't even poop in peace—who's provoking who here, huh?!*

MY HUSBAND AND I SLEEP IN A COFFIN

Could You Be
a Little More
Conscientious, You Pig?

THE SAME SOUND, like a woman keening, echoed from the side hall. This was also one of Wen Fengjin's pet monsters, who'd let out this cry as an alarm whenever grave robbers appeared. The origin point from which her voice rang out would be where the robbers were located.

Upon hearing the woman's wail, Wen Fengjin's face instantly paled. He quickly started rushing back the way he came.

Mian Deng! Those grave robbers were heading towards where Mian Deng was!

Meanwhile, Wang Xiaomie was speechlessly watching the dude in front of him brandish a black donkey hoof in his face while loudly crying on the floor. *Dude you've been yelling for like ten minutes now, aren't you tired?*

Wang Xiaomie opened his mouth, starting to say "I—"

I'm not a bad guy...

The grown man in front of him wailed: "*Don't come near me aaaaaaaaaaaaaahhhhhhhh!*"

Wang Xiaomie was speechless. He kept awkwardly squatting there, doing his best to adjust the angle so he could pull down his clothes; everyone was male here, sure, but what would he do if the guy saw?

Maybe his movements created some sort of misunderstanding, but the dirt-faced dude let out a roar before yelling "It's over for you!" And then struck Wang Xiaomie in the head with the black donkey hoof he'd been brandishing!

Bonk!

A totally unharmed Wang Xiaomie stared at him, dead-eyed.

The dude was shaking all over as he said, "No way! Why isn't this zongzi hurt?! I must not have hit it hard enough!"

He then raised the hoof high above his head and brought it down with full force. Wang Xiaomie was close enough that he could even hear the swish of wind as the black donkey hoof swung towards him.

Fuck, I can't tell if you're trying to fix the zongzi in place or frickin' bash it to death!

Wang Xiaomie's face paled drastically. It was true that, after becoming a jiangshi, his body had become sturdy enough to take a much worse beating than before—and he wasn't particularly afraid of pain—but that didn't mean his head would be able to handle a blow from this hoof! If his skin wasn't thick enough and he ended up with a caved-in head, wouldn't that totally damage his looks?! In his terror, that donkey hoof seemed almost to emit a glittering, frosty light.

Lizardman Mu Yi, who'd been overhead all this time without being told to attack, suddenly widened its scarlet eyes at the sight of the living human making motions to attack. It was only an instant away from leaping down with its bloody mouth opened wide to bite this human's head in half!

Wang Xiaomie, seeing this, quickly tugged at the swinging black donkey hoof—but he'd underestimated how strong he now was, and found himself tugging the hoof right out of the guy's hands. "Don't move!" he yelled loudly.

The crawling monster above their head froze on the cusp of pouncing, and the man—totally clueless to the fact he'd barely avoided death by a hair—stood there white-faced, staring at his empty hands. *Oh no, this zongzi's cultivation is too advanced, it even took my black donkey hoof!*

Wang Xiaomie saw that the grave-robber guy was about to faint and, still lacking any paper to wipe his butt with, hurriedly raised his voice to say, "Don't panic! Don't panic! Don't worry, I won't hurt you, I was just using the restroom, I have no idea how you came dropping in on my head. Bro, I'm seriously in need of toilet paper right now, if you give me some toilet paper I'll give back your black donkey hoof! I'll even tell you how to get out of here! How about it?"

The guy seemed almost to be in a trance, looking at Wang Xiaomie's very ordinary squat and his clearly abnormal apparel and skin tone, before managing with some difficulty to ask, "A zongzi...can shit?"

"So what if I can? Don't go discriminating against zongzi!"

The guy went silent at that, processing who knew how much mental anguish in his mind. Eventually, he wiped his face with one hand, making it even darker with dirt. He heaved the contents of his backpack onto the floor and dug up a pack of Qingfeng-brand paper, handing it to Wang Xiaomie. And it was unopened, too.

"Thanks!" This guy really had a good heart, actually giving him what he'd asked for! Wang Xiaomie accepted the paper with genuine gratitude.

The young grave robber watched as this big zongzi really took the paper, opened it with a practiced hand, and began to use it. If his face were expressive enough, it would definitely have "hhhhhhhhh" and "Who am I where am I why can even zongzi use toilet paper now" written all over it.

Wang Xiaomie was going to wipe, but that burning gaze made him look up with some embarrassment, saying, "Bro, you're kinda making me feel awkward, the way you're watching me, so I'd appreciate it if you turned around."

"Oh!" The also somewhat embarrassed guy quickly turned around.

Wang Xiaomie breathed a sigh of relief at finally getting to finish wiping. He stood up, taking the black donkey hoof with him as he left the little latrine—which didn't even have a door for privacy—and walked over to the guy's side. At least one good thing about becoming a zongzi was that his legs hadn't fallen asleep even after squatting for so long.

As he was thinking this, the guy suddenly leapt up, pressed his hands down on Wang Xiaomie's shoulders, and said with a loud laugh, "I've figured it out! You're a guy my ge hired to come to this tomb to scare me, right?! This was all to stop me from following them on their grave-robbing trips from now on, wasn't it?! Hahaha, I'm a genius!"

How else could your average zongzi speak so clearly? How could it shit? How could it go around not attacking the living? This can only mean this is one of my ge's mates that he sent over to scare me!

"Haha, you must be one of the guys who works at my ge's shop! It must've been hard for you to squat here for so long. Hurry and return my black donkey hoof, I'm definitely gonna find the Fish Pearl."

Who knew what scenario he was imagining, with that bright, toothy grin of his? What Wang Xiaomie did understand was that the guy had decided he was human. *That's fine*, he thought to himself, as he handed over the donkey hoof. But immediately after handing it over, he caught a glimpse of his own hand and realized it was completely covered in black pigment!

"Gods! Don't tell me this donkey hoof of yours is dyed black!" *And here I was wondering why this dude's face was getting blacker the more he wiped it with his hand!* With a weary look on his face, Wang Xiaomie said, "Bro, no matter how poor we are, I'm pretty sure you can't go fooling people with a dyed donkey hoof." *Do you think all zongzi are fools? Tut-tut. You're really trying to trick the dead...*

The guy's face stiffened, and he scratched his head with an awkward laugh. "I, I didn't know, okay? We didn't have any left in the house, so I bought it on Bingxixi..."

Wang Xiaomie was speechless. *Heheh, that's impressive work.* He was certain by now that this guy was pretty young, and you could tell at a glance that he hadn't paid the subscription fee for his IQ.

"Oh right, you must be a new guy my ge recently recruited, right? How come I don't remember seeing you before?" the man casually asked.

Wang Xiaomie shook his head. "I don't work for your ge. My name is Wang Xiaomie, and I have no idea who your ge even is."

"Oh, I'm Zhen Bei—if you weren't hired by my ge, then who are you? Don't tell me..." His gaze turned wary as he continued, "Don't tell me you're also a grave robber?!"

No, I'm the poor grave owner who's getting robbed...

My Husband and I Sleep in a Coffin

13

Oho~
It's Over

*A*ND ZHEN BEI? *You know that's slang for "bad luck," right? Dude, it's a wonder you're brave enough to rob a grave after giving yourself a name like that...*

"Forget it. Just go ahead and consider me another grave robber, I guess." Wang Xiaomie let out a sigh and, remembering the little monster named Mu Yi that was drooling on the ceiling over this guy's head, added, "Let's go somewhere else to talk."

Wang Xiaomie led him out of the little room, then earnestly and quite maternally said, "Zhen Bei, bro, I can see that you're young, and prying open your ancestors' graves is sure to lead to retribution. When my hus—oh wait no, when my partner gets here in a bit, he'll tell you the way out, so you should leave as soon as you can."

"So you have a partner too, huh." Despite the filth on his face, Zhen Bei's expression was surprisingly bright as he replied, "No way! My dage got blinded by poison and can't see anything. Only the Fish Pearl in this legendary mausoleum can save him! So thanks for the warning, but I absolutely have to get the Fish Pearl for my dage!"

"Blinded by poison?" Wang Xiaomie saw that all the man's gear was by no means cheap. Most of it looked professional. It appeared the rest of the guy's family was also in the same line of business.

"It's just..." As expected, Zhen Bei started mumbling and couldn't get out a word of explanation, chuckling awkwardly a couple times before going silent.

Wang Xiaomie understood that everyone had their secrets, so he had no intention of probing further. Instead, he took a moment to ponder it over. The Fish Pearl? Wen Fengjin had pulled out every precious treasure in this mausoleum for him to play with at one point or another. Why had he never heard of anything that could help someone recover their sight?

"Do you know what this thing looks like, if you came to somewhere so dangerous to find it?" Wang Xiaomie asked.

"Of course I do! I'm not an idiot." He pulled a photo out of his backpack and proudly showed it to Wang Xiaomie, saying "See, I secretly photocopied this from my erge's place—this is the last Fish Pearl we discovered, but it's already been used."

We've just met and already you're willing to hand me such important data? Does your ge know what a naughty kid you are?

Wang Xiaomie wordlessly took the picture, looked at it for a moment, then frowned. The Fish Pearl in the picture wasn't very big, and didn't have any distinguishing features to speak of. It was just a white bead about the size of a mung bean, the only difference being that there was a tiny bit of black in the white of the pearl, making it look just like one of the bulging round fish eyes from which it got its name.

This thing... looked really familiar for some reason!

Oh, right!

Wang Xiaomie smacked his left fist in his right hand, pulled a long, embroidered red hair tie from his head, and held one end up between them both. A string of little white beads with black dots on them hung from the end of the hair tie, looking exactly like the Fish Pearl in the picture.

They were both left speechless. Zhen Bei's mouth gaped wide open, his eyes bulging until they were practically about to pop out of his head; he pointed a finger at the hair tie in Wang Xiaomie's hand, his face so red with suppressed excitement that he couldn't even speak.

Wang Xiaomie fixed his long hair and jade crown, which had come loose due to the hair tie's removal, and said, with his mouth twitching at the corners, "You're *sure* these are the Fish Pearls that can save your dage's eyes?" Weren't they just a decoration on his hair tie?

"This is it, it's the Fish Peeaaarrlll! Oh my fuckin' god!" Zhen Bei energetically jumped up and down in all excitement as he continued, "This is my family's main line of business, you think I wouldn't know?! That's the Fish Pearl! And there's so many of 'em! Fuck! I can save my ge's eyes now hahaha, and how do you have so many? Can you give me one? Can you, can you, please, I'm begging you, the down-on-my-knees-pleading kinda begging you!"

Try actually getting on your knees before you say that, Wang Xiaomie thought to himself, unsure whether to laugh or cry at the sight of the guy repeatedly shaking his clasped hands up and down with a pitiful look on his face, just like a little dog repeatedly making a "thank you" motion while begging for treats. It made it hard to reject him.

Besides...I've got a whole chest full of hair ties like this! Wang Xiaomie thought of the multiple large chests which Wen Fengjin would open when doing his hair for him every day. They not only contained hair ties like this, but a ton of men's hairpins and jade crowns too. But seeing the emotional look on Zhen Bei's face, he decided to keep that knowledge to himself. Under Zhen Bei's longing gaze, Wang Xiaomie snapped a string on the ribbon, dropping a bunch of little Fish Pearls into his hand, then picked out a big one to give to Zhen Bei.

Why not give a few more? Because Wang Xiaomie still understood the meaning of the phrase "An innocent man will commit crimes for wealth." Often, giving someone too much could be a bad thing.

Luckily, Zhen Bei truly was a sweet, naïve little cutie. Not only did he show no dissatisfaction at being given a single pearl, he was actually as happy as a puppy handed a meaty bone, happily clutching the pearl with a face full of excitement and gratitude. "Thank you Xiao-Mie! You should come find me if you're ever in S City, I promise I'll have you flying high with the royal treatment! I'm serious!"

Oh come on, Wang Xiaomie thought to himself, *With how sweet and naïve you are, you'd probably send me flying right into a trash heap.*

Before he could finish his thought, the overly emotional Zhen Bei came forward and pulled Wang Xiaomie into a big ol' bear hug!

Before Wang Xiaomie could push him off, he caught sight of Wen Fengjin at the other end of the passage, a hideously distorted look on his face. He was probably trying to go for a smile, but with his narrowed eyes all black and visibly bulging with veins, his expression looked even more twisted than ever!

Wang Xiaomie nearly peed himself with terror, woodenly looking at Zhen Bei, who was still sprawled over him. *Yup, it's over. This is a big ol' scene of adulterers getting caught in the act!*

"Fengjin...er, if you'd just let me explain..."

Zhen Bei jumped off him and turned around with a puzzled look on his face: "Who're you talking to, Xiao-Mie...whoa! When the fuck did someone show up behind us—huh? If you know him, then doesn't that make him your partner?" And then, an almost diabolical finishing blow: "Haha, your friend has a really weird look on his face!"

Yeah, weird, and it'll be even weirder after he's chopped us into dumpling filling... Wang Xiaomie buried his face in his hands.

Wen Fengjin said with a cold smile, "Friend? Heh~ Is that how Shixiong referred to me? Shixiong really is just as elegant as he was all those years ago. But have you forgotten that you're already married to me? Yet here you are in this tomb, getting cozy with other men! Betraying your feminine virtues!"

Wang Xiaomie was speechless. *The heck do you mean by "betraying feminine virtues"?!*

Zhen Bei, being stupidly adorable, said: "Huh? What's all this about?"

Faced with the sight of an adulterous wife (*nothing of the sort!*) and a damned third party (*he isn't!*), Wen Fengjin decided to shut the door and set Mu Yi loose. "What are you waiting for, Mu Yi! Get that creature who stepped into the mausoleum and tear it to shreds!"

My Husband and I Sleep in a Coffin

14

Call a Psychiatrist!

"WAIT, FENGJIN! He really did just come here to look for something! Look, it was this..." Wang Xiaomie held up his hand and waved the hair tie he was holding, stopping him before that quiet gurgling sound could get any closer.

Zhen Bei, meanwhile, was completely lost as to what was going on. He didn't know why the little friend he'd just made had started arguing with his partner, but instinct told him that guy they were facing was not someone he should be picking a fight with. Zhen Bei quickly stuffed the Fish Pearl into his bag, then hid behind Wang Xiaomie, half peering around him to watch how things went down.

The sight of the hair tie in Wang Xiaomie's hand not only failed to calm Wen Fengjin's anger, but actually made his face grow even scarier. In the time period Wen Fengjin hailed from, a man's gift of a hair tie, or a woman's of a handkerchief or hairpin, was considered a declaration of love; conversely, to ask for one meant an active attempt at courtship.

But Wang Xiaomie didn't know any of this. He watched with terror as Wen Fengjin suddenly began to laugh, saying in a low voice, "I've changed my mind, Shixiong, I don't want Mu Yi to kill him anymore..."

Wang Xiaomie let out a sigh of relief. "It's really great that you underst—"

Wen Fengjin tilted his head with a smile. "Mmhm, don't worry, Shixiong, I'll do it myself."

Phew. That's a real weight off my—wait, like hell it is!

Wang Xiaomie watched as Wen Fengjin slowly lifted a hand. His wide, black-and-red sleeve filled up despite there being no wind. Those billowing red clothes, the drifting dark hair, and that deathly pale face, combined to produce spellbinding beauty. Even at a time like this, Wang Xiaomie couldn't help thinking *Gods, he's so hot!*

A second later, before he could get his bearings, a gust of air suddenly and forcefully pushed him away. Until now he'd never imagined that someone might be capable of simply waving a hand and using powerful qi to slap another person into the wall. In an instant, he was squatting down on the floor, while Wen Fengjin was suddenly between them, grabbing Zhen Bei's neck with one hand!

Fuck! He knows the Flash spell?!

"You aren't worthy of demanding my shixiong's hair tie!" Wen Fengjin's grip on Zhen Bei's neck was tight enough that it was about to snap it. Zhen Bei's feet were no longer touching the ground by this point. He was in visible pain as he scrabbled ineffectively at Wen Fengjin's arm.

"Don't be afraid, Shixiong, I know you hate him too, so I'll do away with him for you, all right?" Wen Fengjin's voice lilted at the end of that question, carrying with it a youthful joy, as if he were asking for permission to eat a piece of candy. He even turned to smile at Wang Xiaomie in the middle of his grim act. Wang Xiaomie was scared silly by that deadly aura and the casual tone in which he spoke of taking lives. He leaned against the wall, dazedly watching Zhen Bei as he struggled.

To his shock, the grown man's desperate twisting and tearing didn't seem to move Wen Fengjin at all! He hadn't been kidding when he said it: he really was going to kill Zhen Bei. Wang Xiaomie finally accepted this fact.

"Ugh..."

The pained noise emitting from Zhen Bei's throat was what finally brought Wang Xiaomie back to reality. He hurriedly picked himself up off the floor, and hugged Wen Fengjin's arm with all his strength. He was shaking all over as he yelled, "It wasn't the hair tie! It was the beads on my hair tie! Look, it's these..."

Wang Xiaomie cupped the beads in his palm, holding them up in a panic for Wen Fengjin to see. Wen Fengjin frowned as he looked at the few Fish Pearls lying in that pallid hand.

"He said his brother can't see and needs a Fish Pearl to heal his eyes, so he came here looking for these! So let him go! Let him go... I'm begging you, please..."

Wang Xiaomie was willing to admit that he was an average person. He feared death, feared murder, feared the loss of life, and also feared those who would commit such crimes. Even if it made him seem weak and useless, Wang Xiaomie couldn't harden his heart enough to simply watch as a human life was extinguished before his eyes.

I'm just an average guy... With Zhen Bei's struggling already starting to weaken, a trembling Wang Xiaomie tearfully pleaded with his would-be murderer, who just yesterday had seemed so normal.

It wasn't until Wen Fengjin exposed his malevolent fangs that Wang Xiaomie finally realized what Wen Fengjin was, and what he himself was as well. Neither of them could be called human anymore. His eyes were unable to cry. How could a body for which both life and the passage of time had ceased to exist be capable of producing tears?

Wen Fengjin stared dumbfounded at the near-crying person before him—at Mian Deng, tearfully yet persistently pleading with him... This face instantly became one with a memory of the past. Back then, the scene had looked much like this. He'd killed all his hypocritical sectmates, one after the other, and his shixiong had kneeled at his feet in just the same manner, begging him with that same despairing, woeful look on his face.

And what had happened next? He'd still turned all those people into cooling corpses. Shixiong had gone away, never to return, and he never saw him again...

Wen Fengjin was thrown into a panic. He seemed to transform into an entirely different person as he tossed Zhen Bei aside, his expression shifting into one of alarm and distress at an unnatural speed as he squatted down on the floor and hugged Wang Xiaomie.

Wang Xiaomie shuddered once in his embrace, and Wen Fengjin hugged him harder in response. "It's okay, Mian Deng, don't be afraid... It was my mistake, I was wrong, don't be angry with me, okay? Don't leave me, okay? I'll let him go, I'll let him leave, I'll give you anything you want, just don't go... You'll forgive me, won't you? You've always been so understanding of others, and so prone to tenderheartedness... Mian Deng, I was wrong, I'll carry you back... Why won't you answer me, Mian Deng?"

The lack of expression on Wang Xiaomie's face could not conceal his fear. He was as stiff as a lamb faking death after a fright. Wen Fengjin, meanwhile, seemed to have wilfully gleaned whatever response he wanted, for he smiled as he picked Wang Xiaomie up and started carrying him back. He even lowered his head to lovingly nuzzle Wang Xiaomie's hair on the way back, inhaling his scent with the tip of his nose.

Wang Xiaomie, lying in that icy cold embrace, carefully swallowed a mouthful of saliva, too fearful to move.

"Look at you. You must be angry with me again, or why would you go so long without talking to me?" Wen Fengjin's complaint was spoken with a tone of gentle rebuke. A strand of his long hair fell from his face as he lowered those pretty, feminine features, those black orbs rolling once and the corners of his mouth tilting upward in a smile—but veins bulged noticeably in his eyes...

"I—I..." Wang Xiaomie was unable to restrain his fear, his lips still trembling despite his repeated stuttering. He was unable to get a single complete sentence out through his chattering teeth.

But Wen Fengjin acted as if he actually had heard Wang Xiaomie say something to him. The next thing he said was, "I know, I know, I'll have Mu Yi take that person up to the tomb passage above. He came here with others, so I'll tell Mu Yi to chase them all out together, don't worry, heheh. Did I do well? Mian Deng?"

That settles it, this guy's definitely got problems! And to top it all off, it's the mental illness kind of problem! But Wang Xiaomie didn't dare resist, instead hurrying to play along with a quick "Very well."

Wen Fengjin's features relaxed at that, and he cheerfully continued forward. They'd been walking for a good while now, and Wen Fengjin had been carrying Wang Xiaomie the entire time, holding him in a firm, tight embrace that seemed to imply he was afraid he'd run away.

Just when Wang Xiaomie—too scared to even breathe, heart figuratively pounding with fear—finally caught sight of their familiar destination, Wen Fengjin stopped moving. Wang Xiaomie looked up and saw Wen Fengjin's chin held at a tense angle, the abnormal smile on his face gone like so much smoke, replaced by an expressionless detachment as he looked down at him with a question. "By the way, Shixiong, did he come in as you were using the latrine?"

"Yes..."

"Did Shixiong have anything covering him at the time?"

"Not really..."

"That's no good...If Shixiong was seen by others, I'll die of jealousy..."

Every hair on Wang Xiaomie's body stood on end as Wen Fengjin continued, "Therefore...I must give Shixiong a tiny little punishment..."

15

I Want to Eat Your Pancreas

A FEW TUBE-SHAPED LIGHTS lit the deep and quiet tomb passage. The group which had just repelled the long-haired monster now sat resting, leaning crookedly against the passage walls. Each of them bore various degrees of injury; the most wounded among them was unconscious and breathing rapidly, hands pressed against his wound.

One of the men was down on one knee, the ancient bronze sword he'd been wielding lying by his side. If not for this sword, which was normally used for warding off evil, there was no way he would have been able to fend off that terrifying monster. But though the monster may have retreated, his tagalong kid brother Zhen Bei had fallen into a trap! He felt at the floor with his fingers, a hint of anxiety coloring the normally cold, hard expression on his face.

"Erge, Xiao-Juzi's injuries can't wait any longer..." another injured man impatiently said. "We're only at the mausoleum's entrance and things are already so dangerous—this is way beyond the kind of work the few of us can handle! Who knows what'll happen if we stay any longer!"

The guy who'd just been called "erge"—Zhen Mu—furrowed his brow at that. "So you're saying we should just leave Zhen Bei to die?!"

"...That's obviously not what I meant, it's just..." *It's just that if you fall into a trap in a place this dangerous, there's no knowing if you'll be lucky enough to survive!*

But this obviously wasn't something he could say so directly. The sturdy man let out a sigh as he slightly motioned at his companion, then squatted by Xiao-Juzi, their most heavily injured member, and started giving him water.

Zhen Mu looked at this youngest member of the team, then hit the ground with a fist. After a moment of silence, he picked up his sword, stood up, and said to his mates, "Let's go. We'll take Xiao-Juzi to get emergency treatment, then I'll get the guys waiting on the surface to come try again with me. Alive or dead, I'm gonna find him, whatever it takes!"

The team finally visibly relaxed a bit, gathering their things and quickly preparing to head out with the wounded, while an ashen-faced Zhen Mu shouldered his pack and brought up the rear.

Suddenly, a repeated string of gurgling sounds came from the tomb passage. It sounded like the noise someone might make when they were being strangled!

"Something's coming!" Zhen Mu yelled, drawing his sword. And then, while everyone was seized with panic, a huge, red lizard-like monster hurled something humanoid at them. Before Zhen Mu could do anything, the monster unexpectedly turned around and left.

"Aiyo, my poor back—!" The thing that hit the floor let out a shriek of pain and managed to get to its feet with effort. It spat out a glob of saliva while supporting its waist with a hand, saying, "Ptooey! I ate a mouthful of dirt! Huh? Erge, I've finally found you!"

"Zhen Bei?! What're you doing here?!"

A surprised Zhen Mu joyfully helped up his little brother. But before he could say anything more, Zhen Bei pulled a small bead from his backpack and yelped, with uncontrolled and childlike excitement, "Ge! I found the Fish Pearl!"

"What?!"

"This is the punishment you were talking about?"

Wang Xiaomie, dressed in a white inner robe with his pants left off to the side, squatted as he dunked his ass in a basin of water. If he'd been holding a bottle of Fuyanjie women's antibacterial wash, he would probably have been minutes away from singing the commercial jingle about the health benefits of a quick wash.

Having originally expected to get strung up and beaten, a long-faced Wang Xiaomie now found himself disconsolately washing his butt instead.

Dammit! I seriously just can't win!

"What's wrong? Does Shixiong find this lacking? Must I absolutely do something to Shixiong in order for him to be satisfied?" Wen Fengjin asked with a derisive smile, making as if to pull off Wang Xiaomie's clothes as he continued, "If that's what Shixiong wants, I will of course aim to please..."

Wang Xiaomie's entire body jolted at the mere touch of his hand; having just been scared shitless not long ago, Wen Fengjin now needed only to smile at him for Wang Xiaomie to lose any notion of acting up again, still wrapped as he was in lingering fear. The mood between them, which had finally become somewhat relaxed, instantaneously returned to its original tension. In fact, Wang Xiaomie was now even more afraid of Wen Fengjin than he was before.

At the sight of Wang Xiaomie's listlessly lowered head, Wen Fengjin slowly stopped smiling, his free hand curling tightly into a fist...

Wang Xiao-Zongzi was still squatting down, scrubbing away, when he was suddenly pulled into a hug. The other man crouched with one hand wrapped around the back of his head, the wide palm easily pressing Wang Xiaomie's head into his shoulder. His other hand reached into the basin to press against a certain soft area made chilly from the water.

Hm?! Hm!!

"No need, no need! I can wash it myself—oh fuck don't touch I'll do it—*ah*!" Wang Xiao-Zongzi let out a shriek, thinking *Oh my god, the big zongzi's molesting me!* He started twisting like a worm in the big zongzi's arms, but was sadly unable to escape the steel trap which was the big zongzi's embrace. In the end, he gave up the struggle, and allowed himself to get gently scrubbed by the big zongzi's claws.

After a good long wash, both the areas which should have been touched and those which shouldn't had all been thoroughly felt up by the big zongzi. Afterward, he even picked up Wang Xiaomie the same way you would a child, and started gently drying him off with a towel. "I don't want anyone else to touch Mian Deng, nor will I allow anyone else to see your body; if Mian Deng is seen, you'll be soiled... Anything that is soiled should be thoroughly cleaned. If your skin is soiled, I'll wash it off, if your flesh is soiled, I'll carve it free, if your heart is soiled, then I'll rip it out and toss it away... All right, you're clean again, Mian Deng..."

Wen Fengjin tossed aside the towel and wrapped his arms tightly around the pantsless Wang Xiaomie, affectionately tugging open the collar of his robes and pressing his own chest against the other man's. The thin white inner robe transmitted the warmth of those two icy cold chests to each other. "You smell so good, Mian Deng. I want to eat you up—will you let me have a bite?"

Wang Xiaomie was speechless.

"Haha, I'm only joking..."

Of the two, Wang Xiaomie's chest was slightly colder. Wen Fengjin's, while also cold, still held a weak heartbeat.

Wang Xiaomie looked at the willfulness and mad infatuation in Wen Fengjin's eyes and gulped with some difficulty. *If anyone ever tries to tell me this guy isn't sick in the head, I'm gonna throw a fit! In what universe does this look sane? This is clearly schizophrenia with a side of late-stage psychosis!*

"Are you hungry, Shixiong?"

"I, I'm not hungry, I just ate..."

"No, you're hungry, you need me." Wen Fengjin suddenly lowered his head and gave him a cheerful smile. His black pupils widened and the bloodred pattern on his forehead became nauseating to look at.

Wang Xiaomie shook his head—for some reason, he actually was somewhat dizzy, unable to stop his eyelids from falling shut, as if he were sleepy. In the moment before his eyes closed, he blearily saw Wen Fengjin tug open his collar to reveal his neck, slicing a long cut across it with a fingernail...

Didn't that hurt...?

"Eat up, Mian Deng. Just look at you, always saying things to anger me when you really mean the opposite, heh. But how could I ever be angry with you? Once you wake, you'll be just as accepting of me as you were before..."

Wang Xiaomie's lips touched something soft. He gave it a tentative lick.

Oh, it was bitter...

My Husband and I Sleep in a Coffin

16

The Youth Are Ambitious

I NTANGIBLE CLOUDS wound around the chain of mountains and soaked a little black multistoried building, in which a handsome and gentle-looking youth in pale-green robes held a scroll in his hands, gazing fondly at the tiny tots below him as they studiously worked on their memorization.

When his gaze swept over one among them, a tiny child with bruises on his face and an evasive expression, he paused a moment, then smiled a helplessly amused smile. "We'll end the lesson here today." He put down the scroll, and the bunch of tots immediately cheered as they always did before swarming around him with repeated calls of *Da-shixiong, Da-shixiong*.

As he struggled to disperse the bunch of rowdy children, the scent of pinewood carried on his veil, and those wide, pale-green sleeves drifted over to the youth in the back of the class, who was a little bigger than all the other children.

The youth was expressionless as he put his texts away. Despite how young he was, his feminine features and unique eyes made him look especially gloomy and hard to get along with. Whenever he looked at anyone, there seemed to be a supernatural aspect to his gaze, which made people uncomfortable for reasons they couldn't explain. This, combined with his background, meant that this still-young child was treated with cold detachment in the secluded mountain schoolyard.

But Da-shixiong—who was well on his way to adulthood—wasn't afraid. He looked at the still-growing boy, still half a head shorter than him, and the skinny, gloomy little child was unable to resist immediately brightening with a smile. He had been putting on an expressionless face, but now his face was bright red, innocently blinking his eyes as he spoke up with a quiet, halting voice. "I won the fight..."

"Yes, I'm sure you did, but you didn't come out of it looking any better yourself."

The child finally raised his head with an indignant shout, revealing a panda-like black eye. "Mian Deng-shixiong!"

A moment of mutual silence, then: "Pffthahahaha—!"

"Shixiong!" The little boy, angry with embarrassment, clenched his little hands as he threw himself with full force into the arms of his gently smiling shixiong and hugged that slender waist with all the force he had. That soft and gentle youth in his pale-green robe thus found himself trapped in a tiny embrace.

"I hate you, Shixiong!"

So said the boy whose face was currently buried in Mian Deng's chest...but the way he so energetically nuzzled him, and the bright red tips of his ears, said something else entirely.

"Your eleventh birthday is coming up. Is there anything you want? Hm?"

Mian Deng lowered his gaze. His face—fair as the finest jade—was filled with doting as he ran his fingers through the boy's scattered locks, carefully picking out bits of broken leaves. He didn't need to ask to know that these were picked up from rolling around on the ground during the aforementioned fight...

"Can I have anything I want?" The boy in his arms raised his head, his eyes—longer and narrower than that of the average person, with irises that nearly filled the entirety of the sclera—brimming with shining hope as he asked, "Can I really pick anything at all?!"

"Of course," he replied.

The boy was as happy as if he'd suddenly been given the entire world, and said, "Then I want Shixiong to be my wife in the future! When I grow up, I'll definitely marry you, okay, Mian Deng-shixiong?!"

His dumbfounded shixiong let out a laugh once more. "The heavens have yin and yang as complementary forces, little dummy. Men can't become husband and wife with other men. Now, I don't want you saying such things again, do you hear me? It violates the natural order, and if Shifu catches you saying it, he'll likely get angry and punish you."

The already angry little boy loudly shouted, "You're a liar, Shixiong, you clearly said I could make any wish I want. If the world won't allow it, then I'll change its rules myself one day!"

His shixiong's smiling demeanor immediately changed. "Silence! Anyone can say such things in private, but you are not allowed to, understand me? You absolutely cannot speak this way!"

The boy's eyes immediately filled with tears upon being scolded, but as that unnatural gaze turned to Mian Deng like the eyes of a little fawn, he couldn't help feelings of affection.

"Shixiong's a liar..."

This little boy never cried when he was bullied for his background and feminine looks, not even when he was shoved to the ground and beaten until he bled. No matter how great the humiliation or punishment he suffered, he would always glare back in defiance every time. Yet he now silently spilled those precious, gem-like tears without restraint. Mian Deng's heart immediately melted. He gently hugged him, saying helplessly, "All right all right, I accept, is that good enough for you?" *This will just become something I can tease you about once you grow up, anyway.*

The boy cheered up again and started wiping his tears away with a sleeve, when suddenly that little face stiffened, and he said in an earnest tone, "You have to wait for me, Mian Deng, I'll definitely take you as my bride one day!"

His shixiong lightly rapped his head as he replied, "You're supposed to call me Shixiong, you little hooligan!"

"I don't care, Mian Deng, promise me!"

"Okay okay, I promise... I'll wait for you, Fengjin..."

I'll always wait for you. Wait for you to grow up, when you'll have the strength to protect yourself and those you care for... Until then, I will always open my arms to you. You must live and grow up, Fengjin.

Within the casket, Wang Xiaomie's red-and-black wedding dress fell loosely down to his elbows. Reddened kiss marks spread from behind his ear, down his chin, all the way to his fragile chest, and deeper places beyond. His thin shoulders were gently touched by a pair of full, beautifully shaped lips, his scattered black hair entangling with that of another...

The pain of getting bitten woke him with a bleary start. For a moment, he didn't even know where he was. "Fengjin...I think I had a dream."

The man above him paused a moment before responding, his low, husky voice grazing his ears: "I also had a dream, and it was quite a good one..."

The unbearably low, masculine laugh made Wang Xiaomie hunch his shoulders as he attempted to gently push the other man away. "Stop it..."

Wen Fengjin hummed noncommittally. Every time he pressed close to that flat lower belly, the person beneath him shivered, so he did it over and over in pure amusement. Beneath that loose collar lay an even more attractive view, but Wen Fengjin didn't go any further—he'd already met the limit of how much Wang Xiaomie could handle from him today. He closed the loose collar himself. "This is the last one..."

A raspy laugh and a moan were swallowed together; when Wen Fengjin lifted his head again, he softly sucked Wang Xiaomie's lower lip between his own, giving off a reluctant vibe of not yet being satisfied.

The sound of rustling clothes quieted, and the man atop Wang Xiaomie activated the mechanism in the casket's inner wall, causing the great lid to slide open and allowing the intoxicating scent of that tree of blazing peach blossoms to pour into the space.

Wang Xiaomie raised a hand to cover his mouth, looking even more alive in the tree's proximity. He had a blushing expression, a lively glint in his eyes, and a flush to his face from their recent intimacy.

With his robe pulled open to directly reveal his chest, the beautiful, feminine man looming above him had a more unruly air than usual. After stepping out of the casket, he reached a hand out to Wang Xiaomie, those full lips widening in a smile. "Come, Mian Deng, I'll do your hair."

My Husband and I Sleep in a Coffin

17

Hubby,
a Heart For You

WANG XIAOMIE GOT UP and took his icy hand. He stepped out of the coffin, stretched, and followed the other man. He was then carried across a long, long iron chain to reach one of the side halls on the cliff wall.

Standing before a bronze mirror, Wang Xiaomie watched as Wen Fengjin tied his belt and fixed his clothes for him, smacking his lips as he exclaimed to himself, *What a good man!*

Next, he was pressed to sit upon a round stool. The man behind him, with loose robes still exposing his chest, picked up a comb with practiced ease. After his hair was brushed into perfect style, Wang Xiaomie crossed his thumb and forefinger and gestured to the man behind him.

"Hubby, a heart for you."

Wen Fengjin responded with a close-lipped smile on his bewitchingly handsome face before lowering his gaze to continue securing his hair tie. Those long, slender fingers gently wrapped around the locks, as if afraid to cause him any pain.

Heheh~ I'm so glad I got to meet such an attractive and thoughtful husband in this lifetime. This is something I could never ask for while alive, wouldn't even dare imagine in my dreams—who woulda thunk that after I died I'd have a big house to live in, riches beyond my wildest imagining, and someone to care for me like I was the apple of his eye...

Wow, even if I went cold right now, I'd go satisfied... Er, that's not right, I think I went cold a long time ago actually.

Wang Xiaomie sat on that stool, fully appreciating his fortune in spending his unlife with a simp.

"Oh right," he said, "if it weren't for that Zhen Bei guy from before, I would never have known how amazing all the little beads on my hair tie are. It would be better to store such treasures away—just think of how painful it'd be if we lost one. Did you know how much these beads are worth?"

"Of course I did."

"Yet you casually sewed them onto hair ribbons?"

"Wearing Fish Pearls will often result in improved eyesight."

"...That sounds like a waste of good resources to me." *Dage, I've already closed my eyes in Eternal Sleep, what do I need this for?*

"Shixiong deserves only the best."

As he said this, Wen Fengjin finished tying on a red embroidered ribbon embossed with gold and added a jade hair crown. His tone of voice was very matter-of-fact, to the point that he didn't even seem to think before saying it. Wang Xiaomie sat there on the stool, a wooden expression on his face. *Mama, I think I'm in love.*

Once his hair had been dealt with, Wang Xiaomie stood up from his seat, but Wen Fengjin made no move to tidy himself up, instead hugging him from behind with his chest still fully exposed. In the bronze mirror, he could see the man leaning affectionately against him, head resting in the crook of his neck.

"By the way, Mian Deng, do you still remember the incident with the grave robber from the other day?"

Wang Xiaomie was itching to touch the other man's long, smooth hair, which was lying on his shoulder. He was taken off guard by the question: "Why are you asking about that again?

Of course I remember it. I was using the bathroom when a guy suddenly fell from above, um... He didn't look like a bad guy, and was looking for a Fish Pearl to help recover his big brother's sight, so I gave him one in the end, but I know we can't have other people knowing about the mausoleum, so I had Mu Yi send him out... Is there something wrong?"

"Nothing."

"To tell the truth, I was actually pretty touched. I know I said I'd partner up and live with you back when we were eating hot pot, but I didn't expect you to actually trust me so much. I know the mausoleum is basically our house, and even though the robbers had their reasons, they were still here to steal stuff—but you didn't blame me for letting them go... Thank you, Fengjin."

"It was nothing; I'll consent to anything you ask of me."

The seemingly gentle Wen Fengjin—face still buried in Wang Xiaomie's shoulder—let slip a twisted smile, his black eyes carrying joy within their dark depths...

I thought he was a gloomy zongzi at first, but he's actually a really good guy, Wang Xiaomie thought to himself with some embarrassment. Because he felt bad about what had happened, he'd been doing everything he could to fulfill Wen Fengjin's requests. After all, putting aside the fact he'd sided with an outsider, he'd even given away one of the mausoleum's treasures...

And it was less than a day before Wang Xiaomie, who was absolutely shameless in his fondness for good-looking guys, was already chuckling away inside the casket, wanting nothing more than to exchange kissies with Wen Fengjin every day.

The guy's a good person, rates highly in the looks department, is good in the sack, smart and obedient, teases me, dotes on me—I'd be a fool to let a catch like this get away!

Besides, what's there for a pair of grown men to hem and haw over? In Wang Xiaomie's mind, he was already in a relationship with Wen Fengjin. And perhaps Wen Fenjin would think, smiling: *In my mind we should already be having children.*

"Oh yes, what was it you dreamed about today, Mian Deng?" Wen Fengjin suddenly asked.

Wang Xiaomie told him, then somewhat uncertainly asked, "Do you think...I might really become a different person?"

"You won't become a different person, you'll always be you," Wen Fengjin said with far too much certainty. "You're just remembering scenes from the past. In the future, you'll remember even more of our time together."

Wang Xiaomie nodded with a frown. That dream had been far too real, and he wasn't quite sure if it was because his recent adventures had caused him to remember his past life, or if he was witnessing this body's memories.

Wen Fengjin continued, "But today actually is my birthday..."

"Huh?! You should've said so earlier! Your birthday... Ai, we can't buy cakes now, and there's not really anything to eat in the mausoleum..."

Not to mention the thought of doing anything romantic. *Wanna blow out birthday candles and make a wish? Heheh, sorry, all the lights in our tomb are mermaid-oil lanterns—nevermind blowing them out, they've been burning on their own for over a thousand years and still haven't burned out!*

At Wang Xiaomie's disappointed face, Wen Fengjin suddenly said, "Since today is my birthday, and you've been cooped up in this mausoleum for a long time, I plan to take you outside to look around tonight."

"Outside?!" Wang Xiaomie's eyes widened at that. "Boss, we're jiangshi now! Big zongzi! The kind that hop around roaring and biting people in movies! If anyone sees us we're gonna get captured and turned into research subjects." And even if that didn't happen, the two of them were basically spending their days watching over a gigantic treasury; what if someone robbed them while they were out?

But on the other hand, he really wanted to go outside...

"Above our grave is an unbroken chain of tall mountains with complicated terrain, which should currently be covered in desolate and uninhabited forest. If we're only out for a few shichen..." Wen Fengjin straightened up, fingers slowly sinking into the black hair of the person before him, and just as slowly combing through it. "Besides, I'd really like to see the sunrise with you once...okay?" He then gave Wang Xiaomie a gentle smile.

Wang Xiaomie thought: *Yesyesyes! Drool... This zongzi sure is attractive!*

MY HUSBAND AND I SLEEP IN A COFFIN

Who Is It
You Want?

Around moon hung in the inky-blue sky, outlined by sparkling stars and the Milky Way; unlike the light of the sun, it spilled onto the earth with a chilly softness. Dimly discernible clouds curled around the mountain forest and its mist-sodden black buildings, the dew heavy in the deep night. The blazing-red clothes the couple wore reflected reddish-gold colors under the moonlight, fine dewdrops collecting on their faces and dripping downward.

Wang Xiaomie stared in a trance at the old, weed-ridden cobbled road before him, as well as an old building which—though reduced to a pile of rotting wood—could still be vaguely discerned as what was once an elegant schoolyard.

"What's the matter, Mian Deng?" Someone wrapped their arms around him from behind, forcefully pulling him into an embrace.

It was Wen Fengjin. He looked at the abandoned ruin as well, a distant expression on his smiling face.

"It's nothing, I was just thinking this all looks kind of familiar... I never thought there'd be an ancient building like this atop our grave." Wang Xiaomie looked at the marks left by the place having been burned once, unsure why he felt so strangely hurt by it. Unfamiliar emotions were caught in his throat, neither rising nor falling, giving him an indescribable sense of sorrow. "It looks a little like the place in my dream..."

"You're overthinking it, Shixiong. Have you forgotten? The sect was perfectly fine when we were attacked, how could anything happen to them?" He lowered his head, saying gently, "The surrounding area is full of gathered spiritual energy and the location of a dragon's vein, though sadly it was once occupied by a bunch of disreputable scum. I took it upon myself to deal with them all, and built the underground mausoleum here. Shixiong, would you say I did a good deed? Hm?"

Wang Xiaomie kept gazing at the remains of that magnificent building, absentmindedly saying, "...It really was a great deed you did."

Wen Fengjin's lips slowly widened; his feminine yet handsome face took on a savage and morbid smile. His gaze was fixed unwaveringly on Wang Xiaomie's furrowed brow, unexpectedly feeling a sliver of delight at his pain!

Shixiong, look, those scum who opposed us are all dead. I burned all those dirty rats to ashes and built our underground palace here, so that even in death, they will have to watch how we'll be together forever...

"Don't look anymore, Mian Deng." The demon's pleased smile was buried in the darkness of night, saying the gentlest words with the wickedest expression. "There's nothing worth looking at here. This place is dirty—how about we go over there to wait for the sunrise?"

"Huh? Okay." Wang Xiaomie rubbed his chest as Wen Fengjin steered him over to a great tree a good distance away. Under this tree were also some stone seats, as well as a stone table which was shattered in one place. Wen Fengjin pulled out a handkerchief to clean off the dust before sitting down with Wang Xiaomie.

This great tree was flourishing on one side and withered on the other, its thick branches—too wide to hug—probably strong enough to climb without issue.

The mountain breeze brought the delicate scent of verdure to Wang Xiaomie's nose, and he breathed a sigh of relief, his feelings of depression wiped away in an instant as he finally regained a sense of joy. For some reason, this spot was pleasantly cool to sit in, as if the tree were emitting cold air.

"Fengjin, what kind of tree is this? It's giving off a fresh, chilly scent, like a mint tree or something!"

Wen Fengjin froze for an instant. When his long, narrow eyes turned to look at him, there was a barely noticeable flash of an enigmatic smile in their depths. He swept a gentle gaze over Wang Xiaomie, wide sleeves falling away to reveal a pallid arm and slender, bony fingers as he rested his chin in one hand. "This is just a normal tree," he replied in a soft drawl. "If Shixiong finds it cool, that's likely because..."

"Because what?"

"Because this tree is where I hung that bunch of degenerates... One hundred and seventy-three people swaying in the breeze. One of the branches even broke under the pressure. Oh, right, and after their necks were snapped from the drop, their drooping heads made it seem like they were looking down at whoever was below them. Yes, it was really quite amusing. Heh."

Wang Xiaomie was struck speechless.

Wh-wh-wh-what the fuck?!

A cool breeze blew from behind him. It felt almost like someone's gaze piercing his back...

Wang Xiaomie leapt up with a scream, and was just about to run when Wen Fengjin reached out to grab his waist and pull him back into his arms; his attempt to struggle free was then immediately interrupted when he heard Wen Fengjin burst into loud laughter. "I was joking," he said.

Those black irises commanded over half the area of his eyes. Within them, a thick sense of tenderness and love surged with great force at the sight of the fawn-like, panic-stricken look on the face of the person in his embrace. "Haha, you really are cute."

Cute, my ass! Wang Xiaomie rubbed at the goosebumps that had risen along his skin. "You can kill someone if you scare them enough, you know!"

"But you already died a long time ago, Shixiong."

"...Don't go assuming I won't bite you to death." *You think you're the only one with a mouth here or what?! Bark bark bark!*

Grimacing, Wang Xiaomie wildly waved his fists at him, only for his hands to get caught in the other man's grasp. Wen Fengjin kissed those pale and cool fingertips with great interest, blinking innocently up at Wang Xiaomie, who looked moments away from fluffing up like an angry cat. "All right, where would you like to bite?"

You're not supposed to look forward to it, you dick! Ptooey!

As he was struggling fruitlessly to escape Wen Fengjin's arms, he heard the man's voice sound over his head: "I had another reason for bringing you here today, Mian Deng—look."

A tiny pair of golden scissors and a red-patterned, gold-embossed hair ribbon were placed in Wang Xiaomie's hand.

"Have you heard of the hair binding ceremony...? What I want isn't to live forever; what I want is to be bound with you as husband and wife for as long as we live... We'll help and depend on each other in good times and bad, never abandoning each other no matter what form we take, always keeping each other in our hearts. Shixiong, I once said to wait for me, and that I'd definitely come

back to marry you. I've done it—so now will you make that long-ago promise a reality, and join me as my wife?"

The thick mountain mist churned like white ocean water, the stars in the sky losing their luster. The moon was about to leave. A few rays of orange light brought with them a warmth to dispel the cold and damp, projecting upon the couple in their red wedding robes...

In this moment, Wen Fengjin looked so warm, his eyes narrowed in a smile, his expression no longer carrying its usual dark ruthlessness. His handsome, feminine face was an absolutely dazzling sight. Wang Xiaomie was momentarily put in a trance. It was as if he was seeing that stubborn child in the schoolyard again, insisting on marrying his shixiong. In this instant, he had the false impression that he'd loved this man for a long, long time...

He took the scissors with a sigh. "You had this all planned from the start, didn't you."

"To openly and honestly be bound in marriage with you, here beneath the sun, has long been my obsession. Everything I've done has been for the sake of this day. For the day that you would say, in full consciousness, 'I do.'"

Wen Fengjin lowered his eyes, revealing a thin, sad smile for the first time since they'd met. The gaze he pinned Wang Xiaomie with made it seem like he'd just been crying.

In truth, Wen Fengjin himself likely hadn't realized that his usual expression always carried with it a sense of ruthlessness, regardless of when he was hugging or kissing someone else, or even smiling. There was always a sense that the dream would be shattered in an instant, and he would take someone else down with him. Wang Xiaomie had figured out early on that this wasn't a kind man, but he was hopelessly intoxicated by the lovesick gaze with which Wen Fengjin looked at him...

I really am a love-deprived, looks-obsessed dog.

Wang Xiaomie laughed a bitter laugh, reached out a hand to pull their long locks together, then bound their hair with the ribbon. The long raven strands wove together as one. Wang Xiaomie's hair was soft and a little thinner than Wen Fengjin's, which was somewhat coarser to the touch. People often said that those with soft hair had good tempers, while those with coarse hair had more definite judgment.

The sun gradually rose and everything around them stirred to life, the plants raising leaves so green they were like individual pieces of jade. Water dripped from the leaves, and birds made sweet and gentle cries in the fresh air above. The golden-orange light began to shine...

One man embraced another sitting on his lap, resting his head in the crook of the other's neck, slowly swaying as he sang an ancient melody in his low, husky voice, and watched the person before him use slender fingers to twirl their intertwined hair into a single thin braid. Golden scissors cut off the braid, thick as a little finger, both ends bound together by the red ribbon.

The song ceased, and Wen Fengjin's arms wrapped tightly around his body, the braid gripped tight within his hand. "Mian Deng, call me Fengjin this once..."

Wang Xiaomie was a little bashful, but still acquiesced: "Fengjin..."

"Mian Deng, tell me you love me..." The low voice seemed to have changed in tone.

Wang Xiaomie hemmed and hawed for a good while before quietly muttering, "I, I, y'know... I love you."

The final two words were so quiet as to barely be discernible. The man behind him didn't respond for a long time, but just when Wang Xiaomie began to think that Wen Fengjin hadn't heard him, a few drops of something struck the side of his face and his shoulder...

Hm? Was it raining?

Wang Xiaomie wanted to reach a hand out to catch the drops. He suddenly raised his head, saying, "Fengjin, it's rain—"

"Don't look!"

A cold hand covered Wang Xiaomie's eyes.

Wang Xiaomie lowered his head in a daze. His mind endlessly replayed the image of that face—which always looked so cold and detached, no matter what was going on—losing its normal façade to reveal a blank sorrow and despair like the face of someone who had been pushed off a precipice, those black eyes swimming with wetness...

Wen Fengjin was crying. And it absolutely wasn't the look of someone crying with joy.

Why? He'd done everything he was asked, so why?

After a long time, the man behind him released him and stood up, carefully tucking that strand of hair into the bosom of his robes, his usual gentle mask once more on his face as he said in a soft voice, "Let's go, Shixiong, it's time we headed back..."

As he was led by the hand on the long walk home, Wang Xiaomie pursed his lips and quietly asked, "Do you want Mian Deng's feelings... or mine?"

The man in front of him stopped, then gripped his hand with greater force. "What are you saying? You are Mian Deng. Let's go home..."

Looking at that broad back, Wang Xiaomie let out a sigh. His heart had gone completely cold.

19

Removing
the Mask

A FTER RETURNING UNDERGROUND, Wang Xiaomie dispiritedly leaned against the great tree, feeling somewhat unreasonable. His heart was seriously crushed right now. Reason and emotion were two little people fighting on his shoulders.

Little White said, *Does he really love me? Or just my past life as Mian Deng?*

Litte Black said, *That's a stupid question, isn't it? The answer's obvious—you're nothing to him! The guy he's been obsessively pursuing is his shixiong Mian Deng, not you, Wang Xiaomie!*

Little White put on a pathetic look. *But Mian Deng is me, and I'm Mian Deng... You make it sound like I'm just a substitute.*

Little Black rolled his eyes. *Heheh, how could it be the the same? Even if you are him, did you experience their powerful romance? Do you really think you can just blend right in? What Wen Fengjin is seeing through you is a memory, not the present...*

This one sentence stabbed Wang Xiaomie in the chest like a dagger, and a barbed one at that, splattering blood everywhere the moment it was pulled out.

A defiant Little White said, *But Fengjin's always smiling so gently at us, and the way he looks at us is really soft too.*

Little Black sneered. *Fengjin? Why're you talkng like you're both so close? You've experienced plenty of social snobbery in your life,*

Wang Xiaomie...did you play dumb so often that it's become a habit? Have you really not noticed how ruthless and gloomy that guy is? Him, smile? It's all an act, don't you get it? Don't tell me you can't see it! With that fake smile of his, his acting skills are even worse than that bunch of jerks you call relatives. For all you know, he'll turn around and start giving you the cold shoulder, you fool!

Little White started wailing loudly at the scolding, while Little Black looked triumphant at having come out on top. Wang Xiaomie, leaning against the peach tree, lowered his gaze and chuckled bitterly to himself...

Who says people who often laugh foolishly won't feel pain when they're hurt? Who says someone content with his lot can stay strong when he loses it? It's all a bunch of crap, I'm clearly suffering more than anything...

"What's wrong, Mian Deng? Are you feeling unwell?" An excessively feminine and handsome face approached him. The tiny, blazing-red mark on his forehead startled Wang Xiaomie from his thoughts.

At Wen Fengjin's worried gaze and furrowed brow, Wang Xiaomie said without thinking, "Ah, it's nothing."

I'm just feeling a little heartbroken and tearful, with a side of wanting to hang myself and die for a bit. There's no need to worry about me, I'm fine, just look at my goofy smile—thus was the hypocritical answer he gave in his head.

"How could it be nothing, Mian Deng, what's wrong? You look like you're about to cry..." Wen Fengjin gripped his hands, took a step closer, than gently, lovingly kissed Wang Xiaomie's forehead. "Is there something I shouldn't know?" He suddenly paused, his voice getting even lower as he asked, "Mian Deng, did you remember something again?"

Wang Xiaomie looked at those eyes so full of love they were almost overflowing, and those hands gripping his with such care. He shook his head, saying, "I haven't remembered anything."

"I see. That's fine, you don't need to rush it. Plus, even if they *are* memories, there are times where you may remember wrong—if you do remember something, make sure to tell me, you hear?" Wen Fengjin said with a light smile.

"I know..."

Wang Xiaomie found this whole thing somewhat strange. Why did Wen Fengjin have such a conflicted attitude about him recovering his memories? He seemed simultaneously happy, yet on guard against something.

For some reason, the sight of his smiling face made Wang Xiaomie inexplicably agitated, as if the expression on that face were painted over plaster. He had a feeling that the real Wen Fengjin wasn't like this; wasn't this gentle, careful person who was incapable of anger. Surprising even himself, Wang Xiaomie said, "Stop smiling. It's such a fake smile..."

He regretted saying this the moment it left his mouth. He regretted it even more when Wen Fengjin's suddenly widened eyes and stiffened smile gave him a start of fright.

The two fell silent. The repressive atmosphere made it stiflingly difficult to breathe. It was also difficult for Wang Xiaomie to see the expression on Wen Fengjin's face, because he'd lowered his head again. He looked pretty hurt, though...

Oh no! What the heck is wrong with me?!

Wang Xiaomie hurried to apologize. "I'm sorry... I, uh, just now there was something wrong with my head, don't take offense..." He quickly changed the subject, loudly saying, "Oh right! What happened to that lock of hair from earlier? I hope we didn't lose it."

Wen Fengjin raised his head again, a faint smile on his face. His deep, chilling gaze was cold enough to give Wang Xiaomie a full-body shiver.

Suddenly, he smiled, all lively. "Don't be afraid, Shixiong. Today is our wedding day. How could I ever be angry with you?"

Could you try saying that again after putting away the sharp teeth in your smile, sir? Wang Xiaomie pouted as he complained in his head. *You say you're not angry, but it's only when you're angry that you call me Shixiong.*

"I've put the hair away in a box in the casket—that box is where I keep all my most precious things." As he spoke of the box, the big boss's savage facial expression began to relax.

His most precious things, huh... Wang Xiaomie's eyes lit up.

"Does Shixiong want to see it?" he asked.

"I—I kind of do..."

He nodded with a smile, saying, "All right, then. I won't show you."

Wang Xiaomie was struck speechless. *Are you really gonna hold a grudge about this, Boss?! What you're doing is hiding off-book accounts, you know that?! If you get caught you'll have to kneel and scrub clothes with a washboard! Don't you know that letting your wife handle the accounts is how you keep hold of your money?! You just made a solemn pledge of love with me and already you're hiding money! Wehhh, I'm so miserable. The big zongzi's an unemotional jerk, ptooey!*

Once he'd had enough amusement at Wang Xiaomie's expense, Wen Fengjin went to get water so he could wipe Wang Xiaomie's face and rinse his feet as well, having fully resumed the appearance of a good man. He rubbed the slender feet in his broad hands and let go just as Wang Xiaomie ticklishly shrank back.

"Go to bed. I'll always be by your side."

Having now cleaned himself up as well, Wen Fengjin's gaze softened. He lay together with Wang Xiaomie in the casket, and the box filled with his most precious treasures was placed right by Wen Fengjin's pillow. There weren't really any sources of entertainment in the mausoleum, and with the added problem of Wang Xiaomie's daily drowsiness, they spent pretty much every day sleeping in the casket.

As he lay in a bitter-smelling embrace, Wang Xiaomie entertained himself with the thought: *Who is this hug for? You never know, maybe it's for me.*

Once Wang Xiaomie fell asleep, Wen Fengjin slowly opened his eyes within the pearl-lit casket. He sat up and—in the faint light of the pearls—lay atop Wang Xiaomie, holding himself up with one arm and lifting the other to bite open his wrist, then gently placing the injury in the mouth of the man beneath him.

The body he'd raised habitually accepted the blood offering and began to swallow.

After some time had passed, Wen Fengjin pulled back his wrist, caressed his beloved's cheek, and gazed at him in infatuation, imagining kissing his skin, nose, and forehead as he affectionately, carefully rubbed a thumb against his lips.

The expression on his face was cold and detached, as if his smile were a mask he'd just pulled off. This gave his handsome, delicate face an added level of unyielding ferocity, but those abnormal eyes were far more gentle than usual, his regular false gloom having entirely disappeared. The effect instantly transformed the fallen demon lord into an immortal standing by the Heavenly Lake of Tianshan.

Cold and heartless, yet carrying the warmth of an eternal infatuation with a single person—this was the real Wen Fengjin.

"Shixiong, did you remember something again today?"

Whenever he was with Wang Xiaomie, he always spoke with a higher tone, as if manufacturing a sense of happiness—only for the influence of his personality to make it sound more unnatural than glad. This gave him the affect of a strange clown. It was enough to make one's scalp tingle. Now that he was alone, Wen Fengjin's voice was husky, low, and unhurried, a combination which could truly make any listener's heart race.

After he asked his question, the soundly sleeping Wang Xiaomie instantly opened his eyes, bloodred eyes staring blankly upward as he haltingly replied, "No."

"Then why were you unhappy today, Shixiong? Are you hiding something from me?"

"I was...worried that...the person...you like...is Mian Deng. I want the person...you like...to be Wang Xiaomie..."

Wen Fengjin shook his head, saying, "You're wrong—the person I like has always been you. You don't understand, Shixiong; it isn't that I now have you after Mian Deng, but that having you here gives me the Mian Deng I so love. The one I love is you. It's always been you..."

But I've told too many lies, done too many things I cannot tell you. That's why I want to do everything I can to be the kind of person you like, and as quickly as possible, make it so that you can't leave me...

"Ah, right." Wen Fengjin placed a hand on his own face, which held a peculiar expression. "Is my smile really so fake?"

"It is."

"But didn't you say you love people who smile often, Shixiong... you liar...?" Wen Fengjin's lips curled slightly upwards as he used the palm of his hand to brush Wang Xiaomie's red eyes shut. "Sleep, Shixiong, I really am very happy today."

Wen Fengjin lay down by his side, placed his own hands neatly on his abdomen, and gradually closed his eyes as well.

My Husband and I Sleep in a Coffin

You're the
Only One

PERHAPS BECAUSE OF that cutting of intertwined wedding locks, Wen Fengjin found himself dreaming of the past.

A cold-faced Wen Fengjin stood with his feminine red robes flying in the wind. He was looking at a tiny, younger version of himself, who in turn watched as his father was paraded down the street to his execution. His father, a man who once held the high position of Regent of the Northern Kingdom, treated as a god incarnate by the common people, and who had assisted the emperor in his rise to power, was ultimately carelessly accused of colluding with another country.

"Have mercy, Your Majesty. Send this guilty servant's son to the Xuanfeng Academy, merely barring his children from employment for the next three generations..."

Because of a groundless accusation that somehow managed to be supported by all sorts of "evidence," those storytellers who circulated songs throughout restaurants and teahouses now spoke with righteous indignation of the hundreds of people who comprised the regent's household, and the people who'd once wanted to erect a tablet of merit for his father had immediately turned around and started calling him a brigand. Praise be to His Majesty's benevolence for even allowing the brigand's family line to continue.

But was this benevolence or malice? Forcing a four-year-old child to watch his entire family be beheaded one by one? What kind of benevolence would send him to the illustrious Xuanfeng Academy, to obtain great learning and ability, yet be unable to be employed for the next three generations of his line?

The adult Wen Fengjin looked on with indifference as his parents knelt under the blade, the people around them cheering and flinging garbage at them, his younger self—barely four years old—able only to wail as he watched.

Afterwards, the spit-upon child was sent to the Xuanfeng Academy deep within the mountains. And was the academy as illustrious as they said? This four-year-old's first day was spent being called a traitor's seed, getting held down by others as they tried to press his head into a chamber pot, while a bunch of children barely older than he was clapped their hands and laughed.

"Make him drink it! Hahaha, make him drink! See his eyes? How could a human have eyes like that?!"

"That's how you know he's a brigand's kid, hahaha..."

This was how that young child spent half a year—always finding urine or other things splattered on his bed, his meals constantly being knocked to the ground, his teachers always chasing him from the classroom to stand outside as punishment while they taught, so that the skinny, tiny, dirty child could only put his ear against the wall to eavesdrop on their lessons. And when he was caught, he'd be beaten with a bamboo plank...

Wen Fengjin, his hair black as ink, watched these scenes without the slightest change in expression or even so much as a sliver of anger in his eyes. The tiny child stumbled his way to the age of seven, when—sneaking around the back of the mountain to curb his hunger with stolen wild fruits—he caught sight of the academy's director and their da-shixiong.

The child had only ever caught a glimpse of their shixiong, because he didn't study or attend lessons in the same place as the younger children. But their shixiong was gentle as jade. Though he'd earned a name as someone unparalleled among gentlemen at a young age, he was always smiling, his pale-green robes and veil just like the clouds and mist which wrapped around the mountainside...

The first time he ever saw him, little Fengjin's face stayed red for a very long time.

He heard the academy director say, "How has your task gone?"

Da-shixiong replied with a smile on his lips, "It's been three years—the boy is quite fortunate to still be alive after all this time, but I've already given instructions to the children and teachers. Don't worry, Laoshi, he will not have a good time. Nor will he be able to pick himself up afterward..."

After watching to this point, Wen Fengjin stared tranquilly ahead at the genially smiling Mian Deng, nothing but disgust visible in his eyes, and an incomprehensible sneer on his face.

From that moment on, the tiny Fengjin became hard-hearted and aloof, no longer resigning himself to his suffering. He began to fight back like a feral dog, without a care for the injuries he sustained.

Another year passed before he once again came across that jade-like gentleman of a da-shixiong. He was sitting on a stone seat, smiling as he looked up at the freshly planted gingko tree above. A dumbfounded look crossed his face when he turned his head to see Wen Fengjin behind him.

A gust of wind rose, gently lifting that black hair, light-green robe, and veil; a subtle smile showed itself on that handsome face with its limpid eyes. In this moment, he was no longer like the mist around the mountainside, but a fresh wind after the rain.

As the older Wen Fengjin watched this, the mark on his forehead went a brilliant red. The indifference on his face was erased as—overcome with reminiscence—he gently lifted his hand as if to touch that carefree youth...

Shixiong said, "Little boy, who are you...?"

The child curled his hands into fists, his gaze like that of a wolf cub. "Shouldn't you know who I am?"

Shixiong was momentarily thrown off by this, an embarrassed look on his face as he replied, "Ah... haha, there are so many children in this academy. Er, isn't it normal for me not to remember them all? Let's get to know each other again—I'm Mian Deng, what about you? What's your name...?"

He got up, then stooped over the wary-eyed child, the smell of pine instantly filling the surrounding air as he gently patted the child's head, smiling. "I did hear them say there was a child in the outer courtyard whose eyes were really unique."

Little Fengjin angrily knocked his hand away, abjectly covering his eyes to evade his shixiong's gaze, only for his hands to get pulled away the next moment as the man before him—who had once given him three years of nightmares—spoke to him like someone completely different. "What unusual eyes... Many remarkable people throughout the course of history have had traits that marked them as different from others. I'm sure you'll go on to be someone remarkable, too..."

Perhaps the sun was particularly blinding that day, or perhaps the weather was just too nice, or that youth's smile far too soft...

"Well? Tell me your name again, and this time I'll make sure not to forget it."

Little Fengjin stared in a daze for a long time. The red-clothed adult Wen Fengjin behind him smiled.

They spoke in unison: "Shixiong—Mian Deng—remember this: my name is Wen Fengjin..."

From this moment on, an extraordinary person plummeted into a black and bottomless abyss. There, he became the inextinguishable light held within the heart of the child named Wen Fengjin who dwelt at the abyss's core.

Someone lives in my heart. He likes people who smile, and so I often smile. He likes kind people, and so I've become an expert at pretending. He likes stalwart people, and so I wear a suit of armor. He likes righteous people, and so I've peeled off my own wolf pelt, exchanging it for the kind honesty of a lamb.

But I was born to feed on flesh and blood, so I have no choice but to tell one lie after another so I may cover his eyes, carefully experiencing the taste of being loved, and absorbing the warmth from his body.

I've never thought myself pitiful. I'm quite fortunate, in fact. I love him...and yet, the day will inevitably come when the lies come to light. Which is why I've resorted to every means possible to keep him firmly imprisoned within my heart, even if it means tainting my light with filth.

The now awake Wen Fengjin turned on his side to look at the person behind him: skin so fair it seemed it might tear at the slightest touch, the line from his smooth, full forehead down to the tip of his nose giving the viewer an impression of softness and delicacy, those closed eyes lined with dense, curved lashes. His tender lips were tightly shut.

"It's another day in the mortal realm, Mian Deng."

In the moment you opened your eyes and said in a panic that you were called Wang Xiaomie, your eyes regained their clarity. When you softly called me Fengjin as I requested, I knew.

You've returned...

Wen Fengjin lowered his head to gently capture the man's lips in his own, his movements as careful as if he were holding a treasure that might melt at any moment. He maintained that position until the molestation caused the sleeping man to awake.

Wang Xiaomie opened his eyes with irritation and much difficulty. "Ugh...what are you doing?! Don't go interrupting people's dreams first thing in the morning!"

"Mian Deng."

"Ah?"

"I suddenly want it."

Wang Xiaomie stared back with a wooden expression on his face: *Want what? To die? As if, you undying old bastard of a boss.*

But he never expected Wen Fengjin to suddenly turn affectionate, lowering his eyes and rubbing softly against him in a manner completely unlike his usual odd or gentle behaviors, like a big cat putting aside its pride for the first time to ingratiate itself with its owner. Wen Fengjin rubbed back and forth as he nestled against him, wordlessly tugging at his clothes.

Wang Xiaomie couldn't even get out a single "meow."

Besides, no matter how you sliced it—the vibe Wen Fengjin was giving off right now was that of a wolf, not a kitty-cat!

Did a year pass while my eyes were closed? How'd Boss get yet another split personality?! Also, try reading the room, Boss! I still wasn't on speaking terms with you when I went to bed, you know!

Wang Xiaomie hurriedly grabbed at the clothes which Wen Fengjin had pulled open. "Did I miss an episode or did you just fast-forward? Fuck, stop tugging! I know you're just into your shixiong Mian Deng, you animal! I'm Wang Xiaomie! We otaku will never be slaves—if you keep this up, I'm gonna start yelling! *I'll never be a substitute!*"

Wang Xiao-Zongzi, suddenly being shucked of his leaves, let out what the zongzi world called a final roar of integrity! But it was of no dang use. The undying big zongzi seemed to turn bipolar the moment they had a disagreement, his eyes sparkling despite his expressionless face as he peeled off zongzi leaves with single-minded devotion.

The instant Wen Fengjin bit him, Wang Xiaomie raised a hand and struck Wen Fengjin's face with a resounding *slap*. His clothes were a mess, anger was written all over his face, and his fists were clenched as tight as could be!

"You're a big fat liar! You said you could accept me and start over, but I bet all you actually want is to look at me and think of your damn shixiong! Wen Fengjin, you better get a good idea of who exactly I am!"

Wang Xiaomie didn't want to quarrel. He'd already decided that if Wen Fengjin could accept this brand-new version of him, then he was willing to start over from the beginning. But if the other man was only looking through him in search of a shade of Mian Deng, then it wasn't gonna work out. Men had dignity too! He'd rather starve to death than eat someone else's leftovers!

"Ha, hahaha..." To his surprise, Wen Fengjin—head turned to the side from the slap—started laughing loudly, an excited light sparkling in his eyes as he said, "It's the same. Your slap is the same as it was back then!"

Oh no, I've knocked his marbles out.

Wang Xiaomie gulped as the man above him suddenly became gentle again, his lips curving upward and those abnormal irises filled to the brim with undiluted love. He leaned toward the absolutely terrified Wang Xiaomie, the two of them staring into each other's eyes, and said, "I don't like this body at all, but ever since you've occupied it, everything has changed. Since it's affecting you so much that it's undoing our previous closeness, let me tell you this: there was never any past or present life in the equation, the one I love has always been you..."

This bewitching, willful man suddenly pulled them closer. Wang Xiaomie stared in astonishment at his reflection in the man's eyes, one finger pressed against his chest.

Lips opening and closing, Wen Fengjin spoke.

"The person I loved one thousand years ago was named Wang Xiaomie. You call me a liar, but you are the worst liar of all!"

"Wh-what are you talking about?"

"Heh."

Wen Fengjin pulled him up and opened the casket. He reached over to pick up the box by his pillow, and did something to open it with a *click*. As if in a trance, Wang Xiaomie looked inside to see their hair and a few other small trinkets, as well as two volumes of noticeably ancient, scattered personal letters.

Wen Fengjin extracted the topmost book and quickly closed the box before handing those letters to him. "Look."

"Wh-what is..." Wang Xiaomie dazedly accepted the book, which felt as if it might break apart at the slightest touch.

He flipped it open to the words on the first page, and immediately gasped in surprise. *"Th-this can't be!"*

21

Keep Living
With a Smile
(Sob)

WHEN WANG XIAOMIE reached for the leather-bound notebook by his pillow, it was with shaking hands and a blank mind. This notebook was one he'd dug out of the robbers' backpacks in that one side hall. Because he'd been isolated from a young age, without any friends or family, and couldn't stand being lonely, he'd picked up the habit of keeping a diary, which could amuse him for a bit whenever he had nothing to do.

The two books' composition and design were entirely different, one noticeably ancient, the other clearly modern. But they both had the same words written in large font on the cover!

"Wang Xiaomie's Diary."

Wang Xiaomie was struck speechless. *This childish mark of ownership, this handwriting so ugly it looks like the footprints of a drunk dung beetle... Yup, that's my writing, no mistaking it.*

Wang Xiaomie woodenly flipped open the two books.

The first page of the left one read:

"Today is my second day playing wife for a guy in a mausoleum. I'm hungry..."

And on the first page of the right one:

"Today is my second day transmigrating into ancient times and playing someone's shixiong. I'm hungry...eheh~!"

He was left speechless again. *The heck is "eheh" supposed to mean! You even added a tilde!! Fuck your tilde, you fucker!*

Wang Xiaomie slapped the books shut, shaking like he had Parkinson's disease. *There's no way. How could I write something like this? How could something clearly written by a guy who's touched in the head have anything at all to do with someone as talented, elegant, and good-looking as me? I've definitely never gone to the past or met Wen Fengjin before, and I definitely don't have any memories of it...*

Calm down—you gotta stay calm, Wang Xiaomie—!

And so he flipped to the second page of his own diary.

In order to prevent other people from sneaking peeks at my diary, I've decided to use pinyin! Why not use English, you ask? Because I don't know it, ahahaha! Aren't I a genius? Wink~

Stay calm, you've absolutely gotta stay calm, stay—what the #%ing #@$%W—"wink," my ass!

Putting aside whatever secrets this notebook might reveal, just reading the girlishly chuuni narrative voice was enough to make Wang Xiaomie bury his face in a hand, feeling it sting with shame.

Off to the side, Wen Fengjin blinked at him, saying, "This book is full of your casual writings. I don't recognize the majority of what it contains, but there are some odd symbols in there, as well. Years ago, I gathered all the scholars and subordinates I had who were proficient in foreign languages. Countless people studied this notebook, but not a one of them was able to discern what was written in its pages. Now that I have you here yourself, Shixiong, maybe you can read it to me."

Wang Xiaomie was again speechless. *Let's see—that many people plus it being public plus them studying it together... oh, it's basically an extended public execution. Hi, mortuary? I'd like to have myself cremated, is that cool? Yeah, that's right, I've been dead a long time now, and I'd like to get another death for myself today.*

"Is something wrong, Shixiong? Why aren't you reading?"

Wang Xiaomie looked down at the notebook, flipping to another page.

"The food in this academy's beyond tasty! The royal we must recite a poem for the occasion: Head chef masterfully bakes/osmanthus candies, buns, and cakes/If I had to pick a flaw?/It would be nice to have meat in my maw. Tut tut, we are truly too talented, baahahahaha! Farewell!"

Wang Xiaomie could not bear it. *Don't look! All of you, shut your eyes! This idiot isn't me—he isn't me—!*

Meanwhile, Wen Fengjin was still urging him on. "Since Shixiong isn't reading aloud, I suppose you must have discovered something."

"I have indeed made a discovery," Wang Xiaomie replied.

"Oh?" Wen Fengjin smilingly asked, "And what is that?"

Wang Xiaomie smiled as tears rolled down his cheeks: "The fact that I really am an idiot." [justkeepsmiling.jpg]

Wen Fengjin looked stunned by this. "Shixiong is saying things this Fengjin doesn't understand again. But now that you've seen it, I assume Shixiong understands the situation as well."

Wang Xiaomie nodded with extreme seriousness, then flipped through a few more pages. Much of the writing was stuff along the lines of: *"I saw that kid today. Who would've thought the future villain who'll plunge all existence into the abyss of misery would be a kid like this?"* or *"Ai, I've realized that there's no way to reveal that thing's existence through speaking or writing, but I'll do my mission properly, either way. If I fail, I'll have my memories erased and die again, which is way too harsh..."*

There was also: *"Little shotas are so kawaii! I'll make sure to raise him into a well-rounded kid!"* and *"What the heck is up with this* setting? Raising him from a tiny kid into a big villain, then becoming said villain's unattainable crush... Come on man, isn't that beyond dumb? Stupid xx!"

After getting halfway through this notebook, Wang Xiaomie set it down, buried his head in his hands, and spent a good few hours recovering, while Wen Fengjin spent the whole time keeping him company by his side.

Wang Xiaomie shook his head. Hard as it was to believe, and dumbfounded as he was, now that he'd read this diary, his mind was tying together all the different transmigration and reincarnation stories he'd once read online. He understood, more or less, that his past self had, for whatever reason, been bound to a system. Whenever the diary mentioned "that thing" or "stupid xx," it was probably referring to said system. His mission, meanwhile, had probably been to care for the supervillain, give the villain some warmth during his miserable childhood, and teach him to become a good person...

At this thought, Wang Xiaomie glanced up at Wen Fengjin.

Sensing his gaze, Wen Fengjin—in his brilliant red-and-black robes—unconsciously gave him a bewitching smile. Those dark eyes, those upward-curling lips, that little red pattern on his forehead... this was the epitome of a guy who at any moment was going to say "this venerable one demands your worthless life today."

Wang Xiaomie thought: *Boss, which of those educational tests do you think you can pass? PE?!*

Ai, that's why there was no point asking. The system wasn't blind— one look at what the big boss had grown up to be like and it would simply wave its hand, erasing his memories and sending him back to the modern world.

For all he knew, his inexplicable death was also this system's fault. And Wen Fengjin said that after he died, he'd built this underground mausoleum, collected all sorts of rare treasures, and even planted a pining tree or whatever. He'd genuinely waited for him in this mausoleum for over a thousand years. Wang Xiaomie traveling from modern to ancient times, meanwhile, was something the system could achieve in an instant. For all he knew, he'd failed his mission and died the night before, then been immediately summoned into this body by Wen Fengjin, who'd been waiting for a *really* long time...

Damnit, why was it that the more he thought about it, the more he and Wen Fengjin were like the BL version of the movie *The Myth*?!

If things were really as he supposed, then the fact that he had a system sure was nice—past or present, all it needed was a word from the system. But what about Wen Fengjin? How had he spent these thousand-plus years guarding his corpse?

Knowing himself, Wang Xiaomie figured there was a good chance he'd carelessly gotten close to the guy because of his mission, originally thinking he could muddle his way into becoming the kid's unattainable crush...only to end up foolishly turning their relationship into the ambiguous thing it was now.

And given how stubbornly infatuated Wen Fengjin was, on top of everything else. *Looking at it another way, if you threw me underground and left me there with nothing but a corpse for company...*

Fuck. Wang Xiaomie rubbed at his arms. Forget one or two years—even half a month would be too much for him to handle! A grave robber could show up and he'd excitedly talk the guy's ear off with pointless babble. No wonder Boss Wen had a different face every day, like he had bipolar disorder or something. It was all caused by ~the pressures of life~.

He flipped right to the last page, and found that the only thing written in the diary was that it was the day of Wen Fengjin's coming-of-age ceremony. The rest of the diary had unexpectedly been ripped out by someone.

Beside him, Wen Fengjin narrowed his eyes as he reached over and took the diary from Wang Xiaomie's hands. He said, "The pages here were already damaged when I got it. Seeing as Shixiong has now seen it, I'll be taking it back for safekeeping."

Wang Xiaomie scratched his head. "But isn't this my diary? And it looks like there's another volume in that box, too—can I see that one?"

To his surprise, Wen Fengjin's face instantly darkened at those words, the pasted-on smile completely disappearing like the ebbing tide, his long, narrow, inhuman eyes holding back a bone-chilling *something*. His response gave the impression he was trying to be a little more gentle, but the icy, lowered tone of his voice only served to make him that much more terrifying. "Is Shixiong drawing clear boundaries with me now? Also, you are wrong—that book isn't your writing, it's mine."

"I clearly saw it said Wang on the cover..."

"Shixiong."

"Ah?"

"Don't go angering me now, okay?"

I, Wang Xiaomie, in all the years I've been alive, have never before met someone capable of saying "okay" in a way that just oozes bloodthirst...

"Shixiong, when you first came to this body and replaced the real Mian Deng all those years ago, I noticed it. That's why the person I wanted to be close to from the time I was seven years old, the person I wanted for myself, was that soul from lands unknown. I rejoiced that you had come at all—so much so that I prayed constantly that you would stay for all eternity. I feared that you might be one of those deceased who'd been reincarnated in another's corpse, and so every day, I helped you defend your secret, cleaning up every mistake you made that might give your identity away."

Which is why, as well as those people from before, the assassins that damn emperor sent to kill me on the day of my coming-of-age ceremony—and the academy director, who'd realized you were acting strangely and demanded to have you dealt with—were all killed by the old guard my father had left for me.

What made that day different from the others, however, was that you found out about it. That was probably when you began to distance yourself from me...

Wen Fengjin tilted his head, placing a hand against Wang Xiaomie's cheek as he stared at him with an unwavering gaze. As Wang Xiaomie looked on in terror, his mouth pursed into a long, thin line before curving upward at the corners.

"Now you know my secret, Shixiong, so...are you still going to distance yourself from me? Do you still think the one I love is merely the previous owner of this body?"

Wang Xiaomie wildly shook his head, as if afraid that if he didn't respond quickly enough, the boss would decide to give him a lover's suicide for a present.

Plus there was nothing worse than discovering your current boyfriend was actually your past one, especially when from an outsider's perspective, *you* were the scumbag in the relationship! The other guy had patiently waited for him for so long, only for it to turn out that Wang Xiaomie had completely forgotten him! He'd even told him, "Don't use me as a replacement!"

Wang Xiaomie gulped. *Wen Fengjin really has an amazingly good temper.*

Just as he was thinking this, Wen Fengjin said, "Shixiong, I've suffered so much all these years..."

His intonation had the bitterness of a jilted girlfriend. This, combined with his scary tone, made him sound like one of those female ghosts in movies who went "Ah~ I died such a tragic death~"

Wang Xiaomie said: "...I was wrong! And besides, I don't have any memories right now anyway, so h-how was I supposed to know? Oh, right—and why didn't you show this to me earlier?!"

Wen Fengjin's expression changed ever so slightly, after which he relaxed and replied, "You'd only just awoken, and the memories of your previous death were so painful, I didn't want you to remember them again."

"So that's it, huh." Wang Xiaomie recalled what he'd said about how they'd been hunted because of that immortality elixir, and then been tortured or something. More importantly, the story had ended with him dying, which he was sure would have been a huge blow to both him and Wen Fengjin, albeit in different ways.

No wonder he doesn't want me to remember it. This chain of incidents left Wang Xiaomie's tiny brain totally muddled. He sat in the casket, head aching, as he slowly tried to work it all out.

Seeing how quickly Wang Xiaomie believed him, and the clueless look on his face as he sat there, Wen Fengjin's smile deepened.

The blood sacrifice I performed back then was left incomplete. Without the control the sacrifice would have given me, what will I do if Shixiong remembers all those things I did to you and tries to leave again?

And also...a Shixiong who feels remorse and wholeheartedly devotes himself to me here in the mausoleum... I like that quite a lot. If I don't restrain myself, I'll probably hurt him, huh.

Heh.

22
Tough Love

WEN FENGJIN had originally expected that, having learned the portion of the truth he'd purposely revealed, Shixiong would be filled with remorse and then whole-heartedly devote himself to him, ultimately giving him both his heart and his body, after which they'd live a happy, lovey-dovey life, exchanging words like "Fengjin, I'm cold," and "I'll hug you, Shixiong," for the rest of their days.

However, our little top from ancient times—Big Boss Wen Fengjin—clearly had no idea of the way in which modern people did relationships. Before getting on the Boss route, Wang Xiaomie was a pitiful baby shrinking with terror, who whined and cried when bullied.

But after learning that he was the boss's beloved moonlight darling, Wang Xiaomie turned into a beast with his mouth constantly curving upward, smile gradually turning savage! The disparity was as great as your partner before and after marriage.

"Xiao-Wenzi, do the laundry."

Wen Fengjin thought: *Xiao-Wenzi?!*

"Xiao-Wenzi, I pulled that sword rack out to use as a clothes-drying rack."

"...What happened to my Liaoyue Sword?"

"Huh? Oh, I tossed it on the floor!"

Wen Fengjin was speechless.

"Xiao-Wenzi! Mu Yi stole those snacks I got last time, you've gotta make him give them back!"

Wen Fengjin, again, speechless.

"Xiao-Wenzi, these mermaid-oil lamps have been burning all these years and still haven't burned out. If I put one on the floor to use for hot pot, will it... whoa! I'm on fire! Quick, come put it out, Xiao-Wenzi!"

A blazing Wang Xiaomie ran wild around the room, yelling loudly. Wen Fengjin sighed, not a trace of his usual bewitchingly vicious expression left on his face. He rushed over to catch Wang Xiaomie—who was acting like a puppy with its tail caught in someone's fingers—in his arms. With a wave of his hand, a great stone floor tile suddenly shattered, and the flying dirt instantly extinguished the lantern.

Wen Fengjin hugged the tearful little creature in his arms, looking at a burnt tuft of forehead hair which was curling wildly from the flames, and the accompanying innocent look on that face.

A frowning Wen Fengjin was just about to say something when Wang Xiaomie's eyes widened, and he puffed up his cheeks. "What are you doing? You're planning to scold me, aren't you!"

Wen Fengjin stayed silent. Tough love was reduced to nothing more than this.

Half irritated and half amused, Wen Fengjin couldn't help pinching his nose as Wang Xiaomie kept grumbling "audacious" complaints. His teeth itched to bite into that face—to bite that smooth, soft skin, that lively figure he'd yearned for night and day, even if said figure's skin was cold.

Some kind of warmth gradually spread through Wen Fengjin's heart.

Afterward, Wang Xiaomie began to notice that he was seeing fewer smiles on Wen Fengjin's face. Those twisted, psychotic smiles went away and were replaced by a sort of exasperated, amused yet irritated expression as he put down whatever he was doing to attend to the repeated calls of "Xiao-Wenzi." He was frowning, but he was happier than ever before.

After purposely wreaking havoc, Wang Xiaomie looked at Wen Fengjin's expression, which was gradually growing more lively, and quietly laughed behind his sleeve. *If you're unhappy, I'll do anything to make you warm. I may be cheekily causing trouble, but I just want to make sure you aren't so lonely...*

There was a type of angel in this world that took the form of a romantic partner who was bizarre and constantly causing trouble, yet always gave you a kiss afterward to cheer you up. To deal with a little creature such as this, who could be naughty yet admit their mistakes, and was constantly melting your heart with cuteness, there was no need to hit them—all you had to do was give them a good hard kiss.

When they went to bed at night, the man who'd previously been constantly copping covert feels of the boss would now openly feel him up, circling around him as he freely touched away. *Get that man molested!* Wang Xiaomie thought.

Wen Fengjin looked at the head pressed against his chest, the thighs carelessly riding his lower abdomen, and those quiet, clearly fake snoring noises. He suffered through enduring this treatment, and even being spoken to with disdain, as Wang Xiaomie exclaimed, "Why's your body so cold!" *Hmph, I'll give him the cold shoulder!*

Wen Fengjin stayed silent. The falsest advertising in all of history: Rather than marrying the gentle shixiong he'd expected, he'd wound up marrying this lousy Wang Xiaomie.

Boss Wen, unable to endure any more of this, decided to push Wang Xiaomie off him, only for Wang Xiaomie to bare his teeth. "Do you not like me anymore? Huh? Say it! Bark bark bark!"

"...Stop barking, Xiaomie."

"...Bark bark bark!" *I'll bite you to death!*

Wen Fengjin had, without realizing it, become incapable of calling this suicidally cheeky creature "Shixiong" or "Mian Deng." His unnaturally black eyes began to fill with a sweet love as he changed from a man who looked up to his shixiong to an "old" man who endlessly doted on his beloved little bastard.

One day, Wang Xiaomie was so bored he'd started playing with mud. The mausoleum lacked pretty much everything—including both electricity and Wi-Fi—but it certainly wasn't lacking in gold, jewels, water, and mud. Wang Xiaomie had once even asked Wen Fengjin, "An underground river this long should have fish in it, right?"

Wen Fengjin had paused before responding, "I did toss a few of the more hardy types of fish in there all those years ago, but they're for defending against grave r—"

"Wow! There's fish! That means we can finally have fish to eat!" A jubilant Wang Xiaomie immediately started looking for fishing equipment, completely failing to listen to whatever else Wen Fengjin was going to say. He then pulled up a big fish with a human face and black hair, giving him two days' worth of nightmares full of human-headed fish grinning cheerfully at him. *I was a fool for believing that a mausoleum would have normal fish!*

From that day onwards, Wang Xiaomie never again mentioned catching or roasting fish to eat. And now he obediently molded his mud, with the end goal of making only two things, both cremation boxes—one for Wen Fengjin and one for himself. Whenever they happened to get found by some pro in the future, and dug up out of the dirt, they could put these boxes to use.

He'd recently begun having dreams of the past. Though he always woke up with a bitter taste in his mouth after those dreams, Wang Xiaomie credited it all to that weird tree.

Perhaps it was because his lost memories were beginning to awaken, but he'd also been spending longer and longer periods away from the tree. He'd even gotten to know a lot of Wen Fengjin's "little cuties." Those adorable little oddities sure were something... Compared to the rest, the bloody lizardman, Mu Yi, really was the most attractive of the bunch.

Wen Fengjin held his hand as he introduced him to them.

"This is Mu Er." She was a female ghost who could give Sadako a run for her money, being pale all over, with sticky black hair, and a terrifying visage to boot. Apparently, she lived underwater.

"This is Mu San." This one didn't even have a humanoid shape at all. It looked just like some sort of tree fungus that'd grown a face and hands. Seen from a distance, it looked like a walking, *you* know, ahem, that thing all men know... Also Wen Fengjin said absolutely not to touch the sticky fluid on its body, which could instantly turn a living person into a puddle of water, leaving only their clothes behind.

"This is Mu Si."

"This is Mu Wu."

"This is..."

After that series of introductions, with ten tomb-guardian monsters all pointed out, Wen Fengjin smiled and said, "Aren't they adorable?"

The crew of weird monsters all laughed together, which sounded like a cacophony of howling and cackling.

"...Mmhm, super cute," Wang Xiaomie said. They'd have no problem getting enough participants for a "scariest monster" ranking list.

Wen Fengjin gently patted his head. "Make sure to bring them along when you walk around the mausoleum, understand? The location of this place is ultimately not known to us alone, and the number of grave robbers is irritatingly high, so you must be careful not to let yourself get hurt."

Bring them along? Do I have them walk ahead of me while I hold on to a rope? Bro, are you aiming for a dog walk or a Hyakki Yagyou demon parade?! What do you think those grave robbers are gonna say when they see this big ol' family? Huh?!

Wang Xiaomie gazed expressionlessly at the terrifying family before him, and they gazed eagerly back at him in turn. "Sorry, they're too ugly for me."

When this big ol' gang of tomb guardians starts crying like this, they actually sound kinda pitiful... As if! It's like a flood of unnatural noise pouring into my ears! Fuck!

He asked, "...Could we dial it back a little?"

The gang seemed to say, *No way, Master's watching!*

He looked up to see Wen Fengjin smiling cheerfully—he was watching right there by his side, see? "Xiao-Wenzi..."

"Hm?"

"Giddyup!"

That day, Wang Xiaomie not only rode around a good half of the mausoleum on the back of a Xiao-Wenzi so gloomy there were storm clouds above his head, but also got to walk ten monsters from out of a horror flick.

Having found a way to entertain himself, Wang Xiaomie picked up the habit of having to take a stroll around the tomb before going to bed every night. After ten days of this, Wen Fengjin had even lost weight (cough).

But it lead to him discovering an interesting phenomenon: big lizard Mu Yi and big mushroom Mu San seemed to have some bad blood between them. Every time they went on a stroll, Mu Yi would always crawl on the ceiling or wall of the tomb corridor, then sneakily spit at Mu San. Mu San impassively endured each shot— but Mu Yi would then laugh at his silence, which would anger the mushroom-like Mu San enough that he'd begin secreting corrosive sticky liquid, which in turn was hot enough that Mu Er and Mu Wu, beside him, would start howling in distress...

This is making me feel like I'm watching a gosh-dang troublemaking husky!

"Don't pay them any mind. Mu Yi and Mu San were at odds even in their previous lives," Wen Fengjin said quietly as he carried Wang Xiaomie on his back, sweeping his gaze over the two in front of them.

Mu Yi whined as he fell from the wall and obediently started walking, while Mu San stopped secreting acid.

The group of terrible monsters, who wielded such awe-inducing power within the gloomy tomb and scared countless people to tears with their inhuman visages, now shuffled obediently forward like kicked puppies.

Amused, Wang Xiaomie chose this moment to tease Wen Fengjin. "Dad, you're being too hard on the children."

Wen Fengjin was thrown off by this, eyes widening in bewilderment. "What did you just call me?"

Wang Xiaomie couldn't fully see Wen Fengjin's face from up on his back. He said, with a laugh, "Dad! I mean, don't you think the two of us plus all of them is kinda like a family of three...no, of twelve? With a loving mother and a stern father?"

Wen Fengjin didn't respond for quite a long time, nor did he take another step forward. When the big monsters ahead all turned back to look curiously at them, Wang Xiaomie tilted his head and leaned over to try to see the look on Wen Fengjin's face. "What's wrong, Xiao-Wenzi?"

"Nothing." Wen Fengjin seemed to have suddenly regained his senses. He hefted Wang Xiaomie up on his back before silently continuing to walk.

"Fengjin? Seriously, what is it?"

"It's nothing, Xiaomie..."

"Hm?"

"Or should I say...Mom..."

That husky, laughing voice gently brushed across Wang Xiaomie's senses, instantly turning his face red and plunging the air into silence once more, though this time the silence was a sweet one.

When they returned to the towering platform, Wang Xiaomie and Wen Fengjin climbed into their casket together. The two of them lay there, neither of them sleeping. This time, Wang Xiaomie didn't casually reach over, making the near-imperceptible sound of Wen Fengjin's lone breathing sound infinitely louder than usual. The blazing scarlet peach flowers of the blooming tree above could be seen from within the open casket.

A somewhat cold and bony hand gently covered Wang Xiaomie's.

"You—"

"You—"

The two of them turned their heads to look at each other. Something dense and sweet poured into their surroundings like so much malt sugar—cloying, and difficult to breathe in...

Wen Fengjin suddenly smiled. His delicate, handsome, somewhat wicked face now totally tranquil, he moved closer with a heavy-lidded gaze, and Wang Xiaomie shut his eyes, waiting quietly.

Those pale pink lips finally touched...

What sort of feeling was that, you ask?

The kiss started with a tongue invading his mouth. Once gentle, the man became like a starving animal when he received permission to proceed, his tongue powerfully thrusting as he hurriedly pressed himself flush against Wang Xiaomie's lower belly and started tearing at his clothes.

A pale, soft chest and a wedding dress spread out against the casket floor. The red and white made a distinctive contrast as the two of them tore at each other with rushed kisses.

The man above him hurriedly panted as Wang Xiaomie was compelled to lift his chest and submit to having the pale-pink nubs on it pinched and rubbed. Wen Fengjin's other hand held tight the back of his head, entangling their tongues with a seemingly bottomless hunger, pulling and licking at each other, clear spit sliding from mouth to neck.

When they separated enough to swallow, a glittering and translucent strand hung between them, tying them inseparably together until—not waiting for it to break on its own—it was snapped by their next impatient kiss. They didn't need to breathe, but Wen Fengjin's ruthless power, and the way he licked at the roof of his mouth as if wanting to rip him apart, made Wang Xiaomie involuntarily sob. That burning gaze gave him the impression that he'd already been pressed against the floor, compelled not only to open his body but also to wantonly scream and beg for more.

Even so, the man above him was going to violate him without the slightest mercy.

"Oomph—"

There was more spit than he could swallow, and his tongue hurt a lot too; Wang Xiaomie was close to tears when he was finally let go, and the man above him moved to kneel with legs on either side of his waist.

The naked Wang Xiaomie pressed his legs together as intense pleasure travelled from the tips of his toes to that hardened place, burning its way up his pinch-reddened chest to his neck, and searing hotly at the back of his ears.

Beneath the immortal tree, Wang Xiaomie—in possession of a humanlike sense of touch—chewed on his fingers as the man above him took hold of his member.

"Fengjin..."

"Don't worry, leave it to me... It's beautiful, not the slightest bit shameful..."

"Mn..."

The stimulation of that chilly hand made him want to shiver, but once those fingers wrapped around his shaft and began slowly stroking it, Wang Xiaomie instantly stopped breathing, biting his arm as he narrowed tear-filled eyes. The man bent over him like a powerful beast of prey, one hand lazily stroking his manhood. He ran one nail over the tip and covered the opening, only to let go when Wang Xiaomie was about to arch his back in an attempt to thrust upward.

At his dissatisfied thrusting, Wen Fengjin let out a low laugh before taking a nipple into his mouth, pressing against the little nub and slowly circling it with his tongue. The little thing instantly turned hard as a pebble, leaning this way and that with the tongue's motions as its owner whimpered ingratiatingly.

After sucking at it like a teat until it swelled, Wen Fengjin licked his lips, his odd eyes flashing with light. The red mark on the brow of his beautiful, feminine face made him look terrifyingly and devilishly seductive. Slick wet lips approached Wang Xiaomie's evasive, teary eyes and drank those in as well.

"It aches, don't touch my eyes—*aaahh*—!"

The large hand busy with his member suddenly quickened its pace. The wetness coming from his shaft acted as lubricant, and the movements made sticky, slapping noises. He let out a low cry and quickly started biting his arm again, abruptly arching his back high with hurried breaths.

When he climaxed, he was unable to form any words at all. All he could do was tense his body and stretch upward with everything he had, eyes wide and mouth open as he was taken over by that virus called pleasure—a feeling powerful enough to make him spasm. In the instant his genitals shot their load, the electric jolt of it made his entire body go numb.

It was here that Wen Fengjin bit down on his greatest weakness—the back of his ear—and started sucking on it with great force. Wang Xiaomie's eyes were as wide as they could possibly get, tears quickly welling up at the corners as he spasmed, gasping desperately despite the fact he wasn't in need of oxygen. He had the pressing feeling that his very soul was about to get sucked away...

He was brought to the highest point, then weakly fell back down again, finally recovering his senses after a very long climax. He watched through blurry tears as the man kneeling over him took a moment to adjust his position. And then slowly began to untie his belt.

The great red robe came down, and Wen Fengjin tugged off his jade crown. His long raven locks fell over his wide, well-muscled back as he quirked his lips, casting a sidelong glance from that sinfully handsome face.

His pants were pulled down low, causing a certain something to jump excitedly out and point at Wang Xiaomie's lips.

"Lick," he said. "I'll hurt you if I go in like this. Won't you wet it for me?"

Wang Xiaomie's narrow chest rose and fell, his mind in a haze of passion as he partially propped himself on his elbows and lifted his head to take Wen Fengjin's member into his mouth, carefully giving it a shy, inexperienced kiss.

The man above him grunted, then gave his hair a hard tug.

Wang Xiaomie wasn't frightened, only embarrassed, as he gazed at the large, ferocious fellow before him. Then he stuck out the pink tip of his tongue to give it a lick.

The grip on his hair grew even tighter.

Wang Xiaomie smiled to himself, purposely stretching out his tongue to touch those dangling balls, then quickly licking a straight line from root to tip...

"Do you want me to thrust into your mouth?" asked a hoarse and somewhat angry voice. Wen Fengjin, his expression colored with burning lust, grabbed hold of him and then thrust himself into Wang Xiaomie's mouth as threatened, ruthlessly ramming once against his tongue and throat.

Wang Xiaomie immediately gagged, tears forming in his eyes and his throat burning with pain. This time, he didn't dare play games. His mouth enveloped that long pole, and he slowly swallowed as he clumsily polished it with his tongue. The man above him just as slowly pressed Wang Xiaomie's head into his crotch, thrusting into his mouth at a much more gentle pace. His pubic hair brushed against Wang Xiaomie's face, making him unable to suppress his excitement. Spit began trickling from his busy mouth, the rod now soaking wet from his caresses. Finally, Wen Fengjin stopped moving, and pulled out as Wang Xiaomie panted for breath.

It was time for his other mouth to take a turn.

Wang Xiaomie was pinned forcefully against the wall of the casket, his legs propped up against Wen Fengjin's shoulders. Wen Fengjin's fingers were already inserted and playing with his opening. He bit down on his lips, constantly trying to evade the other man's gaze, even with his pallid face now completely red.

"Don't look away... Look at me... Turn around..."

As Wen Fengjin gave this command, he bent down, pulled out his fingers, and pressed his burning rod against the opening instead. He then breathed out against Wang Xiaomie's ear, smiling as he said, "Watch how I fuck you, hm? Will you? Having you watch will excite me all the more. Unless you *don't* want me to enter your body with even more force, and then..."

Did he not want that? Not only did the shameless talk fail to soften him, but his spent member falteringly spat out more liquid in an attempt to rise again.

"Pfft, hahaha, Shixiong is so cute—I'll satisfy you right now, okay? Let Fengjin rail you until you break. If Shixiong can't persevere any longer... then just cry out for me..."

"Don't—don't say any more—" Wang Xiaomie cried as he watched his own ass gradually swallow the man's length. As if playing a mean prank, Wen Fengjin got halfway in before suddenly raising his head, immediately catching sight of Wang Xiaomie's pleasure-drowned face.

Heh, this is so humiliating. I might as well die and end it all right now.

The man above him laughed loudly before finally penetrating him to the hilt. Wang Xiaomie shuddered from head to toe.

Now that he was inside, Wen Fengjin's expression became excited. The light in his eyes, and the way he looked like a wild beast let loose from its cage, made Wang Xiaomie tremble all the harder. "I-if I call your name, will you really stop?"

"I will..."

This answer was accompanied by a frenzied, breakneck thrusting, with him pulling forcefully free each time before stabbing all the way back in with a wet noise. With Wang Xiaomie's legs on his shoulders, Wen Fengjin pressed his head down to make him watch as he was fucked to tears by that hard rod turned black with blood, each thrust quickly slapping against his buttocks and lower abdomen.

The slapping and splurting noises continued without cease. Wang Xiaomie was so lost in pleasure that his hands were fisting in the clothes beneath them, gasping out puffs of hot air as he moaned wantonly. The gland buried deep in his lower entrance sent out enough pleasure to kill him, pleasure more intoxicating than any alcohol or drug. He'd already lost all dignity and shame, the folds of his ass stretched as far as they could possibly go. The intense pace at which he was being fucked pulled out his soft inner flesh before pushing it back in again.

Wang Xiaomie gave a sticky moan. Being so satisfied during his first time made him lose his mind with passion.

Half an hour later, Wen Fengjin came inside him. The man pumping his seed into Wang Xiaomie laughed as he climaxed, then thrust into him once more.

"...?! You—"

"Don't worry. As I said, if you get scared, just tell me and I'll stop." The man deceived him with these words, then covered his mouth before he could react. "I'm telling the truth—if I hurt you, all you have to do is call my name..."

Wang Xiaomie, whose mouth was covered, made a muffled noise. "...Mmph!"

An even more powerful thrust! Wang Xiaomie was ruthlessly shoved right into the wooden wall of the casket. The wolf in sheep's clothing revealed his true fearsome face and fucked him until he was tearfully crying an endless series of muffled wails, his ass and buttocks completely red. *I'm going to die, wah, I'm gonna die—let me go, I'm begging you—*

The intense slapping of bodies and the stimulation of watching himself get penetrated made Wang Xiaomie sob weakly as he screamed. Wen Fengjin parted his legs, his thick rod drawing out the liquid secreted by Wang Xiaomie's inner walls and spraying it all over their clothes.

Finally, they reached a point where Wang Xiaomie was staring blankly at nothing as his body swayed along with his partner's ramming movements. He no longer knew how much time had passed.

Wen Fengjin pulled out his still-twitching length, and came onto his face. "Does it taste good?"

The man chuckled. Those flashing red eyes seemed to force their way into his line of vision.

"If Shixiong doesn't say anything, then that must mean he hasn't eaten his fill. I'll just have to feed Shixiong one more time..."

"Mmph!"

23

Red Bean
Rice

WANG XIAOMIE LAY spread-eagled in his coffin, gazing at the carved and colored images of auspicious clouds on its inner walls with a blank look in his eyes. He hadn't even found time to put on his clothes: His little zongzi was bared to the world.

Large swathes of strawberry-colored marks ran from behind his ears to the tips of his toes, like a full-body tattoo.

Wang Xiaomie thought: ...*I'm practically zongzi-disabled now.*

The culprit, meanwhile, sat on the edge of the casket with his back to Wang Xiaomie—blazing-red clothes wrapped around his lower half, his sturdy back and envy-inducing hourglass waist exposed, his black hair dark as ink. He was currently humming a tune to himself, tapping a rhythm against the casket as he sat. To put it simply—he was in an *explosively* good mood.

Just look at how he, Wang Xiaomie, lay dumbly there, like his body had been hollowed out. And then look at the guy over there, who felt not the slightest twinge of back pain or anything like it, looking so triumphant his metaphorical tail was practically arched in the air with pride!

Wang Xiaomie felt a tiny ember of something called jealousy light up within his heart. He gritted his teeth and called out, "Xiao-Wenzi..."

"Hm?" Wen Fengjin looked back at him. The dazzling smile on his face nearly blinded Wang Xiaomie.

Wang Xiaomie thought: *Are you really that happy, Boss? You're practically breaking character here, believe you-Mie!*

Wen Fengjin repositioned. He moved from sitting on the edge of the casket to stand on the floor, draping himself over the casket' lip with one hand caressing Wang Xiaomie's cheek. One might call his gaze and expression endlessly affectionate and extremely gentle, like he wanted nothing more than to bury the object of his affection deep within his own chest.

"Xiaomie, yesterday..." As he spoke, Boss Wen straightened his face in an attempt to force himself back into character, but couldn't stop himself from smiling regardless. His eyes glittered bright as he tightly grasped Wang Xiaomie's hands. "I was very happy yesterday, I'll take care of you for the rest of eternity, I swear I'll take responsibility! I'll never betray your affection or trust!"

Wang Xiaomie was speechless.

"Oh, right, we've already been married a while now, haha."

"..."

Not even that femininely bewitching face could hold back his somewhat foolish smile. *Don't be like this, Boss, you're scaring me.*

Wang Xiaomie gulped as he heard Wen Fengjin say, "In our Northern Kingdom, the first night a girl loses her virginity, she's expected to have a bowl of red bean rice. Though we have no red beans in our tomb, I did acquire other ingredients from those grave robbers. Here, I'll help you get dressed before I go make the rice for you."

Wen Fengjin helped Wang Xiaomie out of the casket, lovingly dressed him with his gaze lowered, then picked him up, causing his long black hair to fall in a curving wave which looked like the softest embroidery against his red wedding dress.

Lying against Wen Fengjin's bosom with steady arms wrapped around his shoulders and legs, Wang Xiaomie felt moved beyond words. *My hubby's the handsomest, lovingest hubby ever!*

Upon reaching the riverbank where they'd previously done laundry, Wen Fengjin carefully set him down and said, "Wait here for me."

"Okay." Wang Xiaomie blinked and obediently nodded, eagerly watching as Wen Fengjin got out the pots and things they'd been using, lit a fuel tablet, and started boiling water for porridge.

But while he was making that porridge, Wen Fengjin also mysteriously insisted on hiding what he was doing. By the time Wang Xiaomie got a good look, the beans and rice had already gone into the pot, and the lid was already shut tight.

Wang Xiaomie was so tickled by this that he was grinning at the thought, feigning indifference as he grumbled, "Tch~ Why are you keeping it a secret? Not that I'm curious either way."

Wen Fengjin smiled at that but did not reply.

After the last night, there seemed to be little pink flowers dancing through the air every time their eyes met. A red-faced Wang Xiaomie thus turned his head away.

Wen Fengjin hid a laugh, the thrill of flirtation written all over his face.

Cooking the porridge would take a very long time, and the atmosphere was a quiet one. Wang Xiaomie kept struggling with the desire to look at Wen Fengjin, but whenever he turned his head—heheh, Boss Wen would be looking right back at him, looking pleased as punch.

Aiyo~ What an *awfully* amazing first time!

Wang Xiaomie suddenly stood: "I-I-I, I'm going to the riverside to play with mud!"

Wen Fengjin was momentarily thrown off, then nodded with a smile on his lips.

Wang Xiaomie walked mechanically over to the river and squatted down a good distance away from him. He started using river water to play with the mud, molding it into all sorts of random shapes as he recalled the events of the day before, unable to stop himself from chuckling to himself, his face a bright red.

Drool~ Wen Fengjin has such a strong waist~ Drool~ Last night~ Eheheh~

When he came back to his senses, he looked down to realize that the mud in his hand had been molded into the shape of Wen Fengjin's dick.

Aaahhh!

Wang Xiaomie immediately squashed it flat. Smoke poured out his ears. He wanted nothing more than to crawl into a hole in the ground. His eyes shone wet and a blush colored his pretty, delicate face as he covered his mouth with the back of his clean hand.

...Mom, it really is hard for a man in the throes of ♥♥♥ to control his thoughts after getting a taste of adulthood for the first time!

Unbeknownst to him, Wen Fengjin—watching from a distance as he made all those embarrassed expressions—slowly opened his mouth to bite his lower lip.

Mmhm, he's extremely cute. Mmhm, I so want to fuck him.

This ancient, undying man, eternally caught in the throes of ♥♥♥, was even less able to control his thoughts.

As the foul stench of love filled the atmosphere, the porridge finished cooking. Its warm, delicate fragrance suffused the air. Wen Fengjin opened the lid and stirred it lightly, a satisfied expression appearing on his face. "Xiaomie, come and eat."

"Right, okay!" Wang Xiaomie hurriedly put down the mud, washed his hands in the ice-cold river, and excitedly headed over. Red bean rice! This was the first time anyone beside his grandma had ever cared for him, and cooked a meal for him to eat!

Wen Fengjin served the hot, fresh-cooked porridge, blowing on it as he said, in a low voice, "This is the first time I've made this dish as well. Just eat what you can, don't burn yourself."

Wang Xiaomie smiled like an idiot at the gentle look on that face. "Don't worry, I can handle it! I'll make sure to eat it all!"

"That's good—careful, it's hot." Wen Fengjin looked just as happy as he handed him the porridge.

Wang Xiaomie, so happy he was practically soaring, accepted the bowl with gusto. His eyes sparkled as he lowered his head to eat, and then... And then, silence.

"..."

Wen Fengjin, who had already taken a bite, noticed Wang Xiaomie sitting stiffly there without eating. He asked with a frown, "What is it, Xiaomie? Is it not to your liking?"

"...It's not that. Earlier, you said you couldn't find red beans, but found something else instead, right."

"That's right."

Wang Xiaomie expressionlessly plucked a fresh green mung bean from the bowl with his chopsticks. "So you used mung beans as a replacement?"

Wen Fengjin tilted his head. "Mung beans relieve inflammation and internal heat. Is there anything wrong?"

Wang Xiaomie silently lifted the bag of mung beans off the ground. On it was written: "Grave-robbing exclusive mung beans! Soaked in specialized holy water for forty-nine days, can be eaten or used to control big zongzi jiangshi. Give a good review on receipt to get two yuan in cash back."

The heck do you mean by "grave-robbing exclusive mung beans"?! The heck do you mean by "soaked in holy water for forty-nine days"?!

It's supposed to be talisman-blessed water, you gosh-dang fools! And how do you think the mung beans feel about having to soak for forty-nine whole days?! Just watch them sprout and see how you like it! Good review my ass... For you, only bad! All the bad reviews!

He and the mung bean stared at each other. "I'm super kyoot!" the cute little green bean seemed to say to him. "Eat me an' you'll turn gween too!"

Wang Xiaomie smiled and buried his face in a hand. Two wide lines of tears ran from his eyes.

After my first time doing the deed, my big zongzi husband gave me, another big zongzi, a bowl of holy water mung bean porridge. Can I burn a husband like this? Would burning him be illegal? I'm asking online, this is really urgent!

"Eat up, Xiaomie." Wen Fengjin was even urging him on.

Wang Xiaomie picked up the bowl and thought about slapping it down on his head, but after pausing to consider their respective power levels, he put it back down with a sigh. "Oh, Xiao-Wenzi..."

"Hm?"

"Do you know what it means to wear a green hat, or be called green[2]?"

Ancient Boss Wen Fengjin shook his head with a frown.

Wang Xiaomie picked out all the beans in his bowl, giving them to Wen Fengjin with a kindly smile. "You're the one who worked hard yesterday, so you should eat more. I'm happy with just the porridge."

---

2   A Chinese idiom that means to be cuckolded.

Wen Fengjin's expression softened at the mention of the night before. Unexpectedly, he started putting the beans back into his bowl. "You should eat more as well. After all..."

As he chewed on a mouthful of mung bean porridge, Wang Xiaomie could feel the mung beans relieving heat, just as advertised. Even his heart had gone cold.

Maybe it was that jiangshi really couldn't eat mung beans after all, or maybe the mung beans really had been soaked in holy water, but that night, a familiar feeling began to overtake Wang Xiaomie's stomach. He got to his feet with a dark look on his face, which darkened even further at the sight of Wen Fengjin looking perfectly fine!

Unfair! How come whenever we wanna fill our bellies, I end up fatter than him—wait, no, I mean how come I'm the one who gets diarrhea?!

"What's wrong?" Seeing him suffer, Wen Fengjin frowned worriedly. "Say something, Xiaomie, don't scare me."

"I'm fine..." Wang Xiaomie gritted his teeth, hands over his stomach. "I need to use the latrine."

Wen Fengjin stared blankly for a moment, then remembered how he'd been this way last time as well. He immediately picked up Wang Xiaomie, fetched the same paper from the side hall, then rushed off to the same latrine as before.

"I'll wait at the door."

Wang Xiaomie nodded carelessly, paper in hand, before running into the little room. He squatted over the pit with a rumbling stomach and a pained look on his face.

Ai, one of these days, Wen Fengjin's going to poison me to death! At least this time there won't be a big guy falling from the ceiling, right...?

Wang Xiaomie looked at the stone tile above him, thinking about when he'd met Zhen Bei.

Haha, there's no way that could ever happen. After all, he's already found the Fish Pearl. Plus, there's no way anyone could ever fall for the same trap twice in a row~

Wait! Why do I suddenly feel like I raised a really weird flag by saying that? Hold on, he's not actually going to come plummeting out of nowhere and prove me wrong, is he?!

Wang Xiaomie stared nervously above him, but by the time he'd finished emptying his bowels and wiped his butt, not a single strange thing had fallen from the ceiling.

Silly me~ Like I said, that would be way too big a coincidence ~

As he thought this, Wang Xiaomie cheerfully pulled up his pants and walked over to the door—only for Wen Fengjin to suddenly appear. He pulled Wang Xiaomie behind him as he lifted his head to glare angrily at something up above.

At this same moment, the stone tile on the ceiling of the room suddenly made a familiar noise before immediately flipping open!

"Wayayayaaaah!" a familiar figure screamed. He hit the ground with a *thump*, then started whining. "Aiyo, my poor back~"

He deftly picked himself up off the floor, shaking his head and stumbling about as if dizzy. He'd likely rattled his head in the fall. He loudly spat out the dirt in his mouth, brushing himself off while he was at it. All in all, it was quite a while before he actually thought to look around.

And so the three of them abruptly made eye contact. Zhen Bei stared in blank shock for a moment before a wide smile made its way onto his face. He even waved as enthusiastically as a bright-eyed husky!

"Hi! Xiaomie! I'm back again! Did you miss me?!"

The other two were rendered speechless.

Wang Xiaomie stared silently at Zhen Bei for a long moment before gently slapping his own mouth. *That's what you get with your bloody big mouth! And as for you...what are you, a frickin' beast summon or something?!*

MY HUSBAND AND I SLEEP IN A COFFIN

214

Winning the Tomb Master's Heart

WHILE BEAST SUMMON Zhen Bei greeted them with all the closeness of a dear friend, Wen Fengjin sneered. "You again? To think you dared return!"

He shifted in place, preparing to land a killing blow. Wang Xiaomie hurriedly pulled him back, while Zhen Bei quickly waved his hands, saying, urgently, "I didn't come to graverob this time, I'm here to tip you off!"

Tip them off? Wang Xiaomie blinked: "What do you mean?"

"Don't listen to his nonsense. If this man can get past Mu Er and find his way here again, he must certainly have some tricks up his sleeve. Get out of my way, Xiaomie. I don't want to hurt you— trust me, I'll have this cleaned up quickly." Wen Fengjin—who had been looking at Zhen Bei with the cold and indifferent gaze of a venomous snake—turned to Wang Xiaomie and ruffled his hair with lowered eyes, cajoling him gently.

Wang Xiaomie, however, knew the ruthlessness beneath Wen Fengjin's warm façade. When he said "clean up," he probably really did mean there would be not one hair left of this guy.

"Mu Er? Who's that?" Zhen Bei waved a hand, saying, "Forget that for now! Listen, I really am here to repay you—I brought you guys some important information! Also, you're actually the masters of this thousand-year-old tomb, right? I told my brother about it when I got back, haha. He guessed you must be the shixiong the tablet mentioned, who died in a battle over an elixir of immortality, and the demon lord who died for his love of his shixiong."

He pointed at Wang Xiaomie and Wen Fengjin in turn, then proudly rubbed the tip of his nose.

"I'm not afraid of zongzi, though, plus Xiaomie doesn't seem like a bad guy, and I owe you guys for saving my dage too. Now that that dead-faced guy's threatening my ge to come dig up your grave, the least I can do is sneak over here to tell you about it!"

"Died for love... and a demon lord, too?" Wang Xiaomie stared pointedly at the back of Wen Fengjin's head.

Wen Fengjin stiffened, then quietly cleared his throat. "The tablet was carelessly carved. You needn't believe what it says."

Could anyone really get careless about carving a tablet that big? Wang Xiaomie covered his head with a sigh. *Forget it... After reading that diary, I already know that this guy grew up weird.*

That said, he did care quite a bit about the big news Zhen Bei had just given them. Still holding Wen Fengjin back, he asked Zhen Bei, "What do you mean by important information? Who's digging up our grave? Also, how did you conveniently manage to fall right in front of me..." *I was so shocked, I thought I'd learned a weird summoning technique.*

Wen Fengjin stood between the two, hesitating for a moment after Wang Xiaomie took hold of his hand. Ultimately, he didn't pull free of that icy cold hand, though he still looked at Zhen Bei with cold disinterest. "Answer my shixiong's question, brat."

"Brat?" Zhen Bei's eyes bulged in offense as he pointed at himself, saying, "I'm twenty-four years old!"

Wang Xiaomie rolled his eyes. "I'm over 1,300 years old. Him? Also over 1,300 years old. *At our age, the two of us could be in a museum exhibit.*"

Zhen Bei was speechless for a moment, then said "...Okay, fine." He scratched his head, then stepped a little closer. "I'm actually—"

"Not another step!" Wen Fengjin glared at him, "Unless you want your head and body in separate places."

Grave robbers were treacherous and crafty, and not all such daredevils had evil countenances. In the thousand years since the mausoleum's creation, there had indeed been a few talented individuals who managed to make it into the depths of the tomb. When they were caught by Wen Fengjin, they would instantly abandon all dignity to beg him for their lives, but the moment he let down his guard, they would quickly attack. Some of them were even willing to use their comrades' lives as bait if it would help them kill the master of the tomb.

Zhen Bei felt a chill down his neck at Wen Fengjin's cold and venomous glare. His forehead dripped with sweat. In truth, he was actually so nervous he could barely breathe. That was a zongzi, after all! A thousand-year-old bigshot-jiangshi who'd previously tried to choke him to death without batting an eyelash! The fear of that near-death experience meant just looking at those weird black eyes of Wen Fengjin's was enough to make him go weak at the knees.

However...

Zhen Bei thought of his goal, then swallowed in an attempt to wet his stress-dry throat, and said, with an incredibly forced smile, "I honestly don't mean any harm... If you don't believe me, I'll toss away my backpack!"

Wen Fengjin looked at Zhen Bei's stupidly open smile and sneered. "All right. It would be best if you removed your coat as well—also the dagger in your boot, and the talismans inside your shirt."

"...Fuck, how'd you know about all that?!" A dumbstruck Zhen Bei put his hands over his chest, instantly giving himself away with his actions.

Wen Fengjin immediately grasped this opportunity to mock him. "See, Xiaomie, this is how shameless grave robbers all are—which is why there's no need for you to believe their lies."

Wang Xiaomie couldn't decide if he should be laughing or crying right now. "Fengjin, let him finish."

Wen Fengjin snorted softly as he turned to glare irritably at Zhen Bei again.

Wang Xiaomie continued, with a yawn, "Hurry up and say your piece, bro, I need to go back to sleep, and we left the casket open— I dunno how I'm gonna deal if a bug crawls in while we're gone."

"Oh come on, there's people coming to dig up your grave and you're still planning to sleep?!"

"What else do you expect me to do? Do you know how many people come digging around here every year? If it weren't for the fact there's no way to make them pay an entry fee, I'd have set up a tourist attraction by now!" *The backpacks left behind by grave robbers in that one side hall are piled higher than a mountain! Mu Er—that's the water-ghost little jiejie who wails to raise the alarm when intruders show up–has practically cried herself hoarse. And Mu Yi is constantly dragging all kinds of backpacks back from the outermost areas of the mausoleum. One perfectly good lizardman, turned into a hamster!*

"I gotta say, have you guys been reading too many novels or some-thing? These people must be stupid, constantly obsessed with digging up other people's graves instead of doing anything productive with their lives... Most of you can't even make it past Mu Er to the mausoleum's main entrance, but you keep sending in more!"

He kept being woken by Mu Er's crying, thinking he was about to have a fight to the death with grave robbers, just like in the movies. But every time this happened, Wen Fengjin would briefly open his eyes, close them again, and say, "Go back to sleep. Mu Er has already taken care of it."

Wang Xiaomie stared speechlessly at Zhen Bei. "Even gamers who camp for roaming bosses don't work this hard!"

Zhen Bei scratched his head at this talking-to. "That's 'cause this place has lots of treasures, though," he chirped quietly.

Wang Xiaomie was indignant. "Bullshit, we don't have any treasures here! Just look at yourselves! Living on the surface, getting to go on the internet and watch TV whenever you feel like it, and buying takeout whenever you're hungry and eating whatever you want!" *As for us? We don't have so much as an internet connection or a cell phone, and we have to live by candlelight! We don't even have any food to eat—we have to survive by picking garbage out of equipment packs every day, wehhh~*

"Y-you know about using the internet and watching TV...?"

"Of course I do! I'm a zongzi who keeps up with the times!"

"Oh...but your hair ties all use Fish Pearls for decorations... Sell just one and you can have it easy for life."

Wang Xiaomie and Zhen Bei both stared speechlessly at each other, each seeing envy in the other's eyes. Ai, those in drought would die of thirst and those being flooded would die from drowning; if an impassive Wen Fengjin weren't standing between them, the two of them might even have tried to hug.

"How about I give those things to you? Then you trade them for money and get a few more cell towers built on the big mountain over our heads, and maybe mail me a generator or something while you're at it..."

"Yeah, sure! I could even help you buy some snacks online!"

"Whoa, you really are a great guy, bro!"

"Heheh, no problem! How about we exchange WeChat info?"

"Sure, let's—oh, I don't have a phone."

"Oh...it's fine, I'll bring you one next time!"

"Wahhh! Bro, you're awesome!"

Just as the two were about to exchange bear hugs and declare their brotherhood, a dark-faced Wen Fengjin grabbed Wang Xiaomie by the back of his collar. Smiling through gritted teeth, he said, "Shi. Xiong!"

Wang Xiaomie startled, realizing now that he'd strayed from the point. Zhen Bei—who acted perfectly natural when talking to Wang Xiaomie—seemed to sense a danger alert popping up above his head when he looked at Wen Fengjin's face. Without a thought, he lost all nerve to continue talking.

Wang Xiaomie gave a couple of forced laughs in Wen Fengjin's direction, blinking his eyes adorably as he put on his best good-boy act. Wen Fengjin let out a snort, looking much calmer than before: "Don't talk about unrelated things."

"Got it!"

Wang Xiaomie stuck out his tongue the moment Wen Fengjin looked away, and Zhen Bei was no longer quite as on guard as he was before, either.

After all that pointless chatter, they finally returned to the main topic. "Forget everything else for a minute, how exactly did you manage to get around Mu Er? I haven't seen anyone able to get this far lately—and why is it that you always manage to show up right when I'm using the restroom?"

Zhen Bei awkwardly scratched his head. "I never saw this Mu Er you mentioned...but when I'd gotten halfway through, I kept feeling like someone was following me, only for nothing to be there when I turned my head. Just when I started walking again, I got the feeling something was about to attack me... and then next thing I knew, I'd stepped out onto thin air and landed in some place I didn't recognize. I thought I'd died! But when I actually stopped to look, it turned out to be the same hallway where my brother and I got separated last time! So I purposely touched the trap I'd set off by accident last time, and then rolled my way down here! Heheh, who woulda thunk I'd have such good luck? I really did run into you two the very minute I got down here! And here I thought I was gonna have to walk a really long way to find you. I made full preparations and came ready to risk my life and everything, y'know!"

Wang Xiaomie expressionlessly looked at Wen Fengjin. "Do you believe that?"

Wen Fengjin looked up at the ceiling as he replied, "This little room and its latrine were built by the craftsmen who built the mausoleum. It *is* possible that those craftsmen actually used the latrine as cover to create an escape route for themselves. It isn't necessarily that Mu Er failed to discover him, but that she thought she could deal with this lone straggler on her own, not expecting him to fall down here just as she was about to make her move. She must have assumed he'd fallen into another trap, and so stopped paying him any mind."

Wen Fengjin seemed to recall something, his face twisting momentarily before he continued, "After you left this mortal coil, Shixiong, I once met another person whom I simply could not kill, no matter how hard I tried. He had terrible luck on the face of it, and wound up in one mishap after another, but always managed to blunder his way into getting some good out of it in the end!"

That...was probably the protagonist, huh... *Fuck!*

Wang Xiaomie looked at Zhen Bei. "Dude, you're much too lucky for someone with that name!"

Zhen Bei abashedly scratched his head: "Heheh, it's no big deal. The main reason I came here this time was to tell you guys about how Corpseface's gang's coming next week to rob this grave..."

Following this, Zhen Bei very seriously explained to them how this all began because their family had worked as appraisers of precious items for generations. His ancestors had saved a few valuables over the years, eventually opening a few shops in A City; their family was relatively well-known in antiques circles.

Zhen Bei's oldest brother happened to be particularly talented on this front, able to tell whether an item was real or fake at just a glance—he was even better than a machine! One day, a guy with a corpse-like face suddenly paid a call to this brother and gave him a wooden box. When Zhen Bei's oldest brother opened this box, poisonous smoke poured forth and blinded him.

They'd originally planned to turn the bastard in, but his brother was against it. In the end, Corpseface gave them a copy of the mausoleum map and told them to look for the Fish Pearl there. Last time, Zhen Bei had secretly followed his erge and assistants here, and fortunately run into little zongzi Wang Xiaomie, who bore humans no ill-will. He'd even managed to easily get his hands on a Fish Pearl, thanks to Wang Xiaomie's kindness.

After they returned to the surface, Zhen Bei told the others about what had happened. This made his dage and the corpse-faced man assume expressions of delight. They asked him over and over again to describe what he'd seen to them. They even repeatedly wanted him to tell them the details of Wang Xiaomie's and Wen Fengjin's appearances, personalities, and whether or not they were capable of human thought.

An overwhelmingly confused Zhen Bei eavesdropped on his dage and the corpse-faced man that night—only to discover that his dage actually wanted to break into the tomb, together with Corpseface.

Zhen Bei curled his hands into fists as he said in a low voice, "My dage has always been extremely obsessed with precious antiques and secret passages to underground tombs ever since he was a little kid. But it wasn't until then that I realized he'd already hired a whole bunch of teams to come here, all of which had failed—up until the day that corpse-faced man found him! I don't know what he said to convince my dage to go to the field himself. He even hired a whole bunch of men for the job. I heard the guy say he didn't want the treasures, but he did want the heart of the tomb master."

Wang Xiaomie was stunned. He squinted at Wen Fengjin. "What's all this about? Don't tell me this is an ex you owe something to! Geez, they're even about to come knocking on our door!"

Wen Fengjin was speechless.

Before Wen Fengjin could explain himself, Zhen Bei hurriedly said, "It's not that kind of heart! It's the physical kind! He wants to eat the heart of the tomb master, who ate a celestial elixir and doesn't age or die! They say that if you eat it, you'll gain the tomb master's powers, and also become unable to age or die!"

Fuck! They're digging up hearts!

MY HUSBAND AND I SLEEP IN A COFFIN

He Has Such a Nice Personality

"**T**HAT'S INSANE!"

"Yeah... Anyway, my goal's really simple. That guy doesn't look like a good person to me, and this mausoleum's not that easy to get into..." Aside from all the monsters guarding the tomb, Wen Fengjin was practically a demon incarnate himself! Last time, Zhen Bei had nearly been choked to death before he could even figure out how the guy got there! Zhen Bei rubbed his neck as he looked at Wen Fengjin and Wang Xiaomie, saying, "If possible, I'd like you guys to spare my dage in return for my having tipped you off!"

Wen Fengjin began laughing lowly. He slowly walked over to Zhen Bei. Under Zhen Bei's increasingly pale-faced gaze, those eyes—largely occupied by their black irises—curved into a smile as he asked with great amusement, "You're asking us to let him go?"

"That's right."

Just as he said this, some great and terrifying force suddenly left Zhen Bei incapable of movement. Zhen Bei's eyes widened. Even breathing required so much effort that he felt himself breaking into a sweat. Unable to move anything else, he swiveled his dark eyes over to look at Wang Xiaomie.

Wang Xiaomie, meanwhile, felt no discomfort whatsoever. In fact, he was currently wondering to himself why Zhen Bei had suddenly frozen up.

Does that mean I'm the only one here feeling this?

Zhen Bei watched weakly as Wen Fengjin curled his index finger, pointing it at a spot about a centimeter from his right eye.

"What makes you so sure I'll help you, hm?" With his red clothes and ink-black hair, Wen Fengjin looked like a vengeful ghost. The pressure in the air around them contracted even further, until Zhen Bei started to think he was about to suffocate to death.

At that moment, Wen Fengjin spoke low enough that only the two of them could hear, his tone laced with both disgust and light laughter. "Besides, the truth is that you have no real interest in convincing me to let your brother go, do you...?"

Zhen Bei, pain still written all over his face, gazed at Wen Fengjin without a hint of understanding in his eyes. "What are you saying—*cough*!"

Wen Fengjin's face went completely blank at that. "What's all this about repaying kindness and tipping us off? Heh—you do indeed want to give us this information, but for what purpose? Let me guess... It's because you discovered in your previous meeting with my shixiong that he was actually a perfectly normal person, with far too much unnecessary benevolence in his heart. He was nothing at all like the ruthless and bloodthirsty evil creatures you imagined would be in this tomb, and appeared to lack even an ounce of strength... Despite meeting me, you regretfully discovered that you were actually able to leave the tomb uninjured. How could such a benevolent tomb master help you to kill someone?"

Wen Fengjin's finger touched his forehead, chin lifting slightly with an expression cold as frost: "You worried that your brother and his friend might truly accomplish their goal, and so decided that you may as well tip us off. This way, though we might not kill him, we probably wouldn't leave him unscathed. A single, heavily injured man, all alone in this isolated underground space, could be taken advantage of by anyone who happened across him at such a time..."

It was like the whispers of a demon from hell, cruelly exposing the darkest depths of man's heart before breaking out in mocking, raucous laughter. At this point the fear on Zhen Bei's face faded away like the tide; though his generally open, sunny face was still pale from lack of air. Covered in a cold sweat, he managed to say with some effort, "You're going to kill me in front of him..."

"Of course. That familiar scent of yours makes me want to vomit." A strange shade of red gradually began to spread across Wen Fengjin's already abnormal eyes as he continued, "It might be a bit inconvenient, but even if I do actually kill you, he won't remember it tomorrow."

He won't remember? Why, do you mean the legends are true?! Aside from becoming immortal, did the tomb master really gain other powers too?! So that's how it is... Haha, so that's how it is...

"You can't kill me! I know—"

Zhen Bei quickly said something in a low voice, causing Wen Fengjin's pupils to contract with a vicious suddenness. "All you have to do is help me, and I'll happily give it to you!" he finished.

It was at this point that Wang Xiaomie began to realize something was wrong. He frowned and scurried closer, placing a hand on Wen Fengjin's shoulder as he asked, "Fengjin, what are you doing?"

In that instant, the fog-like redness in Wen Fengjin's eyes immediately dissipated, and Zhen Bei felt the abnormal pressure suddenly disappear as well. He fell to his knees, hands on his throat as he violently coughed and gasped, sucking in air with all the energy he had, and giving Wang Xiaomie a real fright in the process.

"Oh my god, don't tell me you've got asthma, bro!" Wang Xiaomie hurriedly squatted down to lend Zhen Bei a hand of support, only for Wen Fengjin to pull him backward into his arms with such great force that Wang Xiaomie found himself losing his footing.

"Don't bother with him."

For some reason, Wang Xiaomie had the strangest feeling that Wen Fengjin's words carried a bone-deep chill. It would be a very long time before he came to understand that this was deeply suppressed bloodlust.

At the moment, Wang Xiaomie simply watched with anxiety as Zhen Bei started to dry heave. There was no way he could ignore this! His condition was too scary to be left unattended. Wen Fengjin was still firmly holding him back, but he still carefully called out, "Zhen Bei, Zhen Bei? Are you feeling any better?"

Zhen Bei, who'd been dry heaving for a good while now, waved a hand without lifting his head or getting up from his kneeling position. "I'm fine..." His voice sounded completely different, perhaps because of all the coughing he'd been doing.

Wang Xiaomie reacted to this with a single "Oh," unable to say anything else before Wen Fengjin turned him around in his arms, basically using his own chest to block Wang Xiaomie's line of sight.

"What're you doing?"

"It's too dirty, don't look."

"Huh?" Wang Xiaomie's mouth twitched—what was he calling dirty? Then again, they'd been chatting at the entrance of a latrine this whole time... Could it be that Zhen Bei'd gotten nauseous from the smell?!

After gasping for a while, Zhen Bei finally stood up, covering his mouth with the back of his hand. He looked a lot worse off than he had a moment ago. Still, that sunny smile was pure as ever as he said, "I'm fine now—plus, this guy already accepted my request!"

"Wen Fengjin promised to let your brother go?! I didn't hear anything!" Wang Xiaomie was completely lost. "What in the world did you guys do?" He looked up at Wen Fengjin's chin and the jut of his Adam's apple as he asked, "Fengjin, did you really agree to that?"

Wen Fengjin hummed vaguely in response before saying, indifferently, "You don't like blood, so I'll just have Mu Yi and the others repel them."

"I'm just not really used to it, is all..." Having become a zongzi, it was possible he'd have to fight a battle to the death against grave robbers one of these days. But he couldn't help his biases. Wang Xiaomie, lowering his voice, said secretively, "But we can't let them bully us, either—one of the guys Zhen Bei mentioned sounded pretty formidable. He even wants to rip out your heart! If we do have to fight, it'll be our last option." He pursed his lips, an intelligent light flashing in his eyes as he continued, "So even if we do anything to him, it'll be justified self-defense. Besides, we've been dead for years now, and who ever heard of laws that apply to corpses?"

Wen Fengjin stared blankly at that, his arms loosening their grip for a moment before wrapping tightly around him again, though this time much more gently. "Has Shixiong forgotten that I don't actually count as the dead?" Wen Fengjin asked with amusement.

Okay fine, you're an immortal old man, happy now? Wang Xiaomie rolled his eyes. "You're over a thousand years old. I don't think they could bear to make a thousand-year-old grandpa sit in jail. If you work hard at living a few more years, you can level up from 'millennium turtle' to 'eternal tortoise'! Then you can set a new Guinness World Record or something. When that happens, they can put the two of us on display in a museum. I'll be the never-rotting male corpse next to your walking fossil!"

The more he talked, the more he could visualize it in his head. Wang Xiaomie found himself laughing. Wen Fengjin also chuckled gently at the sight of Wang Xiaomie so cheerful.

"Did you get all that? I'm not a bleedingheart—if they really do hurt you, then even if you do attack them, I'll still be on your side!" Wang Xiaomie gazed up at him with a resolute expression as he continued, "So even if you did something, there'd be no need to hide it from me, understand?"

Wen Fengjin lowered his head to meet Wang Xiaomie's gaze, fingers twitching for a moment before the corners of his lips slowly pulled themselves upward. "...I wouldn't lie to you, Shixiong."

I'm sorry, but this, too, is a lie, Shixiong.

Wang Xiaomie smiled once again upon hearing Wen Fengjin's promise.

Zhen Bei was still panting as he wordlessly stared at the pair's backs. That strange ability of Wen Fengjin's had made his chest ache and his head dizzy, along with the added desire to vomit... The master of this mausoleum truly was formidable. Luckily, he could be used.

Despite clearly being an undying monster and a transformed corpse, they embraced each other with as much feeling as if they were real human beings. The sight led a soft smile to make its way onto Zhen Bei's face. *Disgusting. Aw man, it's so disgusting, I wanna barf.*

Zhen Bei's smile was a dazzling one.

After Wang Xiaomie and Wen Fengjin were done conversing, Zhen Bei finally scratched his head and approached with some awkwardness, saying, "Thanks again, guys, I never thought you'd actually say yes. I don't know how I can thank you, Xiaomie, and also you... Thank you. I sincerely ask that you make sure to spare my dage."

He gazed at Wen Fengjin with a look as clear as crystal.

Wen Fengjin smiled, or something like it. "All right, I'll make sure to spare your dage."

"That's great!" Zhen Bei's mouth split in an grin so warm and so excited that he practically looked like a golden retriever.

Wang Xiaomie couldn't shake the feeling that something was off. It was like the ocean on a cloudy day—clearly calm, yet terrifying all the same.

Zhen Bei said, "They've decided to make the journey a week from now, but they'll be here two days before that to do some preparation. I'll come along with them then."

Wang Xiaomie blinked, pulling himself out of Wen Fengjin's arms as he asked, "You want a map?"

Zhen Bei shook his head: "There's no need for that. I'm content with you guys being able to answer my unreasonable request. On top of that, even after hearing that I'm going to come rob your grave, you still haven't killed me..." He lowered his gaze, then looked up again, saying with all seriousness, "Thank you, Xiaomie." After this, he suddenly started laughing and said, "Haha, sorry, your name's just way too unserious."

"That's all because my grandma said a kid with a humble name is more likely to live to adulthood..." Wang Xiaomie grew angry with embarrassment. "Your name's not any better, y'know!"

Wen Fengjin stroked his hair comfortingly. "You have a very pretty name."

Zhen Bei chuckled. "According to my mom, my dage's the one who named me."

"Huh?" Wang Xiaomie was at a loss for words. "I can't believe your brother had the guts to name you that, and your mother had the guts to go with it!"

"You got that right... Oh, right, I've gotta go! I snuck out to come here, and it's been a few days since I disappeared from home; if I don't get back soon, I'm definitely gonna get a scolding from my erge!"

Zhen Bei suddenly started scrambling to pick his backpack up off the floor, throwing it on as he scrubbed the dirt off his nose. "Hey, uh, I don't know how to get out of here. Could you guys, y'know..."

Wang Xiaomie was about to say something, but Wen Fengjin preempted him by indifferently saying, "I'll have Mu Yi escort you out."

"Huh?" Zhen Bei shrank back fearfully. "Not the big lizard!"

Wang Xiaomie tried to placate him: "Mu Yi always does what Wen Fengjin says, so don't worry—he won't try to sneak a bite out of you."

"Oh phew, that's good to know."

Something strange hid in Wen Fengjin's expression as he swept his gaze over Zhen Bei's smiling face, before turning to face the tomb passage with closed eyes. After a moment, a guttural sort of gurgling emerged from within its depths. The bloodred lizardman, Mu Yi, crawled out before them.

As Zhen Bei was about to leave with the lizard, he suddenly turned his head and said to Wen Fengjin, "Once my dage gets out safely, I'll repay you."

He then turned back and left, following Mu Yi.

Wang Xiaomie watched his figure recede into the distance, only for a large hand to turn his head away. "Stop looking."

The look on Wen Fengjin's face was a chilly one. Wang Xiaomie, assuming he'd gotten jealous, said with a grin, "Don't go getting any silly ideas now—I was just thinking he has a really good personality. He might be a little foolish, but he fought his way here for the sake of his brother. Say, if I had a personality like his, do you think you'd like me even m—"

Wen Fengjin was silent.

"Oh fuck Boss, what kinda look is that?!"

Wen Fengjin thought: *Hurk.*

My Husband and I Sleep in a Coffin

Would You Be Scared of an Extra-Thick Halo?

INCE ZHEN BEI'S last visit, Wang Xiaomie had realized something incredibly fun. He could say something like, "Wow Zhen Bei's got such a good personality, I want—" and Wen Fengjin would purse his lips, a terrible look on his face.

He would continue, "What would you think if we had a child like Zhen Bei—"

And Wen Fengjin's pursed lips trembled, his Adam's apple bobbing wildly.

"What if—mmmph!"

Wen Fengjin put a hand over his mouth, and after a long moment of recovery, finally said "Xiaomie...shut up."

Wang Xiaomie wriggled out of his arms like an earthworm, grinning with a crafty look in his eyes. "If you don't tell me why you don't like Zhen Bei, then I won't stop talking!"

The fact that Wen Fengjin hated Zhen Bei was something Wang Xiaomie had just discovered the day before. It had to be why he got such an ugly look on his face whenever Zhen Bei's name was brought up. But the two had clearly never met before, so what was the cause of Xiao-Wenzi's terrible expressions? Wang Xiaomie was dying (metaphorically) of curiosity. But no matter what he tried, whether by threat or by se—ahem, by you-know-what—Wen Fengjin stayed as tight-lipped as ever.

Looking at his bright-eyed lover, who had curiosity written all over his face, Wen Fengjin's frown relaxed. He was also beginning to find it funny how worked up he was getting over mention of that man's name. Still, it was a long while before he finally said, "Xiaomie, you need to keep your distance from him. He is nowhere as simple as he appears."

Wang Xiaomie rolled his eyes. "But you won't tell me what exactly is so bad about him, so how am I supposed to know if he's good or not!"

"You want to know?"

"Of course!"

"Come here."

Wen Fengjin sat down beneath the freely blooming pining tree, resting an arm on one lifted leg, and motioned to Wang Xiaomie.

Wang Xiaomie walked to sit by his side, leaning against him. Wen Fengjin wrapped his right arm around Wang Xiaomie's shoulders before speaking in a cold tone which did nothing to hide the disgust and dislike he felt. He told the story of a big boss who'd been lying at home, diligently working to revive his shixiong, only for people to keep inexplicably showing up at his door and starting trouble while shouting "Die, demon lord!" and other similar epithets. Among these people was one who left Wen Fengjin with mental scars that would never fade.

"I killed him a total of twenty-nine times. Throwing him off a cliff six times, stabbing him through the heart seven times, crippling all the vital channels of his body ten times... I even nearly chopped off his head a few times. But none of it worked. Every time he fell off a cliff, he wound up finding some kind of hidden treasure. It wasn't until after I'd pierced his heart seven times that I realized he was born with his heart on the right side. Every time

I crippled his channels, some reclusive master physician would come out of the woodwork to heal him. The next few times I killed him, I made sure to give him what were definitively fatal wounds… But it didn't make the slightest difference. No matter what I did, he always managed to have some fortuitous encounter that saved him, allowing him to come back to face me once more."

Wen Fengjin's lips pressed tightly shut at this point—yes, it really did make him nauseous.

Even Wang Xiaomie had horrified goosebumps after hearing all this. *What the fuck! How much money did they sink into this guy's damn protag halo! Are you a top-tier VIP member or something?! This isn't even a halo anymore! It's more like you've stuck a whole god on top of your head! No wonder Wen Fengjin wants to hurl when he sees someone like that. It's like he opened the door to find the guy he'd already killed a billion times over was standing there in front of him again. Eek! How scary! This is getting into horror-movie territory here!*

Any normal person who had that many near-death experiences would have broken down ages ago. But *this* person seemed to have no emotions whatsoever. He acted as if he were born for the sole purpose of killing Wen Fengjin.

Wen Fengjin said, "He didn't seem like a human being to me, but rather, some kind of twisted automaton. That thing was always smiling, no matter the circumstances. As if it had never, in its existence, experienced any emotion other than 'justice' and 'hope'. The human named Zhen Bei shares certain similarities to that person. Even the sense of nausea I feel around him is extremely similar."

At this point Wang Xiaomie felt his scalp go numb as he had a sudden thought. If his past self was chosen by the system to educate Wen Fengjin into a well-rounded good citizen, then what happened after he failed his mission?

That guy wasn't created by the system to kill Wen Fengjin, was he?! Fuck! This is seriously scary to think about, for real...

"...But you really are amazing if you managed to eliminate a guy like that," Wang Xiaomie said.

But Wen Fengjin shook his head. "I never did kill him."

"Huh?! Then how—" *How did you survive to this day without him pestering you to death?*

Wen Fengjin then smiled: "I am unaging and undying. His lifespan ran out when I was a mere 150 years old."

Wang Xiaomie was silent. So simply being better at living could actually be an advantage, huh? He suddenly thought of a line he'd once read. *"The old woman took a drag of her cigarette and said, 'All the doctors who told me to stop smoking back then have already passed away!'"*

To think this story would have such an ending. It was actually kinda sad...

"But, Xiao-Wenzi...what exactly did you do after I died?"

After all, the system didn't just decide to go back to your childhood in an attempt to straighten you out—it even made an extra-thick-plot-armored hero in an attempt to kill you, or at least disgust you, if nothing else.

Wang Xiaomie gazed curiously at Wen Fengjin.

Wen Fengjin froze under his gaze. After what felt like half a day had passed, he turned his head and graced Wang Xiaomie with a pure and innocent smile, saying, "I don't know. I was hard at work reviving you the whole time, Shixiong."

All Big Boss Wen had done was kill people—massacring entire sects and clans and families—and ultimately even overshadowing the Northern Kingdom for a hundred years before finally burying himself for good. He didn't know what had happened at all!

Wink!

Wang Xiaomie, who'd been unceremoniously kicked back home by the system after failing his mission, thought, *If I believed what you said just now, I might as well try to shit while doing a handstand.*

He more or less understood now that Wen Fengjin had ended up with PTSD thanks to the extra-thick-plot-armored hero. It wasn't that he hated Zhen Bei—

(Aside, Wen Fengjin: I absolutely hate him)

—it was that simply laying eyes on a person like that gave him a headache. It was just like the saying went: be bitten by a snake one morning and you'll be afraid of coiled rope for ten years.

Having sated his curiosity, a now comforted Wang Xiaomie yawned. "Oh right, Zhen Bei said they were going to come dig up our grave in a week." Ai, what kind of life were they living now? Even getting grave-robbed was being done by appointment.

"Mmhm." Wen Fengjin nodded, indifferently adjusting their positions as he continued embracing Wang Xiaomie: "Would you like to sleep a while?"

Wang Xiaomie nodded as well. "All right...I *am* a little tired. I don't know why, but lately I keep feeling like my 'charging tree' isn't working as well anymore." He used to be good for two hours after five minutes of charging, but now he had to sleep for half a day at least. "But what about the grave-robbing thing?"

"There's no need to worry about that. I have everything planned out."

Wen Fengjin hugged him tighter with a smile. The continuous fragrance of peach blossoms enveloped them as the scorching-pink blossoms blazed with radiance. A few petals floated down to land upon a winding river of inky-black hair, making a beautifully perfect adornment.

The man beside him was already asleep, leaning against this pining tree with neither pulse nor breath, his features tranquil and his skin snowy white. It was impossible to tell just by looking that this was actually a corpse.

Suddenly, veins and blood vessels slowly started to swell beneath his snowy skin. A bruise-like mark appeared on his neck, near his chin.

It was a patch of livor mortis.

"I told you before—there is no way to refine a body without a soul into either a puppet or a jiangshi. It will rot, even when transformed into a walking corpse. There are things which can be done if you wish only to preserve the body and prevent it from decaying, but the corpse-stabilizing beads and the pining tree can only maintain its surface state. The moment the body leaves their protection... Even if the immortal tree really can summon his soul back to the body and maintain it there, at best, he will wake but be unable to move. And at worst, the body—along with the corpse-stabilizing beads and the soul—will all dissolve to dust."

"How do I bring a corpse to life?"

"You need a particular kind of medicine."

"Tell me."

"Yes, milord..."

Wen Fengjin started quietly humming an ancient tune from the Northern Kingdom as he lifted the now unrecognizable person whose face was covered in veins, placed him upon his lap, then unbuttoned his collar and slit open the side of his own throat.

The bitter scent of medicine mixed with the slightly sweet fragrance of peach blossoms filling the air. The person in his arms opened scarlet eyes before quickly burying his face in Wen Fengjin's neck and sucking on it with great force. The ancient, husky-voiced tune obscured the bestial, gulping sounds.

Perhaps out of weakness, Wen Fengjin shut his eyes and stopped humming, his slender, bony fingers slowly sinking into the other man's long, inky hair as he gently caressed the silken strands.

After a long while, the person in his arms once more regained a liveliness to his skin. Those scarlet eyes closed as he lay back in Wen Fengjin's arms with a frown. Wen Fengjin brushed the red bloodstains off his lips with a finger, then pressed the back of a hand against his forehead.

"It's all right now. Everything is fine... Once they enter the tomb, I'll make sure to get my hands on that object. Then we will no longer need to stay beneath the ground. Wherever you may wish to go, no matter where it is on this earth, I will go there with you..."

After saying this, he lowered his gaze, lovingly pressing his cheek against Wang Xiaomie's forehead. An unnatural color, like red mist, spread across his eyes.

"I'm sorry, Shixiong. I'll have to lie to you again—but I cannot allow a single one of those men to leave here alive!"

The scene: the Zhen household.

Zhen Bei, a pack still on his back, paused the moment he crossed the threshold of this old house on Antique Road, his expression going momentarily blank before transforming into a dazzling smile.

"Erge!"

Zhen Mu looked up from where he leaned, arms crossed, against a doorpost behind the vermilion front gate. He was wearing a formfitting black outfit, his short black hair swaying in the wind, the forceful gaze beneath it softening somewhat at the sight of Zhen Bei.

"You're back? What godforsaken place did you run off to without even a note? I told you before not to head out to the fields with that lot—you'd be better off staying home and studying antiques like you're supposed to."

Zhen Bei chuckled, saying, "Are you really telling me off when you're in the same line of work, Erge? Besides, we have Dage to do the antiques research. I don't have his talent, so I might as well not waste the effort."

"That's bullshit, you've got a *lot* of talent." Zhen Mu's smile dampened slightly as he walked over to throw an arm around his little brother's shoulders. "In a few days, I'll be accompanying Dage on a trip below. Let's have a meal together—we might not have another chance in the future."

Zhen Bei poked his brother in the chest with a smile. "What's that supposed to mean? You make it sound like you're never coming back or something! If we're eating out, though, you're paying!"

Zhen Mu laughed aloud at that, helplessly lifting a scar-covered hand to gently muss his little brother's hair. "You brat—when's your brother ever made you pay? Huh?"

"Heheh! You're the best, Erge!"

Zhen Mu went with him to put away his luggage. After that, the two left the old and silent Zhen manor with much talk and laughter.

In a wooden chair in the drawing room sat a tall, thin man with a face so devoid of expression it seemed a mask. Beside him sat a gentle and refined man in his thirties, with such an extremely calm and youthful face that it gave one the impression of extreme softness—Zhen Hao.

"You're sure this will work?" Zhen Hao asked the man as the two studied a map and text on brocade silk.

The man nodded. "Don't worry. Can you not tell if this map is genuine or not? All the things those people had in storage were fakes, but this one genuine article was left to me by my shifu.

"Those two little brothers of yours have ventured in, and even survived to bring back a Fish Pearl. If your brother's telling the truth, and the two masters of the tomb are capable of rational thought, just like living humans, then that means the legend is true, and there are more precious treasures than you can count in there. With my personally selected men and your erdi accompanying us, it shouldn't pose us any problem at all. The main issue here is that the traps and tomb-guarding monsters in the mausoleum are relatively troublesome to deal with. But with this map, we can avoid those threats entirely.

"You've already personally experienced the power of the Fish Pearl. And those treasures you've never seen before, some of which have only ever been mentioned in unfinished books, are going to be a million times more valuable than a Fish Pearl. They're all waiting for you within the tomb... Can you honestly say you don't want to take a peek?"

The expressionless man stiffly curved his lips in an attempt at a smile. Zhen Hao clenched his fists tight at this, his eyes narrowing as he said, "Make all your preparations. We'll head out as soon as possible!"

The man nodded in satisfaction. "By the way, bring both of your brothers. They won't turn traitor on us at the last minute though, will they...?"

There were no family bonds when treasure was involved, let alone brotherly love! Zhen Hao snorted a laugh, saying, "Don't worry. They're practically my dogs—obedient to the last."

The man collected the silk as he glanced indifferently at him. "That's good, then..."

My Husband and I Sleep in a Coffin

Defending the Grave Mound

BACK UNDERGROUND, Wang Xiaomie stood with rolled-up sleeves at the entrance of a certain side hall, gazing at piles of gold and jewels stacked so high they were spilling out of the room. The sight failed to send him wild with joy. In fact, he let out a sigh instead. Then he began to dig, like a dog, through the riches in resignation. Any gems or ornaments, he piled to one side. What he wanted was to find some sort of weapon in there!

"Xiao-Wenzi, come help out!"

Wen Fengjin walked over from somewhere else, watching his sweet little zongzi energetically digging a hole with his butt up in the air, and said with a slight smile, "Xiaomie, don't raise your butt so high."

Wang Xiaomie turned to glare at him with a dark look on his face. "Are you perving on me?! Hurry up and give me a hand already! Hmph—do you see the big bosses in the movies going around without weapons? There's only a couple days before they come to dig up our grave mound, and here you are, acting like you don't have a care in the world."

"It's not like either of us can go outside. Waiting for them in the mausoleum is a perfectly normal thing to do." Still, Wen Fengjin did in fact roll up his sleeves, joining the search.

"Even so, we've gotta be prepared. Otherwise, what'll we do if you can't beat them?"

"I'll still have Shixiong then, won't I?" Wen Fengjin replied with a smile.

"And what do you expect *me* to do? Call the police or an ambulance for you?" Wang Xiaomie didn't even look up from what he was doing. Suddenly, his eyes lit up. He pulled out the thing in his hand to see...

A tiny vest made with golden thread?!

"What's this supposed to be?! I can't believe you even collected vests, that's way too deranged!" Even if it was made of gold, that didn't mean he should be ripping people's clothes off, after all.

Wen Fengjin was silent for a moment before saying, "Xiaomie... that's a gold-weave armor vest."

Wang Xiaomie was struck silent. G-gold weave armor vest? Like that super cool, weapon-proof thing? He lifted up the little vest and silently stuffed it into his pocket. Cough, ahem, he was keeping this.

A somewhat abashed Wang Xiaomie continued digging for treasure, changing the subject as he did so. "Aiya, there's so many good weapons and things around here. You should've gotten a separate hall to keep them in. Just look at what a pain it is for us to have to dig them out of all these average jewels and riches."

Wen Fengjin paused, then pinched his brow with a sigh. "Xiaomie..."

"Huh?" Wang Xiaomie looked at him with wide and watery puppy eyes.

"Have you forgotten that you took apart the sword rack to use as a drying rack, and turned the armory into a laundry room?" Wen Fengjin looked down at him, saying, "And it was you who had Mu Yi toss all those weapons in here..."

Wang Xiaomie was filled with grief and regret at the memory of his bratty behavior! Then he looked up at Wen Fengjin with a grin. "Yeah, I did it! What're you gonna do about it? Are you gonna scold me for it?! *Bark bark bark!*"

The wild arrogance of his manner and the savageness in his features expressed such a mule-headed refusal to repent that it made Wen Fengjin's hair bristle. *What am I supposed to do about my little zongzi constantly barking like a dog? It's so cute. Can I fuck him? If I fuck him, will that fix it?*

Faced with such a wildly frenzied (and adorably fuckable) Wang Xiaomie, Boss Wen chose to bow his head, quietly continuing to accompany him in his rummaging.

The clinking sound of metal on metal went on without pause. After a long time, a certain someone asked: "That Liaoyue Sword of mine..."

"Stop being so petty! I'll have it dug out for you in a minute! Hmph!"

It took a day of rummaging, during which they called Mu Yi to help out as well, before they finally got most of the valuable burial swords, other weapons, and defensive equipment all sorted into the main hall.

Wang Xiaomie, sitting on a stone-tiled floor so clean he could see his reflection in it, was so exhausted at this point that he lay right there. Wen Fengjin leaned against a pillar with half-closed eyes, clearly having expended a lot of energy himself.

As for poor Mu Yi, he couldn't even keep a grip on the wall anymore. The lizard fell to the floor with a *plop* and panted like a dog with his tongue out. If it weren't for the fact he was still breathing, Wang Xiaomie might have thought the guy had dropped dead.

After a short rest, Wang Xiaomie sat up and looked listlessly over at Wen Fengjin. "We've pretty much dug up everything, haven't we..."

Wen Fengjin nodded: "This is it, more or less. A few items may possibly be on the lowest level, but what we have here is enough. Xiaomie, I told you before that you don't need to worry about the mausoleum. I'll find a way to deal with those grave robbers myself."

"I know, I know." Wang Xiaomie placed a hand on Mu Yi's somewhat scary-looking head, petting it the way one might pet a puppy, while Mu Yi made a mumbly attempt at a purr in an ugly-cute sort of way. "I'm just doing it for some peace of mind. It was fine before Zhen Bei gave us a date, but after learning the day they were coming, I feel like there's a timer ticking away my life... Besides, I just have this feeling of foreboding, somehow." And this feeling of foreboding had been growing stronger the closer they got to the arrival day.

Wen Fengjin looked at him with a fixed gaze. "Xiaomie..."

Wang Xiaomie interrupted him with a laugh as he said, "I know, I don't think you're going to do anything shady or fail to take care of this whole situation. I'm just kinda worried about that guy Zhen Bei mentioned. He wants to take your heart, after all—and if he can say a thing like that, then I'm sure he's got something backing him up."

He'd even had a nightmare the night before, in which Wen Fengjin was caught and had his heart ripped out. The bloody scene had scared Wang Xiaomie straight back to wakefulness. His hands were shaking for a good while afterward, only calming down again at the sensation of the other man's familiar embrace.

Wen Fengjin walked over to half squat by his side, reaching out to press a hand against his cheek, his thumb gently rubbing at the corner of one eye. "You don't need to worry about me. I am undying and unaging. No matter what happens, I'll be able to survive it."

Wang Xiaomie lowered his head, saying, "Even if you're undying and unaging, you probably still have weaknesses somewhere. If you got your heart ripped out, would you be able to grow it back?"

Wen Fengjin's lips slowly curved into a smile. Those black irises, which dominated the greater portion of his eyes, reflected the figure of his most beloved as he said, "I'm a little happy."

Wang Xiaomie looked up again to shoot him a glare. "Happy about what? Happy about getting your heart ripped out?!"

Wen Fengjin laughed in that deep voice of his, saying, "I'm happy that you worry about me, and care about me." *You've once again given me that warmth—that warmth I didn't dare ask of you after the things I did in the past.* "I'm even more determined now not to let them get their way."

Wen Fengjin pulled Wang Xiaomie into his arms. At the sensation of his own full embrace, and Wang Xiaomie's trusting reciprocation of it, he breathed out a silent sigh of deep satisfaction. His eyes narrowed, smile deepening.

Finally...the day I wished for has finally come... It is impossible that anyone could stop me and Shixiong from being together. If anyone tries to stop me, I'll make him suffer a life worse than death!

Back at the Zhen household, a number of extraordinary men and women sat within the drawing room of the old and stately manor. Though they all seemed friendly on the surface, none were paying any attention to each other.

In the hosts' seats were the old master of the Zhen family and his wife, with Zhen Hao and the stiff-faced man sitting down to their left, and Zhen Mu and Zhen Bei down to the right.

"All of you are well-known experts in your field. It is the Zhen family's great honor to welcome you to our home today. Your assistance here will not be forgotten. Yan-xiansheng, my eldest son Zhen Hao mentions you quite often."

Old Master Zhen smiled at the man next to Zhen Hao, who merely nodded slightly in response, his stiff face devoid of any real expression. Old Master Zhen had been told the man was left unable to move his face due to an injury he'd sustained underground, and so thought nothing of this, instead moving on with the pleasantries.

The grave robbers below, quite respectful of their financial backer, were at least paying attention to what he said. A bold-looking woman in the group below, who had a thin, small young man in his twenties with her, looked over at Zhen Mu with a smile.

Zhen Mu, sensing this burning gaze, turned his head slightly to evade it. The woman laughed quietly, then started toying with her fingernails out of boredom. The skinny young man behind her, meanwhile, looked at his shifu with a helpless sigh.

When the rest of the speech was almost over, Madam Zhen—who hadn't spoken a word this entire time—suddenly said with a worried look, "Zhen Mu, Zhen Bei."

Zhen Mu and Zhen Bei turned to look at her.

Madam Zhen said, "I can't stop your dage—though I don't know why he'd suddenly want to go rob that grave. It's such a dangerous place... Zhen Mu, you're good at this, so make sure to watch over your dage once you get there, do you hear me?"

Zhen Mu lowered his gaze. Despite his fierce features, he had a sedate and gentle heart and, when faced with his mother's clear directions, nodded his head by habit.

Madam Zhen gave a small smile of satisfaction at that nod. She had some faith in her second son's skills, after all.

"And you, Zhen Bei." At Zhen Bei's foolishly smiling face, Madam Zhen frowned deeply. She began to chide him. "Just look at how scatterbrained you are! Still constantly relying on your dage for advice at your age! Don't go causing trouble for your dage while you're down in that tomb, do you understand me?!"

Zhen Bei shrank back at that. Zhen Mu—with a somewhat unpleasant look on his face—unexpectedly spoke back to their mother for once. "Ma, Zhen Bei isn't a fool, he's just been an honest person since he was a kid. You shouldn't keep scolding him all the time."

"*You!*"

"All right, that's enough!" Old Master Zhen interrupted his angry wife, saying, "We have business to discuss, and you're pulling us further and further off topic! Are you trying to make a laughingstock of us in front of our guests?!"

Madam Zhen looked away in a huff. It wasn't until this point that a smiling Zhen Hao quietly consoled his mother, saying in a gentle voice, "Ma, I know you're saying all this for our sake, but Ba is right. I'll go to your room later to sit with you a while."

Madam Zhen smiled a bit at that. Old Master Zhen's expression also grew cheerier to hear his beloved eldest son speak up. He brightly gave a few last words of advice to the group before standing up and leaving the room with his wife.

The man with facial paralysis—Yan-xiansheng—stood and motioned at the others, gathering everyone so that he and Zhen Hao could tell them the planned harvesting procedure, distribute some tasks, and answer any questions about equipment and the departure time.

Whether consciously or not, when the group gathered, they left Zhen Bei and Zhen Mu cut off on the outside.

Zhen Bei's mouth twitched, and he quietly whispered to Zhen Mu, "Erge, do you think Zhen Hao's an idiot or what? The people here might all be experts, but not a single one of them works for our family. Now Zhen Hao's even purposely alienating the two of us. If that corpse-faced Yan guy betrays us later, all three of us are doomed!"

Zhen Mu looked thoughtfully at the smiling Zhen Hao, standing amidst the group. Zhen Hao, catching his gaze, smirked proudly then gave them both a disdainful look.

Zhen Mu lowered his gaze and patted Zhen Bei's head with his large, heavily scarred hand. "Don't worry, Erge will protect you. You'll always be the first one I protect."

Zhen Bei's smile was a dazzling one, and he nodded energetically. "Right!"

He looked over at Zhen Hao, who silently mouthed at him, "You're a fool."

Zhen Bei kept smiling, scratching his head as if he hadn't understood his brother's words. Zhen Hao laughed disdainfully at this sight, mentally asking himself why he was bothering to communicate with an idiot.

Their departure time was quickly confirmed. The equipment and necessary supplies would be arriving soon.

Meanwhile, in the depths of the mausoleum, Wen Fengjin smiled as he leaned against the pining tree with folded arms, watching Wang Xiaomie wave around a short yet plucky dagger.

"Xiaomie, I suggest you use the previous dagger rather than this one," Wen Fengjin said.

Wang Xiaomie looked at the glittering dagger in his hand, then at the jet-black rusty dagger on the floor. He raised an eyebrow as he replied, "No matter how you look at it, this one looks like it's better!"

"A weapon's grade doesn't depend on how clean or shiny it is. Only new blades or ones meant as accessories are going to be notably shiny—they call it a *thief's light*. In reality, a genuine sword is heavy and durable, with a fine cutting edge, which will only reveal the *precious light* of daily use after it is wielded for a long period of time. Soft swords are a unique exception, of course."

"Ah? I didn't know that." The ignorant Wang Xiaomie looked at the dagger he was holding, which was even encrusted with jewels. It had "gaudy" written all over it.

He silently picked up the jet-black dagger on the ground, then continued gesticulating at the air with an expression much like that of a puppy baring its fangs, as if he was ready, at any moment, to risk his life fighting that bunch of mean thugs who were coming to dig up his grave!

Wen Fengjin slowly and silently covered his mouth with a hand. *Look at Shixiong, acting threatening in such an infantile way... Tch.*

MY HUSBAND AND I SLEEP IN A COFFIN

Enlightenment

O N THE MORNING of the fifth day, the foggy, wild mountains were incredibly quiet. A group of people deftly put up a few green tents in a weed-ridden grove, and brought into them a great many boxes.

A frail young man slowly scattered insecticide powder in a circle around the area, then turned to see his shifu calmly using a sword cloth to slowly wipe a straight-edge hunting knife as long as her forearm and three fingers wide.

"Shifu, it's so hot today. Why don't you go in the tent?"

"The tent's too green," the woman absentmindedly said as she looked over her knife.

The skinny young man was momentarily rendered speechless by this. He sighed. "Shifu, if you don't want to stay with them, then just say so. These are tents, not hats. It doesn't matter if they're a little green or not, you'll still have to go inside to sleep once night falls."

The woman squinted at him, saying, "So you've got the guts to talk back to your shifu now, huh? Is it because I haven't been beating you? Hats and tents both go over your head the same, and they're green as a softshell turtle! Also, remember what I said, you damn brat: aside from that serious-minded Zhen Mu, you can't trust a single one of these ghoulish, man-eating bastards!"

The skinny young man was called Xiao-Luo. He was still quite well-behaved in this respect, so he happily nodded as he replied, "I know. I haven't acknowledged anyone here besides Zhen Mu, Zhen Bei, and Shifu."

"Not Zhen Mu and Zhen Bei, just Zhen Mu."

"Huh? Why's that?" Xiao-Luo was dumbfounded.

The woman narrowed her eyes: "That Zhen Bei... I get the feeling there's something really evil about him."

Xiao-Luo scratched his head as he thought, *Ai, this is probably Shifu's feminine sixth sense acting up again.* But he took her advice to heart regardless. He'd been taught by his shifu for many years, after all, and valued her words over anyone else's. With this in mind, he picked up the plastic-packaged insecticide and returned to the tent, deciding to do another check of their equipment.

Meanwhile, the woman's face lit up at the sight of Zhen Mu coming out of the tent with his bronze sword in hand. She hurriedly waved a hand at him, saying, "Zhen Mu! The Zhen family's erge! Over here! We haven't seen each other in ages and you won't even say a hello? Get over here and let me have a look at Changfeng!"

Zhen Mu looked like he wanted to evade the woman, but upon hearing her mention his weapon, he schooled his expression and walked over, saying in a quiet voice, "Lei-jie."

Lei-jie smiled happily, saying a single "aye" in response before putting down her own weapon and taking the ancient brass sword from Zhen Mu's hands. She then carefully unsheathed the sword, and brushed a hand over the Changfeng characters seemingly imprinted into its blade.

Lei-jie came from a long line of swordsmiths. Craftsmen treated such valuable works with a sort of unbridled frenzy, some going so far as to sacrifice themselves for the sake of forging their life's greatest work. It was exactly because of Lei-jie's obsession with antique swords that she'd entered this line of work.

"After all this time, you're still as beautiful as ever..." Lei-jie said softly to the brass sword. The love and care of successive owners had kept the sword from oxidizing or weakening. In fact, it was just as sharp as the day it was forged. Lei-jie had even given it a full-service maintenance twice. If it weren't for the fact that Zhen Mu was unwilling to part with his treasured possession, and had previously saved the life of her disciple Xiao-Luo, Lei-jie would have given anything at all to get the sword into her possession!

Lei-jie carefully wiped the body of the sword with her sword cloth, checking the grain of the blade as she did so. The sword cloth, made of special materials, also produced a quiet humming sound as it slid over its edge.

Zhen Mu sat silently on a nearby rock, watching as Lei-jie did her inspection.

After a long while, Lei-jie suddenly said, "The Zhen family's oldest son, Zhen Hao...did he ever get injured when he was little?"

A befuddled look crossed Zhen Mu's fiercely handsome face; after a moment of serious thought, he responded, "No."

"Oh." Lei-jie continued, "Then why does he look so much like a damn idiot to me?"

Zhen Mu was stunned silent.

Lei-jie squinted as she closely inspected the sword, while indifferently saying, "I've always been frank with my words, so don't take offense or anything. I'm just an old lady, and I don't have the best sense of judgment. But everyone in the circle knows that old bastard Yan is the kinda guy who'll eat you up and leave not even bones behind, and that lot who work under him are all bloody bastards. Meanwhile, that brother of yours is groveling in their wake and giving them whatever they want with an idiotic smile on his face. The way I see it, he's gonna die in there, sooner or later! And your poor devil of a mother wants you to protect him? Is that even possible? It'd be a blessing if you even made it out alive yourself."

Zhen Mu was silent for a moment before replying, "I know this is your warning to me, so thank you, Lei-jie."

"Tch." Lei-jie, knowing he was as expressive as a piece of wood, said nothing more. She reluctantly handed him the Changfeng Sword she was so fond of as she said, "Well-meaning advice won't do much for a guy who's already doomed. Watch out for that little brother of yours." Swordsmiths like her were particularly sensitive to the blades and spiritual energy of weapons. They were similarly sharp when it came to people, as well.

"My little brother..." Zhen Mu shook his head: "My little brother is a good kid, Lei-jie, you're overthinking it. Also, if I die down there, this sword will go to you. So could you help me watch over him and make sure he gets out safely?"

Lei-jie looked him over, then said, "Aiyo. What are you saying? I'm not trying to pit you against each other or anything. Besides, if *you* can't manage it, how do you expect me to rescue your brother?"

The normally expressionless Zhen Mu gave a rare smile at that. "Lei-jie, others might not know it, but I'm no stranger to your skill. If it weren't for those famous weapons, you'd never have come here."

Lei-jie scowled at him. She cast a covetous glance at the Changfeng Sword in his hand once more, then finally gave him a languid reply. "Ai... If only I could manage to see the Liaoyue Sword and Kaiming. Then even if I died in there, it'd be with a smile on my face!"

Zhen Mu let out a sigh of relief at this response. He gave her a proper smile.

Within the tent, Zhen Hao slowly fanned himself with a paper fan, looking entirely unwilling to move as he listened with half-closed eyes to the man named Yan deploying his underlings.

"Xiao-Li, you're good with your hands. You and the Zhen family's little second son Zhen Mu can take point. If anything seems off, send a signal and retreat immediately."

"Yes, sir."

"Tiezi and Chun Lei, you two will protect Zhen-xiansheng."

The two men named Tiezi and Chun Lei nodded with grins on their faces. "Don't you worry about a thing, Yan-ge."

"Lastly, let me mark the positions of the traps for you to avoid. We'll also have to leave someone on the surface as backup. A-Shui, you stay behind."

"Got it. Leave it to me, Yan-ge."

"Mm, by the way, what about that woman and her disciple?" Zhen Hao asked with a frown, opening his eyes.

The man stiffly turned his head and spoke without any real inflection to his voice. "They're coming with us. The woman and her disciple are real tough characters; let them do what they want. Either way, for safety purposes, they'll be working according to our arrangement."

"All right." Zhen Hao nodded reluctantly.

In the depths of the mausoleum, Wen Fengjin looked at Mu Yi and the rest of his former subordinates—now tomb-guarding monsters—who were all lined up before him. "The enemy's strength is unknown. You're free to investigate them, and kill them as well—but Mu Yi, remember to let in the men who have the same scent as last time. Those men absolutely mustn't be killed. Understand?"

"Gegege." Mu Yi gurgled in his throat, while the monsters behind him all made similar noises of obeisance.

"Very good." Wen Fengjin nodded with satisfaction. "Now go to each of your guard points and remember what I told you."

The terrifying monsters all obediently turned and left the tomb passage at great speed. Meanwhile, Wen Fengjin turned his head to find Wang Xiaomie standing right behind him.

"Xiaomie?" Wen Fengjin was thrown off by this, his eyes darkening despite the smile that graced his face. "How long have you been here? I didn't hear you coming."

Wang Xiaomie rubbed the sleep from his eyes, exhaling at Wen Fengjin's question: "I just got here—I didn't see you anywhere when I woke, so I came over to look. Did Mu Yi and the others just leave? What did you tell them to do?"

Wen Fengjin kept smiling as he walked up to Wang Xiaomie and pulled his hands away from his face, then carefully used his own fingers to brush at the corners of Wang Xiaomie's eyes. "Don't rub at your eyes so hard, you'll hurt them."

"Okaaay." Though Wen Fengjin hadn't answered the question, Wang Xiaomie didn't pay it much mind. He lowered his hands and raised his face, eyes shut as he obediently let Wen Fengjin brush them for him.

"If my assumption is correct, they should be coming down here tonight to scout the area, but won't venture too far in. Make sure to keep my dagger on you at all times, understood?"

"I know." Wang Xiaomie pulled away, tossing his head. When he opened his eyes again, he really did feel better. He reached into the bosom of his robe to pull out a dagger. The blade was pitch-black and primitive in design, lacking any sort of inlay or carved patterns.

Its only distinguishing mark was the name "Kaiming" written on its round-headed hilt. "See, I've been keeping it on me."

Wen Fengjin took his hand and slowly walked back together with him.

Wang Xiaomie waved the dagger and sighed. "Do you really think it'll be any use for me to carry this thing? Every inch of lost reach is an inch of more danger, so wouldn't this be the death of me? They could have my head pressed to the floor and I wouldn't even be able to reach their bellies."

Wen Fengjin chuckled as he explained, "The dagger Kaiming was once known as a divine weapon. It was created by a master swordsmith, then given to an assassin and used to kill an incapable ruler. Because it bore the hope that it would eliminate a tyrant and save the country, it earned the name Kaiming, referring to the phrase for an enlightened sovereign. This dagger is abnormally sharp, can slice other divine weapons in half, and has previously killed a great many foolish monarchs and nobles. If a wicked person is in the vicinity, Kaiming will emit heat in warning."

"Huh? That's so cool!" The pitch-black color of this blade instantly seemed both simple and sedate. Every scratch upon the dagger seemed to speak to the many ups and downs it had experienced in its life.

Suddenly remembering something, he blinked at Wen Fengjin. "You said it'll get hot when there's bad guys around, so how come it's not reacting when you're right next to me? You better not be making an ass of me!"

Wen Fengjin was taken aback. "...Shixiong, I'm actually a good person."

Wang Xiaomie fell silent, looking at Wen Fengjin in his brightly colored red-and-black robes. In response, Wen Fengjin automatically donned a smile which he thought was gentle, but was actually bewitchingly evil. With his dark gaze, his quirked lips, and that eye-searing little red mark on his forehead, he looked like a strikingly realistic final boss brought to life!

"...Tell the truth." Wang Xiaomie poked him in the chest with the dagger.

"I *am* a good person," Wen Fengjin said with a wooden expression on his face, "Kaiming even acknowledged it."

The dagger poking at his chest suddenly heated up with a hum.

They both stared in silence.

Wang Xiaomie slid his gaze away from Wen Fengjin's face, which was too beautiful for him to behold. "I said, tell me the truth."

An unpleasant look crossed Boss Wen's delicate, handsome face. Under Wang Xiaomie's wordless stare, he finally told him the truth. "All right... The truth is that after first acquiring the dagger, I'd often carry it with me in winter because it amused me. I'd use it to...keep warm."

Wang Xiaomie looked at the increasingly hot dagger in his hand. He could almost feel its sorrow and anger at having been used as a portable heater for so many years. No wonder it couldn't be bothered to heat up around Wen Fengjin these days—it'd probably gotten so used to the scent of the boss's scumbaggery that his presence made it want to cry!

29

You Dare Kick the Boss's Butt?

THAT NIGHT, a dozen or so grave robbers prepared to enter the underground, following the path they'd previously made. After getting the ropes down, advance scouts Xiao-Li and Zhen Mu tossed in a few light sticks, watching as the dim lights descended away from them. It was a long time before they finally heard the faint sound of the sticks hitting the ground. It didn't seem like they'd be all that useful as light sources, since all that could be seen from the surface were the tiniest specks of illumination.

"Damn, how deep *is* this?"

"Beneath this thousand-year-old tomb is an underground palace as huge as a proper building—big enough that it stretches underneath this entire mountain range. Just think about how much space you'd need to fit a building that grand, and you can imagine how deep it is."

For ease of entry, the mouth of the hole wasn't a vertical drop, which meant that nobody could see inside all that well. Gazing down into that bottomless pit, Zhen Hao was unable to hide the excitement and impatience in his eyes. He yelled at the squatting pair: "What're you spacing out for, then?! Hurry up and get down there!"

Xiao-Li grinned cheerfully at him, not moving an inch. It wasn't until Yan-xiansheng slightly nodded at him from behind Zhen Hao that he finally said, "Got it, boss! Right away." He then fastened the buckle at his waist and slowly slid his way down on the rope.

Just as Zhen Mu was about to head down as well, Zhen Bei pulled him back and shoved something into his hand: "Erge, this is for you."

Zhen Mu stared dazedly at the little pouch sitting in the palm of his hand: "What's this?"

"A protective charm," Zhen Bei said with a smile. "I specially went up the mountain for it."

Looking at that tiny cloth pouch, a faint warmth welled up within Zhen Mu's eyes. He mussed Zhen Bei's hair with a gloved hand. "Thanks, Xiao-Bei."

"You're welcome!"

After Zhen Mu went down, Zhen Bei kept squatting at the entrance of the hole, gazing in with obvious worry on his face.

"Heh, you knew to give Zhen Mu a protective charm, but didn't think to give your dage one?" Zhen Hao asked, smiling down at the squatting Zhen Bei.

Zhen Bei looked up with agitation as he said, "No no, I brought one for you too, Dage! Look!" He then pulled a little pouch from a pocket, holding it out as if presenting a precious treasure. "I'm worried about both you *and* Erge, so you gotta make sure to get back safe, Dage."

Holding the pouch by its string, he enthusiastically attempted to put it around Zhen Hao's neck. Zhen Hao looked at the dusty pouch and the foolish smile on the quickly approaching Zhen Bei, then knocked his hands away with a look of disgust.

The resounding *slap* left the back of Zhen Bei's hand slightly red. The pouch fell to the ground. Yan-xiansheng glanced coldly at them before returning his gaze to the entrance, while the underlings behind him broke out in malicious laughter.

"A thing like that? You might as well wear it yourself!"

"Who knows where that dusty old thing has been? Disgusting!"

"Oh..." Zhen Bei lowered his head, looking somewhat hurt, like a big golden retriever that had just been kicked. He bent to pick up the pouch, only for another hand to snatch it up before he could.

As it turned out, Xiao-Luo had been unable to keep watching this. He handed the pouch to Zhen Bei and whispered, "Don't pay any attention to that blockhead brother of yours, just keep it for yourself."

"Thank you." Zhen Bei managed a somewhat bashful smile, but didn't accept the pouch, pushing it back at Xiao-Luo instead. "You take it, then. It's really effective. I'm sure it'll protect you from harm!"

Xiao-Luo laughed in surprise, nodding as he tucked the pouch into a shirt pocket and even patting the pocket afterward to show that he'd treasure it. "Thanks, I'll take good care of it."

"Right!" Zhen Bei nodded happily.

Zhen Hao coldly watched the two, rolling his eyes as he muttered to himself, "Idiots."

The rest of the group was unaffected by this short scene.

It wasn't until a pair of clear, sharp whistles sounded from below that the stiff-faced man finally quirked his lips up into an awkward smile. "They've done it! We're all heading down."

At his words, the men immediately forgot everything else. Each of them quickly and smoothly tied on their ropes; in an instant, all but Zhen Hao had slid their way down. Once Zhen Hao had gone down as well, Lei-jie finally called Xiao-Luo to come along, leaving Zhen Bei as the last of them all.

He stood at the entrance, gazing into the distant depths with a dark gaze. In the gloom, his face looked as cold as if he'd been possessed by a ghost. A-Shui, who'd stayed behind, shuddered upon catching an accidental glimpse of it. But when he turned his head for another look, he saw Zhen Bei's expression wasn't cold at all. He was clearly smiling like a fool!

A-Shui—angry at the thought that he'd been frightened by this big idiot—kicked Zhen Bei in the rear as he said, "What are you staring at over there?! Get going, you dumbass!"

Zhen Bei stumbled a moment, then turned to look at him, laughing at the sight of A-Shui's somewhat nervous expression. He nodded. "Sorry, I'm still a little scared, haha. I'll go down right away."

After watching Zhen Bei dawdle his way down like he really was a little scared, A-Shui relaxed, muttering a few curse words before tugging at the ropes to ensure they were secure. With that done, he then leisurely headed back to the tents to sleep.

Gazing up from the depths of the hole they'd descended into, the view was enough to make the men feel as if their world had been reduced to a gaping abyss beneath a great cliff. Before them was a great stone door, which seemed almost to join this world to the one they'd just left. The stately portal before them was suffocatingly tall. No matter how far back they tilted their heads, the men couldn't see its top. It was illogically disheartening, while simultaneously filling them with awe. Someone less brave might have wanted to stop right here and go no further, too fearful to take a peek inside.

"This...is the legendary thousand-year old underground mausoleum?!" Zhen Hao stared fixedly at the stone door, his hands shaking as they brushed over the engravings carved into it.

Even Yan-xiansheng, behind him, was breathing slightly faster. Though Zhen Bei and Zhen Mu had been here once before, they couldn't help marveling every time they saw this door.

A gaping Chun Lei asked Tiezi, "How the heck did they even make this thing?! It's so tall... Could the ancients all fly or something?"

Tiezi rolled his eyes, then calmly turned to look at Yan-xiansheng, waiting for their boss to lead them inside.

"Considering how cool just the *door* to this place is, I'm getting kinda scared. 'Cause what's inside...can't possibly be easy, can it?"

"Hey! If you're chickening out, then leave. It'll mean more for us when we get to splitting the goods!"

"Fuck off, I didn't mean it like that!"

The excitement of being about to uncover a little corner of splendor got the men all carelessly joking around. Far at the rear of the group, however, Lei-jie was tightly gripping her disciple's hand, her gaze fixed upon that door!

Xiao-Luo twisted his face into a grimace. "...Shifu, at this rate you're gonna sacrifice me to heaven before you even get through that door!"

Lei-jie recovered her senses just to slap him upside the head, saying, "Shut up! Sacrificing your teammates nets you boundless magic power—so watch yourself, or I really might burn you alive, you little bastard."

"Come on...we're going in!" The man named Yan waved a hand with undisguised excitement, and the group exploded in joyful cheers, shimmying in through the spot where Zhen Mu had previously cracked open the door.

Zhen Mu and Xiao-Li carefully made their way forward at the head of the procession, each with one hand on their respective weapons and the other holding a Wolf Eyes flashlight, while Zhen Hao and the rest trailed behind.

Xiao-Luo surreptitiously asked Lei-Jie, "Shifu, does this mean we've made it in past the mausoleum's front door? That easily?"

Lei-jie snickered at that: "The mausoleum's front door? Heh. What you've just stepped through is nothing but a city's main gate. What's more, lots of people have come through here before.

How could it *not* be easy? There's no knowing how many of them died in here—it's possible you're stepping on someone's remains even now."

Xiao-Luo shut his mouth, but his gaze was noticeably more guarded than before. The skinny young man now exuded an unexpected sharpness, like that of an unsheathed sword.

After their figures vanished into the pitch-black, stone-paved cavern, a smooth portion of wall suddenly began undulating like water within the darkness before finally transforming into a pair of transparent, jellylike people. These two figures huddled, their whispered conversation sounding like intermingled chirps.

[Did you smell which ones had that scent Mu Yi mentioned, chirp?]

[Yeah, there's three in total with that scent, chirp!]

[It was the sword-wielding one in the front, the tall skinny one at the very back, and the short wax gourd next to the woman, right, chirp?]

[Not right, chirp! Not right, chirp! Not a short wax gourd, it's a little bean sprout. He's not fat at all, chirp.]

[You're right, you're right! Mu Shi is amazing, chirp~]

[Heheheheh~ Mu Jiu is amazing too, chirp~]

[Then what about the other people, chirp?]

[Obviously, we kill them all, chirp!]

The two jelly people once again transformed into transparent liquid and slowly disappeared into the wall.

Beneath the blazing blooms of the pining tree, peach blossoms fell like sparks of flame. Within the abyss, atop a platform, stood a peach blossom tree and a red coffin. It was like the start of a poignant romance.

And beneath the tree, the protagonists of this poignant and romantic tale were—barbecuing.

It happened like this: Once he learned that his dagger, Kaiming, could emit heat, Wang Xiaomie was struck by the brilliant idea of getting out the vacuum-packed beef and lunch meat he'd previously uncovered, then washing Kaiming and handing the freshly cleaned dagger to Wen Fengjin.

As he watched Kaiming get increasingly hotter, Wang Xiaomie's eyes practically emitted a light of their own. A wicked expression revealed itself on his face.

He then stuck a piece of meat on the dagger's blade with an audible *plop*.

Wen Fengjin was speechless. *In this moment, I actually feel some empathy for a dagger.*

If the dagger Kaiming could speak, the first words out of its mouth would be *Fuck you!*

Wang Xiaomie picked up a piece of cooked meat with his home-made chopsticks and put it in his mouth. *Mm, delicious!*

He remembered to feed Wen Fengjin as well; Wen Fengjin's beautiful face was somewhat wooden right now, but he softly opened his mouth and ate the proffered meat.

Feeling the heat in his hands—strong enough to radiate through cloth—Wen Fengjin had a feeling like he'd just eaten what little there remained of his conscience.

Wang Xiaomie continued to press his advantage as he ate. "Aiya, look at Kaiming! It's so hot it's started steaming! Just think of how many bad deeds you must have done to make it do that!"

To think the world actually contained such a completely shameless person! Boss Wen fell silent, staring at his shixiong's face and thinking for the first time that this puppy of his was really quite diabolical!

I'd like to self-destruct real quick here, just to blow this damn idiot to smithereens, Kaiming might have said.

After finishing off the meat, Wang Xiaomie tossed the chopsticks, piled the mess of packaging and cans off to one side, then took Kaiming back with a cheerful grin, carefully wiping the oil and residue off its blade.

Now that it was in his hands, Kaiming finally began to cool down. Wang Xiaomie looked at the dagger with a loving gaze as he tenderly caressed it. "You really are something great~"

And Kaiming? The dagger let out a hum, and burned Wang Xiao-zongzi hard enough to make him yelp.

Wen Fengjin, watching all this from the sidelines, was quietly chuckling to himself when his smile suddenly froze on his face. He narrowed his eyes and looked off in a certain direction—the direction in which the grave robbers had just broken in.

The outermost perimeter of the mausoleum was Mu Shi and Mu Jiu's territory. This being the first day, it was probably best not to kill anyone. After all, what if they decided not to come in?

Wen Fengjin lowered his head, the look on his face like a smile, yet not. "Xiaomie."

"Huh?"

Wen Fengjin's expression softened as he said, "It's time for us to sleep."

30
First
Blood

THOUGH THEY'D ONLY managed to reach the passage Zhen Mu passed through on his previous visit, over two days of exploration, the man named Yan used the traps they encountered to ascertain their exact position on the map he had with him.

Everything was ready on the night of the seventh day. The group once more entered the mausoleum.

"This was the deepest point we managed to reach." Zhen Mu stopped and turned to look behind him, saying, "It was here that I met a monster that looked like a long-haired female ghost. And then up ahead..."

The procession all stopped and looked at the man named Yan.

"What do we do, Boss?" Xiao-Li cheerfully asked.

The stiff-faced man took out his map and carefully pored over it, while Zhen Hao said with a frown, "What do we do? Obviously, we keep going forward! Didn't you say that sort of thing was unavoidable, Yan-xiansheng? And we haven't run into a single creature in the past two days."

"That's not your average zongzi, or any of the other evil creatures you might find in a tomb. It's a tomb guardian."

"Don't get impatient." The man cast Zhen Hao a lukewarm glance. Perhaps because his face was stiff to begin with, his expression looked particularly cold right now. He turned to give a slight nod to Xiao-Li and Zhen Mu. "We'll keep going. The map only shows a portion of the traps, not all of them. As for the tomb guardians, they're not marked at all. But this isn't our first time running into a situation like this, and we've gone through a good number of graves without a map at all. A little thing like this isn't enough to make us panic."

His calm and indifferent tone effectively calmed down the nervous members of the team. Zhen Hao pulled a long face, wordlessly shooting Yan-xiansheng a glance before following the group in their continued forward march. At the back of the line, Lei-jie snickered with narrowed eyes, her quiet laughter prompting Xiao-Luo behind her—strictly defending his shifu's back—to cast a glance at Zhen Hao. His normally warm gaze carried a faint hint of a sneer.

"Shifu, he's too much of a hindrance. In a place as dangerous as this, he may slow us down..."

"No touching, you little brat."

"...Right." Xiao-Luo lowered his head, and Lei-jie reached over to muss his hair.

How long had it been since she last saw someone who let all their resentment and arrogance show on their face? Lei-jie smiled, eyes narrowed. He really was pure, in a certain sense of the word.

"This mausoleum sure is huge. How long've we been walking at this point?" Chun Lei quietly asked.

Tiezi nodded. "It doesn't help that we've got to rely on the boss's pointers to evade traps, and watch out for any tomb guardians while we're at it."

"These tomb guardians *are* real though, right? We haven't seen any female ghosts or anything yet." Tiezi rubbed his face, then said, "Hm? Is it because we're too far underground? Why do I hear water? Fuck, I just got a drop in my mouth!"

Water droplets? Oh, that made sense—they were deep underground, and also beneath a mountain, so it wouldn't be strange for there to be plenty of underground river water.

Plus... Chun Lei rolled his eyes at him, saying, "It's because your mouth's too big, you idiot!"

"Fuck off." Tiezi spat a few times, then stopped to pull a canteen from his backpack so he could wash out his mouth—only for Zhen Hao, who'd been walking behind them with that long face of his, to bump him aside without even bothering to look up, nearly knocking Tiezi's canteen to the floor. "Move, don't get in my way!"

Tiezi's face immediately contorted, but Chun Lei pulled him back before he could say anything. "Don't start any trouble!" Chun Lei shook his head slightly, then used his eyes to signal: *Boss is watching*.

Tiezi sneered angrily, then firmly spat in Zhen Hao's direction. He muttered through gritted teeth, "Shit, once that Zhen Mu is gone, I'm gonna make him pay!"

As he was saying this, water droplets began to drip from above again. But with how angry Tiezi was now, he couldn't be bothered to care—it was just a few drops of water, let them drip all they want!

At this moment, Xiao-Li and Zhen Mu suddenly told the group behind them, "There's a dead end up ahead!"

"A dead end..." Yan-xiansheng stepped forward to feel the wall.

He was just about to say something when Zhen Hao suddenly raised his voice. "What's going on, Yan-xiansheng?! Are you unable to point us in the right direction, even with a map in your hands?"

Once he said this, every last person in the area was immediately thinking the same thing: *This man must be soft in the head*. Why else would he be picking a fight with Yan-xiansheng in front of them all?

Zhen Mu frowned, then sighed. Lei-jie's smile grew wider then before. Some of the men exchanged glances: *Is Boss gonna off him?*

Yan-xiansheng's face was even colder than before. He lowered his gaze and pulled out the map, ignoring everyone around him as he carefully ran his hand over the seamless wall, looking for a mechanism within it.

"Tch!" Chun Lei and Tiezi turned their heads with some disappointment.

Zhen Hao, meanwhile, curled his hands into fists. *I'm going to teach that Yan bastard a lesson in respect once we get out of here!* he thought to himself.

Zhen Bei, who hadn't said a word since he came down, stood in a spot out of reach of the light sticks and raised his head, looking up at the high ceiling of the pitch-black tomb passage. As he looked, a foolishly sweet smile slowly made its way onto his face.

Ah... They're here.

"Oh, right! Who's in charge of guarding the outermost tomb passages?" Wang Xiaomie turned back to look at the man currently hugging him.

"Hm? It's Mu Shi and Mu Jiu," Wen Fengjin replied in his low voice, as he kept brushing his lips and chin against Wang Xiaomie's neck.

Wang Xiaomie, getting somewhat restless from this pestering, struggled to push him away as he grumbled. "You mean those two jellyfish?"

They were so soft, and even made chirping sounds. He had to admit they were pretty cute.

"They can transform into a liquid like water and permeate into the bodies of their targets, who feel no pain at the intrusion. Mu Shi and Mu Jiu will then begin eating them from the inside—organs, intestines, and finally flesh, blood, and fat. They don't eat the skin, however, so in the end...all that's left is an empty husk."

I was a real fool for calling them cute, Wang Xiaomie thought with a gulp, a wooden expression on his face.

Pale lips curved upwards as Wen Fengjin hugged Wang Xiaomie hard. His handsome, womanish face pressed unforgivingly against his neck, the tip of his nose twitching as he sniffed at something.

"...Seriously, why are you so annoying today?! Sniffing me up and down like this...do I stink or something?" Wang Xiaomie couldn't take any more of this. Turning his head, he gripped Wen Fengjin's neck as though he was about to hit him.

Wen Fengjin looked calmly down at him. His smiling expression and the unnamable emotion in his eyes inexplicably caused Wang Xiaomie to blush. Faltering, Wang Xiaomie bared his teeth. "W-what do you wanna say?! You're not allowed to sniff me like a dog with a bone!"

"A dog sniffing a bone...that's not a bad analogy." Wen Fengjin placed a hand on the ones gripping his neck, then licked his lips with the tip of his tongue, saying, "Though I wonder if Shixiong will allow me to eat him?"

Such a back-breakingly lascivious expression... Wang Xiaomie was speechless. *My Xiao-Wenzi must be possessed today. Yes, that's definitely it!*

"Don't come near me! Kaiming's even started to heat up! What sort of evil designs do you have?!" Wang Xiaomie loudly wailed as he ran around the casket.

Wen Fengjin chuckled in that low voice of his as he leisurely pursued him. *What evil designs? Mn... Those would be lustful ones, most likely.*

Wen Fengjin swept his long, narrow eyes over the pining tree off to the side, then turned his gaze back to Wang Xiaomie, who was watching him on full alert.

...Come quickly. I can barely wait any longer. The man who wants my heart... My shixiong just happens to need a new sacrifice, as well.

At the outermost perimeter of the mausoleum, the man named Yan said, "Xiao-Li, you and Zhen Mu go take a look around the nearby walls." He then set down his backpack and pulled out a sheet of folded paper.

It was the copy of the tablet inscription.

Xiao-Li and Zhen Mu exchanged looks, then each went to different sides. The perfectly pristine, stone-paved passage was lined with rows of unlit lanterns, but not one of the people present suggested they light one. The majority of lamps or lanterns found in tombs triggered some sort of mechanism when lit. Rather than take that risk, it was safer to rely on light sticks and flashlights to find your way around.

As Yan-xiansheng was absorbed in studying the inscription, their current predicament probably wouldn't be solved anytime soon, so Chun Lei and Tiezi parked their butts on the ground to rest and conserve their energy.

This time, Zhen Hao also said nothing, simply folding his arms as he leaned his back against the wall with an impatience that not even his soft, elegant features could hide.

Lei-jie sat off to one side with her hunting knife, her gaze combing every inch of the wall before them. It was covered in an engraved pattern like great ripples of water. The main entrance of a tomb would normally be carved with religious icons, or pictures of whatever terrible beasts were guarding the grave in order to scare any potential grave robbers away. If not that, there'd at least be carvings depicting the life of the tomb master—how they ascended to immortality, or whatever. This was much too strange...

Xiao-Luo didn't put down his backpack, nor did he sit down to rest. The first thing he did was cautiously look around, after which he walked over to where Zhen Bei was squatting. His shifu had said there was something wrong with this guy, but seeing him squatted silently with downcast eyes, Xiao-Luo still couldn't help but pat Zhen Bei on the shoulder after a moment's hesitation.

Zhen Bei looked up at him in surprise, asking, "Something up?"

"Not really..." Not knowing what to say now that he'd patted him, Xiao-Luo somewhat awkwardly pulled his hand back. After a long moment, he finally squeezed out the words, "This place is pretty dangerous...be careful."

Zhen Bei stared blankly at him, blinked, then showed off a brilliant smile. "Thank you, I'll remember that."

Xiao-Luo assumed he meant he'd remember his warning. He couldn't have known it would be his softhearted kindness that, together with that little pouch, would save his shifu's life...

"Hey, is it just me, or is it dripping even more around here?" Chun Lei rubbed at his arm. Even though a layer of clothing separated his skin from the air, every time a drop of water hit him, he'd feel a tiny sting.

"You're right..." Tiezi looked up at the ceiling just in time for a droplet to land right in his eye. *"Fuck!"* He started wildly rubbing his eyes.

It was at this moment that they heard the dull clack of moving machinery. Everyone, including Zhen Bei and Zhen Mu, snapped into battle-ready positions.

But upon closer inspection, it turned out that Zhen Mu and Xiao-Li had pressed what appeared to be a normal brick in the wall, while Yan-xiansheng stood nearby with the inscription in hand, softly nodding.

The activation of this mechanism also caused accumulated dust and dirt to fall from the wall. What originally looked like a carving of ripples now revealed four hollowed recesses, each with a rotatable round stone in the shape of a beast's head. Each stone was encircled by markings, much like those of a clock.

"A password? Hahaha, this tomb master sure is up with the times! And here I thought we'd have to have Chun Lei blast our way through—after all, I get the feeling that if we made a door we could go in and out of, then *they* could come out through it too," Xiao-Li said with a grin.

Everyone else gathered around the new discovery, looking curiously at the ingenious mechanism.

Zhen Mu said, "Yan-xiansheng, we don't know the password here. If we get it wrong..." *Won't we die?*

Before he could finish speaking, a great rumbling noise suddenly sounded from above. Even the floor seemed to quake beneath them.

"What's going on?! Quick! It's the mechanism! The ceiling's coming down—*aaahhh! What's this?! Aaahh—*"

"What's happened?!" Yan-xiansheng shoved a few panicking men out of his way and stepped forward, only for his pupils to shrink nearly to dots at the sight of the thing on the floor. Even Lei-jie and Zhen Mu burst out in cold sweats.

What lay on the floor was a sack of boneless, fully clothed human skin. And the clothes that skin was wearing clearly belonged to Tiezi!

"Tieziiiii! He's dead—!"

"What the hell's going on?! Are you telling me none of you saw it? How the hell did he get hit?!" The man named Yan roared his question at a completely dumbstruck Chun Lei as the rest of the group unconsciously distanced themselves from the skin.

Chun Lei dully lifted his head, saying, "I-I don't know... We were sitting together just a minute ago, looking at the mechanism on the wall, I... Why is my stomach so hot? My throat—I—urgh—"

His eyes widened and he grabbed desperately at his throat and gaping mouth. He then bonelessly collapsed in front of everyone's terrified eyes as he turned into empty human skin...

MY HUSBAND AND I SLEEP IN A COFFIN

The
Tomb Master's
Invitation

HE DIED.

Died right before their eyes, wailing with a hideous look of terror on his face as he clawed feverishly at his own throat, then giving them all a hollow-eyed look of despair before collapsing like a deflated balloon, bereft of the flesh which filled him, leaving only his clothes and an intact skin...

The surviving team watched all of this in horror. Not even the old hands who'd gone spelunking many times before had seen anything like this! The most extraordinary things they'd faced before were ghost-blown candles, zombies, glazed fire ceilings, and door-sealing sand. Other than those, it was just things like mechanical traps and ghosts banging on walls or covering your eyes. In other words, the things they encountered in tombs tended to be illusions that pushed people to their deaths. Or, to put it more simply: magical attacks and traps.

And the average nobleman's or general's grave wouldn't have any of these things at all. At worst, the door would be a little harder to open, so they could quickly and easily clean the place out in three hours tops. But they hadn't even reached the main gate of the tomb this time...and its master had already given them a huge present!

Zhen Mu and Lei-jie exchanged a glance behind Yan's back, while the man himself stared silently at the skins of his two employees. The rumbling noise above their heads was still going, but the skins on the floor suddenly swelled. With a *swish*, they began circling around the group.

Have you ever seen a child running around in a grown-up's clothes? That's exactly what this was: Two mysterious creatures were running around, wearing the skins of what had been their comrades just a moment ago, and shrieking with childish, chirping laughter as they did!

"Zhen Bei!" Zhen Mu yelled. He unsheathed Changfeng with a *shink* and rushed over to pull Zhen Bei behind him, sharp eyes keeping a close watch on the things on the ground.

Xiao-Luo also grabbed his bag with one hand and reached into it with the other, looking ready to pull out some sort of weapon at any moment as he stood guard in front of Lei-jie.

The man named Yan watched the things on the ground with no expression at all. After a long moment, he suddenly let out a laugh. His remaining subordinate Xiao-Li—also a strong fighter—drew close to his boss with a pair of daggers in hand, looking upon the skins of his comrades with no outward signs of discomfort. In fact, he was still grinning.

This bunch of daredevils had no real affection for each other. If you died, it was because you lacked talent. If anything, the fact he hadn't stabbed his former comrades himself was a testament to his benevolence.

Everyone present revealed their positions in that moment of danger, leaving Zhen Hao to let out an ear-piercing scream as the monsters drew ever closer. "Aahh—*aaahhh!* Yan, you bastard, have you gone blind?! Hurry up and save me! Save meeeee! Zhen Mu, you idiot! Get over here already—*AAAHHHH!*"

Before the man named Yan could say anything, Xiao-Li snorted out a laugh. He'd gained a dislike for Zhen Hao early on. Now, he purposely whistled in the direction of a noticeably unhappy-looking Zhen Mu. "Zhen Mu, your master's calling~"

Blatantly implying that Zhen Mu was a dog the Zhen family had given Zhen Hao as a pet! He wanted to see if Zhen Mu would swallow the insult and rescue Zhen Hao, or if he'd show his ruthless side by coldly watching as the stupid asshole died!

Although... Xiao-Li's grin stretched as wide as an infamous hyena's. *If one of these two Zhens dies, it'll be a good thing for us either way. Ain't that right, Boss?*

He turned to look at the stiff-faced man, only to freeze in stupefaction. Why did their boss look so happy? Did he really find Zhen Hao that annoying?

Any man with a spine would bristle at being so humiliated, but though Zhen Mu had a naturally harsh face, his heart was as steady and enduring as a great mountain. He held his Changfeng Sword in a death grip, his cheeks taut as he gritted his teeth. With Zhen Hao's screams echoing in his ears, Zhen Mu forcefully shut his eyes and banked the fire of his rage. However, just as he opened his eyes once more and was about to step forward, a pair of hands suddenly pulled him back. A dumbfounded Zhen Mu looked behind him, only to see Lei-jie. She released him, uttering an incredibly insincere excuse. "Oh, sorry about that. I just slipped and nearly fell over—it's a good thing you were there to catch me."

Zhen Mu looked stoically to his right, seeing a teary-eyed Zhen Bei tightly gripping his sleeve. Upon seeing his face, Zhen Bei let go, looking as aggrieved as a big, well-behaved dog that was so scared its fur was standing on end. "Ge, I'm scared."

Zhen Mu fell silent for a moment. It was exactly in that moment of obstruction that the pair of creatures laughing shrilly in their stolen skins finally charged toward Zhen Hao. While Zhen Hao screamed like a marmot, the creatures threw the skins onto his face and body with a resounding *plap*. When the soft skin landed on his face, Zhen Hao's scream cut off abruptly with an ugly wheeze, like a stuck cassette tape. Then his eyes rolled upward, and he fell unconscious to the floor with a *thump*.

Zhen Mu's pupils shrank as he hurried over. Now that the two creatures had shed the skins, the group was finally able to see that they were actually a pair of humanoid monsters that moved with flowing, jellyfish-like motions. Despite being transparent, you could still clearly tell that their features were those of young boys, and that they were currently looking right at them with wide smiles on their faces.

When Zhen Mu rushed over to defend Zhen Hao with his sword, he'd originally assumed he was in for a tough fight. However, the two tomb guardians seemed to be thrown off by his arrival—not only failing to attack but even taking a step back in retreat.

"...Ch-chirp?" *This guy has the scent Mu Yi mentioned!*

"...Ch-chirp?" *We can't eat him, no... Master would get really mad...*

Under the baffled stares of the people around them, the two tomb guardians muttered away, whispering to each other just like human beings...

Wang Xiaomie might have found their clumsy, childish behavior cute, but in the eyes of these people, monsters who could chat with each other were all the more terrifying!

"Shifu..." Xiao-Luo tightly gripped the weapon in his bag with one hand as he said, "These things are much too strange. If we don't act now, we might end up getting killed by them in the future!"

"Shut up!" Lei-jie pressed down on his shoulders, her gaze fixed upon the two monsters. Suddenly, she called out in a low voice, "Look!"

Xiao-Luo quickly looked over to see the two tomb guardians abruptly cower, as if they'd encountered something they feared. They instantly melted into the ground, transforming into a mobile puddle of water and disappearing from sight.

...?! The group stared in complete astonishment at Zhen Mu, unable to even pay any mind to the still-lowering ceiling.

What the fuck, when'd this guy get so OP?!

Mu Jiu and Mu Shi, who'd fled as quickly as they could out of fear that they'd kill the wrong person and get a scolding from Wen Fengjin, chirped as they ran.

Zhen Mu himself was just as confused, with no idea why they'd suddenly fled.

On the other hand, monsters running away was never a bad thing. With their greatest threat gone, the exit behind them was now open as well. Zhen Mu had no time to think. He quickly hefted Zhen Hao onto his back, then shouted to the man named Yan: "Yan-xiansheng! Do we run now or not?!"

The man named Yan stared blankly for a moment before putting on a thoughtful look. He said, without any noticeable emotion in his voice, "Why run? The password isn't hard to guess. According to what's noted on the silk and the tablet inscription, the tomb master set the password to be the year most important to him...

"In the year 1326 of the Northern calendar, he came of age and left the academy. In 1328, he gathered his old guard and established Anlou. In 1330, he strengthened his forces and slaughtered both the court and commoners in bloody revenge. That same year, he became the demon lord of Anlou. In 1334, he obtained the elixir of immortality and was encircled by his enemies. The same year, he and his shixiong fled back to the academy. They failed, his shixiong perished, he ingested the elixir himself to gain an undying, unaging body, and the next year—in 1335—he slaughtered his shizun and fellow disciples, wiped out all clans suspected of being involved with them, eliminated officials with influence, forced the emperor to retire, and raised a new one to power. In the year 1445 of the Northern calendar, construction of the mausoleum was completed and he had the coffin interred, burying himself in the same box as his shixiong and dying for love within the tomb..."

"Whoa, this guy was seriously infatuated if he did that much all for his shixiong... He's totally a good man!" Zhen Bei blinked innocently as he said, "My guess is the most important one's gotta be either 1334, when his shixiong lost his life, or 1445, when he had himself buried with his shixiong."

Lei-jie nodded in agreement. "But we don't know exactly which date is most important to the tomb master, and if we guess wrong..."

But the man named Yan quirked his lips at that, saying, "Actually your guess is only half right."

"Half?"

"Yes, the password *is* connected to the tomb master's shixiong. But rather than everything I said just now, it is actually—the shixiong's birth year: 1308 in the Northern calendar."

Everyone was struck speechless.

Wait, then what the hell did you keep blabbering on so long for?! The ceiling's about to come down and crush us into ground meat, and you're still in the mood to lead us in circles?! Also, is this tomb master a high schooler? Changing both his cell phone's password and lock screen to his girlfriend's birthday?! Fucking hell!

Zhen Mu and Lei-jie expressionlessly stared at the man named Yan, grinding their teeth with great ferocity.

Sensing the awkwardness in the air, Yan-xiansheng quietly cleared his throat, then turned to Xiao-Li beside him.

In that moment, Xiao-Li immediately got the idea. He said, "Wow, Boss, you sure know a lot!"

Yan-xiansheng quirked his lips and replied, "It's nothing, I just happened to have done some research, is all."

Zhen Mu, Zhen Bei, Lei-jie, and Xiao-Luo were stupefied.

This tomb didn't have some kind of defense that lowered people's IQ, did it?

But now that they knew the password, they quickly opened the main gate and left the area they were in, with Zhen Mu carrying Zhen Hao on his back and Zhen Bei still carefully following him.

After passing through the main gate, the surrounding tomb passage began to be covered in colorful drawings and carvings, each individual brick beneath their feet taking on the form of specific totems. If the main gate had been an average unfurnished house, then what lay inside was the mausoleum equivalent of an extravagant manor with all the furnishings included in the sale.

The man named Yan looked at the drawings, fingers tightly curling and loosening again as he gently brushed his hands over the wall.

Wen Fengjin, I've finally arrived... Oh, how I want to see the look on your face when you meet me.

Wen Fengjin, I'll get what I want by any means! Because you owe it all to me!

In the depths of the mausoleum, Wen Fengjin bent down to press a hand against the cheek of the bride now sleeping soundly within the red wedding casket, those fair-skinned rosy cheeks flush with life and that long black hair spread softly beneath him like a spider's silk.

"...Shixiong is always so beautiful. Ever since I was a youth, I've always longed for a future where I could caress your face like this when I woke up every morning. I've already let them in, Shixiong. You'll be able to be free of your fetters soon. You'll no longer have to suffer..."

Wang Xiaomie's eyelids twitched in his sleep, curved lashes fluttering with the movement, but he was unable to open his eyes.

For the next leg of the route, the party passed heedlessly through this spectacularly gorgeous underground palace like they were playing tourist, but not a single tomb guardian came by to stop them.

This freezing-cold crypt was the resting place of the dead. The silence was so complete it made you feel compelled to wrap your arms around yourself. It was impossible for a flashlight to fully illuminate a building this grand. It was like they'd become insects who wandered into an abyss by accident, tiny and insignificant. It made you anxious enough to fill the impenetrable darkness with countless hideously smiling monsters...

"Shifu, for some reason, my heart's still pounding like crazy even though we haven't met a single strange thing the whole way," Xiao-Luo whispered secretively to Lei-jie.

Lei-jie glanced at him, but didn't get the chance to respond. With a *fwoosh*, all the lanterns in the surrounding halls suddenly lit up at once. And the instant these thousand lights set the area ablaze, illuminating the entire palace, they also lit a certain dark area in the distance as bright as day.

Two parallel rows of monsters of all shapes and sizes were revealed, all currently sizing them up with narrowed eyes!

"...Darling disciple," Lei-jie said, "would you tell this teacher when it was that you had your mouth consecrated?"

Xiao-Luo was shocked speechless.

"Why are you all standing around? Get your guard up!" Xiao-Li raised his twin daggers, dripping with cold sweat as he watched the monsters. "Shit, did one of you step on a trap mechanism?!"

At this perilous moment, Zhen Mu placed the unconscious Zhen Hao on the ground and unsheathed the Changfeng Sword, frowning with a hardened gaze.

Yet Yan-xiansheng's widened eyes were glistening with a strange brilliance as he stared at the very front of the palace. Even his stiff face cracked open in a wide smile.

"Put down your weapon, Xiao-Li. It looks like the tomb master has invited us inside!"

My Husband and I Sleep in a Coffin

32
True Nature Revealed

HOW DID IT FEEL to swagger right into someone's home with a bunch of monstrous tomb guardians watching you? It felt like being the student in the very back row getting dragged up to the podium to solve a problem in front of the entire class. The mixture of distress and pleasure was impossible to put into words. After all, who ever heard of a tomb master opening the doors and inviting the grave-robbers to come right on in? They'd come prepared to sustain terrible casualties, only to unexpectedly encounter something like this. If not for the row of monsters standing there drooling at them, it really would have felt like they were guests visiting someone's house.

The man named Yan strode forward. Behind him, pale with fright, Xiao-Li looked vigilantly around him out of the corners of his eyes.

Sweat beaded on Xiao-Luo's brow as he tightened his grip on the thing in his hand, finally pulling his secret weapon out from his backpack and revealing it to the world. As he did so, he muttered, "I suddenly have the urge to turn and make a break for it."

Zhen Bei, still walking behind him, looked over upon hearing his words. But his expression froze in the next instant. He stared at the weapon which Xiao-Luo had been hiding like it was his little treasure all this time, then pointed at it with a blank face. "What's this?"

252 MY HUSBAND AND I SLEEP IN A COFFIN

Xiao-Luo waved the long and slender weapon: "Oh this? It's the Sacred Physics Sword!"

Zhen Bei blinked. *Sacred Physics Sword?* "It's just a crowbar, isn't it..."

Xiao-Luo's expression changed at that, and he replied with all seriousness, "No, this is the Sacred Physics Sword, I had it blessed in a temple."

Even a double-dealer like Zhen Bei felt like he was suffocating at this moment.

A slender, yet callused hand reached out from behind them and smacked Xiao-Luo over the back of the head, "Ignore the chuuni here," a noticeably irritated Lei-jie told Zhen Bei. "This guy'll even yell 'it can you do'[3] when he gets drunk~"

"Shifu! Don't say that!"

"Hm? If you've got the guts to yell at your shifu, does that mean you'd like me to use the Sacred Physics Sword to separate you from your dick?"

Silence fell.

Zhen Bei quietly power walked over to Zhen Mu in an extremely obvious attempt at avoidance. "Please, wait just one moment."

The heretofore unmoving monsters suddenly let out shrill noises, freezing everyone in their tracks with fear. They then watched as a monster which looked like a long-haired female ghost stepped forward with dragging feet to stare gloomily at them. She looked so glum that she practically stank of mold and mildew. The man named Yan's face went even more sour than before.

Xiao-Li was even more frightened. His mind—long stretched taut as a fragile bowstring—instantly ordered him to attack!

---

3 给力噢 (gei li o) is an exclamation which, depending on context, can mean "cool," "amazing," or "you can do it." 奥利给 (ao li gei), which is the same phrase read backward, became popularized in online slang during the pandemic years.

There was a wet squelching sound.

"Aaaahhhh! My hand! Aaaahhhh, Boss!" Xiao-Li grabbed his right hand, which had started melting from the wrist down, and fell wailing to his knees with a terrible look on his face. In that instant, his right hand had already decayed enough to come away from his wrist and fall to the ground.

The perpetrator was one of the monsters gradually closing in around them. It looked like a humongous tree fungus. It had done nothing but spit a single glob of saliva at Xiao-Li's hand—and the appendage had immediately melted right off!

The group quickly raised their weapons and grouped together to stand back-to-back, palms sweating like mad. Nobody could spare the effort to worry about Xiao-Li, who was nearly passed out on the ground, but their fear and the ear-piercing noise of his wails ruthlessly struck their thunderously pounding hearts!

It's over. Are we gonna die?! Was all of this a trap?! So many monsters... If I'd known before, I never would've come here! This isn't a place any human being should be setting foot in!

"You, people, truly have no manners... heheheh. Master said only four of you could enter, so you should decide amongst yourselves who will move forward and who...will stay behind..." The ghostly tomb guardian let out a laugh like something out of a horror movie. "But those who stay behind will become our dinner."

"Eat~ Eeaat~ Hahaha! Eat them!" The two monsters who'd previously turned their companions into bags of skin broke out into shrill-voiced, childish, terrifying cheers. "All ten of us~ Eating togetheeerrr~ We want the organs! The organs are super tasty, chirp, chirp!"

"In that case, I want the heads..."

"Gugu..." *I want their hands.*

"Want, want...eyes..."

"Kakaka!" *No fighting, everyone will get their share!*

The hideous, inhuman monsters circled around them, bloodred eyes staring greedily at their bodies in much the same way long-starved wild beasts might look upon their prey.

Even if you couldn't understand their words, it was easy to recognize their excitement. Once the choice was made, they would tear apart those who remained and feast to their hearts' content!

"Four people?" The man named Yan looked indifferently at Xiao-Li on the floor, then raised a leg and kicked his still-wailing lackey into the circle of monsters, saying blandly, "You can have this one first."

He spoke and acted like he was talking about an object, not a living human. And his own subordinate too. Zhen Mu's and Lei-jie's faces paled. After sharing a look, they both quietly added the man behind them to those they were on guard against.

Xiao-Luo, despite his small and youthful appearance, only jeered derisively at the sight of Xiao-Li's stunned and terror-stricken face. The man named Yan and his underlings were a renowned bunch of bastards—their deaths were a good thing. Then he wouldn't have to worry about this pack of hyenas attacking him and his shifu from behind!

Meanwhile, a horrified Zhen Bei gripped the corner of Zhen Mu's shirt, seemingly worried he might be in the way. He anxiously covered his mouth with one hand as if about to vomit.

"What're you doing?! You bastard! Fuck! I don't wanna die! I'll kill you, Yan, you—"

Xiao-Li picked himself up off the ground, hatred twisting his face until he looked more terrifying than any ghost. He angrily swore, picked up a dagger with his remaining hand, and made to throw himself at the man named Yan and ensure they went down together.

But a second later, the tomb guardians grabbed him by the arms and legs and bodily dragged him back. The sounds of chewing and screams went on for a full minute before finally fading away.

The sound was enough to make your hair stand on end and tremors run through your whole body. Even Zhen Mu was constantly swallowing as the air filled with the faint smell of blood. Lei-jie and Xiao-Luo shut their eyes, and the man named Yan stiffly quirked his lips.

"Ugghh—"

Zhen Bei squatted down and started dry heaving, while Zhen Hao—possibly disturbed by the noise from earlier—gradually stirred to wakefulness, only to get a clear look at where he was and immediately let out a marmot-like shriek! *"Aaaahhhhh!"*

The sound was so shocking that it even caused the man named Yan to tremble. Xiao-Luo was so frightened by it that he gave him a vicious kick, cursing, "What're you hollering for?!"

"How dare you kick me?!" Zhen Hao unexpectedly forgot his fear at this. Standing up to settle things with Xiao-Luo, he reached out to wrap his hands around Xiao-Luo's neck.

Xiao-Luo, in turn, raised his crowbar with a mocking smile on his face. This dumbass had been getting on his nerves for a while now, but now he had the opportunity to feed him to those tomb-guarding monsters!

Lei-jie put a hand to her head and muttered, "Seriously, does this guy even have a brain in his head? Does he think this is his own house or something?"

"Dage, what are you doing...?" A deep frown crossed Zhen Mu's fierce features. He could tell Xiao-Luo intended to do his older brother in for good, and so he reached out to stop him.

Slap!

An open palm viciously struck Zhen Mu in the face.

Stunned, Zhen Mu's head snapped sharply to the side, while Zhen Bei's pupils shrank, fingers curling into tight fists.

Zhen Hao looked at him with a sneer, saying, "You ungrateful son of a bitch—not only refusing to help me but even daring to hold me back! You call this protecting me? And what's going on now? Zhen Mu, you take me somewhere safe right this instant!"

The sated monsters watched the group, as if enjoying a good show.

Yan-xiansheng, Lei-jie, and Xiao-Luo fell momentarily silent at his words, after which they couldn't help but laugh out loud. Lei-jie turned to Zhen Mu and said, "What are you enduring this treatment for? Just off him already."

"...I can't." No matter how stupid Zhen Hao might be, he was still his older brother and a blood relative. Zhen Mu might be inwardly angry enough to beat him to a pulp, but he still couldn't simply watch as his brother was eaten by these monsters.

"Tch! That personality of yours is seriously... Let me tell you something you won't want to hear." Lei-jie continued with a small laugh, "If we can't satisfy these monsters' demands, then it's possible *all* of us will die. And we still need to ditch another two of the six of us... Zhen Mu, who do *you* think is staying behind? What? You aren't thinking you can leave one of us three, are you? Haha."

Of the six of them, Zhen Hao and Zhen Bei were the only ones without any real power. It was obvious who was going to get left behind.

Zhen Mu's pupils shrank as he turned to look at Zhen Bei, quickly pointing his Changfeng Sword at the other three as he strode over to shield Zhen Bei behind him. "Nobody's hurting my little brother! Or else...I'll make all of you stay behind with me!"

Zhen Bei furrowed his brow as he looked uncertainly at them. "Ge..."

Zhen Hao frowned as well. "What are you talking about? Why aren't any of you afraid? Zhen Mu, Zhen Bei, answer my question."

But nobody was paying him any attention at this point—after all, Zhen Mu's stance was very clear now...

Zhen Hao was doomed to die.

As Zhen Mu guardedly watched the other three, Zhen Bei suddenly called out to him. "Erge..."

"What—"

Dumbfounded, Zhen Mu doubled over with a cough as he looked at the fist slammed into his chest. His vision went black as he struggled to breathe. In the moment before his consciousness faded, he raised his head to stare in disbelief at Zhen Bei. "You..."

"You're such a pain, Erge."

Zhen Bei flashed him a brilliant smile as he said, "Be good and close your eyes now, or I might have to make you hurt a little more." His tone flippant and cheerful, he addressed him by name. "Zhen Mu..."

Thump.

Zhen Mu collapsed to the floor, and Zhen Bei stifled a laugh. Using only one arm to lift the man onto his shoulder, he smilingly turned to face an equally smiling Lei-jie.

"You knew all along, didn't you? I hate smart women the most... They really make me sick."

Lei-jie patted her stupefied disciple as she replied, "Twisted monsters in human skin like you are even more sickening. Tch...you stink to high heaven."

"Hahahaha!" A happy smile revealed itself on Zhen Bei's sunny face, as if bathing him in sunlight. His entire person carried a warmth to it. But after narrowing those peach blossom eyes and tilting his lips upward, the words he spoke were the kind that made chills run down your spine.

He said, "You three go ahead. We brothers need to settle some things among ourselves—especially my dage. I'm practically chomping at the bit to see him get torn to pieces, heheh."

"Let's go." The man named Yan coldly turned around, and Lei-jie did the same.

"Where are you going?! Wait! Zhen Bei, you idiot, don't touch me—what are you doing—*ah*!"

Zhen Bei steadied Zhen Mu on his shoulder and reached out to grab Zhen Hao's head with his other hand, smiling softly at his brother as he screamed and struggled to get away. With that hand, he suddenly slammed Zhen Hao's head hard into the ground. Then he pulled out a butterfly knife...

Unable to resist one last backward glance, Xiao-Luo even saw Zhen Bei excitedly lick his lips at the sound of Zhen Hao's screams.

To think the Zhen family were such twisted people! A chill ran down Xiao-Luo's spine as he hurried to catch up with his shifu.

33

Should
I Lie Back
Down?

THE OPEN MAIN GATE of the palace closed once more, and at the head of the group, Mu Yi broke into a wide-mouthed, bloody smile. The ten tomb guardians had already eaten their fill earlier, and now circled around Zhen Bei but did nothing to act. Instead, they sniffed at him, passively watching to see what Zhen Bei would do.

After all, this human had the same scent as them on him~

Zhen Bei tossed Zhen Mu to the ground, deft fingers flicking his butterfly knife a few times, then squatted down to look at the now bloody-faced Zhen Hao. The expression on his face was that of a warm-hearted young man, as if any moment now he might reach to pull a tissue from his pocket and hand it to the fallen Zhen Hao. Of course, what he'd pulled out instead was a knife.

Zhen Hao, sensing danger, stopped swearing as well. He scuttled backward in terror, while before him Zhen Bei stood up and tilted his head, smiling as he followed after him one step at a time. He had the appearance of a homicidal demon from hell.

"Da—! Ge—! Let's play a game togetheerr. Hahahaha."

Zhen Hao bumped into a monster. In this moment, though, he was far more afraid of the little brother he'd once called an idiot!

The pretty butterfly knife rose and fell.

"Aahhh!"

Zhen Bei squatted down again, propping his face on his right hand as he pouted. "It's just one hand. What's Gege yelling so loud for? Although... it does make me really happy!"

"Let me go... Zhen Bei... I'm begging you to let me go, once we get out..." Zhen Hao was in so much pain that his face was a mess of snot and tears, but he still forced out a terrified smile as he attempted to negotiate.

"No need." Zhen Bei interrupted him with the words, "You won't be getting out, Dage."

"You—" Zhen Hao's face immediately contorted, and he swore, "You're nothing but a dog! You're *all* my dogs! I—mmph..."

"It looks to me like you don't want your tongue anymore, either."

Flicking the blood off his blade, Zhen Bei started deftly spinning the butterfly knife in his left hand with three fingers, saying, "That's right. How about we settle some things between us? I still remember how much effort you put into hyping up your skill at identifying antiques, but back when Erge made an imitation article, you actually couldn't tell at all, hahaha! That must've been the first time you ever made such a laughingstock of yourself."

In the span of a second, Zhen Bei's wide smile was exchanged for a cold and impassive look, and he patted Zhen Hao's cheek with his knife.

"Wasn't that just because you're terrible at appraising things? And yet you called Erge into the room and cut up his hands with a knife—Dage, don't you think it would be best if I cut off your hands here too?"

"Mmmmph—!"

"Also, Erge clearly has more talent than you, so you sent him to risk his life robbing graves for you. All *I* did was show the tiniest bit

of appraising talent, and you told all the employees in the house to purposely avoid me, calling me an idiot. A~aaaah~ the more I think about it, the angrier I get... heh!"

"*Mmmmph—!*"

Red liquid gradually spread across the ground, while Mu Yi and the others laughed and whispered to each other. There was a group of monsters surrounding the humans here, and yet the human in the middle was even scarier than the monsters... They watched the show being put on by those humans, listening respectfully to the screams on the stage.

A very, very long time passed.

A completely blood-soaked Zhen Bei stood up, a huge grin on his face and his peach blossom eyes narrowed happily. Blood slid down his chin and dripped to the floor like crimson tears.

"I've had my fun." He casually tossed aside the now blood-sticky butterfly knife, then pulled a handkerchief from his pocket and started slowly wiping his hands, before suddenly raising his head to look at the monsters. "Oh right, thank your master for me—he did exactly what he said he'd do, so of course, I'll do what I promised as well. This man..." He poked at Zhen Mu's butt with the toe of his boot. "I still need to take him outside."

Mu Yi and the others gazed indifferently at him with their bloodred eyes, then turned and instantly disappeared.

Zhen Bei paid no mind to this. He reached out to take the gray pouch from within Zhen Mu's shirt. Inside the pouch was a piece of his own clothing. That day, he'd made an agreement with the tomb master—that those who carried his scent on them would not be attacked.

After tossing the pouch to the floor, he picked up Zhen Mu again and hefted him on his shoulder.

"Although...I'll be coming back in again." Zhen Bei lowered his gaze, a strange light flashing in his eyes as he looked over at where Mu Yi and the other tomb guardians had been just moments ago. "...After all, the mantis stalks the cicada, unaware of the oriole behind~"

Elsewhere, the remaining party was passing through splendid halls, luxurious, animal-eaved, winding corridors like the kind you'd find in an ancient imperial palace, with stone dragon banisters and floors so shiny they were as reflective as mirrors, even row after row of scarlet pillars with coiled draconic designs which were so thick you'd need three men to fully encircle them. Mortal eyes felt underequipped to drink in such profoundly grand and elegant architecture.

Every time they thought they'd reached the end of the road, a guiding mermaid-oil lamp would always light up ahead of them, telling them that they still had a long way to go.

"This mausoleum is practically as big as ten imperial palaces put together! What the heck kind of person is this Wen Fengjin?" Xiao-Luo looked around with infatuated eyes at all the art and vases, any of which could fetch an exorbitant price on their own. And that wasn't even including the ceiling rafters, which were inlaid with countless pearls and jewels.

This time, before Lei-jie could say anything, the man named Yan spoke up first.

"Hmph, this is nothing. Back then, the man held complete control of not just the Northern Kingdom but even the lands beyond it. He'd barely come of age when the jianghu and imperial court became victims of an endless reign of terror, and it only took five years for him to reach a level of power on par with an emperor! Everywhere you looked, there were people who worshipped him as a god. Many were infatuated with him to the point of obsession."

How do you know so much...? Xiao-Luo wanted to say something in ridicule, but chose to keep his mouth shut. Ever since this man sacrificed his own subordinate to take the fall for him, just the sight of him was enough to give Xiao-Luo goosebumps.

But it wouldn't be long before he could no longer be bothered to think about this. Because after passing through the final hall and reaching a certain platform, the light went from a concentrated point to a glow that lit up the whole area. In the moment he saw the scene before him, he found himself entirely at a loss for words—and, he knew, his shifu and that man were just as shocked as he was.

They had reached a massive, empty cave the size of a hollowed-out mountain. It was a size larger than even the Olympic Bird's Nest Stadium, the circular space ridged by raised cliffs thickly dotted with tiered houses and palace halls, looking like the cliffside temples built in tourist areas. And the three of them stood on a single red platform among all these, with a bottomless abyss at their feet.

In the middle of this huge space, surrounded by mushroomlike buildings, was a gigantic stone pillar wrapped in tree roots. Attached to this pillar was a platform the size of a playground, with chains as thick as an adult's waist extending from it in all directions. From where they stood, they could see that atop that wide platform was an old tree, wide as seven men, covered in flowers but lacking any leaves.

What shocked the group wasn't the tree, however, but the splendour of the pink peach blossoms that covered it. And to what degree were these flowers blooming, you might ask? It looked like a blazing pink fire was merrily devouring the tree. The rays of light cast down from above only added to the immortal tree's holy appearance.

And the casket they were looking for lay right below this brightly blazing peach tree.

"Looks like we'll have to go up." Lei-jie licked her drying lips, looking to her disciple Xiao-Luo as she said, "Based on what we've seen, I'm guessing there's not much chance of getting out of here alive today. Even worse, I've led you, my student, to a dead end. Do you hate me?"

"I don't." Xiao-Luo shook his head, firmly saying, "If it weren't for you, I'd have spent my whole life as some petty thug. Shifu...is there no way for us to turn back?"

"Turn back? Does this look like the kind of situation we can just leave? All our skills and talents are totally worthless against this kind of absolute power. I could handle one or two of those monsters from earlier, but a whole pack of them?" Lei-jie glanced over at the man in front of her, who was already stepping out onto the chain without the slightest hint of hesitation, and said in a quiet voice, "This Yan guy's practically been a man possessed since we got here—he's gotta have something up his sleeve if he's this impatient. Remember, Xiao-Luo, when things start kicking off, we absolutely aren't going to make the first move. Keep behind him!"

"Yes, Shifu!"

Between the high platform the chain was attached to and the abyss below, stepping onto this chain was certain to be a path of no return. A fall would shatter your body to pieces. Lei-jie quirked her lips, then took that first step onto the chain...

The man named Yan's face was stiff yet twitching weirdly, his eyes glittering with excitement! A thousand years, *a thousand years*! He was finally going to see that man again!

Wen Fengjin...

He sped up as he thought this. Even though there was an abyss beneath the chain, and the chain was swaying slightly, he continually stepped forward without a visible hint of fear, almost as if he were walking on level ground!

The teacher and disciple followed tenaciously behind him. The moment they set foot on the platform, a huge, swirling gust of wind blew straight up from the abyss, obscuring their vision and rustling the tree of blazing peach blossoms. Those flower petals flew upward like pink sparks of fire, filling the entire space with their flourishing sacred flames.

Under the circle of windblown flowers, beneath the falling blossoms of the pining tree, lay a casket built for two. And beside the casket stood a man looking up at the peach blossoms with his hands behind his back, flower petals swirling around him. The wind blew at his red-and-black, eye-searingly intricate and expensive long robes. A belt outlined his slender waist, a red crown topped ink-black hair, and then there was that pale white neck...

Just like an immortal god.

In the stillness, a silent field of power pressed down on them with such pressure that they struggled to breathe.

By this point, Xiao-Luo and Lei-jie were too shocked for words. Upon seeing this figure, they suddenly lost any doubt they'd originally had about the inscription's mention of magical elixirs and ascension to immortality. The thought "So *this* is an immortal," passed through their minds.

In a trance, the man named Yan gazed at that man's back, his eyes and the muscles of his face twitching, his lips pursed into a thin line, his fingers convulsing and curling.

After a long moment, he suddenly opened his mouth and sucked in a breath. "Wen Fengjin."

The words were quiet as the whine of a gnat, yet seemed to rouse the stranger regardless. The man coldly turned his head, chin tilting slightly upward. His face showed no expression of any kind, though the extraordinary cast of his femininely handsome features gave it a sharply aggressive air. The black irises, which filled most of his long, narrow eyes, gazed at the insects before him without the slightest emotion.

The man named Yan stopped breathing for a moment, gazing back at him from afar. After a very long moment, he began to laugh aloud, the sound both savage and filled with stubborn obsession. "It's really you! It really is—"

His gaze fell upon the casket by Wen Fengjin and his wild laughter became even more unrestrained. He said, sounding demented, "Hahaha—after all these years you're still watching over the same dead man! What pining tree, what revival? It was all a lie! Hahaha! This is all your just deserts—it's retribution for discarding me so long ago!"

"Who are you?" Wen Fengjin frowned at the man. Why did his face look kind of familiar?

But the man named Yan didn't respond, instead pointing at the casket with a poisonous gaze! "What's in there? A corpse? Or a handful of dust? Hahaha, either way, I'm the winner! It's me!"

Just as he said this, a person sat up from within the casket.

The two awkwardly made eye contact. A moment of silence followed them.

The man's laughter came to a sudden stop. His eyes bulged so far they nearly fell out of his head.

Wang Xiaomie felt goosebumps under his gaze.

"Uhh... Should I lie back down again, maybe?"

MY HUSBAND AND I SLEEP IN A COFFIN

34

What Son of a Biscuit Do You Think You Are?

"**T**HIS CAN'T BE...IT'S IMPOSSIBLE! I've taken away half, so why are you still alive? How could you actually have woken up—Mian Deng—!"

The man shook his head in disbelief; when he roared out this name, Wang Xiaomie looked with some shock between him and Wen Fengjin.

"Um, do you know me?" Wang Xiaomie pointed at himself. The man had invoked the name from his previous life—was it possible that he was involved with them somehow? "Fengjin, do you know him?"

Wen Fengjin glanced away from Wang Xiaomie and swept his gaze impassionately over the man's faintly hopeful face.

"No," Wen Fengjin said, "I have no idea who this man is."

At those words, the stiff-faced man's expression immediately began spasming hideously. The bulging-eyed look with which he stared at Wen Fengjin made him look like he'd gone mad. "You don't recognize me..." He roared with laughter as he pointed at Wen Fengjin, saying, "You don't recognize me? You lie! You *absolutely* recognize me!"

Wang Xiaomie gulped at the demonically ruthless look on his face. "Xiao-Wenzi, if you know him, you should say so, right? This guy's giving me the feeling he's about to pounce and take a bite out of us." His frenzied gaze made it seem like they'd killed his father and stolen his wife.

But Wen Fengjin shook his head once more, this time not even bothering to look at the man as he walked over to the casket and gently caressed Wang Xiaomie's cheek with a hand. "Shixiong's awake? I need to deal with some noisy rats in a moment, so why don't you sleep a little longer? Don't worry, I'll be finished soon."

...Hey now, he can hear you. Wang Xiaomie cast a furtive glance at the man. *Fuck! Dage, don't your eyes hurt with how wide you've got them open?!*

But Wang Xiaomie also noticed that when this dage looked at him, he seemed full of envy and resentment!

When this dage looked at Wen Fengjin: a mix of both love and hate...

The dage looked at him again: envy and resentment!

The dage looked at Wen Fengjin again: a mix of both love and hate...

Dearest Mother above! This dang guy can switch freely between two kinds of complete gaze-and-facial expression combos with zero delay!

This was seriously giving Wang Xiaomie the vibe of a heroine seeing the other woman come onto the scene, turning to the male love interest with both love and hate to whine, "Wehhh, you'll regret treating me like this~" then immediately telling the other woman, "You green-tea bitch, just you wait, I'm gonna rip your ■ ■ ■ to shreds!"

There's way too much psychological drama behind those eyes, Wang Xiaomie thought.

Even Lei-jie and Xiao-Luo—who had been trying their best to keep a low profile behind the man called Yan—couldn't help thinking the same thing once they recovered their senses: *Why do I feel like we're accompanying a gal pal as she catches her cheating boyfriend in the act?*

Wang Xiaomie pushed Wen Fengjin's hand away, frowning as he whispered to him, "...You'd better think it over, because I feel like he really does recognize us—though how does he know who we are when we've been alive for so many years?"

The way this guy looked at him was just too strange. It gave him an uncomfortably suffocating feeling.

Wen Fengjin responded with a noncommittal hum, brushing his cheek one last time with his thumb before straightening up again. "You're the ones who wanted my heart?"

"No, not them, just me." The man named Yan's gaze was sharp as knives, his tone scathing. "Should I be saying such heartlessness is to be expected from you, Wen Fengjin? Back then, you had eyes for no one but that good-for-nothing shixiong of yours. And after your shixiong died, you still had eyes for nothing else but that corpse—heh. I did so much for you, yet now you don't even recognize me."

Wen Fengjin's expression momentarily froze.

"What, have you finally remembered me?!"

As the flames of hope reignited within the man's gaze, Wen Fengjin half closed his eyes, his hair raven black, the red mark on his forehead as bright as fresh blood. He turned his head, long slender fingers carelessly brushing some fallen peach blossom petals from his shoulder. This attitude seemed to convey that both the man's words, and his very existence, were as worthy of recall as the dust on that shoulder.

Pinching a petal between his thumb and forefinger and tossing it to the ground, Wen Fengjin quirked moist pink lips into a smile and said, "Are you a being deserving of this venerable one's remembrance?"

That's a real good badass act. Wang Xiaomie, sitting in the casket, silently made a note in his little mental notebook. *I've learned something new today.*

The man clenched his fists in a death grip, gritting his teeth so hard that his cheeks bulged. He quickly relaxed, however, and even forced those hard-to-use nerves in his face to once again form a smile. "It's fine if you don't remember me. All that matters is that *I* remember *you*, Fengjin." His smile was scary, his tone now both affectionate and discomfiting. "You would never have obtained the elixir of life all those years ago if it weren't for me. If not for me, you wouldn't have needed to keep watching over him after he woke, living out your days within this underground palace. Let me guess why you haven't returned to the surface? Haha, it's because if he strays from this pining tree, from your blood, he won't be able to continue living! Hahaha."

The man named Yan suddenly turned to point at Wang Xiaomie, saying, "Mian Deng, you're nothing more than a living corpse now. Smelling death on yourself every day must be quite painful! Hee! It's all because I ate half the medicine that was given to you back then! Look at me—I've also lived a thousand years. Do you know how that medicine was made? It's—"

There was a chaotic gale of wind as Wen Fengjin suddenly swept before the man and gripped his neck in his hands, cutting off both the man's words and his breath.

"So it was *you*. To think you would even dare show yourself again."

The black irises which nearly filled Wen Fengjin's eyes changed to a brilliant red, and his fingers tightened their grip. The crisp *crack* of breaking bones echoed within the cavern.

When Wen Fengjin let go, the man collapsed bonelessly to the ground. Wen Fengjin, meanwhile, didn't even spare the body a passing glance before turning to walk back to the casket and saying to the dumbstruck Wang Xiaomie, "Xiaomie, give me my sword."

Wang Xiaomie stared blankly at the corpse of the formerly rude and frenzied man where it lay on the floor. It felt almost unreal, the way he'd come in like a lion and gone out like a lamb. It was like when your opponent was trash-talking you, and you suspected it was all cover for him to pull out some special attack and destroy you in an instant...only for him to suddenly get knocked down by a brick just as you were cowering in fear.

It was a goddamn hollow feeling. He almost wanted to pick up a brick and cosplay Wang Dachui!

And Wang Xiaomie wasn't the only one thinking this, either— Lei-jie and Xiao-Luo were also staring in wide-eyed shock, their jaws practically hitting the floor.

"...Shifu, didn't you say he had something up his sleeve?" Xiao-Luo's mouth twitched.

"...Apparently, what he was relying on was trash talk." It was too bad he'd run into an opponent who simply said *Fuck off, I don't wanna hear it*. Lei-jie buried her face in a hand.

"Wait, is that it? And what did he mean by all that? What medicine, what corpse stench? Why didn't I know about this?" Wang Xiaomie looked uncertainly at Wen Fengjin. He'd had the premonition that this man was about to say something which would overturn the world as he knew it, but Wen Fengjin had purposely stopped him from saying it.

Just as he was thinking this, the man on the ground suddenly moved!

Xiao-Luo yelled out the words Wang Xiaomie was thinking. "What the fuck! He came back to life!"

He watched in terror as the body began to twitch and, after a while, swayed back to a standing position like a zombie in the movies. The man's hands wrapped around his own neck, making crisp, bone-cracking noises, like he was realigning things in place.

Wen Fengjin tapped Wang Xiaomie's forehead, saying, "Come back to reality, Xiaomie, and hand me my Liaoyue Sword."

"Huh? Oh right!" Wang Xiaomie hurriedly pulled the Liaoyue Sword out from within the casket and handed it to Wen Fengjin, muttering a cowardly line unbefitting of a genuine zongzi. "How the heck did this guy get back up again?!"

"He cannot be killed by such methods alone. It seems the situation has become slightly complicated, so hide inside the casket for now. This man is insane. I'll answer your questions once I've dealt with him."

Wen Fengjin wore a kind expression, his eyes reflecting the image of Wang Xiaomie's somewhat nervous face. He did not spare even a sideways glance at that reanimated monster. As he gently pulled the Liaoyue Sword from its sheath, an excitement Wang Xiaomie couldn't understand flashed through his eyes. He quietly said, "It seems that Zhen Bei fellow wasn't lying after all—soon, I'll truly be able to revive you, Xiaomie."

Wang Xiaomie was taken aback by this: "What does that mean... What does truly reviving me mean?" *Haven't I already been turned into a jiangshi? Aren't I already back from the dead?*

But Wen Fengjin didn't answer him. He gripped his sword, the sheath falling to the floor. Strands of ink-black hair blew in the wind, emanating ice-cold killing intent amidst a sea of red as a powerful aura burst forth from him. It became hard to breathe, as if an invisible fist pounded against your chest, and a buzzing noise filled your head.

Even Wang Xiaomie felt this from where he stood behind Wen Fengjin, never mind the strange man facing him, who straight-up staggered and nearly fell to his knees. Behind him, Lei-jie and Xiao-Luo gripped their chests as they went down on their knees, pale-faced, blood dripping from their noses.

But the man only froze for a moment, then seemed to adjust to the pressure, as if he'd turned on invincibility mode, and even donned an aura just like Wen Fengjin!

"...You call me insane?" The man's clothes fluttered in the icy wind as he laughed lowly. His face and skin turned a bluish-gray, slow enough for the eye to track. His veins surfaced one after the other, pulsating on the surface of his skin—a terrifying and hideous sight. His eyes, once normal, became the same shade of red as Wen Fengjin's. "Wen Fengjin, tell me, which of us is the real madman? Have you forgotten the sin of murder which you once committed, as well as the fact that you slaughtered your master and sect?"

"Shut up."

Wen Fengjin held his sword in one hand, swinging it in an arc like the full moon as he suddenly attacked.

The man, unable to dodge in time, actually tried to catch it with the flat of both palms!

"Fuck! A perfect empty-handed blade catch?!"

"Shit! Do you think you're Guo Jing or something?!"

Two yells of shock sounded simultaneously, after which Wang Xiaomie and Xiao-Luo made distant eye contact with each other.

Comrade!

Huh? Xiao-Luo froze in momentary confusion. *Isn't he a thousand-year-old zongzi? How does he know this joke?*

But before he could figure this out, the intensity of the fight drew the gaze of everyone in the area.

That first attack had nearly chopped the man's arm right off—but in the next instant, the wound unexpectedly healed at an unprecedented speed. The man then reached for his own waist, and actually drew a soft sword.

Wen Fengjin became entangled in battle with him. Their swords flashed with dizzying light, the clear sound of clashing weapons echoing with an endless hum. To the eyes of an average mortal like Wang Xiaomie, it was practically a battle between immortals. The sheer array of moves and light effects on display left him dazzled. If he'd been the one to step up, he probably wouldn't have blocked a single strike.

Wen Fengjin's attacks, in particular, brought world-shaking killing intent with every move, while his opponent relied on his powerful healing ability, dodging when he could and simply tanking it when he couldn't.

The strange thing was that every wound Wen Fengjin gave him was more than enough to be fatal, but barely drew any blood. It was as if...

Wang Xiaomie put his hands over where the celestial sword Kaiming was hidden in his chest. It was as if he were just like Wen Fengjin...

Having been stabbed once again, the man ignored his injury and continued to hack at Wen Fengjin with no regard for his own condition, as if he wanted to trade a life for a life.

35
An
Unexpected Turn
of Events

"**Y**OU LOOK LIKE you're afraid I'll say something, haha. Let me guess what's going on." Amidst the storm of swordplay and murderous intent, the man dodged an attack meant to slice off his head, and viciously said, loud enough for everyone to hear, "It's because he's lost his memory, isn't it? Hahaha! I'm more than familiar with the power of that elixir! You're relying on blood and the medicine from all those years ago to nurture him, but you're simultaneously controlling him—otherwise, how could the man who once hated you so bitterly be so docile?"

Wang Xiaomie looked at Wen Fengjin with a stunned look on his face. *What's all this about control? Why would I hate him bitterly? Aren't we sect siblings who supported each other in our youth?*

But Wen Fengjin coldly continued his advance, showing no emotion at those words. In response, his opponent braced himself against the full-body agony, the soft sword in his hand dancing with increasing intensity and twisting itself around the Liaoyue Sword. If Wen Fengjin hadn't immediately knocked it away, it might even have twisted off his fingers!

"Hahaha! You really are a pitiful bastard, Wen Fengjin! It's too bad the medicine that should have gone to your most beloved shixiong was stolen by me! You want it back? Go ahead! Kill me and take my heart, then you'll have the other half of the medicine!

However...if I kill *you*, I'll finally be able to turn this inhuman body back to my original form. You need my heart in order to fully revive your shixiong, while I need what remains of your heart to turn myself back into a normal human being."

The combatants separated once more to stand on opposing sides of the area. Because both of them had quick-healing abilities, you could only tell by the tears in their clothing that the two had in fact injured each other at all; the man's clothes were shredded to tatters, while Wen Fengjin's right sleeve, as well as his side and shoulders, were now torn enough to reveal his skin.

"Fengjin!" Wang Xiaomie anxiously unsheathed the dagger Kaiming.

"Don't worry," Wen Fengjin said with a comforting smile, before turning to look at the stiff-faced man and saying, "You cannot defeat this venerable one, Yan Chun—you came here just to die!"

"Haha! You're overthinking it, Wen Fengjin. In the thousand years since you tricked me and served up the elixir to someone else on a silver platter, do you know how many hardships I had to endure before I found a way to survive with the power of that medicine? Do you see what sort of monster I became in the end—a monster that can be called neither man nor ghost? Tut tut... You've finally remembered my name." Yan Chun felt at his inhuman face with a cold smile. "You're being very cold to your former spouse, hm? Haven't you told your shixiong about the relationship we once had?"

Wang Xiaomie's eyes widened. "What does he mean by spouse?! Huh?"

He looked at the middle-aged man named Yan Chun—that square face, that expression stiff as a corpse, all those wrinkles that came with the passage of time, that sexy bit of stubble...

Wen Fengjin rapidly turned in an attempt to explain himself. "Shixiong, let me explain, I—"

But Wang Xiaomie didn't show any of the jealousy or indignation he'd expected, or even any disappointment, for that matter. Instead he said, in a voice filled with both disdain and a mix of hard-to-describe emotion: "Woooww, you've got some real strong tastes..."

Even the rubbernecking master-disciple pair on the sidelines reacted with the exact same look.

"Huhh."

"Ewww."

Wen Fengjin fell silent for a moment, then lifted his head to glare at Yan Chun with powerful, murderous intent blazing in his eyes. He yelled, in a tone that could be described as anger born from humiliation, *"This venerable one will kill you!"*

And so the two once more came to blows.

This time, Wen Fengjin's swordplay was even stronger than before, and the man quickly found himself unable to hold his own against it.

While the two were tangled inseparably in battle, Lei-jie and Xiao-Luo were having a whispered conversation with each other, to the effect of:

"Whoa! It's the Liaoyue Sword—the Liaoyue Sword—! Fuckin' shit! Kaiming! *Kaiming!* It's the immortal weapon Kaiming, fuckfuckfuck—!"

"Shifu, calm down! Don't just look at the swords, don't you see the cultivation level on that big zongzi? Stop looking, we're better off running!"

"No! If you're leaving, you're going alone, I've gotta get a feel of Kaiming's little face if it's the last thing I do~ Tch tch tch, ugh, I wanna feel it!"

"...Shifu, we're about to lose our lives... While they're locked in battle we should take the opportunity to—"

"You're right! While they're locked in battle, we should take the opportunity to quickly circle around to the back. The zongzi in that casket's got a clean air about him, I get the feeling he's nowhere near as messed up as the other two! Let's hurry and go cop a feel! If I die I'll effin' die on Kaiming's blade!"

Xiao-Luo was speechless. *If you want to say he looks easy to bully, then just say it straight...*

He wordlessly looked up at the sky. *Ai, when my shifu sees immortal weapons, there's seriously no helping her.*

On the other end, it seemed like things had come to a conclusion. Yan Chun fell to the floor with the Liaoyue Sword through his chest, a bit of red trickling from his mouth, his soft sword shattered as well. But the terrifying look with which he glared at Wen Fengjin—who gazed indifferently down at him from above—made it seem like he could neither feel pain nor the approach of death.

He reached out his hand as if trying to touch something, but because he was nailed to the ground, and the man above him had no intention of showing compassion, the hand fell fruitlessly back to the ground.

"Heh, heheheh. Wen Fengjin, when I was young, I acted on orders to search for the immortal elixir...yet you cheated me for your shixiong's sake. Giving me the authority to move into your home... There were so many people who admired you to the point of insanity, I thought I was special. I thought that disobeying orders to join your side was the best thing I could have done—I thought I'd succeeded.

"Yet you turned and gave the elixir I'd obtained to your shixiong... He'd gotten injured following you and could no longer cling to life.

When I learned the truth, I hated you more than anything in the world. Who could have known he'd go on to die all the same...?"

He vomited up blood, then broke into violent coughing. The heart was the greatest lifeline for these imbibers of the elixir of immortality. With such a grevious injury to his weak spot, his power was gone as well.

Wen Fengjin lowered his head.

"Such beautiful eyes, lofty, as though looking down upon insects." Yan Chun started to laugh, "But I don't want to be an insect. I want to be someone who can stand by your side the way your shixiong does... When he died back then, I was so happy to hear he'd given the elixir to you. He must have wanted to punish you—after all, not only did you imprison him, you even killed all those he most cared about.

"When I saw you lose all reason and begin to mutilate yourself, my heart was filled with both distress and joy! You, too, got to taste the pain of loving that which you could not obtain! You were even more lowly than I was before him!"

As the man roared with unbridled laughter, Wen Fengjin squatted down, grabbing the sword by the hilt and pulling it from his chest. A gasp emanated from Yan Chun's throat, but he continued using his now-distorted voice to tell of his thousand years of obsessive infatuation...

"...Later, you found that old man, as well as a method to preserve corpses. Then you continued, unchanging—every day, your gaze, your heart, your every emotion was focused on reviving your shixiong. But I heard...hahaha! I heard! That old man's words."

"I told you before—there is no way to refine a body without a soul into either a puppet or a jiangshi. It will rot, even when transformed into a walking corpse. There are things which can be done

if you wish only to preserve the body and prevent it from decaying, but the corpse-stabilizing beads and the pining tree can only maintain its surface state. The moment the body leaves their protection... Even if the immortal tree really can summon his soul back to the body and maintain it there, at best, he will wake but be unable to move. And at worst, the body—along with the corpse-stabilizing beads and the soul—will all dissolve to dust."

"How do I bring a corpse to life?"

"You need a particular kind of medicine."

"Tell me."

"Yes, milord..."

"It was your heart!" Yan Chun used the last of his strength to grip Wen Fengjin's wrist just as he was about to rip out his heart. His furious eyes seemed about to bulge out of his head as he continued, "To think it needed half your heart, doused in immortality elixir! And you actually believed him! You actually *gave* it to him, even! What's so great about him?! Why can you go to such lengths for him! *Why?!*

"Hahaha, but so what if you gave it to him? I still stole the other half of the medicine! And after I took it, I became half a dead man, a monster that's neither man or ghost! When I was mistaken for a corpse and buried, when I lost my old face, I swore—I wanted you and your shixiong to die! If you refuse to love me, then I won't allow anyone else to have you either! Why did you think I so readily agreed to help you achieve your aims? I searched for you all those years just to watch as you, Wen Fengjin, lose that which you love once more!"

Wen Fengjin furrowed his brow. But just as he was about to throw off Yan Chun's hand and take his heart for himself, Yan Chun suddenly yelled out in a certain direction, "What're you waiting for! Kill them! *Kill them!*"

Two loud noises came tearing through the air!

Wen Fengjin hurriedly turned with widened eyes, shouting through the hideous cacophony of Yan Chun's proud laughter. "Shixiong—"

A minute ago, Wang Xiaomie had been gripping Kaiming, Yan Chun's words reverberating in his mind. The story that spilled from his lips was entirely different from the one Wen Fengjin had told. *My head... it hurts.*

Wang Xiaomie put his hands over his head as he shook it with some force. The motion didn't matter, but in the process of doing it, he suddenly realized a pair of strangers had furtively snuck up behind him. He turned just in time for all three of them to make eye contact!

"What're you doing?!" Little Puppy Wang tightly gripped Kaiming as he pointed it at the grave robbers with trembling hands, wanting nothing more than to loudly yell, *Hubby, they're stealing our base!*

But Wen Fengjin was clearly extremely busy dealing with that Yan Chun person, so Little Puppy Wang quickly gathered his courage and started gesticulating with the dagger, doing his best to imitate hoodlums on TV in hopes of scaring them off. "Don't come any closer! Or else it's not gonna look good for you guys!"

With his pretty, delicate face, even a fully adorned set of ancient robes couldn't hide his childishness.

Xiao-Luo was silent, not just unintimidated, but on the verge of bursting into laughter.

Lei-jie was even worse—her eyes focused unwaveringly on that swaying dagger, nearly drooling as she did so. "Eheheh~ Little darling!

Come on and lemme cop a feeeel~" As she said this, she lifted a huge blade and came charging forward!

Wang Xiaomie was stunned. ....*Xiao-Wenzi! There's a pervert here! Yamete—!*

It was at this exact moment that two gunshots rang out from behind him. The explosive cracks were amplified by the cavernous space they were in, making them sound like bolts from above.

It was also at this same time that Wen Fengjin let out a shout of despair!

"Shixiong—"

He wailed as if he were weeping a river of bloody tears. Wang Xiaomie could never have imagined that the cold and supercilious Wen Fengjin, who gave off a sense of scorn even when smiling, was capable of making such a trembling, despairing sound...

Wang Xiaomie turned to look blankly back at him.

Someone pinched off this moment in time so that all sound faded away, leaving just the bullets in the air, and the look on Wen Fengjin's face.

Lei-jie, who was closest to him, paled slightly. She hurriedly rushed forward, raising her great blade to slash at Wang Xiaomie's forehead.

Pow!

"Pff!"

A bullet capable of splitting his head open embedded itself in the blade Lei-jie held in front of his forehead, while the other passed through his chest, leaving an uneven hole behind.

The impact of it caused him to stagger backward a couple steps before being caught by the person behind him.

The flow of time resumed. Red blood seemed to suddenly remember to react as it gushed audibly from the exit hole in his chest, pain impatiently following at its heels.

He collapsed into the arms of the person behind him. Someone loudly yelled something, but he couldn't hear clearly, his ears filled with constant noise.

In the moment that Wang Xiaomie closed his eyes, he felt as if someone had frenziedly pulled him into an embrace, and was letting out a heartrending roar.

"*No, Noooooo—! Don't—Shixiooonnngg—!*"

36

That
Bitter Time

THIS HAD BEEN a monstrous lie from the start. All the happy things he'd described were false...

Wang Xiaomie stood in a high place, stupefied yet indifferent gaze fixed upon the lifeless assassins below him...as well as a certain shidi of his, with whom he'd once been bound together by the system. The youth he'd raised as lovingly as a little brother was holding a bloody sword, looking panicked as he watched his shixiong emerge from behind the rockery with a stiff smile plastered on his face.

That was the year in which Wen Fengjin came of age, as well as the year in which he learned that the various shidi who'd mysteriously disappeared from the academy were spies planted by the emperor. It was also the year in which he belatedly came to recognize the unbearably foul things that had been hidden behind the happy laughter and cheerful voices he'd seen around the academy. Everyone was putting on an act. Everyone was hiding ulterior motives...

Wang Xiaomie watched as a panic-stricken Wen Fengjin tossed aside the sword and rushed behind the rocks to hug him and desperately attempt to explain himself. The men removing the bodies respectfully retreated into the shadows, their bearing both modest and well practiced; it was obvious that this was far from their first time dealing with corpses.

"Shixiong, I, I never wanted to kill them, it's that damn emperor who wants to kill *me*! Honest, I mean it... Don't ignore me... Shixiong."

Having only just come of age, he still looked like an inexperienced youth. Faced with the eagerness and panic in this youth's eyes, which were beginning to well up, Wang Xiaomie's heart couldn't help but melt. He hugged the murderer tightly as he gazed in terror at the bodies on the ground.

Like any average person who'd just discovered that a loved one had committed murder, he was both in disbelief and utterly terrified. While his mind was a total blank, a voice in his heart was firmly saying, *He's a good boy, he'd never do something like this*—groping for excuses and reasoning before shakily telling himself to simply forget it all.

"It's fine... I know they were assassins, don't be scared, I won't say anything."

We're in ancient times, and the kid was only acting in self-defense. He's already very scared... I need to help him, I need to protect him...

Even though Wang Xiaomie in the past was himself terrified, he still considered himself the older one. And he did his best to steady himself in an attempt to give the shivering youth in his arms some comfort through his body heat.

But all his mistakes began with this one act.

The Wang Xiaomie of the present watched impassively as his past self enveloped the youth in a hug. But the face buried in the crook of his neck as they embraced wasn't teary-eyed in the least, nor did it show a trace of panic. The only things he saw on that face were upturned lips, and the abyss-like iciness in those abnormal eyes.

But this was merely the beginning—Year 1328 of the Northern calendar.

Perhaps the lofty emperor was unsatisfied with killing Wen Fengjin's entire family, sending him to the academy, and telling the people there to torment him, for he then decided to take back that final bit of hypocritical benevolence and thoroughly wipe Wen Fengjin from the face of the earth.

Naturally, Wen Fengjin wasn't the kind of pitiful child who'd tolerate such things. He'd already assembled his father's old troops. This year, Wen Fengjin left the academy, stepped out into the jianghu, and established Anlou.

Separated for the first time, Wang Xiaomie and Wen Fengjin insisted on sending each other daily letters by pigeon. The system, meanwhile, urged Wang Xiaomie to hurry up and complete his mission, or it would kill him.

It was true that Wang Xiaomie was an average person. But he wasn't stupid, and he knew perfectly well that Wen Fengjin had left the mountain in order to exact bloody revenge. He had the lives of over two hundred of his family members weighing him down; he'd watched with his own eyes as his parents were beheaded as a child; when he entered the academy, countless so-called innocent children decided—at the academy director's suggestion—that bullying him would be fun, and performed terrible acts of cruelty as a result.

Why should *this* child be the only one who had to swallow his resentment and take all the ill-treatment with indifference? Just because he was going to exact revenge on a lot of people when he grew up?

Wen Fengjin's childhood was a hate-filled nightmare. He often had terrible dreams of returning to that blood-soaked past. So until he turned ten, Wang Xiaomie would always carry the emaciated, fierce-eyed child into his own room and coax him to sleep there. He even learned a nursery rhyme from the Northern Kingdom. Afterward, even when Wen Fengjin had grown up, Wang Xiaomie would occasionally hear him hum this tune to himself when he was resting...

So how could Wang Xiaomie not care for him? People's hearts were flesh and blood. From the moment he first began protecting that child, from the moment Wen Fengjin first looked at him with a gaze full of affection and trust, Wang Xiaomie could no longer be neutral.

Ever since that day—though he often tried to persuade Wen Fengjin not to kill people on the face of it, and always scolded him for being too ruthless—deep down, he knew that hatred burned within Wen Fengjin's heart, and that hatred had long since turned him into an Asura.

With the old troops his father, the prince regent, left behind, Wen Fengjin quickly expanded his influence, throwing the world into chaos in a few short years. He slaughtered both courtiers and common folk in the pursuit of his revenge, earning himself the title of Anlou Demon Lord.

But this ruthless reprisal was met with a grand counteroffensive. Though Wen Fengjin was born with great natural gifts, like his abnormal eyes, the nation and the jianghu had accumulated power of their own as well. Wang Xiaomie, idling his days away in the academy, overheard from the other disciples' conversations that Wen Fengjin had been successfully stabbed and wounded, and that his current whereabouts were unknown.

Anxious, he hurriedly left the academy.

The academy director had looked at him and said, "Mian Deng, you were once my most favored disciple, but the things you do now bring me nothing but disappointment. Do you truly wish to help that beast? If so, then don't ever return here! Once you pass through this gate, you will no longer be my disciple!"

"Xiansheng, he isn't a beast, he's a human being." Wang Xiaomie cast one last glance at the academy and the furious director, then determinedly made his exit.

As for how he found Wen Fengjin? Well, the system had been impatiently urging him to complete his mission for quite a long time now. One might even say it wanted nothing more than to stick wings on him and send him directly there.

With the system's guidance, Wang Xiaomie quickly found Wen Fengjin in a brothel. Practically green with jealousy, he stood before a gaggle of flirtatious women, thinking, *Fuck, I was so worried about you, and this whole time you were just fooling around at a brothel?!*

But when he showed them his token, and was taken to see Wen Fengjin with a bandaged chest in a place underneath the brothel, any anger he'd had disappeared in an instant. As the bitter scent of medicine filled the air around them, Wen Fengjin's eyes practically shone when he caught sight of Wang Xiaomie. But his joyful expression was quickly exchanged for one of anger. "What did you come here for, Shixiong?! Don't tell me you don't know it's dangerous here!"

"So you still remember that I'm your shixiong? Then why didn't you say a word to me after getting so badly injured?! Do you know how damn worried I've been about you?!"

"But I don't want you to be in danger!"

"And I don't want *you* to quietly die somewhere I don't know about, so you might as well just let me go with you! If we're going to die, then we can just die together and get it over with!"

Wen Fengjin and Wang Xiaomie stared at each other with faces flushed from anger.

After a long moment, Wen Fengjin's gaze softened, filling to the brim with a gentleness that gave Wang Xiaomie butterflies. "I won't let you die, Shixiong."

"Mmhm...I know!"

It probably started somewhere then. They clasped that young bud of emotion carefully to their breasts. The increasingly obvious way in which Wen Fengjin looked at him after he came of age was enough to make even the dense Wang Xiaomie understand how his shidi felt about him.

And just when Wang Xiaomie was pacing to and fro with his tiny, newly unfurled feelings cupped in his hands, hesitating over what to do...that emperor unexpectedly sent his own shadow guard to pursue and capture them. The stronghold at the brothel was discovered.

What happened afterward was in fact just as Wen Fengjin previously described. They ran as frantically as if they were being chased by jackals, Wen Fengjin's subordinates dying one after the other, until it was just the two of them left.

Every time they reached the end of their rope, the shadow guard would hold back, letting them escape with their lives. Perhaps that crass-minded emperor had ordered them to do so. By this point, no part of Wen Fengjin's body remained untouched. Broken bones and internal injuries made it difficult for him to breathe and half the flesh of his arm had been carved away to expose ghastly white bones. Even if it ever grew back, this arm would never be the same again. The wound on his belly had burst open from the strain of carrying Wang Xiaomie on his back, and those scant few layers of cloth could not staunch the blood pouring out like a waterspout...

Wang Xiaomie was even worse off than that. Aside from its map function, the shitty system did nothing but beep death threats at him every day. But then he defended Wen Fengjin from a shadow guard's hidden weapon, injuring his lungs and breaking both his legs in the process. The blow he took from that shadow guard destroyed his internal organs.

He wasn't going to make it.

At this point, even the system shut its mouth. It'd probably given up on him a long time ago.

Only Wen Fengjin kept evading those shadow guards' humiliating cat and mouse game, drenched in blood from head to toe as he carried him to the academy.

The ichor dripped from their bodies like rain, pattering across the stone steps as they climbed. The blinding sun burned them from above, air humid as the mountains brewed a real rainstorm. Wen Fengjin had long since reached his limit, and only the desire to save Wang Xiaomie was keeping him going.

With Wang Xiaomie on his back, the pair looked as miserable as walking corpses.

"...Shixiong, everything's going to be okay... We've almost reached the academy. It's fine if they don't let me in, as long as they can save you... Don't sleep, Shixiong...don't sleep...Fengjin is begging you..."

When he didn't hear a response, Wen Fengjin began to cry. Wen Fengjin, who'd wanted nothing but revenge, who'd never lowered his head, bent his back, or once admitted defeat despite the entire world wanting to oppress and torment and kill him, was now choking on tearful sobs. He said, "I'm begging you, please, don't sleep, Shixiong..."

Salty tears flowed down his blood-stained face, washing a single clean line.

Wang Xiaomie wanted to pat his head, but found himself unable to, so he decided to crack a joke, to tell him not to cry, that he hadn't shut his eyes. But blood poured out the moment he opened his mouth, staining Wen Fengjin's shoulder.

"Shixiong?!"

"Nn..."

After a long pause, the only response he was able to make was a single nasal sound. But this one sound was enough to become the single source of Wen Fengjin's strength. He climbed much faster than before, enduring the agony, as an ever-growing rain of blood wound up the long mountain stairway.

They were halfway up when the long-brewing mountain rain finally began to fall, about as welcome as frost upon snow or oil poured on flames. It was as if the heavens above truly didn't want them to live. Wang Xiaomie half narrowed his eyes under the beating of ice-cold droplets, his vision already starting to fade. He really couldn't take any more...

Wen Fengjin had to have noticed this. He wanted to take Wang Xiaomie off his back and hug him tight against his chest, but one of his arms was already whittled to the bone, the rainwater whitening what little flesh remained. He didn't dare stop. Right now, he was moving entirely on willpower alone; if he stopped, it was possible that he'd never get up again.

The pervasive, bone-chilling mountain rain soaked through them as Wen Fengjin, lips pursed, finally arrived at the academy on the peak.

"Shixiong, we're here! You'll be saved, don't be afraid, you'll be saved in no time!"

Wen Fengjin agitatedly placed him on the ground as he spoke, then staggered up to pound his fists against the main gate.

37
The Sin
of Avarice

IT WAS A YOUNG BOY who opened the gate. Upon seeing the pair, looking like storybook yaoguai who'd climbed out of the grave, he let out a scream of fright. Wen Fengjin grabbed him with one hand, splashing droplets of watery blood all over the boy's body. "Call the academy's doctor! My shixiong... Mian Deng-shixiong has been heavily injured..."

"Mian Deng-shixiong?!" The boy knew his academy's da-shixiong, and as frightened as he was, still snuck a glance at Wang Xiaomie on the ground, finally recognizing his face beneath all the wet hair and dried blood. "Oh! It really *is* Mian Deng-shixiong! You guys wait here, I'll go call someone right away!" He then ran inside in a flustered panic.

An exhausted Wen Fengjin sat down and leaned against the gate, using his one good arm to tug Wang Xiaomie into his bosom. The eaves of the entryway shielded them from the rain.

His fingers were ice-cold yet still moved gently as he brushed the long damp hair from Wang Xiaomie's face, then enveloped his head in an embrace, softly pressing a cheek to his temples.

"Everything will be better soon. Just hold on a little longer. Those people hate me, but they should still be able to extend their aid to you..."

...But what about you? How are you going to evade the shadow guards hidden nearby and get back down the mountain with your body like this? You're obviously planning to die on your own!

Wang Xiaomie struggled to grip Wen Fengjin's clothes, but lacked even the strength to open his eyes or speak. Wen Fengjin hugged him and said, "As long as Shixiong lives on, I'm willing to do anything..."

No! Wang Xiaomie minutely shook his head, shameful tears dripping from his eyes as his senses began to fade. Finally, and weakly, he closed his eyes.

But they were both wrong.

Neither of them received any aid from the academy that day. The boy did indeed call someone, but that person was the academy director, who gazed impassively at Wen Fengjin and his once-beloved disciple.

"I said before, once you leave through this gate, you are no longer my disciple!"

The open gate closed once more. Wen Fengjin began pounding and banging on the door like a madman, his fists leaving bloody prints with each blow.

"Save him! He's your shixiong, isn't he?! Save him, I'm begging you..." Wen Fengjin's pupils shrank as he stared at the nearly closed door. He fell hard to his knees... "Save him."

That arrogant head pressed down upon the mud-soaked stone tiles, and the door stopped closing. The director slowly quirked his lips upward as the boy and disciples behind him gazed upon his back with some concern. "Xiansheng, Shixiong is..."

"Hmph." The director raised a hand, turning around with a sneer. And the gate between them shut with a bang.

A freezing torrent of pouring rain, a body filled with pain and injury, a journey paved with humiliation, and a severed sliver of hope...

Wen Fengjin, head still lowered, dug his fingers into the stone path so hard that they left deep, bloody grooves. His face twisted into a manic smile. His odd black eyes filled with bloody veins.

Perhaps the last vestige of his humanity was thoroughly erased that day. What survived was a soul forced into distortion.

"I won't forgive you..." Wen Fengjin hugged Wang Xiaomie, looking at the gates with tilted head, and raised his lips into a wide smile as he said, "I'll never forgive you! Hehehe*hahaha*! Even in death, I will never forget all the humiliation I suffered today—I'll kill you all—all of you—*every last one of you!* I'll have you buried together with my shixiong, with me—"

His despair was so deep it seemed ready to take physical form. The irises that filled most of his long, narrow eyes were now a bloody scarlet as they stared so angrily at the gates that tears burst from their corners.

He enunciated one word at a time: "If I survive, I will slaughter your entire sect! I will never show kindness to anyone else ever again, I will make the entire Northern Kingdom taste my pain! *Aaaahh*—"

Wang Xiaomie watched from above as Wen Fengjin threw back his head and roared. His lips moved for a moment, but to no avail, as something hot flowed ceaselessly from his eyes...

These were his memories. This was all cruel reality.

Those years were far too painful to bear. Even with each other to lean on, what little body heat they could share did nothing to defend them from all the people who opposed them, or from the cold unfriendliness of the world.

Back then, Wang Xiaomie—living alone after being abandoned and forgotten by everyone around him—traveled to the ancient past, where he met Wen Fengjin, who was equally tormented by the entire world. The two tragic souls kissed each other's wounds and

gave each other warmth, but ultimately succumbed as their paths to survival and hope were cut off one by one.

The memory he was witnessing jumped ahead to when he woke in a room suffused with a bitter aroma.

Somehow, they'd both survived.

According to Wen Fengjin, they should have died that day. But perhaps they weren't fated to meet their ends just yet, for Wen Fengjin's subordinates—Mu Yi, Mu Er, Mu San, and the rest—broke through the shadow guards with them, and used the best available medicine to keep them alive.

He and Wen Fengjin had both been wounded to their very cores, but Wen Fengjin had abundant internal energy and a strong body, so he ultimately made it through after a long period of unconsciousness. Wang Xiaomie, on the other hand, was just a substandard weakling. Not only did it take almost a month for him to wake from his coma, but he was still slowly dying, even if they were using powerful medicines to keep him going for now.

The day he woke, Wen Fengjin silently placed a hand against his cheek. In that moment, Wang Xiaomie felt that Wen Fengjin had changed. His neck, head, and fingers were all swathed in bandages as he smiled at Wang Xiaomie and said, "Shixiong, I'll avenge you, okay...?"

Half a year later, Wen Fengjin carefully took Wang Xiaomie into his arms and once more carried him up the stone steps to the academy. But this time, they sat in a palanquin high above the masses and watched as the countless piteously wailing residents of the academy were killed by hanging.

That day, it was their turn to listen as the people of the academy mourned. The director, in particular, was treated to torture at Wen Fengjin's own hands before finally breathing his last.

A trembling Wang Xiaomie covered his ears and shut his eyes, not daring to look at those faces as they approached their deaths, or to hear their cries of despair.

Wen Fengjin, however, laughed heartily as he gazed upon this hell on earth with full appreciation.

It was in this moment that Wang Xiaomie's fear of Wen Fengjin was born.

He hated those people as well, but the majority of them were innocents. What wrongs had the ignorant children of the academy ever committed? He couldn't accept it.

Wen Fengjin quickly noticed his aversion and fear. He was no longer the person who once treated him with such gentle softness, but radical, savage, unreasonable, and heartless, exacting revenge with unbridled fervor. Countless innocents lost their lives in the cross fire.

And Wen Fengjin—whose eyes were blinded by hate and the need for slaughter—was already incapable of being reasoned with. Due to Wang Xiaomie's escape attempts and resistance, Wen Fengjin even had him imprisoned in his room.

Wang Xiaomie wouldn't be able to live for much longer. He was taking medicine daily, and the effects of that medicine were growing briefer the more he took it. When the physician was at a loss for what to do, it was probably because he knew there was no way to keep him alive any longer.

Then Wen Fengjin did *that* to him...

As he watched this portion of his memory play out, Wang Xiaomie turned red from head to toe, covering his face as he cursed through gritted teeth, "Shameless!"

Now, it seemed he no longer cared all that much about such things. But with the pair already arguing, and more at odds than they'd ever been before, Wen Fengjin's use of force served to thoroughly rupture their relationship.

He didn't know what happened after that. Because not long after, he was lying in bed, waiting for death.

Wang Xiaomie was momentarily dazed. He'd remembered meeting Yan Chun before, though at the time, Yan Chun had looked nothing like he did now. Back then, he had been absolutely gorgeous, the kind of glamorous that had a fierceness to it. He'd looked arrogantly down at the bedridden Wang Xiaomie and said some nonsense words, then been taken away by Wen Fengjin. But it was also after his arrival that Wen Fengjin found the elixir of immortality.

This was probably a common failing of the dying. Lying in bed for so long with nothing else to do, a bored Wang Xiaomie began revisiting everything he and Wen Fengjin had gone through together.

To be honest, it was then that he stopped hating Wen Fengjin. He was already going to die, so why take things to heart? The most important thing was that the system had determined he'd failed his mission and was going to have him obliterated.

So when Wen Fengjin fed him the elixir, he used his mouth to pass it back to Wen Fengjin.

When the look of despair crossed Wen Fengjin's face, Wang Xiaomie opened his mouth to explain. But the next instant, the system wiped his memories and ejected him from that world.

The scenery around him became a sea of darkness.

Floating in the air, Wang Xiaomie thought to himself, *I'm guessing that after I died, Wen Fengjin believed I gave him the elixir as a form of revenge. Ai...*

Stretching himself in midair, Wang Xiaomie shut his eyes and waited for his second death to happen. He'd already seen his life flash before his eyes, so it was probably about time to die.

After some time...Wang Xiaomie, still floating in the darkness, furrowed his brow.

Some more time passed. Wang Xiaomie couldn't stop himself from scratching his head.

Yet more time passed...

Wang Xiaomie thought: *Fuck! The reaper this time around is seriously bad at his job! I've been floating here practically half the day, why hasn't he shown up to take me?! Do I not deserve a name anymore, just because I revived once and turned into a jiangshi?! I'm leaving a bad review!*

Huh? Is it just me, or does something smell bitter? It's kind of a familiar scent, too.

Wang Xiaomie's consciousness faded away amidst this medicinal aroma.

"Tut-tut, that sure is some deep love you have," Zhen Bei said, as he gazed at the man firmly pinned to the pining tree with sharp weapons pierced through both hands. His eyes, with the way they drooped at the corners, were the perfect definition of what they called "peach blossom eyes." Even when he wore no particular expression at all, he still looked as if he were smiling warmly.

Around him, Lei-jie and Xiao-Luo were crumpled on the ground, the pools of blood beneath them making it difficult to guess if they were alive or dead. Meanwhile, there was nothing but a pile of tattered clothing in the spot where Yan Chun had been, along with a handful of something like white sand.

Wang Xiaomie was leaning against the side of the casket with his eyes shut tight and his lips coated in blood. His clothes had a bullet hole over the chest, through which you could see the broken skin and tissue reforming themselves.

"If that bitch hadn't gotten in the way just now, both my bullets would have pierced his body—the force of that could've instantly shattered his head and liquified his chest. But I shouldn't have expected any less from an undying monster. Even after losing so much blood to Yan Chun's attacks, you were still able to injure me badly."

Zhen Bei laughed as he spat out a blood clot that had risen from his chest cavity. One of his legs was broken, and the left side of his chest was caved in, but he was still alive, even managing to stand upright with his weapon for support.

The weapon in question was a strange one: Its body was a coppery-gold, its handle as long as a spear, and there was a palm-sized, horizontal copper cylinder on one end, making it look like a strangely proportioned, long-handled little hammer.

It was with this strange weapon that he'd returned to the mausoleum and, with that idiot Yan Chun's assistance, heavily injured these two sickening monsters.

"I know... Hah... I know the weak point of monsters like you is the heart—but I'm shocked that you'd stubbornly ignore my attacks just to feed him your blood and Yan Chun's heart. It's a good thing you're stupid, or else defeating you really would've been a challenge..." He swayed a couple times as he moved to balance on one leg, then used the long, thin weapon to poke at the chest of the man pinned to the pining tree. "Don't you agree, Wen Fengjin...?"

Wen Fengjin was nailed to the tree with a piece of wood hammered through each palm. His red crown was shattered, his red-and-black robes were a mess, and that winding length of long black hair had actually turned snow-white.

He raised his head slightly, snowy hair falling against his gradually greying cheeks. His scarlet eyes and the red mark on his forehead were still as brilliant as ever, but the huge gash on his throat, deep enough to reveal his windpipe, made it temporarily impossible for him to speak.

"Who ever heard of a human being devoid of greed? The world is filled with people like me, false and filthy and endlessly hurting others to satisfy ourselves." Zhen Bei looked down at him with narrowed eyes, his smile so wide it seemed almost to reach his ears, as he bent down to viciously say, "Don't worry, everything in this mausoleum of yours will belong to me.

"And as for you? You'll soon become dust, just like Yan Chun, and so will your shixiong!"

I'll Beat
Your Ass You
Sonuvabitch!

"A LL RIGHT, there's no need for too much trash talk. You can get going with your mind at *ease*!" Zhen Bei—who wasn't much better off himself—stumbled as he lifted his weapon and prepared to swing it down.

Wen Fengjin's hair was snowy white, the loss of too much lifeblood leaving his body too weak to break free of his bonds. All he could do was hang there from the tree.

In that moment, everything seemed to slow down...

Zhen Bei's face-breakingly wide smile, his raised copper-gold, long-handled hammer, and Wen Fengjin's bluish-gray skin, covered by silver hair. Bright red splattered across the ground, some still trickling, some not.

The ever-whirling wind blew sparks of peach blossom petals up into the air. Their intoxicating floral scent mixed with the raw sweetness of blood to create a nauseating odor.

Ah... Seeing him look so miserable really makes a guy happy~

Zhen Bei was already chuckling to himself when someone suddenly placed a hand on his shoulder!

"Young man, have you watched basketball before?"

When that faint voice made its way to Zhen Bei's ears, he froze in place, his smile stiffly plastered to his face. This was impossible!

How could there be anyone behind him right now? He'd already done away with everyone!

As he was turning his head, the voice behind him said:

"If you have, then you should know that there's a kind of situation called...a buzzer beater—!"

Pow! A fist ruthlessly struck Zhen Bei's conveniently turned face.

The strength behind the blow instantly warped Zhen Bei's face. The sound of cracking bones rang out clear as a bell. His body was sent flying through the air, hitting the ground with a dull *thump* and then rolling a good distance. His weapon clattered as it was kicked, flying into the abyss below the platform!

As Zhen Bei was tossed into the air, he got a clear look at the person who'd been behind him...

The blazing pining tree bloomed like a great flame. Countless peach blossoms wrapped around him in a powerful gust of wind, agitating that intricate, bright-red ancient-style wedding dress and that head of long raven-black hair.

It was Wang Xiaomie. It was the other tomb master, now fully awakened.

Wang Xiaomie let out a chuckle, slowly curling his fingers into a tight fist as he looked over at where Wen Fengjin was pinned to the tree, then turned his head and spat out a mouthful of someone else's blood.

Again. It's happened again—why does everyone always want us to die? Why can't they just let us live our lives in this mausoleum! Do we just not deserve it or something?!

Wang Xiaomie walked over to Zhen Bei with a dark look on his face, one foot planted on either side of his waist as he looked down on him from above.

After the battle with Wen Fengjin, Zhen Bei was completely spent of energy. His vision had gone blurry from the unexpected blow, his red-and-black face a terrible sight to see. His main weapon was now gone as well...

"Xiaomie...listen to me, it's not what it looks like... When I got here, Yan-xiansheng was already a pile of dust, and you were injured and being defended by Wen Fengjin—he already seemed really off then! And Lei-jie and Xiao-Luo were facing off against him..."

Zhen Bei frowned, a pained look on his face. He gazed seriously at Wang Xiaomie as he said, "Lei-jie told me to run then; she said that Wen Fengjin suddenly went berserk because you'd gotten injured, and was trying to kill them all! Lei-jie and Xiao-Luo risked their lives to get him pinned to that tree... I, I really had no choice, Xiaomie." Zhen Bei looked miserable, his eyes reddening at the corners, choking up slightly as he shook his head: "I'm seriously injured too, so that was the only thing I could do, or he'd kill all three of us once he recovered..."

Wang Xiaomie gazed impassively down at him.

It was at this point that Wen Fengjin behind him recovered enough to somewhat raise his head, staring fixedly at them with scarlet eyes. "Shi...xiong...kill...him..." *He's not a good person, don't trust him, Shixiong, he'll hurt you...*

Sadly, it was impossible for Wen Fengjin to get these words out through the terrible gash in his throat. All he managed was a few wispy gasps.

"See! He's already gone crazy! He wants to kill *everyone*!" Zhen Bei yelled fearfully.

Wen Fengjin pinned Zhen Bei with an angry stare as he struggled to free his wrists. He couldn't let anything happen to his shixiong.

He knew how horrifying a sight it must be to see him struggling with all his might, even at the risk of completely running his wrists through, his eyes bright scarlet, hoarse wheezes coming from his gaping mouth.

So when Wang Xiaomie frowned and said "I've recovered my memories," Wen Fengjin froze in the middle of his struggles, the light in his eyes slowly fading...

Shixiong has remembered everything? He remembers the parts I was trying so hard to hide from him... Shixiong won't ever trust me again, will he...?

It was like a flame being doused by unexpected rain. Wen Fengjin's entire body sagged with dejection.

Zhen Bei didn't know what was going on with these memories Wang Xiaomie said he'd recovered, but the sight of Wen Fengjin giving in to exhaustion filled him with wild joy. He raised his head to look at Wang Xiaomie again, his soft hair and innocent face giving off the impression of an injured stray dog.

"I'm not lying, Xiaomie, honest. I know you probably don't believe me. How about this? Since you're now awake, we can leave this place together, if you're not willing to kill him. We can just take Lei-jie and Xiao-Luo with us!"

If I can leave, then I can kill this disgusting monster any way I want once I've recovered!

Zhen Bei gazed pleadingly at Wang Xiaomie.

Wang Xiaomie sighed, still standing over him with one leg on either side of his body, then squatted down to grab Zhen Bei by the collar, pulled something out of his robe, and pressed it to the dumbfounded Zhen Bei's face. Expressionless, he said, "All people might be able to lie, but this thing can't. Is it hot, friend?"

Zhen Bei contorted with pain—the thing pressed against his face was the immortal weapon Kaiming!

"To tell the truth, Zhen Bei, you're a pretty good actor." Wang Xiaomie tucked the dagger back into his bosom. His smile did not reach his eyes as he raised a fist and struck with perfect aim at that false countenance!

"I'm gonna teach you what it means to be in awe today, you little shit!"

Pow! A left hook!

"This is what you bloody get for thinking you could beat up my little Wenzi!"

Pow! A right hook!

"How dare you fuckin' snipe at us from behind!"

Pow! Pow! Pow! A mixed combo of left and right hooks!

"And you even effin' dared play tricks with *me*! Your mom might not know what a beast in human skin you are, *but your daddy Kaiming sure does*! I'm gonna beat your ass, you sonuva bitch!"

Countless blows rained down so fast they were leaving afterimages. Ever seen your cat frantically slap someone? That's what this was.

By the time an exhausted and panting Wang Xiaomie finally staggered back up, Zhen Bei was lying like a corpse on the ground.

"Damn, his face was actually pretty sturdy," Wang Xiaomie grumbled to himself. He shook his numb and stinging hands, then caught his breath and walked over to a lifeless-eyed Wen Fengjin, reaching out to pull as hard as he could at the nails.

Once those two nails came loose, Wen Fengjin leaned back against the tree, his head still low.

"All right, that's enough of that." Wang Xiaomie patted his face. "You can stop with the dead look. It's because I recovered my memories that I've managed to confirm one thing."

Wen Fengjin raised his head, gazing at him with a look like his heart had already turned to ash.

Wang Xiaomie squatted in front of him, resting his chin on one hand as he placed the other on Wen Fengjin's cheek, then grinned in a way that let a single canine poke out from between his lips, eyes curving with his smile.

He said, "I confirmed that I've long since forgiven you. Whether its my past self a thousand years ago, or the me that's here right now, I've always really liked you, Xiao-Wenzi. We'll still be together in the future too, and this time, we'll never part again!"

In those times of pain, we embraced each other for warmth. And we'll do the same now, entangling ourselves with one another.

Beneath the pining tree, with peach blossoms flying around them, Wang Xiaomie opened his arms in their big wide sleeves and pulled Wen Fengjin into a tight hug, pink petals landing on their wedding clothes and atop their mixed black-and-white hair.

As Wen Fengjin leaned his head against Wang Xiaomie's shoulder, his eyes widened slightly, then closed again as he wrapped his wound-ridden arms around Wang Xiaomie in a death grip!

The two hugged in mutual silence for a while.

The wounds on Wen Fengjin's neck and arms began healing at a hundred times the speed of a normal human's.

Once they were done healing, Wang Xiaomie let go of him to rub at his own nose with some embarrassment. Wen Fengjin's eyes were filled with too many emotions. It almost gave Wang Xiaomie goosebumps when he looked at him.

"Don't look at my hair, Shixiong," Wen Fengjin suddenly said with a frown.

"It's fine, it's so pretty, it's not ugly at all!" *I have a thing for white hair, after all! This long silver hair is fine as hell, okay?!* Wang Xiaomie laughed foolishly as he picked up a lock of that hair, drooling as he thought, *Wow, silver hair~*

"As long as you like it." Wen Fengjin hugged him tight, rubbing his chin against the top of Wang Xiaomie's head. He'd gone through so much, with so many huge ups and downs, but in the end, he now knew his shixiong didn't hate him. He really was going to turn into a big, sticky beast at this point, wanting nothing more than to envelop Wang Xiaomie entirely with his body and stay motionlessly intimate for as long as he could.

And Wang Xiaomie patted his back, feeling nothing but tender affection for his poor, unfortunate, big gray wolf.

However...

The woman on the floor suddenly coughed, lifting her head to look at the pair and firmly stretching out a hand as she said, "*Cough...* Hey, uh...I think I can still...still be saved..."

Having said this, she then fainted once more.

Wang Xiaomie said, "I didn't think she was still alive..."

Wen Fengjin made a noise. "Mhm..."

"She sure is strong..."

"Mhm..."

The two were silent for a moment, when Wang Xiaomie suddenly leapt to his feet. "That's not a dang answer. Get to saving them already!"

Wang Xiaomie hurriedly dragged Wen Fengjin into helping up the woman and the youth who was with her. While he was at it, he also had the unfortunate Zhen Bei ruthlessly tied up like a dumpling with a rope from their backpacks.

He hadn't forgotten that when Zhen Bei sneak-attacked him, it was this woman who'd used her own weapon to block the bullet aimed for his head. If it weren't for that, he'd definitely be dead by now.

Wen Fengjin added, "When Zhen Bei arrived, this woman and her companion repelled him for a while together. That makes them our saviors! I never would've thought she'd actually help us, and also..." Wang Xiaomie wasn't stupid—he took out Kaiming and tried it against the woman. It wasn't hot.

"Save her!" he said, with prompt decisiveness.

Wen Fengjin was currently in a very good mood, or he wouldn't have cared if these people lived or died. As such, he reached out a finger and dabbed it against the still-wet blood on Wang Xiaomie's chest, then wiped the blood on the woman's and the youth's mouths.

W-was it really this easy? Wang Xiaomie stared wide-eyed at Wen Fengjin.

Wen Fengjin shortly explained, "Our blood carries the power of the immortal elixir. Just a small amount is enough to help an average mortal recover from wounds like these."

Indeed, their blood carried with it the bitter scent of medicine. Though, wasn't this just a little *too* good? The sight of himself and Wen Fengjin covered in blood gave Wang Xiaomie the painful urge to cut off all their clothes to preserve it.

As he watched the pair unconsciously lick the blood on their lips and start to recover from their wounds, Wang Xiaomie breathed a sigh of relief. "All right, we've saved them, and we've managed to survive. Next, we should do something about *him*..." Wang Xiaomie walked to the prone Zhen Bei and said, with some hesitation, "How do we deal with him?"

"Naturally, we can't let him leave this mausoleum alive." Wen Fengjin looked at Zhen Bei, his long and narrow eyes filled with disgust. He moved to immediately pierce the guy straight through the heart, only for Wang Xiaomie to pull him back.

"Wait, wait! Xiao-Wenzi, you promised me you wouldn't kill anyone anymore!" And that included even Zhen Bei.

Wen Fengjin frowned, but slowly pulled his hand back, looking very dissatisfied at not being able to personally stab his enemy to death. "Then tell me how else we're going to do this."

"Mn, I actually do have a plan..."

It wasn't that Wang Xiaomie was kind to a fault, but that he'd realized the reason things like a "system" and "plot-armored hero" had showed up a thousand years ago. It was likely because they considered Wen Fengjin to have committed the sin of murder far, far too many times.

Besides, they were in the modern era now. If they were going to go live on the surface, Wen Fengjin's current habit of killing anyone who crossed him was absolutely not gonna fly!

So Wang Xiaomie looked down at Zhen Bei, gave his stupid head a pat, and chuckled to himself. "It just so happens I need to be a good role model for my little Wenzi, so I might as well practice on you first! Don't worry, I'll make sure to arrange things nice and aboveboard for you!"

39
Activating Land Mode

A T THREE IN THE MORNING, a commonly seen white freight truck stopped in front of the police station of a certain small town. Its trailer opened as if something had kicked the doors open with great force, and a lumpy object was sent flying through the police station's front door.

This white freight truck then zoomed away, leaving only a trail of exhaust in its wake.

Wang Xiaomie sat in the back seat of the truck, leaning against Wen Fengjin's shoulder as he toyed with a Polaroid camera.

"The pictures and the weapons he brought with him were all tied up with his body; the weapons have his fingerprints on them too. Grave-robbing, murder, unlawful possession of a firearm... I think we'll be able to see him on the news in a day or two."

For a guy like Zhen Bei, who was so fond of hiding behind a mask of pretense, what better punishment was there than to expose him for all to see? Take away all avenues of escape, then finally let him find justice at the hands of a bullet? What people in his line of work feared most wasn't dying, but entering that place which was even more terrifying than death, unable to ever taste freedom again.

In the passenger seat, Xiao-Luo turned to look back at the cheerfully smiling Xiaomie, and felt a chill run down his spine.

He was extremely curious as to why a thousand-year-old zongzi in an underground mausoleum would know all these modern tricks, but ever since he and his shifu were rescued from the brink of death, just the sight of Wen Fengjin and Wang Xiaomie instilled Xiao-Luo with panic.

His shifu was the only person in the world who could have two big zongzi sitting right behind her and still be in a good enough mood to hum a tune while driving!

This strange four-man team had come to be two days ago. That day, they woke up within the mausoleum to discover that that weirdo Zhen Bei had already been beaten silly and tied into a mahua pretzel, and Yan Chun had turned into a pile of dust. Xiao-Luo and Lei-jie gaped in shock as they watched the two zongzi directing monsters to sweep the tomb like an average family cleaning up the aftermath of a robbery. The huge, terrible creatures now almost seemed like chibi mascots, obediently clearing rubble, fixing up broken mechanisms, and even knowing to sweep up the dirt they left behind as they walked.

That scene was *too* normal, *too* mundane. So when they saw Wen Fengjin frowning at a footprint on the reflectively shiny mausoleum floor, Lei-jie and Xiao-Luo felt an inexplicable sense of remorse.

Sorry...if we'd known the tomb master was germophobic, we would've brought shoe covers. Although...who the shit ever heard of a jiangshi who knows to clean the floor after chasing off grave robbers?!

But none of this was the important part. The important part was that that man called Wen Fengjin had already changed into a clean outfit, a red crown in his silver hair. His gaze was focused entirely on the floor they'd soiled with their footprints, not sparing them a moment's notice.

It was as if they were a pair of decorative vases. The kind that was covered in dust and not particularly liked by their owner, to boot.

Lei-jie and Xiao-Luo were silent. *In this moment, we suddenly feel like we've suffered an insult to our dignity as grave robbers, heh heh.*

They looked at the big monsters around them, then at Wen Fengjin—who still refused to pay any attention to them, and radiated strong "don't talk to me" vibes—and pitifully withdrew into a corner. *We don't dare ask anything, and we don't dare say anything either.*

When they'd finished giving themselves a full-body inspection and discovered to their surprise that their injuries were healed, the other master of the tomb appeared.

Wang Xiaomie's hair was still a little wet. Dressed in a different set of clean red wedding robes, he walked over to them with hot cups of water on a tray and a pleasantly surprised smile on his face.

"Oh good, you're finally awake! Thank you for helping me and my little Wenzi, have some hot water to drink, haha, we don't have any tea leaves down here so I could only steep some peach blossoms—go ahead, give it a try!"

They looked at Wang Xiaomie's soft face, that gentle smile, and those two cups of steaming hot water...

The tomb master made tea for us grave robbers?! And he's even smiling at us?!

Dearest disciple, have we walked onto the wrong set? Are we actually paying a visit to relatives?

Shifu, wake up! We don't have any relatives who can give their guests tea in thousand-year-old imperial painted porcelain cups!

Lei-jie and Xiao-Luo looked at the museum-worthy teacups they were holding, and for a moment, were silently conflicted over how exactly they were supposed to drink from them. *What do we do if our hands are shaking? What are we supposed to do when this whole thing feels so much like we're dreaming?*

Wang Xiaomie didn't understand why the pair had gone silent. "Go on, drink up. You've slept for a long time, so have some hot water and I'll get you something to eat."

They looked at Wang Xiaomie's harmless, pure, and jade-like eyes.

It was the more open-minded Lei-jie who took the first sip of tea, after which Xiao-Luo wordlessly followed her example. The warm liquid slid down their parched throats into their stomachs, warming their entire bodies, and helping them to relax.

Disciple, does this big zongzi actually seem pretty friendly to you too?

Uh-huh, he's much more human than Zhen Bei.

As they were thinking this, the bound Zhen Bei turned out to still be alive. He let out a quiet groan, as though he was about to wake.

Before Lei-jie and Xiao-Luo could react, the still-smiling Wang Xiaomie lifted the bothersome hem of his skirt, walked over to Zhen Bei, and quietly called out, "One, two!" And then he kicked him right in the skull!

Zhen Bei's eyes rolled back and he fainted.

Lei-jie and Xiao-Luo nearly spat out their tea.

Wang Xiaomie went on to step on Zhen Bei's head, then turned to Wen Fengjin to say, in the same tone, as if he were complaining to his husband about a chronically leaky pipe, "Fengjin, why did he wake up again? Don't you think his healing skills are too strong? It's so annoying~"

Wen Fengjin turned back while in the middle of directing Mu Yi and the others in repairing the mausoleum. The cold, detached look on his face instantly melted away to reveal an exasperated yet incredibly doting smile.

"He probably got blood in a transaction with Yan Chun, but it will lose its effect very soon. Also, Xiaomie, don't lift up your clothes like that, and remember to dry your hair."

He paused a moment, ultimately deciding to put his work aside for now. After taking a cloth from Mu Yi, he personally wrapped it around Wang Xiaomie's long hair to slowly soak up the water.

"'Kaaaaay~" Wang Xiaomie lazily drawled, then suddenly leaned back against him, laughing as he rubbed his wet hair against Wen Fengjin's chin.

Wen Fengjin lifted Wang Xiaomie's long hair with both hands, somewhat ticklishly narrowing his eyes, but his gaze and smiling face were indulgent to the max.

Lei-jie lowered her teacup. *I don't want to eat this dog food.*

Xiao-Luo finished off his tea before nodding emphatically.

It wasn't until Wang Xiao-Zongzi and Boss Wen were done with their PDA that Wang Xiaomie remembered to go back over to Lei-jie and her companion again. "Right, why did you decide to help us back then?" he asked Lei-jie.

Lei-jie was thrown off by this question. She toyed with her teacup for a long moment, mulling it over, before replying, "Because I'm not a resourceful person, so I prefer to follow my instincts when I do things. To put it better, I do as I please; to put it a worse way, I straight-up just don't use my IQ."

Xiao-Luo made a great show of nodding along with folded arms beside her, only to get a slap over the head from Lei-jie, who didn't even turn around to do so. *See that? My shifu's intuition is so good she's practically got a third eye!*

"I've got real good instincts that've saved my life a whole bunch of times. Back then, I chose to save you with no hesitation whatsoever because compared to Zhen Bei, who gave me a weird feeling from the start, I'd much rather help you guys."

Lei-jie flashed a smile in a display of mature frankness, as well as that tenacity particular to women, then raised her cup as she continued, "Looks like my instincts were right as always."

Wang Xiaomie laughed aloud at that. He really did like people like this, both strong and independent, who seemed like they would shrug off a heavy rain of gunfire and just keep on walking.

"Let's make a deal," Wang Xiaomie said, looking at Lei-jie.

He gave a quick summary of the details of this transaction: To put it simply, they wanted to go to the surface, but he and Wen Fengjin didn't have the required resident identity cards. Add to that the fact that they'd been away from society for far too long, and it would probably be difficult for them to even find a place to live.

But they had untold masses of gold and riches. So he wanted Lei-jie to solve his and Wen Fengjin's housing and identity problems, and as repayment, they'd let her pick anything she wanted in the mausoleum for herself. While they were at it, she could also help them sell some of the things in the mausoleum to exchange for the currency commonly used on the surface.

Lei-jie hesitantly lowered her head to ponder all this for a moment, while Wen Fengjin coldly watched the two humans. He certainly wasn't as docile and considerate to outsiders as he was with Wang Xiaomie. *If they dare to reject Xiaomie, I'll just have them stay here for eternity,* Boss Wen thought silently to himself.

"Oh yeah!" Just as everyone was hesitating, Wang Xiaomie suddenly remembered something and smacked a fist against his palm, surprising the other three into staring blankly at him for a moment. They watched as Wang Xiaomie ran over to a corner of the hall, picked up a very long stick, and came back to them.

That thing might have been rather *too* long, because when Wang Xiaomie walked with it, he gave off the impression of an overly energetic puppy that looked like it was going to fall head over heels at any moment. The object in his hands knocked a good many times against the ground before reaching the rest of the group.

Seeing Wang Xiaomie's lightly panting expression and its accompanying soft smile, Wen Fengjin endured until he could endure no more, then reached out to pinch his cheek with thumb and forefinger.

Honestly. He was far too cute.

When a confused Wang Xiaomie looked at him with head tilted, Wen Fengjin lowered his right hand, then lifted both hands together to pinch both delicate cheeks at once.

Sorry. Actually, I still want to pinch you a bit. Yes, I might need to keep going just a little longer.

The interaction was quickly interrupted, however, because Lei-jie—who moments before was giving the impression of a powerful and gifted woman—let out a loud yell, then threw herself at the dirty, knocked-about thing on the floor which Wang Xiaomie had just brought over. Her eyes were so bright they were all but shooting lasers!

Wang Xiaomie poked his head out from behind Wen Fengjin. With his cheeks being tugged out of shape, his words were garbled when he spoke: "Uh, you wook wike you weally wike Kaiming, bu' I can't give you Kaiming; this sword got 'witched in the fight wid Zhen Bei, so you can have id~ Heh heh, no need do tank me—Shao-Wenzi, shtob bulling my mouth, my saliva's dri—id's dribbing—*shlurp! Shlurp! Id's dribbing out!*"

Wang Xiaomie hurriedly sucked in his drool, then pushed Wen Fengjin's hands away. His pale, white face even had cartoon blush fingermarks left on it.

Wen Fengjin covered Wang Xiaomie's mouth with a hand, falling silent under Wang Xiaomie's questioning gaze. *I can't control my hands.*

This time nobody tried to interrupt Boss Wen, who'd become clingier than ever since their "eternal parting," who wanted more than ever before to hide his treasure to keep for himself.

I Want a Bed

LEI-JIE WAS GOING WILD with ecstasy over the sword in her arms.

"Fuck fuck *fuck!* The Liaoyue Sword—the frickin' Liaoyue Sword—*they gave it to me! Fuck fuck fuck! The Liaoyue Sword's fuckin' mine—!"*

Xiao-Luo looked at the deranged smile on his shifu's face and pressed a hand to his forehead. *Have you ever seen someone go crazy over winning five million yuan? My sword freak of a shifu is currently acting like she's won a hundred million.*

"The Liaoyue Swoooooorrrd! I'm dying here! Heart pills, heart pills! They gave it to me—the Liaoyue Sword—to *me! Awooo—*shit, you could work me like a horse an' I wouldn't care! *Hahahaha!"*

Lei-jie wasn't even listening to the words coming out of her own mouth as she hugged the sword, smiling a genuine gigawatt smile, so happy she was about to explode into rainbow fireworks. It was enough to make any bystander jealous.

Now that she had the Liaoyue Sword, Lei-jie was not only willing to help get them to the surface—she wouldn't even mind getting them into the sky.

Wen Fengjin and Wang Xiaomie had Mu Qi—a monster who could eat ores and spit out a liquid which would change into a sturdy wall after a while—fortify all the parts of the mausoleum that needed fortifying, then put Zhen Bei's mysterious weapon in storage.

As they were putting it away, Wen Fengjin commented that it was unique. It was with the help of this weapon that Zhen Bei was able to injure Mu Yi and the others and charge in here. That's right—he didn't quietly sneak back in. He'd charged in by force, nearly killing Mu Yi and the others in the process. It was a good thing Wen Fengjin managed to give them some blood in time.

Wang Xiaomie frowned, saying, "One man taking on ten monsters—from that perspective, Zhen Bei really does have some balls."

But Wen Fengjin only shook his head and showed him that copper-gold little hammer: odd, thin, long-handled and fist-sized.

Wen Fengjin waved the little hammer around and smashed it into one of Mu Liu's broken-off tentacles. It was clearly an ordinary blow, but the tentacle unexpectedly started to sizzle, as if it was getting eaten away by acid. On top of that, it very quickly turned to dust.

Wang Xiaomie was stunned. *You're telling me a thing that can turn physical attacks into magical attacks actually frickin' exists?! I didn't transmigrate into some bizarre fantasy world, did I?!*

"This isn't your average weapon, it's one that has genuinely been empowered with blessings. According to my memory, only that old man was ever able to do such a thing. I don't know how he got his hands on this, but it appears not all the humans on the surface are average people."

So Wen Fengjin said.

But this question was very quickly forgotten. After all, they had a far more important matter to deal with. After doing some basic tidying, Wen Fengjin had Mu San carry their casket up to the surface.

Lei-jie, who'd gone ahead to assist, was not the only one stunned by this development. Wang Xiaomie was terrified as well. "Wait, why are you carrying out this casket?! We don't have anywhere to put it! Plus it isn't as if we won't have beds once we're living on the surface."

"No." Wen Fengjin became unexpectedly stubborn about it. "Shixiong and I shared this coffin together for a thousand years. I cannot leave it."

Wang Xiaomie made a final attempt at arguing as he looked at the casket. "It isn't as if we're never coming back..."

Wen Fengjin shook his head: "...No, this casket is more than satisfactory."

Wang Xiaomie felt like Wen Fengjin was the perfect spokesperson for those people who insisted they couldn't sleep well in a different bed, always needing to bring along their favorite bed (casket) wherever they went.

This also meant he'd never be able to escape the fate of sleeping in a casket for the rest of his life. *How wonderful...* Tears immediately started falling from his eyes.

There was no helping it. Lei-jie had no option but to trade the Land Rover she'd driven over for a freight truck big enough to contain the huge two-person casket.

And thus Zhen Bei was sent where he needed to go to be put on trial. Afterward, they quickly left the place, traveling nonstop overnight over rural village paths in order to avoid any trouble, and managed to get to Lei-jie's house in B City after two rushed days.

Freight trucks were not rare in these mansion-filled suburbs. What with traffic and shopping not being particularly convenient here, people often bought large furniture and the like online.

Moreover, Lei-jie choosing this area as a place to live meant that their neighbors weren't exactly going to be common people—which meant in turn that no one would question the actions of other residents. This neighborhood's one ironclad rule was that no one stuck their nose in each other's business.

When the security guards saw Lei-jie's face, they quickly and silently opened the front gate. Lei-jie finally breathed a sigh of relief once she drove into her own villa. She then turned to the other three who'd sat through the two-day bumpy ride with her and said, "We're here, everyone out."

She was the first out of the car, opening the door to the house before nodding to Wang Xiaomie and Wen Fengjin behind her. "Don't worry, this place is totally safe. I'll give you guys this house to live in from now on; you'll have a lot of freedom here, and nobody will go around asking you questions, either. That casket of yours, though...

"If my eyes haven't deceived me, that thing's gotta be made from some special kind of wood, and is probably heavier than steel. There's no way for any of us to lift it. How about I call some guys to come over and help us carry it in?" she said tentatively.

Wen Fengjin shook his head: "No need." He then turned around and copied Xiao-Luo's actions to open the truck's back door, revealing the casket covered in a moisture-proof tarp.

Wang Xiaomie gazed at that casket and felt full with conviction, his mind filled entirely with: *I want a bed, I want a bed, I want a bed.*

Wen Fengjin raised his arms slightly and his robes began to rustle on their own. After a few seconds, a thundering howl sounded, as if his sleeves had shattered the very air!

He then slapped his hands against the casket, his palms sticking to the nearly one-ton object as if held there by some sort of magnetic force. The huge, heavy, two-person casket was lifted as easily as if it were made of air or bubbles!

That's right, he lifted it...

Wang Xiaomie swore with his perfectly good vision that he definitely saw something like the flash of inner energy in wuxia films when Wen Fengjin slapped that casket. Wen Fengjin lifted the thing as easily as if it were a plastic bag.

Seeing the three people who stood by the doorway, their jaws practically touching the ground, he frowned. "What are you standing around for? Out of the way, it's pretty heavy."

Sorry, but the way you're carrying it makes it look like it's not heavy at all!

They still hurried out of the way so Wen Fengjin could carry it in. Wang Xiaomie scurried in after him. After all, their "bed" was so heavy, it wouldn't do to go smashing the floor tiles with it.

Behind them, Xiao-Luo picked up his jaw and prodded his shifu's shoulder. "Shifu."

Lei-jie turned her head: "What?"

Xiao-Luo surreptitiously whispered, "Is this really alright, Shifu? Just look at the power he has—that's a thousand-year-old zongzi! What if one day, he stops being satisfied with this and sneaks out to drink someone's blood or eat their flesh, then turns other people into zongzi, then one person infects the next, and... then the whole city gets turned into jiangshi in the span of a single night?! We'd be condemned throughout all of history!"

Lei-jie was silent for a moment, then just as surreptitiously whispered, "Y'know, Xiao-Luo..."

Xiao-Luo hurried to bring his ear close to listen. "Go on, Shifu."

"Did you...watch *Train to Busan* behind my back?! I told you to watch fewer damn zombie flicks! Just look at this frickin' head of yours—ai—there's no saving you, you're beyond help."

Xiao-Luo was speechless. *It can't be that I'm overthinking things, it's gotta be that Shifu's been bought over by them. That's gotta be it! Weeehh.*

Cola,
Fried Chicken,
and Hamburgers!

"THIS IS A CELL PHONE. It lets you communicate with people over a thousand li away and can also order takeout—oh, takeout is when you have other people send you food—

"Here's some instruction manuals, they're all related to household electronics, umm—I bought a bunch of children's reading materials at the store earlier, I think you guys'll need these. Also a hundred-word picture-recognition book, since you probably don't understand modern Chinese characters.

"Here, we've got some clothes I bought with Xiao-Luo, and these are snacks, cans, and a bunch of other edibles.

"Oh right! There's also this card! This card was set up under my name, it's got five hundred thousand on it. Obviously, I know the Liaoyue Sword is worth far more than that, this sum isn't even worth the scratch marks on the sword, but you can use it for now. The password is—"

Lei-jie pointed out everything in the house, giving them a basic explanation of each and every object with a woman's patience. Xiao-Luo even demonstrated to Wen Fengjin how to use things like a TV, refrigerator, washing machine, and heater.

Wen Fengjin looked on with folded arms and a lidded gaze, appearing entirely uninterested in the proceedings.

Of course, if Xiaomie were the one doing the explaining, he'd probably be wrapping his arms around Xiaomie's waist, smiling as he looked at all these strange objects. But now? Our Boss Wen was watching as an increasingly sweaty Xiao-Luo, worrying that his explanations weren't clear enough, started gesticulating at the electronics with even more energy than before.

A long moment passed. Wen Fengjin made a single tutting noise.

Xiao-Luo thought: *Have I offended him? Eep! I bet that's it!*

Meanwhile, Wang Xiaomie nodded and said to Lei-jie, "Okay, I understand." He accepted the phone and card, effortlessly swiped open the phone under Lei-jie's astonished gaze, and looked over its downloaded apps with practiced familiarity.

Ooh! It's even got Honor of Kings *and* PUBG*!* If it weren't for the fact that Lei-jie was watching, Wang Xiaomie would be registering his own gaming account right now and happily playing a round!

"You sure are a fast learner," Lei-jie said with genuine admiration.

Wang Xiaomie, who was actually a modern-day person to begin with, gave her a smile. That softness and that tiny bit of pride momentarily led the thirty-something-year-old Lei-jie to forget that this was a big zongzi, and instilled her with the urge to put a hand on his head and pat it gently.

He seemed as soft as a small animal. Someone who looked like Wang Xiaomie should have given off the impression of a gentle, family-oriented kind of man when he smiled, but thanks to the foolish soul that dwelled within him, he looked like a puppy no matter what he did.

"You don't need to worry about us. Don't underestimate the intelligence of the ancients, we'll get used to things in no time at all." Wang Xiaomie purposely made it sound simpler than it was, and a brightly smiling Lei-jie nodded in response.

"All right, then you guys can rest in the villa today. As for those things over there," she said, pointing at a package on the floor, "I'll get these grave goods off your hands real soon, and once I've got the money, I'll put every last cent of it on your card."

Wang Xiaomie was thrown off by this. "Why?"

Lei-jie shrugged, saying, "You guys gave me the Liaoyue Sword. As far as I'm concerned, that's the greatest treasure of them all. I'm a swordsmith—the reason I'm always going underground is because I want to see all those weapons of myth and legend, and now I've not only seen one, I even got to keep it.

"It's not good to get too greedy, or I'll end up losing myself. My point is—whatever I do to repay you, you've earned it. So don't worry."

Lei-jie raised a hand and, after a moment's hesitation, patted Wang Xiaomie's shoulder. "To tell the truth, you genuinely don't feel like zongzi or monsters to me, so there's nothing wrong with us being friends. Oh right, and pass on my thanks to that guy—for the Liaoyue Sword, I mean."

"Okay." Wang Xiaomie nodded. Looking at Lei-jie's smile, he suddenly felt that there was still warmth in this world after all. There were always going to be good and bad people. Even in the deepest darkness, you'd always be able to find the sun.

Seeing his shifu motioning at him, Xiao-Luo, who'd pushed himself to the verge of tears after spending so long trying to explain things to Wen Fengjin, hurriedly ran out like someone had set fire to the seat of his pants.

Lei-jie picked up the bag of goods and waved at Wang Xiaomie. "We'll be going, then. If anything happens, you can call me with the cell phone, just press that button, and don't forget to keep your phone charged." Lei-jie gestured like she was making a phone call.

After getting an affirmation from Wang Xiaomie, she looked over at Wen Fengjin behind him. Lei-jie nodded respectfully at this thousand-year-old master of the mausoleum, who'd stunned her from the very start, then left with a practically fleeing Xiao-Luo.

The moment the front door closed, Wang Xiaomie's entire body relaxed from head to toe. Stars shone in his eyes as he sprang into Wen Fengjin's arms.

"*Yahoooo*—I have a phone hahaha, I have the *internet!* I'm gonna play all the games I couldn't before~ And look at all the cartoons and comics I missed! And then I'm gonna order lots and lots of milk tea and hamburgers and cola and fried chicken and crayfish, and, and! We have lots of money now! Let's go on a tour later! We'll visit all the places we haven't been before!"

A wild-with-joy Wang Xiaomie howled enthusiastically as he wrapped his legs around Wen Fengjin's waist. Wen Fengjin supported his bottom, gently smiling as he did so.

Wang Xiaomie suddenly looked down at Wen Fengjin to ask in a panic. "Oh right! Can I eat those things now?! I nearly forgot to ask."

It was as if a single affirmation, yes or no, from Wen Fengjin would extinguish the light from those doglike eyes, and his nonexistent puppy ears would pitifully droop.

"You can," said Wen Fengjin.

In that instant, the man who currently had his arms around his neck and legs around his waist began to all but shoot beams of light from his eyes. Those imaginary puppy ears immediately perked up, and if he had a tail, it would have been spinning like a propeller, sending him straight up into the sky.

Wang Xiaomie released his claws from Wen Fengjin's neck, hands on his hips and laughed with abandon. He turned once again into a little madman as he tapped away at his phone. "Milk tea fried chicken cola! Crayfish burgers maocai! Mwaahahaha—bark bark bark!"

Wen Fengjin, hands still on Wang Xiaomie's perfectly springy behind, laughed in spite of himself as he looked up at him. "Xiaomie, no dog noises."

"Bark bark bark."

"Heheheh..."

A sexily low, husky laugh came from Wen Fengjin's mouth. He was unable to suppress a smile as he walked slowly around the house with his little madman in his arms. Faced with buildings, transportation, and all sorts of weird electronics which were vastly different from what he was used to a thousand years ago, he suddenly felt much better adjusted than he'd been moments ago.

That's right—Wen Fengjin wasn't capable of adjusting to all this in an instant. Even Captain America was at a loss after sleeping for seventy years and arriving in the modern era, let alone someone who'd slept for a thousand.

On the way here, Wang Xiaomie had looked at all the heavy traffic outside, pointed at himself and Wen Fengjin, and said with a laugh, "We're practically a pair of artifacts someone unearthed."

You had to admit, this line was extremely fitting for their current situation.

That night, Wang Xiaomie had a simple bath with Wen Fengjin. They bathed together because he was worried Wen Fengjin wouldn't know how to use the hot water.

Gazing at the naked little zongzi, Wen Fengjin was just about to put his hands on him and do a little something, when he got a handful of purple body wash instead.

"...What is this."

Wang Xiaomie asked, "Hm? Didn't you want body wash? Were you looking for shampoo instead?"

Wen Fengjin was silent.

"Oh, I know!" Xiaomie, thinking he'd figured out what his darling hubby wanted, lay back in the large bathtub and had Wen Fengjin lean against him, then poured a big glob of shampoo on Wen Fengjin's head, saying, "Do you not know how to use shampoo? It's easy! I'll show you how to wash with it."

He pressed his hands down against Wen Fengjin's head and started scrubbing away with wild abandon. Boss Wen, sitting expressionlessly in the tub with his head buried in bubbles, sighed silently.

"Hey! Don't lower your head, it'll get in your eyes that way."

Just when Wang Xiaomie said this, Wen Fengjin felt a sharp sting in his left eye. He closed it against the irritation caused by the aromatic liquid. He raised his head as well, opening his right eye to watch as a startled Wang Xiaomie hurriedly pulled out a towel to wipe his left eye for him.

With the white foam wiped away, and warm steam rising into the air, Wang Xiaomie momentarily paused. That excessively feminine face carried with it a fierce and commanding presence. One of those long, narrow, and unusual-looking eyes was closed, while the other was looking right up at him. Despite having been hurt, his face was overflowing with tolerance.

Wang Xiaomie pursed his lips, then leaned down to plant a kiss on his mouth.

Aromatic shampoo emitted warm steam as their lips pressed together, soft plump flesh sticking and then parting again, carrying with them an exquisite elasticity...

Also...

They were sweet beyond imagination.

Wang Xiaomie covered his mouth and looked away, pink from the backs of his ears to their very tips, while Wen Fengjin quirked his lips into a smile as he closed his eyes and leaned against his lover's belly, entirely lowering his guard.

Honestly, I'm very satisfied with this. As long as I can be by his side, even this will bring me fulfillment... Although, Wen Fengjin thought, *I suppose I might be greedy.* His arm sent up a spray of droplets as it broke through the surface of the water to land gently on the edge of the tub.

Once they were done with their bath, Xiaomie dragged Boss Wen along to put on pajamas, then excitedly used his phone to order a whole bunch of food, covering the table in all his old favorite dishes.

Wen Fengjin frowned at all the overly strong scents tickling his nose. People had actually started paying attention to their health a long time ago, and Wen Fengjin tended to eat very bland foods. In fact, he didn't *need* to eat anything to begin with. As such, he tasted a small amount of the food on display and then put down his chopsticks.

Xiaomie was too immersed in the world of gourmet dining to notice. After eating his way through the whole meal like a whirlwind, he did some simple cleanup, then excitedly pulled out his phone, wanting to listen to music and play games and also look at cartoons and comics. At this moment, he wanted nothing more than to split himself into multiple copies so he could really enjoy himself to the fullest.

Time slowly passed. Engrossed in a game, Wang Xiaomie let out a scream of fright when someone suddenly covered his eyes. He turned to see a gloomy-looking Wen Fengjin. He was originally going to throw a fit at having his game interrupted, but the sight of Wen Fengjin's frosty countenance made him immediately turn coward. "Wh-what's wrong?"

"It's night." Boss Wen stared unblinkingly at him with a disapproving look on his face.

Xiaomie stared blankly back. It was only when he happened to glance out of the window that he realized the entire room was now dark, and also that he had no idea when he'd ended up lying in the casket. He then took a glance at the time. *Oh my god it's practically dawn!* His cell phone was also hot and on the verge of dying.

It was only then that Wang Xiaomie realized he'd been so engrossed in his video games that he'd completely neglected Wen Fengjin. He looked at the noticeably unhappy man and suddenly felt somewhat guilty. Coming to the surface for him was like returning to his own territory, and he'd recklessly gone about his merry way, completely forgetting that this really was Wen Fengjin's first time on the surface. Not just that, but he'd even ignored him in his excitement, leaving Wen Fengjin to sit in vain beside him for a very long time...

Speaking of which, Wen Fengjin didn't seem to have eaten much. He probably didn't care for that kind of flavor, huh... That thought made Wang Xiaomie feel even guiltier than before.

His head drooped, and he set the phone down on the ground outside the casket. Because there was a bed in the bedroom, they'd placed their casket in an unoccupied study with a balcony and French windows. "I'm sorry..." he said, pouting, gazing nervously up at Wen Fengjin as he carefully put on a cute act. "Are you mad at me?"

A sour-faced Wen Fengjin said nothing in response, his anger extremely obvious. When he looked at that so-called cell phone, his affection points dropped to absolute zero!

Wang Xiaomie slumped his head against Wen Fengjin's chest, nuzzling his big ol' skull against him with all his might. "I was wrong I was wrong I was wrong—"

Wen Fengjin kept a straight face as he nuzzled away, but it was less than a minute before he cracked a smile.

Wang Xiao-Zongzi immediately saw his chance, chuckling with his hair mussed into a bird's nest as he shamelessly continued nuzzling against Boss Wen's neck.

Finally, a hand pressed down against his little head, and an exasperated but amused Wen Fengjin knocked his fingers against it. "That's enough, it's time for bed."

"Okay!"

Wang Xiaomie lay down in the casket, wriggling into Wen Fengjin's arms like an insect and cheekily nesting against his medicinal-smelling chest.

After recovering his memories, the invisible barrier of understanding between them had instantly disappeared, and all their interactions were now as practiced as an old married couple.

The two fell asleep in each other's arms, and slept soundly all night through.

My Husband and I Sleep in a Coffin

I'll Send You Spiraling Into the Stratosphere

T HE NEXT DAY, Wang Xiaomie—who'd thought that everything would be better by now—immediately understood that he'd set his hopes too high. And it was because of this.

Wang Xiaomie: "Today we're learning how to integrate with modern society. The modern day isn't like the Northern Kingdom was back then, we're very calm and very peaceful now. We don't have to worry about anything bad happening—the worst that could happen would just be someone stepping on your foot when riding on crowded public transportation, or getting into an argument with a drunk on the street."

Wen Fengjin: ‾∧‾

Wang Xiaomie: "Of course, there's still the occasional unexpected event, like pickpockets stealing your phone or something, so promise me you won't go starting fights willy-nilly. Fengjin, one slap from you could probably send the tops of their skulls flying right off their heads and let passersby get a look at their brains."

Wen Fengjin: ‾∧‾

Wang Xiaomie: "Also, it's important that we keep our powers a secret! Er, and we should do good deeds too, okay? In order to prevent having any more system sort of things pop up, you absolutely can't kill anyone. Right—when someone bothers you, the correct way to handle it is to call the police."

Wen Fengjin: ‾ ∧ ‾

Wang Xiaomie finally reached the end of his patience and angrily flipped the table! "What are you making that face for...? What exactly are you trying to say?!"

Wen Fengjin thought for a moment and said, "No killing people, and if I come across trouble, I should call the police, understood."

Wang Xiaomie raised his eyebrows, unconvinced. "You really understand?"

"I do." Wen Fengjin nodded.

And so—

At the store, a man wearing a black jacket, jeans, and short boots, with long silver hair tied up in a ponytail, both hands stuck in his pockets, and a face so beautiful it was sharp enough to cut, frowned and pulled out his phone as he looked at the people around him who were screaming, wildly taking photos, and even asking him for his WeChat ID.

"Hello, police?"

Wang Xiaomie was stunned silent. *He sure is making waves.*

"Little Gege, are you cosplaying?! Little Gege, do you have WeChat—aaahh so hot!"

"Is your hair real?? Oh my frickin' god, that hair is killing me, it's so sexy!"

"Little Gege, where are you from, what are you and that person with you cosplaying? *Whooaaa! They're actually holding hands!*"

Wen Fengjin had frowned unhappily, made to attack, then remembered Wang Xiaomie's words and stopped himself. But just when he took Wang Xiaomie's hand and started to leave, the crowd exploded with yet another chorus of screams.

Wang Xiaomie had nothing to say to that. These ignorant onlookers simply assumed they were members of some group or other—but gosh these group members' looks were just way too heckin' high-class!

A few girls fixed frenzied stares on Wen Fengjin's face and hair, drooling as they did. A guy with white hair and black clothes was seriously super stylish! And the instant Wen Fengjin and Wang Xiaomie held hands, the fujo emotion of "I'll pay the ten bucks to get you married" began burning in a violent conflagration.

The crowd happily and excitedly snapped photos without the slightest ill will, following them everywhere they went, to the point that random bystanders saw what looked like superstars doing some sort of show and started tagging along to make recordings and join in the fun.

Seeing that the commotion behind them was only continuing to grow, Wang Xiaomie immediately abandoned his shopping plans, making quite the detour before he and Wen Fengjin finally managed to shake off their tagalongs.

But there were still people on the road who'd stare at them astonishment, turning their heads at 200 percent speed to try to sneak pictures. If it weren't for the ugly look on Wen Fengjin's face, which suggested he might rip the top off someone's skull at any moment, it would probably have turned into a repeat of the earlier incident.

After they got home, a clearly displeased Wen Fengjin asked, "Why did they attack me?"

Wang Xiaomie couldn't help laughing at the look on Boss Wen's face as he replied, "Haha, they weren't attacking you, they just thought you were super attractive and stylish, and wanted to get to know you. Taking pictures and asking for your WeChat ID are ways of expressing that they like you. Are you satisfied? If you were an average guy, you'd never get this sort of treatment." If he could have gotten girls to block his way and ask for his number back in college, that would've been enough to give him bragging rights for a year.

But their very first shopping trip ending in failure also made Wang Xiaomie understand one truth. Even with a change of clothes, they attracted far too much attention.

Even if they could hide their faces behind sunglasses... no, forget it. Wen Fengjin was the kind of guy who could still look aloof and ascetic when wearing a jacket and black pants. Adding sunglasses on top of that would just make him even more—*ugh!*

And so that night, Wang Xiaomie went up to Wen Fengjin with a pair of scissors in hand. "Let's cut our hair short!"

This plan was a perfectly good one in Wang Xiaomie's head, but it was met with visceral rejection on Wen Fengjin's part. He stood up and stared at the scissors, frowning so hard a deep crease appeared in the middle of his forehead. "Our bodies and hair are received from our parents. To cut one's hair is akin to cutting off one's head. I won't cut mine, nor will I allow you to cut yours."

Wang Xiaomie fell silent. Never before this moment had he ever been so deeply aware that Wen Fengjin came from an ancient time. In those times, cutting your hair was seen as an extremely humiliating thing, to be refused even on pain of death.

"Unless I die, I will not allow anyone to cut your hair, including you." Those deep, dark irises filled his long, narrow eyes. His gaze burned with anger as he looked over and gripped Wang Xiaomie's scissors with great force.

Exasperated, Wang Xiaomie had no choice but to let Wen Fengjin take the scissors from him before getting pulled into a tight hug by this occasionally too stubborn man, those large bony hands sliding through Wang Xiaomie's long inky hair. Wen Fengjin kissed the top of his head.

"It's perfectly common to cut your hair, you saw how all the men on the street had short hair..." Wang Xiaomie grumbled.

"That isn't my way of thinking, and none of them are people I care about." Wen Fengjin then repeated, as if in warning, "Don't cut your hair, and don't allow anyone else to touch your hair. Or I'll have no qualms about doing something to them."

Wang Xiaomie's mouth twitched. He was a little angry, but he also felt a little bit of unspeakable happiness, probably because the other man cared so much for him.

What am I being so girly for? Wang Xiao-Zongzi thought to himself in disdain. And yet, he still couldn't resist shoving his chilly nose against the man's neck and sniffing the bitter aroma of his body.

Wen Fengjin frowned, massaging that head of long hair. "Do you understand me?"

"I heard you!" Wang Xiaomie complained. "You're so pedantic!"

The accused said nothing in response, emitting a chilly pressure that nearly froze the nearby vase.

At this point, their first expedition outside could be considered a definite failure. They spent the next two days at home studying the Chinese alphabet and pinyin, as well as things like traffic regulations, various uses for currency, et cetera.

It was then that Lei-jie conveniently called to ask how they were settling in, as well as to inform them that one of the items had been sold, and the money would arrive in their account in the afternoon.

To celebrate, Wang Xiaomie decided to take Wen Fengjin to the most highly rated restaurant he could find on his phone for a meal.

Before doing so, Wang Xiaomie even wrote down every possible potential event to watch out for—as well as some necessary phone numbers—in a tiny palm-sized notebook, and had Wen Fengjin keep it on his person.

With all preparations complete, he and Wen Fengjin went out again, this time with face masks on.

However...

Wang Xiaomie looked back at the men and women once again following them and taking photos. Most likely, they'd been mistaken for superstars or famous cosplayers again. But given Wen Fengjin's aggressive, extraordinarily unique looks and that long silver ponytail, it really was hard for him to blend in with the average shoppers on the street.

Luckily, their destination this time was a restaurant and not a shopping center, so they managed to avoid a lot of trouble by leaving their entourage behind to disperse once they entered the restaurant.

Aside from the seats by the window on the first floor, all the tables in this restaurant were private rooms. The reception side of things went pretty well too—even his and Wen Fengjin's weird long-haired attire provoked no unusual reactions from a single member of the waitstaff.

A young woman in the restaurant's uniform quickly recovered from a moment of dazedness to politely ask, "Welcome, may I ask how many of you there are? Do you have a reservation?"

"We do." Wang Xiaomie pulled out his phone and showed the waitress their order form.

After looking over it, she led them with great hospitality to a room upstairs, where they quickly ordered their dishes. After the smiling waitress left with the menus, Wang Xiaomie finally tugged the face mask off his mouth with a gasp and sagged into his chair.

Wen Fengjin took his mask off as well. Though he didn't say anything, the look on his face improved quite a bit.

"Everyone online says the food at this place is light on flavor but the ingredients are extremely fresh, plus their veggie meatball soup is extremely delicious, and their perch is good too!"

"As long as you like it."

Ever since the incident with Yan Chun, Wang Xiaomie's body had become just as human as Wen Fengjin's. There was currently even a bit of sweat on the tip of his nose from the heat. Upon seeing it, Wen Fengjin used a finger to gently wipe off those droplets. "Are you warm?"

"Uh-huh, I was a little bit at first—I'm wearing long hair in weather like this, after all." Wang Xiaomie wiped a hand across his forehead, then looked up. "I'll cool off soon enough though, this room's got air conditioning. There's sweat all over my face and hands—I'm gonna go wash up in the restroom, will you come too?"

Wen Fengjin shook his head.

And so Wang Xiaomie stood up and went to the restroom on his own, rinsing his hands and washing his face with chilly water. When he was pulling paper from the dispenser on the wall, someone gave him a pat from behind.

Wang Xiaomie squinted slightly in an attempt to keep water from getting into his eyes as he looked behind him, but his vision was blurry, and all he saw was the figure of a man motioning at him and saying in an apologetic tone of voice, "My bad, my bad, I saw you had long hair and thought a girl wandered into the wrong restroom, haha, sorry, man."

"Oh, sure, don't worry about it." Wang Xiaomie wiped his face. A man with hair down to his legs was certainly a rare sight, so the mistake was perfectly natural; he paid it no mind and continued pulling paper to wipe his face with.

Upon returning to the room, he lazily sat by Wen Fengjin's side. One of the dishes they'd ordered was served, but just when Wang Xiaomie picked up his chopsticks to serve himself, Wen Fengjin suddenly pinched at the clothing on his shoulder and asked with a frown, "Who did you meet just now?"

"What?" Wang Xiaomie turned his head, his voice muffled by the fried shrimp whose tail was sticking out of his mouth, wagging up and down as he spoke. This looked so silly that Wen Fengjin let go of his clothes, then brushed at that patch with lidded eyes, as if flicking off some dust. "It's nothing, we can discuss it after dinner."

A clueless Wang Xiaomie proceeded to sweep every dish into his belly, his mouth working ceaselessly, while also making sure to add plenty to Wen Fengjin's bowl.

Once they were done, Wen Fengjin finally poured Wang Xiaomie a cup of tea and said, "Someone's trying to track you."

Wang Xiaomie was taken aback. "Huh? Track me? Why?"

"I'm not sure myself, but he's no normal person, despite being easy to shake off." Wen Fengjin sipped his tea, saying, "He probably sensed something different about you, and wanted to try confirming it."

Wang Xiaomie's eyes widened. "Don't tell me it's one of those, like, spirit hunters? Did he discover I'm actually a big zongzi?!"

"No, there's no such thing as spirit hunters." Wen Fengjin laughed. "They're all just a bunch of artisans with interesting skills. I've already broken the thing he left on you. When we leave again tonight, he's sure to follow us."

Wang Xiaomie was even more frightened now. "Are they all this tough?"

Wen Fengjin quirked his lips. "They just have a few screws loose, is all."

Wang Xiaomie hadn't expected his identity to be discovered so quickly. As a result, he found himself unable to sit still, so nervous that he was twisting his arms together. The character for "panic" was practically written right on his forehead. He looked like a cat fluffed up with fear, wanting nothing more than to nestle into Wen Fengjin's arms.

He stayed like this, dripping with cold sweat until nightfall, at which point he left the restaurant with Wen Fengjin's hand gripped in his, head turning every which way like an owl as he checked to make sure no one was following them.

Wen Fengjin smiled to himself at this frightened behavior, but didn't say anything.

It wasn't until he walked into a small alley and turned around that he finally patted Wang Xiaomie on the head. "All right, he should be arriving now."

"Wh-what?" Wang Xiaomie stared nervously at the alley entrance.

Right when he spoke, a backlit figure slowly stepped into the alley. Wang Xiaomie realized it was the man who'd patted him in the restroom.

The man was holding something in his hands. He smiled at them, then suddenly started to laugh. "Hmhm. The two of you have such an abnormal scent about you, it was easy to guess you weren't ordinary people. I'm a genuine disciple of the orthodox school—you should be giving up and surrendering just at the sight of me!"

The sheltered Wang Xiaomie trembled in fear, while Boss Wen sneered aloud.

The man turned red at the sound of this clearly mocking laugh, revealing the small black iron bar in his hand and flourishing it in a series of swishing moves.

"Hah, White Crane Lightning Wings!

"Hah, Black Tiger Scooping Heart!

"Hah, Great Roc Unfurling Wings!"

He then even did a flashy pose, after which came a loud yell of "Wha-taa! Die!" After saying this, he came charging in with an ululating battle cry.

Wen Fengjin pushed Wang Xiaomie out of the way, then narrowed his eyes as he lifted a leg.

Swish!

With a single sweep of that long leg, the man charging at them like a wrecking ball let out a cry of pain. He spun through the air like a propeller and crashed headfirst into an alley trash can.

Wang Xiaomie was stunned silent.

Wen Fengjin thought: *Heh, all flash, no substance.*

43

You're Going to Die

HIS ONE KICK delivered, Boss Wen patted Wang Xiaomie's head and very gently said: "See, that's all you need to do."

Wang Xiaomie stared silently at the man, who was now just a pair of struggling legs sticking out of the trash can. The funniest part of the scene was that the trash can had "No Recycling" written on the outside. The man had thought he was a diamond-tier player, but it turned out he was merely a bronze.

And here I was trembling with fear all night, Wang Xiaomie thought as he put a hand over his face with a tired sigh. "How do we deal with him? He's figured out our identities."

"It doesn't matter. He's a normal human being, and doesn't actually know what we really are; the things he pulled out were also nothing but the tricks of an amateur." Wen Fengjin was smiling, but his gaze was cold and indifferent as it swept over the man, who was still making muffled yells as he recklessly struggled. "If even an unskilled dabbler like this has the nerve to block our path, then it seems that the world truly has become a lot more peaceful these days."

"So we just leave him here?" Wang Xiaomie didn't know how to feel as he watched those wildly kicking legs droop as if breathing a sigh of relief. You had to admit, the guy had zeal.

The two returned home and finished washing up, after which Wang Xiaomie placed a thick mattress and pillows into the casket, then patted his tummy as he lazily laid back inside, yelling "I'm so *satisfiiieed~*"

A low chuckle sounded from above his head. Wen Fengjin was holding a book and leaning over the side of the casket by Wang Xiaomie's head, long silver hair falling in an arc as he looked down at him.

Wang Xiaomie reached out to grab that hair and pull it off its owner's shoulder, then brought it close to sniff it like the little hoodlum he was. "Heheh, what a beautiful girl you are. Come join me for some beddy-bye!"

"Oh, you..." Wen Fengjin, not at all bothered at being called a girl, was perfectly happy to spoil him. He knocked Wang Xiaomie on the forehead, then put down his book and climbed into the casket.

Little Puppy Wang very mischievously rolled onto Wen Fengjin and used the boss's chest as a pillow, casually shifting his position before placing his hands on his nice full belly and letting out a burp. Wen Fengjin softly kissed the top of his head, hugging his puppy a little tighter.

"Oh right, what was up with that guy today?" Wang Xiaomie rested his chin on Wen Fengjin's chest. "Did he have something to do with those 'craftsmen' you mentioned earlier?"

"Mmhm." Wen Fengjin idly brushed his hands through Wang Xiaomie's hair as he simply explained, "I once met a group of people in the Northern Kingdom who were talented at the creation of tools. They could use mysterious methods and ingredients to make all sorts of things that seemed to defy logic. But there weren't many of them, and they put great stock in natural talent. Also...most tool-crafters of their kind have eccentric dispositions, and are slow in the head."

At those words, Wang Xiaomie thought of the man they'd met that night. *What d'you mean "slow"? Wasn't that obviously more like blockheaded?!*

With Wen Fengjin's explanation complete, Wang Xiaomie started feeling a little sleepy. Perhaps because the man had left just such a strange first impression, he didn't give it much thought, quickly falling asleep in Wen Fengjin's arms.

But soon enough, Wang Xiaomie would realize that he'd been too quick to put it behind him. Just because he'd forgotten the other party didn't mean that they'd forget him in turn.

The next few days, he and Wen Fengjin saw that guy practically every time they went outside, stealthily sneaking after them, wearing a big face mask and dark shades even in the scorching weather. He was so thoroughly wrapped up that he seemed even more like a zongzi than they were. It was enough to make you wonder if he was at risk of heatstroke.

Wang Xiaomie wordlessly turned to look back at the guy, who was currently standing barely ten feet away from him, holding a phone and pretending to be a random passerby. Wen Fengjin, meanwhile, was already looking around with a displeased look on his face, probably searching for a trash can.

"Forget it, it's fine." Wang Xiaomie quietly pulled him back. "There's people all over on the street, and security cameras too. He can't do anything to us, so if he wants to follow us, let him do it. It's not as if he can get into the villa."

Wen Fengjin pressed a hand against the twitching vein on his forehead, but ignored the man with an impassive look on his face, instead only giving him another dangerous warning glare as they were about to reach the villa.

Their completely wrapped-up stalker shrank back for a second, then quickly turned tail and ran.

They'd assumed it would end at that, but afterward, it was like the guy lived right by the entrance of their neighborhood. They'd run into him whenever they went out, and he'd trail them every time, and each time, Wen Fengjin would send him flying into a trash can with a sweep of his leg. The man was getting to be on very good terms with those trash cans...but he persisted in showing up the next day without fail.

I can almost see a halo bearing the word "perseverance" over his head, Wang Xiaomie thought. *I'm almost moved to tears here. Amen.* If you wanted an example of the idiom "not turning back until one hits the south wall," this would be it.

Even Wen Fengjin was getting angered by this roach-like behavior. He tried a good many times to deal with him for good, only for Wang Xiaomie to stop him.

He just wanted to live a normal life with Wen Fengjin, doing the things any married couple would do, like eating together and shopping together and going to the supermarket to buy snacks together, maybe taking a stroll after a filling meal, even touring the country if they had the time, then returning to the mausoleum once they'd had enough fun.

Besides, they had literally all the time in the world in which to walk together hand in hand. They'd spent their past lives buried in helplessness and despair. This time around, he wanted to live the simplest kind of life together with Wen Fengjin—not as a legendary master of a mausoleum and an undying immortal, but as a good and ordinary person.

Wang Xiaomie was not a fool. He'd been living on his own since he was a child, so beneath his happy-go-lucky exterior was a powerful and tenacious heart. He sensed no ill intent from the man, and Wang Xiaomie knew Wen Fengjin must understand that as well, which was why he still hadn't killed the guy despite how much he hated being stalked like this.

The problem lay in that he still didn't know why the man insisted on following him and Wen Fengjin. Maybe it was just curiosity?

And then one day, as he and Wen Fengjin were coming home from the supermarket, a light rain began falling from the sky. Wang Xiaomie had seen the weather forecast and had brought two umbrellas with him, but as they were heading home with all their bags, he suddenly thought of something.

That big guy was probably still following them, huh.

He immediately turned. As expected, there was a drowned rat of a man pitifully tailing them. Seeing Wang Xiaomie look this way, he hurriedly pulled out his cell phone, pretending he was a random passerby looking up directions.

...Bro, you've used this method a billion times by now, you know that?!

As Wang Xiaomie thought this, he saw the guy suddenly start to panic, shaking his phone a few times and then trying to wipe it with his hand. It was raining hard, and his phone was an old one; Wang Xiaomie had previously seen that it was covered in marks and scratches.

But even after fiddling with it for so long, Cell Phone-kun's screen stayed black; it closed its eyes, and finally left the land of the living. This time the guy forgot his worries about Wang Xiaomie recognizing him, shoulders drooping dejectedly as he held the martyred Cell Phone-kun in his hands. An all-pervasive torrent of rain crashed over his head, and thunder roared through the air.

Wang Xiaomie thought: *Why does this seem kinda weirdly pitiful?!*

Wen Fengjin cast an indifferent sideways glance in the man's direction, then raised his umbrella with a frown as he looked at the wet tips of Wang Xiaomie's shoes. "We should go home."

"I know, just wait one moment!"

Wang Xiaomie ran over with umbrella in hand.

The man's eyes—the only visible part of him—said that he was at a complete loss as to what to do. He made an evasive movement, as if about to flee, only for Wang Xiaomie to grab hold of him, then hold the umbrella out to him handle-first. "Use this. You don't have to return it. In weather like this, it's best to just go home. You might catch a cold."

Not expecting the guy to be able to voice any thanks, Wang Xiaomie gave him a smile that left one canine poking out, then put his hands over his head and charged back into the cover of Wen Fengjin's umbrella. "All right, let's go," he said with a grin as he shook the water off his hands.

"Why did you give him your umbrella?"

"Because he looked so sad, and personally I can't stand rainy days."

Years ago, it was in a downpour just like this that a man had carried another on his back, walking up that long, long mountain road. At the time, the man being carried had thought, *if only I could hold an umbrella for him.*

But in the end, no one came to cover them from the bone-chilling rain lashing down at them...

Ever since then, Wang Xiaomie hated rain.

Wen Fengjin looked down at him, innocent and gentle black eyes meeting with long, narrow, ice-cold irises. After a long moment, Wen Fengjin simply raised his umbrella without a word, tilting it to cover more of Wang Xiaomie's side.

As he watched the pair leave, the bundled-up man tightened his grip on the umbrella in his hand. There was a complicated look in his eyes as he gazed in the direction they'd gone. After a moment of silence, he then turned around and headed down a different path in the rain.

From that point on, Wang Xiaomie never saw that man following them again.

One month later, Wang Xiaomie was making dinner in the kitchen, wearing a sky-blue apron and wielding a wooden spatula.

Wen Fengjin didn't like strongly flavored takeout, but they couldn't keep eating out all the time either, so Wang Xiaomie—who'd always lived by himself before—took over the job of cooking their meals.

As he was preparing to start the soup, Wang Xiaomie reached for the seasoning jars, only to discover that the salt jar was empty.

"Fengjiiin—Fengjiiiiiin—" Wang Xiaomie shouted in the direction of the kitchen door, and soon enough, Wen Fengjin came striding in, wearing loose pajamas.

"What, did you burn yourself again?" There was a furrow in his handsome brow. The next instant, he was already bending down to lift Wang Xiaomie's long tied-back hair, carefully checking it for any signs of scorching.

"No no, I'm fine." Wang Xiaomie took a step back, saying, "I only burned myself last time because I wasn't paying attention. I called you because we're out of salt." He showed him the empty jar.

The crease in Wen Fengjin's brow smoothed out, and he let that handful of smooth black hair slip free of his fingers. "No problem, I'll go buy some."

"Okay, be quick about it, I'm still waiting to simmer this soup here."

Wen Fengjin nodded and left to put on a change of clothes. Wang Xiaomie wasn't particularly worried about him going out alone— they'd been living here for nearly two months at this point, and WenFengjin was a pretty fast learner too. He was close to mastering basic Chinese, and even learning how to use a cell phone.

Taking Wen Fengjin's speed into account, a trip to the nearest grocery store and back would only take twenty minutes. Still in that same black jacket, matching black jeans and short boots, and with both hands in his pockets, he left the villa.

His formfitting clothes perfectly accentuated his beautifully well-muscled body. The smooth line of his curves, from shoulders to waist to calves, was captivating enough to make anyone start fantasizing on sight. With every step he took, his high ponytail of long silver hair swayed slightly behind him. His rather feminine face, so handsome that it seemed overly sharp, wore a cold indifference that seemed to tell all strangers to keep their distance.

As the number of people taking candid photos and sneaking peeks at him grew, a deep furrow gradually enveloped his red-marked forehead, and his eyes began to darken. The look could be translated as "if you bother this venerable one any further, I'm going to make you regret it!"

If Wen Fengjin had made this face a thousand years ago, who knows how many people would be trembling in fear. But now—

"Whoa he's so HAWT—!"

"OMG what a cool cosplaaaay!"

Wen Fengjin: ￣∧￣

The demon lord once capable of frightening crying babes into silence angrily paid for his bag of salt and hurriedly took his leave.

The streetlights were already lit when he got outside. Wen Fengjin paused a moment, then turned to look over at a tiny path stretching out from the side of the road, from which the cool night breeze was blowing a familiar, sickly sweet scent toward his nose.

Wen Fengjin lowered his long, narrow eyes, expressionlessly staring at the spot for a long time.

One minute later... He quirked his lips, sticking both hands in his pockets, long silver hair swaying slightly in the wind. His handsome face, the red mark on his forehead, and his long slender figure all combined in the dimly lit night to make him look like an akuma sighted in the twilight hour.

He raised his exquisite and expensive boots. The tip of his right foot stepped into the puddle of red liquid and slowly pulled back again, drawing a long, long line of blood across the dusty ground.

As he gazed down at the liquid on the ground and the horribly messed-up person, his eyes, with their massive irises, began to fill with joy...

"You're going to die," he said.

The dark night covered that ruined body. Only the person's chest still moved up and down as bloody saliva dripped from his open mouth; it took all the effort he had to reach out and grab Wen Fengjin's ankle with one hand.

"Save me—"

These two words gurgled within his throat, but failed to emerge.

Wen Fengjin, hands still in his pockets, looked on with all the loftiness of an immortal god as the curtain closed on this life like a flame sputtering out. Yet when he gazed upon the other man's pain and death, the expression which appeared on his face was one that suggested the man had done something to please him...

It was the sort of expression that made chills run down your spine.

The man teetering on the precipice of life and death was overcome by fear so strong it threatened to suffocate him.

But after a very long moment, the already despairing man watched with blurry eyes as this stranger pulled something out of his pocket, and after giving it a glance, said:

"All right. I can save you."

THE STORY CONCLUDES IN

My Husband and I Sleep in a Coffin

VOLUME 2

My Husband and I Sleep in a Coffin

Afterword

To all my dear reader friends,

I'm delighted this work will now be seen by more people, and thankful that you were willing to spend the time to get acquainted with *Coffin*.

This is a story that starts out supernatural, gets a little silly, and gradually turns into a romance. Though the title has a somewhat frightening taste to it (which is the effect I racked my brains to achieve back when I thought it up), it's actually about is how two people are able to find each other, understand each other, and gradually grow to love each other in a seemingly preposterous world. In other words, this is actually a love story, love story, love story (important things must be emphasized three times).

I'm honestly extremely moved by the thought of this work being translated for an overseas audience, and thankful to everyone who reads it. I hope you'll be able to feel the kindness and courage within this story. I also hope that you'll like my protagonist, Wang Xiaomie. He might be a little awkward and fond of talking smack, but deep down, he's very soft, Like anyone else doing their best to live their lives, he desperately desires to be understood and loved.

If you laughed, teared up, or in some random instant, suddenly thought "I somehow don't feel all that lonely anymore" while reading this work, then everything I hoped for when I created it has come true.

It is my sincerest wish that you will also be able to find the light (husband) of your own life, no matter how fantastical or impossible the place in which you find them.

Thank you all.

—WU SHUI BU DU

CHARACTER GUIDE & GLOSSARY

CHARACTERS, NAMES AND LOCATIONS

> The identity of certain characters may be a spoiler; use this guide with caution on your first read of the novel.
>
> Chinese characters may have many different readings. Each reading here is just one out of several possible readings presented for your reference, and not a definitive translation.

CHARACTERS

MAIN CHARACTERS

WANG XIAOMIE 王小咩

Surname Wang; Given Name Xiaomie, "little baa"

A modern-day otaku who has lived alone since he was a child, he wakes up one day to discover his soul was transferred to the body of an undead bride in a thousand-year-old mausoleum.

Weapon: Enlightened (开明/Kaiming): A short knife that heats up when it comes in contact with evil people.

MIAN DENG 眠灯

Surname Mian; Given Name Deng, "sleeping lantern/light"
Titles: Da-shixiong

The original owner of the body Wang Xiaomie finds himself in, Wen Fengjin's shixiong, and the oldest head student at the academy they went to a thousand years ago.

WEN FENGJIN 闻风尽

Surname Wen; Given Name Fengjin, "to exhaust the wind"
Titles: Anlou Demon Lord
A tyrant who terrorized the country a thousand years ago, with an obsessive love for his shixiong from his school days.
Weapon: Voidcrosser (廖越 / Liaoyue): The famous sword of the demon lord.

SUPPORTING CHARACTERS

TOMB GUARDIANS

MU YI 木一 "WOOD ONE"

One of Wen Fengjin's old subordinates, transformed into an immortal lizard creature to guard his master's mausoleum for eternity. Wen Fengjin's favorite.

MU ER 木二 "WOOD TWO"

One of Wen Fengjin's old subordinates, transformed into an immortal rusalka-like creature to guard her master's mausoleum for eternity. Her main job is alerting the other guardians to the presence of intruders.

MU SAN 木三 "WOOD THREE"

One of Wen Fengjin's old subordinates, transformed into an immortal mushroom creature to guard his master's mausoleum for eternity. Secretes acid and doesn't get along with Mu Yi.

MU LIU 木六 "WOOD SIX"

One of Wen Fengjin's old subordinates, transformed into an immortal tentacled creature to guard its master's mausoleum for eternity.

MU QI 木七 "WOOD SEVEN"

One of Wen Fengjin's old subordinates, transformed into an immortal monster to guard its master's mausoleum for eternity. Its main job is repairing/maintaining the mausoleum structure with its spit, which hardens on contact with air.

MU JIU & MU SHI 木九，木十 "WOOD NINE, WOOD TEN"

Two of Wen Fengjin's old subordinates, transformed into childlike jellyfish creatures to guard their master's mausoleum for eternity.

GRAVE ROBBERS

ZHEN BEI 贞北 "FAITHFUL NORTH"

The youngest son of the Zhen family, a family of appraisers. His name sounds a lot like the modern slang for "unlucky."

ZHEN MU 贞木 "FAITHFUL WOOD"

The second son of the Zhen family. A professional grave robber.
Weapon: Long Wind (长风 / Chanfeng): An ancient copper sword.

ZHEN HAO 贞昊 "FAITHFUL SKY/BOUNDLESS"

The eldest and favorite son of the Zhen family. Set to inherit their appraisal business.

LEI-JIE 蕾姐 "FLOWER BUD"

A professional swordsmith who joins grave-robbing expeditions in hopes of seeing rare swords.

XIAO-LUO 小罗 "LITTLE SNARE/NET"

Lei-jie's disciple, a young man.

YAN CHUN (initially introduced as YAN-XIANSHENG) 严先生 "MISTER STRICT"

Head of a gang of grave robbers, known for his immobile facial muscles and harsh leadership.

XIAO-LI 小李 "LITTLE PLUM (TREE)"

One of Yan-xiansheng's men.

TIEZI 铁子 "IRON"

One of Yan-xiansheng's men.

CHUN LEI 春雷 "SPRING LIGHTNING"

One of Yan-xiansheng's men.

A-SHUI 阿水 "WATER"

One of Yan-xiansheng's men.

LOCATIONS

NORTHERN KINGDOM 北国:

The country Wen Fengjin lived in a thousand years ago. Ruled by an emperor.

THE ACADEMY:

An unnamed academy located deep in the mountains, leading it to earn the nickname of "the hermitage." It had connections to the emperor of the Northern Kingdom, and housed a great many students, but they were all wiped out by Wen Fengjin a thousand years ago.

THE MAUSOLEUM:

An underground mausoleum spanning three mountains. Wen Fengjin had it built for himself and Mian Deng. It is filled with countless treasures that often attract grave robbers. Due to its many traps and guardian monsters, few have ever left alive.

A CITY (A 市):

The Zhen brothers' hometown.

B CITY (B 市):

The city where Lei-jie lives.

NAME GUIDE

NAMES, HONORIFICS, AND TITLES

Diminutives, Nicknames, and Name Tags

A-: Friendly diminutive. Always a prefix. Usually for monosyllabic names, or one syllable out of a two-syllable name.

XIAO-: A diminutive prefix meaning "little."

-ER: An affectionate diminutive suffix added to names, literally "son" or "child."

LAO-: A diminutive prefix meaning "old."

-ZI: An affectionate suffix meaning "son" or "child."

-XIONG: A word meaning "elder brother." It can be attached as a suffix to address an older male peer.

Family:

DI/DIDI: Younger brother or a younger male friend.

GE/GEGE/DAGE: Older brother or an older male friend. If you have more than one older brother, your oldest brother would be 'dage' while the second-oldest would be 'erge.' In a modern context, dage is used to express respect for a man about the same age as you.

JIE/JIEJIE: Older sister or an older female friend.

-SHU: A suffix meaning "uncle." Can be used to address unrelated older men.

Martial Arts and Tutelage:

SHIFU: Teacher or master, usually used when referring to the martial arts.

SHIZUN: Teacher or master. For one's master in one's own sect. Gender-neutral.

SHIXIONG: Older martial brother, used for older disciples or classmates.

SHIDI: Younger martial brother, used for younger disciples or classmates.

XIANSHENG: Teacher of academics. In a modern context, xiansheng is used similar to "Mister."

PRONUNCIATION GUIDE

Mandarin Chinese is the official state language of mainland China, and pinyin is the official system of romanization in which it is written. As Mandarin is a tonal language, pinyin uses diacritical marks (e.g., ā, á, ǎ, à) to indicate these tonal inflections. Most words use one of four tones, though some are a neutral tone. Furthermore, regional variance can change the way native Chinese speakers pronounce the same word. For those reasons and more, please consider the guide below a simplified introduction to pronunciation of select character names and sounds from the world of *My Husband and I Sleep in a Coffin*.

More resources are available at sevenseasdanmei.com

Wǒ Hé Lǎogōng Shuì Guāncai

- Wǒ: as in **wool**
- Hé as in **huh**
- Lǎo as in **law**
- Gōng: pronounced like **go**-ng
- Shuì: Sh as in **shh**, ui as in **way**
- Guān: G as in **g**et, uan as in **wan**
- Cai: C as in **ts**ar, ai as in **lie**

Wáng Xiǎomiē

- Wáng as in **wan**ted
- Xiǎo: X as in **shh**, iao as in **yaw**
- Miē: M as in **m**iss, ie as in **yes**

Wen Fengjin
- Wen as in **wen**t
- Feng: pronounced like **foe**-ng
- Jin as in **jin**x

GENERAL CONSONANTS

Some Mandarin Chinese consonants sound very similar, such as z/c/s and zh/ch/sh. Audio samples will provide the best opportunity to learn the difference between them.

X: somewhere between the **sh** in **sh**eep and **s** in **s**ilk

Q: a very aspirated **ch** as in **ch**arm

C: **ts** as in pan**ts**

Z: **z** as in **z**oom

S: **s** as in **s**ilk

CH: **ch** as in **ch**arm

ZH: **dg** as in do**dg**e

SH: **sh** as in **sh**ave

G: hard **g** as in **g**raphic

GENERAL VOWELS

The pronunciation of a vowel may depend on its preceding consonant. For example, the "i" in "shi" is distinct from the "i" in "di." Vowel pronunciation may also change depending on where the vowel appears in a word, for example the "i" in "shi" versus the "i" in "ting." Finally, compound vowels are often—though not always—pronounced as conjoined but separate vowels. You'll find a few of the trickier compounds below.

IU: as in **ewe**

IE: **ye** as in **ye**s

UO: **war** as in **war**m

GLOSSARY

While not required reading, this glossary is intended to offer further context to the many concepts and terms utilized throughout this novel and provide a starting point for learning more about the rich Chinese culture from which these stories were written.

BINGXIXI: A commonly known online nickname for the shopping site Pinduoduo, which advertises itself as selling things direct from the farmer. The nickname came about because many sellers on the site are scammers, and so people started giving the site a knockoff name on par with its knockoff products.

BLACK DONKEY HOOF: Literally the hoof of a black donkey, it is an item which, according to legend, was capable of restraining or controlling a jiangshi. The item is popularly mentioned in the Chinese fiction series *Daomu Biji*, or *Grave Robbers' Chronicles*, as well as an earlier series called *Gui Chui Deng*, or *Ghost Blows Out the Light*.

CULTIVATORS / CULTIVATION: Cultivators are practitioners of spirituality and martial artists who seek to gain understanding of the will of the universe while also attaining personal strength and expanding their life span.

CUT-SLEEVE: A slang term for a gay man, which comes from a tale about the Emperor Ai's love for, and relationship with, his male court official in the Han dynasty. The emperor was called to the morning assembly, but his lover was asleep on his robe. Rather than wake him, the emperor cut off his own sleeve.

FLASH: A location-targeted teleportation spell used in popular MMO *League of Legends*.

"GO TO THE FIELDS": 下地 normally refers to "going to work in the fields/farmland," but in this book is used as grave-robber slang for entering a tomb or mausoleum.

JIANGHU: A staple of wuxia and xianxia, the jianghu (江湖 / "rivers and lakes") describes an underground society of martial artists, monks, rogues, artisans, and merchants who settle disputes between themselves per their own moral codes.

JIANGSHI: Also called "hopping corpses" or "Chinese vampires," jiangshi are a type of undead which appears in Chinese folklore. Said to be formed when a person's soul is unable to leave its body after death, they are traditionally described as having pallid, furry skin (likely due to the presence of mold on actual corpses), and go around draining the life essence of living human beings.

LI: A traditional Chinese unit of measurement, approximating about a third of a mile.

MEITUAN: An online shopping service popularly used in modern China, through which you can buy anything from takeout/delivery to booking hotel rooms, movie tickets, tours, etc.

MERMAID-OIL LAMPS: According to legend, the tomb of China's first emperor, Qin Shi Huang, is lit with lamps fueled by mermaid fat, which can burn for eternity without needing to be relit.

SHICHEN: Before the introduction of western chronology, the Chinese measured a day in twelve shichen rather than twenty-four hours, with each period being named after one of the twelve Earthly branches (used together with the ten Heavenly stems to measure hours, days, etc). One shichen is therefore about equal to two hours.

SYSTEM: A common trope in transmigration novels is the existence of a "System" that guides the character and provides them with objectives in exchange for benefits, often under the threat of consequences if they fail. When Wang Xiaomei was transmigrated into Mian Deng's body in the past, the system issued him a mission contingent on his relationship with Wen Fengjin.

WANG DACHUI: The protagonist of an online comedy series called *Surprise* (万万没想到). He begins every episode with a simple goal such as "become a teacher" or "find a girlfriend," only for things to end in entirely unexpected ways (such as becoming a teacher for a criminal organization, or the girlfriend marrying his father instead).

ZONGZI: A zongzi is a type of Chinese rice dish made with glutinous rice, stuffed with different fillings, and wrapped in leaves (usually bamboo, though this can change depending on availability). It is traditionally eaten during the Duanwu Festival every summer. In this book, however, the term is used to refer to an undecayed living corpse, a use which was popularized by the Chinese fiction series *Daomu Biji*, or *Grave Robbers' Chronicles*, as well as an earlier series called *Gui Chui Deng*, or *Ghost Blows Out the Light*.

ABOUT
Wu Shui Bu Du

THE AUTHOR was born in Chaoyang County, Liaoning Province, China. Growing up in a small shop run by her family, and influenced by all the things she saw around her, she gained a profound interest in all sorts of stories, characters, and details of life from a very early age, and developed keen and meticulous powers of observation. She believes that hidden behind every ordinary day is a bit of magic. As long as you look carefully, you'll be able to find a story that touches your heart.

In 2019, she started trying to capture these daily "miracles" in words, and gradually developed her own unique style of creation. She excels at using peculiar settings as a starting point to depict those emotional bonds which transcend the laws of common sense, and particularly enjoys exploring the sincere yet complicated emotional relationships between humans and their "inhuman" partners. Whether it's a supernatural story, a fantastical chance meeting, or the subtle turn of events that changes a long-dead friend into a lover, they all take on a warm and emotionally moving light under her hand.

Her best-known work, *My Husband and I Sleep in a Coffin*, combines all of her favorite elements: a fantastical setting, a light tone, and an exquisitely delicate love hidden beneath it all. This work has been widely loved since it first began serialization, and the author herself feels impossibly thankful and honored to know it now has the opportunity to go overseas. Regarding her life, the author tends to have a wide range of interests. She likes to read fantasy and mystery books, and loves to observe the little kindnesses that people unintentionally do each other in their daily lives. She prefers rainy days, because the sound of raindrops hitting the window is perfect for letting her thoughts fly. When it comes to food, sweet chocolates and the occasional tiny cake are her best writing companions.

Though she keeps a low profile and rarely makes public appearances, she believes that stories can speak for themselves, transcending language and distance to reach the hearts of every reader. She hopes that with every fantastical, gentle, and slightly weird story she writes, she can allow her readers to discover their own bit of magic within the real world around them.

Her other works include:
Advanced Stage Leopard-Con
Transmigrated Into the Sword of a Babylonian Tyrant
I'm On The Godfather's Menu
Attracting Bees